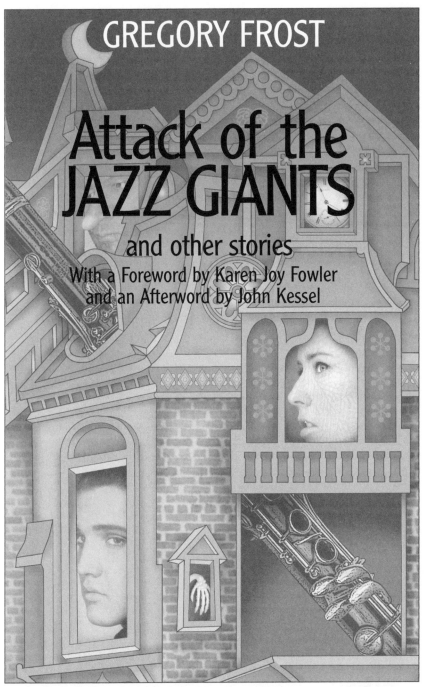

GREGORY FROST

Attack of the JAZZ GIANTS

and other stories

With a Foreword by Karen Joy Fowler
and an Afterword by John Kessel

GOLDEN GRYPHON PRESS • 2005

Copyright © 2005 by Gregory Frost

Interior illustrations copyright © 2005 by Jason Van Hollander

LIBRARY OF CONGRESS CATALOGING-IN-PUBLICATION DATA

Frost, Gregory.
    Attack of the jazz giants and other stories / Gregory Frost ; with a foreword by Karen Joy Fowler. — 1st ed.
        p.   cm.
    ISBN 1-930846-34-7 (hardcover : alk. paper)
        1. Fantasy fiction, American.   I. Title.
PS3556.R59815   A98   2005
813'.6—dc22   2004026627

Printed in the United States of America.

First Edition.

Contents

For Barbara, who's heard it all before.

"Realism is a literary technique no longer adequate for the purpose of representing reality."
—Andrey Sinyavsky

Acknowledgments

First and foremost, I have to thank Karen Joy Fowler for taking the time to write the introduction to this collection. It's not as if she doesn't have her own writing to do. She's probably hoping to get another dinner out of it.

Karen and I are both veterans of many Sycamore Hill writing workshops, which were begun by three people in North Carolina in the mid-1980s. One of the founders, John Kessel, wrote the afterword to this collection, and I owe him a great debt of thanks, not only for the kind words found herein, but also for his abiding friendship. To the rest of the SycHill writers, my gratitude for your wise counseling over the years, from which a few of the stories here have benefited greatly. I won't name names, but you all know your ears are burning.

Finally, I'd like to thank Gary Turner for the invitation, and Jason Van Hollander for being so dangerous with pen and inks.

Foreword

A few facts about Gregory Frost:

1) The first time I met Greg he was wearing a tuxedo. We were at a science fiction convention and he was helping staff the writer's suite. At science fiction conventions you expect to meet: Klingons, vampires, men in chain mail, women in elf ears. At science fiction conventions you don't expect to meet: Cary Grant.

2) Greg is an excellent cook. I've eaten his food many times at Sycamore Hill (a writer's workshop). One year he made a jambalaya for eighteen. Chorizo, chicken, and shrimp, just the right amount of heat. It was a really great jambalaya. I'm not the only one who remembers it fondly.

3) Greg can sing. He can dance. He can do cartoon voices. If you annoy him, he is perfectly capable of reading your own prose aloud to you first as Elmer Fudd, then as Yosemite Sam. This can go on for hours. There is nothing you can do to stop it.

4) Greg has a pair of contact lenses like goat's eyes. Gold with black slit pupils. I haven't seen these for myself. There've been reports. "Deeply unsettling," the eyewitnesses tell me. "You think you'll get used to them, but you don't."

This is the best I can do at describing the stories in this collection:

Imagine Cary Grant. He's offering you some of the best food you'll ever taste. It smells delicious. You take a few bites. It tastes delicious. You look up from your plate to tell him so. He has goat's eyes. Here are the sort of stories a culinarily gifted Cary Grant with goat's eyes might write.

The cartoon voices have nothing to do with this. I just threw them in for verisimilitude.

A few facts about the stories:

1) I once had a writing teacher who told me, as writing teachers generally do, as I myself generally do when I teach, to remember in our stories to evoke all the senses. When I read Greg's stories I'm reminded that we have more senses than just the five. In addition to rich, sensory writing, Greg's work evokes: my sense of justice, my sense of wonder, my sense of horror, my sense of humor.

2) Greg is both a funny writer and an angry one. His sympathies are usually clear; his heart is usually fully engaged. Some people can't get justice in this world and Greg's characters tend to locate themselves among them. Sometimes Greg provides different worlds, places where different justices are possible.

But the work is never simple, never thin, never escapist. You can't miss the writer's unhappiness with the real state of things; the real, unjust world exists as visibly as a shadow to every sentence. Things are not as they should be and, if we allow ourselves the temporary solace of pretending otherwise, still Greg's anger reminds us that we are only pretending.

3) What I love most when I read is to be surprised. I could list the ways in which these stories consistently produce this pleasure, but that would spoil the surprise for you. (A consistently surprising writer is a sort of Zen koan. You can think about this later.)

4) Another thing I love is to travel fictionally. I love to travel for real, too, but the food is not always so good. These stories take me to many places—to New Orleans, to the Maquiladora, to Russia, to Jesusworld, to the planet Recovery, to someone else's (thank God) high school reunion. And all the while I'm time traveling, too, forward, backward, and once in the company of Edgar Allan Poe. He's sort of glum, but he has good reason. Mozart appears (and disappears.) Dorian Gray. Bob Hope. Greek gods. Jazz Giants. The dust and blood of history.

Great fiction is transporting. Transporting fiction is great. Greg's fiction is consistently surprising. Lush, varied in voice and tone. Heart-filled, angry, magical. And transporting. You do the math.

Or read the book. That's what I'm recommending.

Karen Joy Fowler
December 2003

Attack of the Jazz Giants and Other Stories

The Girlfriends of Dorian Gray

WITH HIS FORK, HE CUT THROUGH THE LAYERS of crisp philo dough, lifted and placed in his mouth the slice of *bisteeya*. The flavours of cinnamon, coriander, butter, and almonds flooded his senses—a sweet and tender orgasm to which he gave himself completely, eyes closed, fingers curled tenderly around his utensils. When he opened his eyes again, he was staring right at Alison.

She sat across the table. In front of her were a white bread plate and a glass of spring water with a slice of lemon floating in it. The plate contained three saltine crackers. Alison was trying to look disinterested and unaffected by his meal. But just then her stomach gurgled and he had to keep himself from smiling at its betrayal. She could have had the same meal he was eating or anything else on the menu: He would have been more than willing to order her something, anything. The choice to starve was hers. He could not concern himself with it.

A single rose stood in the small vase between them. It was his particular flourish, that rose. He began his conquests with the rose, knowing that so simple a gesture was an arrow to the heart of the romantic. He promised elegance, thoughtfulness, taste, but above all, romance. After their first date—the first night they'd met after she answered his ad—Alison had confessed that the rose made her toes curl. Tonight, however, it stood as an emblem of distance, a cenotaph of her feelings for him, already buried elsewhere. He knew this would be the last night, knew already exactly how it was going to end. It had ended this way dozens of times before.

He was elegance himself—tall, smoothly groomed, with perfect teeth and long slender hands. He took extra good care of his hands. "The hands of an angel," one of the women had told him. Wasn't it Tricia? Yes, that seemed right. Tricia was always alluding to Christian iconography: hands of an angel, face of a saint, heart of the devil. An annoying habit, actually—he never could have married her. But of course he wouldn't; just as he wouldn't be marrying Alison.

He'd taken her to only the finest restaurants in the city. A night out with him ran to hundreds of dollars, and he never skimped, never hesitated to order the finest meals. Maître d's knew him. Chefs came out of the kitchen to the table and discussed dishes with him. Dining with him was like dining with a celebrity. "If we are going to eat, then we should only ever eat the best," was his mantra. Never would he have dipped below a four star establishment. He was like someone who had just stepped out of a magazine ad for Rolex watches or Dom Perignon, a real live James Bond without the silly devices and world-dominating villains. A man who'd been bred to know the best and settle for nothing less. And by association, what did that make the woman who accompanied him?

How many dinners had they shared before she noticed the first signs of the change? It was three before he saw, but he was watching. Six or seven for her, by his reckoning. When you're in love, you overlook and deny so many seemingly insignificant things.

Like the fact that he was a gourmand.

He not only liked the finest cuisine, he liked as much of it as he could possibly consume in any one sitting. Four courses, six courses: paté de fois gras, bisques thick with cream, lobster-stuffed squid-ink ravioli in a tomato-cream sauce, soufflés, quiches, duck a l'orange, prime rib of beef, cherry compote, tiramisu, bottles of champagne, carafes of wine. Single-handedly he could take out a whole menu.

For all that, his manners were impeccable. It wasn't that he sat slobbering and gnashing, drawing attention to himself as some deranged Neanderthal with a fork might have done. No, he ate demurely, quietly, chatting with her, truly interested in what she had to say (or at least feigning interest so well that she would never notice the difference). Dinner with him lasted the entire evening. The courses came and went—soups, hors d'oeuvres, first course, main course, cheese course, desserts and coffee, liqueurs. She would not have noticed right away that he had eaten an extra course, or more than one dessert, or consumed an entire bottle of wine on his own and helped her with half of another. Simply, he ate. And ate. And ate. And ate.

He wondered if any of them would have stayed with him. He supposed it didn't matter, since he never intended to stay with any of them. But he liked that they always called it quits. Alison was going to call it quits tonight. When they got to the saltines stage, they always called it quits.

He'd been surprised that first night how petite Alison was—the smallest woman he'd had so far, her head barely reached his nipples. And very healthy. She exercised hard, and was proud to show him her abdominals, her perfect, smooth, taut, and round rear, and her well-muscled legs. She was certainly the only woman he'd met who claimed she enjoyed stairclimbers and rowing machines. Such strict attention to her physique included diet, and so she hadn't been prepared for the cream sauces, the nights of sheer ecstatic indulgence in all things edible, the ease with which one got hooked by rich, buttery, fattening foods. He supposed it had been something like springing a trap on poor Alison. By the time she'd mentioned to him—a gentle reproof—that she thought he over-indulged when they went out to dinner, he could only laugh. She told him as if he might be unaware of it himself. In all other ways he was the personification of charm and compassion; a wonderful, thoughtful lover. Of course when he'd offered her the ring she had accepted. On the first date he showed it to her. On the second date, he placed it on her finger. His eating habits didn't dissuade her from accepting his offer of a more significant relationship.

Then the tummy had arrived.

Suddenly she didn't fit comfortably in her electric blue Lycra. Where she had been hard muscle, she began to bulge. The solution of course was to increase her workout and decrease the number of times she ate out with him, both of which she did. She promptly gained another dozen pounds. Soon he had to coerce her into going out, and when she did, she ate the lightest fare—a salad, or something high in protein like fish, while avoiding all starches, breads, and pastas—while he devoured half the planet with his usual zeal, but always solicitous, always asking if she minded that he ate a regular meal, exhibiting such concern that she could say nothing except "of course not." There were many nights when she begged off dinner and he went out alone. It didn't matter. Once she'd handled the ring, she didn't have to be with him.

Now five months had passed and the engagement had run its course. The longest it had ever run was eight months, but Anita had been a much taller woman to begin with. At four months while expressing continued desire for her company, he ceased to exhibit any for the physical relationship they'd shared. Without saying anything directly, he reproached her for her size. He found her 190-pound physique as repugnant as she did. *He* didn't weigh that much. She was only five-feet tall. She couldn't remotely carry this kind of weight around. Just climbing the steps to the restaurant left her labouring for breath. He held her hand and waited for her with the utmost patience and consideration. Never would he give her cause to doubt the sincerity of his concern. Treadmills and rowing machines fell by the wayside. Alison couldn't bend forward enough to row, and she complained of backaches when she used a stairclimber. At five months, the skin sagged on her arms, flowed around her elbows and knees. Her calves literally hung over her ankles. She was gelatin, marshmallow, not human at all. He found it all terribly disgusting, especially as he sat there, indulging himself with a raft of the most glorious foods and never gaining an ounce.

She had tried every diet and gone so far as to experiment with acupuncture and hypnosis. He suspected she had become bulimic. She couldn't become anorexic. Not quite yet anyway.

Nothing had worked. Nothing was ever going to work.

So while he finished the *bisteeya*, Alison told him that she had to stop seeing him, that her world was out of control and she needed to get away for a while. She was going to a clinic in upstate New York where they could help people with her kind of disorder. It was—it had to be—hormonal.

He set down his fork and let her see that he was stunned, crestfallen, horrified. "I do understand," he said. "You have to take care of yourself. Why, it must be awful to have to watch me enjoying food when it's become so miserable for you to eat. That's so awful, Alison. I can't imagine what it would be like to have to stop enjoying food. I don't think I could do it. I'll—I won't have another thing. I'll call the waiter right now and cancel the main course. You should not have to sit here like this."

She agreed with him on that point. But rather than making him end his dinner, she insisted he just allow her to go. "It's better if

I don't see you again, either. I'm afraid—" her eyes glistened with her first tears "—I can't separate you from what's happened to me. I'm sorry." Sobbing, she slid his ring across the table.

She rose to leave the restaurant, but swayed dizzily, and he leaped to his feet and caught hold of her pudgy arm to brace her. He moved as swiftly as someone who had foreseen that she would become light-headed.

He guided her into her coat, then hailed a cab and helped her struggle into the back of it. She clutched his hand, kissed it, then turned her face away. He gave the driver her address and a twenty dollar bill, wished her well, and sent her off.

Once the cab was out of sight, he returned to his table and proceeded immediately to eat the rest of his meal as if nothing had happened, as if there was—and could not have been—a care in the world. Some of the other diners glanced at him with disgust. He ignored them. The waiter asked if the lady would be all right, and he answered, "Eventually. She's having digestion problems." The waiter eyed him peculiarly, and he took that as his cue to say loudly enough for those nearby to eavesdrop: "We've just broken up. So, while I'm sorry that she's feeling ill, I'm not full of tea and sympathy just now. You understand? She's broken my heart and I'm not going to cave in. I refuse." That seemed to satisfy the waiter. At least it lent some justification to his insistence that the dinner proceed. People ate their way out of misery all the time. Didn't they?

Thus he ate and ate as if Alison were still there, as if she or her phantom was being served a portion of everything, too, as if no amount of food could salve his conscience. As if he had one.

In the morning he called the paper and placed a new ad. He needed a new vessel.

The most difficult part was this limbo in between. He had no vessel and he wanted desperately to binge; but he knew that, if he succumbed to his lust, the repercussions would be his alone to bear. That was how the spell worked. It wasn't under his governance. It hadn't really been his idea in the first place.

The whole thing was Rebecca's fault. She'd irritated him into it. At the time, of course, he'd only half-believed in it, and that half was drunk. Magic was silly—Penn & Teller pulling the audience's collective pants down. That was magic to him.

He'd been drinking ouzo, but as Manny had said, "What else ya gonna drink in a bar in Canea on Crete, dude?" In his cups, he'd been complaining to Manny and one of the local men about Rebecca's vanity, her obsession with her model's figure, which included denial of most of the foods he loved, and her complaints about his own softening physique. If she was to deny herself these pleasures, then she expected him to do the same. He wasn't even married to her yet and already she was instituting changes in his life. "Come all the way here just to eat Melba toast? My God, it's hideous!" he'd exclaimed. Mummy and dad were footing the bill for this trip—his reward for graduating with honours—and he wasn't about to spend their money on a diet of figs and yogurt. There was more to it, of course. She'd complained the whole trip about how pathetic and stupid the native population was, these poor little people without even cell phones. The next thing he knew he and Manny were in the company of two locals on a narrow street with a name like Iepela Odoc or something. Well, the word in Greek that *looked* like *odoc* meant "street" but that was as far he could get with his sloshing vocabulary.

He had the money to buy the spell. He could have bought a dozen. He remembered joking to Manny that there was "a special on love potions in aisle five." He didn't so much as feel the amount he was paying, although to the woman—the herbalist or witch, or whatever she was—it must have been a jackpot sum. In her corner of the world, that much money was a fortune. "Travel broadens the mind, not the girth," he'd announced. It was all a lark.

"You don't believe, but yet you pay?" she'd asked. She clearly thought him an idiot. He never got to answer. She asked him to give her something to use to focus the spell upon, and he fumbled in his pockets and pulled out the antique ring he'd bought for Rebecca in Athens—he intended it to be her engagement ring. At least, he had intended that before she started telling him what he could and couldn't eat.

The next thing he knew, he'd been presented with a small chalice and he was thoughtlessly drinking the contents. Whatever it was, it made him double over in pain. His brain cleared enough for him to experience fear—to think she might have played a trick on him and now he would die in a little shop on a back street in one of the oldest cities of the world, murdered by a woman who looked about as old as the city. He had time to hiss, "Manny, you stupid bastard," before blackness shot with stars scooped him up and deposited him back in his hotel room. He opened crusted eyes beneath a spinning ceiling fan, on his bed; it was as if the entire adventure, the whole day, had been a wild dream. He was still dressed. He checked his money belt. The cash he remembered giving the woman was in fact gone—but only that much. The other thousand he had was still there, and so was the antique ring. If it hadn't been for that he might never have believed the journey had happened at all.

He felt no different. He looked no different. Whatever she'd given him, it hadn't killed him. The whole thing was just a mean, drunken digression. Despite which, he gave Rebecca the ring at his first opportunity, and then watched to see what would happen.

Of course it had worked. He couldn't believe how well it had worked. Over her shrill protests, he finished his holiday eating whatever he wanted, as much as he wanted. Within a month, Rebecca had developed a double chin. Dear, vain, conceited Rebecca was swelling up like a balloon and could do nothing to stop it. His pudginess, on the other hand, was vanishing. By the time they left for home, he looked positively trim. That was when he knew.

Once they returned home, it continued. Rebecca tried everything from yoga to liposuction. The latter vacuumed fat off here and there, but couldn't slow down its reappearance. She saw specialists in diet, hormones, metabolism. No one could account for the changes. No one could reverse them. She ate in the zone, adhered to the Atkins diet, and finally, humiliatingly, joined Weight Watchers. The latter thought she lacked the will to lose. She was cheating.

She became reclusive, and within the year was institutionalized. Never for a moment did anyone save Manny have the slightest suspicion what was really happening—and Manny, the instrument of the spell, couldn't say a thing. It was all too sublime.

Finally, Rebecca's clogged arteries had given her a stroke. She hadn't lived long. After the funeral, the family returned his ring to him; it was only proper—he had stuck by her the whole time. At least, when he wasn't eating.

The moment his fiancée was gone, any over-indulging he did came back on him as it would have on anyone. He made himself rein in his appetite. The trouble was, by then he'd discovered he *liked* to eat that way. His body had grown used to rich sauces and huge quantities of food. It ached for more.

Rebecca had a sister, Midge, who liked him. She had always been waiting in the wings, jealous of her older sister. It was the element of sibling rivalry, stealing the boyfriend away from her dead sister that made his part easy. Within weeks they were engaged, and he started eating again. He did so warily, with an eye to Rebecca's replacement, because at that point he wasn't certain the magic would transfer. But Midge wasted no time in following in her sister's elephantine footsteps. The difference was that Midge somehow figured out he was responsible. He suspected that Manny told her, and thereafter he and Manny parted company. Midge soon rejected him. Although she never could have understood what was happening, he had learned never to involve people who knew one another.

And so he had come to the personals page, where potential fiancées abounded—a thousand women of all persuasions looking for the right man, for romance and adventure. He looked for the ones who proclaimed their thinness, their great physiques. He tailored his own ad to attract them. It was easy. They were ducks on a pond.

Two days later, when he looked to check that his ad was listed in the personals, he found Cerise. Her ad was across from his on the page. The title caught his eye.

"THE WAY TO A MAN'S HEART. WiOF, in the middle of life, slender, attractive, loves good food, trained chef, ISO delicious male, 35-45, who wants to savour the flavour. BOX 2356."

The silly "savour the flavour" rhyme ought to have made him dismiss the ad, but instead it crawled inside his head like some tiny, obnoxious nursery rhyme, helixing in singsong around and around his thoughts. "Trained chef" was a taunt, an invitation, a tantalizing dare. He started imagining all sorts of things — of taking her to the best restaurants in the city, watching her pass judgment on the culinary delights as he devoured each one. Letting her pick out the courses one after the other, electing his sauces, hobnobbing with the various chefs. Choosing the very shape of her own undoing.

What was the "O" for, he wondered. Old, maybe, or oriental. Widowed oriental? Slender? Well, for the time being, maybe. He would change that.

He replied to her ad immediately, calling the 900 number and leaving his name, his phone number, and particulars. He finished by saying, "Good food is necessary for all things sensual. How can anyone be a sensualist without appreciating food? You, with your training, can't help but *be* sensual. Of that, I'm certain." He didn't know why, but he was sweating by the time he finished—a case of nerves. Having made the call, he found himself worried about losing her to someone else. The ad spoke to *him*. He wondered if his own ad had affected the women who answered that way.

He'd never had a problem inducing them to accept the ring, which meant that they came to the date with some illusions, some ridiculous hopes that worked to his advantage. And he always began with the rose, that romantic hook. He remained attentive, cultured, never angry or even irritated; he was, he felt, a good lover, always solicitous, as hard, soft, or vocal as they desired. He never looked at another woman, not even when the ballooning began. He was obsessed with watching the changes as he reshaped and distorted her. It was like peering into a funhouse mirror, witnessing a transformation that should have been his own. Behind the rapacious joy of eating and the visceral pleasure of controlling and destroying, he couldn't imagine what he would have looked like by now without the ring, without the magic.

Responses to his ad trickled in, but he didn't answer any of them. He waited for the woman to call him.

As the days ran on, he convinced himself that he'd been rejected, he had lost her. Maybe she'd had an answer before his. Her ad might have been in place for ages. He dug out the section and looked at it again, noting the "Exp. 2/19" date at the end. His own ad didn't expire until the 23rd, so she must have been bombarded with calls well before his own, how could she not have been? Someone had beaten him to her and there was nothing he could do, no way to get her to consider him instead. He thought of calling again, but knew how desperate that would make him sound, and he refused to be desperate. He sank into a depression, and thoughtlessly ate a huge meal to take his mind off her. Of course it did just the opposite, and he gained five pounds on top of everything else. Defeated, he returned to his mailbox and listened to a dozen unappetizing answers. What could he do? He needed a vessel. He was starving without one.

After two weeks she called. A husky, lightly accented voice asked to speak with him. Her name, she said, was Cerise, like the colour. "I loved your reply. You seem to know me just by imagining my cooking. You made food sound as if it were your one consuming passion."

"It is," he said. His palms were sweating. "You—you're a chef?"

"Yes. Oh, not professionally. That is, I don't work as one. But I have been trained here by the CIA, and also in France awhile ago."

The CIA—only someone with his fixation would know to render that as a reference to a cooking school and not a collective of spies.

"What was your specialty?" He felt like an idiot asking it. What had happened to his refinement, his sensibility? His whole façade had deserted him.

"Mediterranean dishes." Then she added, "So, would you like to sample my art?"

He'd intended to ask her to come to Figaro's with him—that had been his original plan, the one he'd used on all the others. Instead he found himself saying, "I would love to," and writing down her address and promising to be there that night.

He hung up the phone and then sat still, his mouth dry, his penis as stiff as if she had just performed a striptease before him. There was something truly wonderful about her. *Absurd*, he thought, *but I believe I'm in love.*

He considered that he might even regret what had to happen to her.

He arrived at 8:00 P.M. sharp. She had a midtown flat overlooking the park, an address that announced her wealth. The doorman called her and he heard her voice answering to let him in. The doorman touched finger to cap and held the door as he entered.

He'd brought a fine Bordeaux with him from his cellar, one that he never would have brought along on a blind first date. It seemed terribly important to make a good first impression. He had his single rose, and the ring was in his breast pocket. He never knew when he was going to convince his vessel to wear it. What was important was that the magic start—that she handle the old ring sometime during the first meal. By the second or third date, he would propose, give her the ring to wear, and then let the rest happen. He'd done it enough times that the process was scripted, events pre-ordained before the first course had been cleared.

The elevator was an old-fashioned cage, and he rode up rigid with apprehension, staring through the bars but seeing nothing beyond his own desire.

Even before he'd reached her door, he could smell spices and sea scents. His stomach fluttered with anticipation at the same time as he realized the wine he'd brought wasn't going to work. He ought to have asked what she was making. It would be interesting to see if she appreciated the gift; they could always drink it the next time.

He lifted the knocker and rapped quietly. She opened it at once.

The moment he looked at her, he knew what the "O" had stood for.

"Olive," he said aloud.

As though she understood his meaning, she smiled when he said it; and he thought he would go blind with lust. For a moment he actually forgot about food.

Her flesh was a deep, deep olive colour. She was as tall as he, and her bearing could only be described as regal. Her cheekbones were high, and as sharply defined as her jaw, which ought to have been too large, too pronounced on such a face but was unaccountably beautiful. Her eyes were lighter than her complexion, nearly golden. Her hair was jet black, yet where the light in her entryway sparkled in it, the hair seemed highlighted with gold, as if she'd looped thin strands through it. Her eyes looked him up and down as she spoke his name and offered her hand. He, utterly besotted, raised it to his lips and kissed it. She smiled again as he gave her the rose, and looked at him a moment over the petals. There were lines of experience beneath her eyes, but they laughed at him, promised joy.

She ushered him in, took his overcoat while commenting on the cold weather, accepted his proffered bottle. As he'd hoped, she noted its vintage with satisfaction: she knew her wine.

She wore a sort of loose, red, ochre, and purple dashiki, belted in gold at her narrow waist, slit along the sides. When she reached to hang up his coat, he glimpsed her breast and realized that she was wearing nothing at all beneath the gown.

She had a bottle decanted already, some cold and golden aperitif, and she poured him a drink, then led him on a tour of her apartment. It was simply decorated in the style of a Mediterranean villa. The walls had been glazed, treated in rough imitation of old plaster. There was a mosaic built into the dining room wall of a fish creature—a kind of seahorse with a bearded human head. It looked like something that might have been uncovered at Pompeii. Whoever had died and left her a widow had provided for her very well.

"I hope you like paella," she said. She placed herself on a divan across from him. Her feet, in sandals, crossed at the ankles. He couldn't help staring.

"You made a paella?"

She shrugged as if to say it was nothing. "I selected the ingredients this morning myself." She sipped her wine. "It's important to have fresh ingredients."

"Absolutely."

"So, please, tell me about yourself."

"Well," he said, and launched into a long-winded autobiography, surprising himself as he told her about his first sexual encounter, about growing up with a sense of superiority over the average citizen because he could read a wine list, because he could recognize quality in objects, in places. In people. At least, that was what he found himself saying. He described his trip to Crete with Manny and Manny's girlfriend and Rebecca, calling it "the transforming event of my life." He very nearly blurted out that he'd purchased a magic charm there—very nearly gave away his secret to a woman who was about to become its next victim—and decided that he'd best go light on the wine.

The dinner became immediately one of the greatest meals he had ever eaten. She had struck the perfect balance among the fish, shellfish, and mussels, the herbes de Provence, saffron rice, and chorizo. Each mouthful was like an island floating on an orgasmic ocean, so good that his eyes closed half the time. He had to eat slowly. She plied him with more wine, a lovely Sauvignon Blanc, and flat bread, and conversation. She described her life as nomadic. She had, it seemed, lived all over. She told him about cooking classes in Paris with artists whose names he'd never heard; about living in Venice with her late husband; about traveling finally to "the New World" for a change not only of scenery but of lifestyles, of attitudes. Of people. She made it sound as if it had all taken centuries. And who had she found but a man who had himself gone to the Old World? To Crete. A lovely place.

She talked and he ate, slowly, steadily, ready to die for another mouthful. He lost count, but she must have fed him three portions. She seemed only more and more delighted as he devoured the food, relishing and groaning and repeating how incredible she was. He would have eaten four or five helpings if his body allowed it, but even with the spell it was still his stomach.

Finally, sated, he sat back, saying, "I believe I have never in my life eaten anything at all to compare with this."

Cerise collected his plate. After a few minutes she emerged from the kitchen with a slender, Turkish-style coffee pot. She set in on the table. It smelled wonderful. His head lolled while he studied the filigree etched into the pot. He fingered the ring in his pocket, drunk with the idea of marrying her tonight. It was absurd, he had to remind himself. He didn't want a wife, only a receptacle, a fiancée. But, dear God, how could he allow her to slip through his fingers? Whether she swelled up like a human blowfish, where on Earth would he ever taste another meal to equal this one? How could he deprive himself of her culinary art?

He mulled it over to no avail. It was a conundrum. Finally, he said, "You are divine, Cerise, your meal was just . . . breathtaking."

"I'm happy to have robbed you of breath," she said, and laughed lightly. She poured the coffee then. It was sweet and strong, an intoxicant to smother the last of his will. He took the ring out and set it on the table.

"This will—this will sound mad, but I am mad, I think. I am madly in love with you." He couldn't quite make it more comprehensible than that, but he pushed the ring toward her.

She saw it and her teeth flashed again in delight. It was a beautiful ring. She took it, slipping it on her finger and admiring it as she said, "I knew when you answered my ad that you were the one I was looking for. The *only* one." She slid around the table, perching beside him. The smell of her was more heady than the scent of the meal had been.

"Oh. Oh, my, my . . ." He couldn't find the right word and embraced her instead. His hands slid like snakes inside her clothing.

She made love as she made food. Everything was fresh, full of spice, hot and overwhelming. He thought of the sea god on her wall and he imagined the face as his own. He was drowning in pleasure, letting himself go completely. He was a ship, she was a storm, and he rode the tempest, too lost to look for bearings, just spinning, spinning, rising and falling.

In the morning when he awoke, he was alone in her bed. This room, like the others, had a sense of antiquity about it. A bronze sun with a capricious face looked at him from the wall. The mirror beside it was edged in verdigris and copper, the reflecting surface marbled with imperfections. When he got up and stood before it, he gasped.

Gasped and looked down.

His belly was swollen. He turned sideways, twisted his face, looked at the reflection, then down at his stomach, then back again. He craned his neck and patted the slight jowl under his chin that hadn't been there the night before.

He looked as if he'd gained ten pounds.

Something was terribly wrong. He couldn't understand it—he'd given her the ring, hadn't he? He thought so, but he'd been intoxicated by her food and drink. By Cerise herself. Maybe he'd just imagined giving it to her.

He checked in his clothing, patted the pockets. Then he turned and circled the bedroom until he spied the ring on her dressing table. He snatched it up. So, she hadn't worn it? But what difference did that make? All the others had had to do was touch it for the spell to take hold, the transformation to unfold. He crumbled under self-doubt: Maybe he'd given it to her too late. Could there be a time limit that he just hadn't encountered before? Damned if it didn't look like the whole thing had been flipped back on him. As if he'd gained for both of them.

Uncertain, he dressed, assuring himself that, yes, the food was superb, more than superb, but not good enough to warrant this. And maybe that was it—maybe it had to be someone else's cooking. He would go home, listen to the women who had answered his ad, select one and start over. Give the ring to some other woman as soon as possible.

He walked out of the bedroom, his mind made up, his story already arranged—walked into a cloud of olfactory bliss: Cerise had baked, poached, cooked, and it was ready and waiting for him. As was she.

The sight of the Eggs Benedict smothered in hollandaise made the blood pound in his temples. She'd brewed more coffee, baked some sort of braided bread that glistened with honey, filled bowls with fruit. Around the corner in the kitchen, she looked up from pouring him a mimosa.

She was naked: She'd cooked breakfast in the nude! She offered him that alluring smile once again, and proudly carried the fluted glass to him. Which he accepted. Her hands slid around his neck, into his hair. She kissed him, tasting of strawberry. Her tongue snaked along his own. His will dissolved.

They ate breakfast in almost complete silence. She treated it as if it were a silent sharing. He tried to remember between bites of egg and ham and buttery sauce what he was going to say to her. He began to wonder if he couldn't continue seeing Cerise. Pick some new Alison or Sandra or Jill or Rebecca to take on this cooking, too! He could have it all—Cerise *and* a vessel—and why not? They never had to meet, or even know the other existed. His eating picked up speed. He ate now almost as a test, just to make sure the spell hadn't taken late. So long as that chance remained, he didn't want to do something rash.

When he had eaten, she served him more coffee, then led him back to her bed. He followed docilely, in something of a daze. His body responded to her touch as before; he grew hard and let her ride him into near exhaustion. It went on longer than he would have thought possible. He couldn't believe that after half an hour he was still erect, still going, still unreleased. Tension, he told himself. Tension.

Finally, after she had experienced repeated orgasms of her own, he joined her. She sat awhile, then lay beside him. He sprawled, twitching like a galvanized frog's leg, unable to coordinate his muscles enough to stand up. His whole body smelled of her now. Even the scent of her sex worked on his appetite, making him hungry for more. He dozed, then woke with a start from a dream of having fallen, to find her sleeping beside him with feline contentment upon her features.

He rose unsteadily, glanced at the time, found his underwear and socks. Before he dressed, he stepped in front of the old mirror again. If anything, he looked fatter than just a few hours before. That wasn't possible, was it? It had to be an illusion—his fear working on him. No one got fat this fast . . . except for his vessels. As if to drive the point home, his pants had to be coerced into meeting. He sucked in his gut and used his belt to keep them together. All right, then, there it was—the spell didn't work on her. Now there was no question. No tempting fate further; he had to get out of here before she cooked another meal for him.

Cerise made a noise deep in her throat, not a moan exactly, more like a few notes from a song being hummed below his hearing. She didn't move, but her golden eyes tracked him. "You are going, my darling?"

"Ah, you're awake. Yes, I have to. That is, I have business that I should have taken care of this morning, and now it's late afternoon, and if I don't do it today, I'll have to wait until Monday."

"Oh." The sound of disappointment. "You'll come back tonight?"

"Well, I—" He could think of nothing to say by way of an excuse. "Of course. Unless there's a problem. If there is, I'll call you."

"All right." She stretched languorously, her black hair reaching all the way to the dimples above her buttocks. Her legs were slightly spread. With her smell clogging his nostrils, all he could think of was how much he wanted to push them wider apart and dive in between.

He made himself turn away. "I'll call," he repeated, but she had fallen asleep, and he fled from his returning arousal and the accompanying fear that if he gave in, he would never get away.

Back home, he stripped and showered, scrubbing hard to rid himself of her maddening scent. He put on fresh clothes, leaving the others in a heap beside the laundry hamper. He would have to bag them, take them to a dry cleaners and get the smell removed.

Comfortable but exhausted, he sat on his couch and dialed his account box and listened to the list of those who had responded to his ad. There were five, and from that list he culled two who sounded the most promising and self-absorbed. He wanted someone vain and stupid right now; someone he could manipulate without having to work hard at it.

The first woman he called was named Gwen. She giggled when he made the simplest joke, said she had never eaten anything like he described and couldn't wait to try. He made a date with her, hung up and called La Parisienne. By luck they had a table. The maître d' knew him of course and was delighted to hear from him. He sat back, sighed with relief, then curled up on the couch and fell asleep. His descending thought was that he had escaped from something terrible.

The new vessel was perfect. She had artificially dyed red hair, and wore an outfit, which she undoubtedly thought appropriate for an evening of fine dining but which was just a few steps shy of a hooker so far as he was concerned. Her jewelry was cheap and gaudy. His ring would be lost within the trappings. Still, it was the easiest thing in the world to ask her what she thought of it, if she liked it. She turned it over, studied the stone—"This is a real one, isn't it?"—and tried it on. He let her wear it all through the soup course. He listened to his body as he ate the rich mushroom bisque, but sensed nothing. Convinced that the bisque wasn't touching him—that it was going where it was supposed to go—he relaxed and anticipated the rest of the meal.

Gwen babbled about her job—something clerical in a photo-mounting company where her manager kept finding ways to touch her. It was all accidental according to him, but she knew better: the man was a sleaze. She was thinking about filing a suit.

He tried to seem interested, nodding, giving her warm smiles of sincere support. His mind, however, refused to focus on her. The main course arrived—he'd ordered a wonderful fillet of beef in a sauce of wine, shallots, and Dijon mustard. When he closed his eyes at the first mouthful, he saw the dining room of Cerise's apartment. It was dark, cold. Leaves were blowing, swirling around the empty room. Startled, he opened his eyes, swallowed. Glanced around himself at the restaurant. The noise of a dozen conversations seemed to echo the hiss of the leaves. Gwen asked, "Are you okay?"

He said, "Of course," and to prove it took another bite. Again, he couldn't help closing his eyes with pleasure, and again the instant he did, he was whisked away to the empty table. But it wasn't empty. Cerise was sitting in the chair across from him, motionless, like a corpse, her face hidden in the shadows.

He opened his eyes and found that he'd dropped his knife. A number of people were looking his way, and Gwen said, "Honey, I think you need an aspirin or something." This opinion seemed to be shared by the maître d', who along with the waiter appeared at his side to ask if everything was all right. He laughed lightly and replied that it was nothing—simply, the meal was so good that he'd been transported by it. The maître d' bowed slightly at the compliment and retreated. The waiter replaced his knife.

"It *is* really good, isn't it?" said Gwen.

This time when he ate, he was careful not to close his eyes. This significantly diminished his pleasure in the meal but he had no choice. He ate thereafter a subdued dinner. When Gwen couldn't finish her Suprêmes de Volaille Basquaise, he didn't even attempt to eat it for her, even though the sautéed chicken breast looked and smelled so wonderful. He ordered dessert over her protest that she couldn't touch another bit; after all, he didn't care what *she* ate, but he presumed that her early satiety meant that the magic was working better than ever. So smug was he over this that he forgot himself again at the first taste of the coffee creme caramel. He let his eyes close.

A fierce wind circled him in the cold, dark dining room. The cadaverous Cerise rocked in her chair, as though buffeted. Her hand, crablike, reached for his across the polished surface. Her voice, a rasp, asked, "How can you leave me? How can you leave me like this?" The final sibilance went on hissing. Her hand caught him and he tore himself free of her grip.

He came to, on his feet, moving, the chair already falling back from him, Gwen with her hands up as if to ward him off. There was creme caramel on her forehead, her arm. He couldn't find his spoon.

The whole restaurant was watching. Silent. He'd only closed his eyes for a fraction of a second, how could so much have happened? He sat down, confused, terrified. When the waiter came this time, he asked quietly for the check, added a generous tip and apologized quietly, explaining that he was on a new medication and was obviously reacting badly to it. This did not remove the worry from the waiter's eyes, but at least it might serve to protect him so that he might return another night, after a few months. Once he'd seen through this . . . this whatever it was.

He apologized to Gwen, who suggested that maybe they should call it a night. She handed him back the ring. He knew she would have nothing further to do with him. He'd thrown food at her, like some sophomoric fraternity twit.

Not far from the restaurant was a small café where he could get a drink. That, he decided, was exactly what he needed. He sat at the bar and ordered a double of Glen Morangie, his favourite scotch. He huddled over the glass, inhaling it, trying to calm down. The smell was, as always, intoxicating. His guard came down for only a moment, but that was all it took to transport him again.

Her bony hand gripped his. "You are mine," she said. "Only for me. You swore. You chose." She leaned toward him and the light from outside fell upon her face—the face of the gorgon. Her golden eyes seared him.

He screamed, lunging back from the bar, pouring scotch over himself. He slid from the stool and fell heavily. The back of his head struck the floor, bounced, and hit it again.

The next thing he knew, someone was helping him to his feet, and a voice asked, "What *bit* you, there, fella?" He heard other voices saying, "Seizure" and "drunk."

"I'm all right," he insisted. "All right." Although his head ached and he felt nauseous. "Sorry, sorry. Medication. Bad reaction." He slapped a twenty on the bar and fled. Four doors away, he doubled over and threw up his dinner. *So much*, he thought, wheezing, *for needing a vessel.*

After that he walked without destination, without purpose, lost in a fog of pain and fear, stinking of scotch, the smell of which reactivated his gag reflex twice more until all he could vomit was air.

Finally he stumbled inside. There was nothing for it but to sleep off the whole experience.

Head hanging, he rode the elevator up and was halfway down the hall before he smelled the food. His stomach rumbled, and he stopped dead and looked around himself. This wasn't his building. His hallway.

It was hers.

He knew where the smell of cooking came from. Somehow he had slipped right past the doorman without noticing, been let in—

no, been *brought* in. He turned and lunged back into the elevator, slamming the cage door closed; then he stood inside, his hands on the bars, the odour of cumin and cloves, coriander and cardamom spinning around his head the way the wind had spun about the table in his vision of her. The smells—how could he ignore the rich—the divine—smells?

He had only to relinquish control and his body took over. His body, now divested of all extrinsic food, wanted desperately to fill itself again. It led him step by step to her door.

He raised the knocker, and the force of it dropping was enough to push the door open further; it had been ajar, waiting for him. He walked in. She was standing in the kitchen, wearing nothing but an apron and her golden sandals, her body the colour of wheat toast, and he went to her, his arm outstretched, the ring between his thumb and forefinger. She turned as if on cue, her own hand raised to let him slide the ring into place. Once she had it on, his arm dropped and he stood, transfixed, unable to move or think, bound to her utterly.

"You love your food too much to do without me, don't you? Even on the telephone, I knew you were the one. You're so like Odysseus' men. They loved their food and drink to excess, and so were halfway to being swine before they even set foot on my island." She turned the ring with her thumb, admiring it. "Complementary magics. Of course, mine is the stronger for being the older of the two, so I can use yours as you have done. *Of course*, you are my vessel and my pleasure, my piggy. For so long as you last. Now, go sit down and I'll serve you." She said it all without malice or cruelty, but gently, with affection.

She turned back to her cooking, to the huge clay pot she'd removed from the oven.

He shuffled past her and into the dining room. Took his seat. A bouquet of roses stood in the centre of the table. There were dry, dead leaves on the tabletop. Circe brushed them aside as she set his plate before him—a mountainous biryani sprinkled with *varak*. "There, my darling, now eat to your heart's content."

Staring at the rice and meats, inhaling it, his terror drowned beneath the ocean of his appetite. He looked into her eyes as his own flooded with tears. It was all going to be his.

Afterword

Girlfriends of Dorian Gray

Blame Michael Swanwick and Marianne Porter for this one. It took wing over dinner at their house one evening, really as a joke that snowballed along until Marianne said, "You should probably write that." You have to understand that these are five of the deadliest words you can ever say to a writer.

She knew exactly what she was doing.

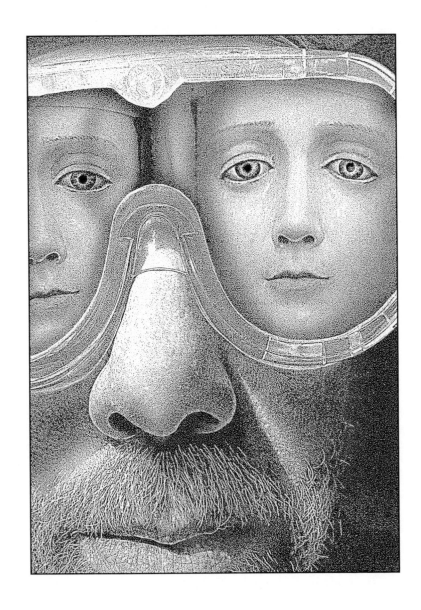

Madonna of the Maquiladora

YOU FIRST HEAR OF GABRIEL PEREA AND THE Virgin while covering the latest fire at the Chevron refinery in El Paso. The blaze is under control, the water cannon hoses still shooting white arches into the scorched sky.

You've collected some decent shots, but you would still like to capture something unique even though you know most of it won't get used. The *Herald* needs only one all-inclusive shot of this fire, and you got that hours ago. The rest is out of love. You like to think there's a piece of W. Eugene Smith in you, an aperture in your soul always seeking the perfect image.

The two firemen leaning against one of the trucks is a good natural composition. Their plastic clothes are grease-smeared; their faces, with the hoods off, are pristine. Both the men are Hispanic, but the soot all around them makes them seem pallid and angelic and strange. And both of them are smoking. It's really too good to ignore. You set up the shot without them knowing, without seeming to pay them much attention, and that's when you catch the snippet of their conversation.

"I'm telling you, *cholo*, the Virgin told Perea this explosion would happen. Mrs. Delgado knew all about it."

"She tells him everything. She's telling us all. The time is coming, I think."

Click. "What time is that?" you ask, capping the camera.

The two men stare at you a moment. You spoke in Spanish—part of the reason the paper hired you. Just by your inflection, though, they know you're not a native. You may understand all right, but you are an outsider.

The closest fireman smiles. His teeth are perfect, whiter than the white bar of the Chevron insignia beside him. Mexicans have good tooth genes, you think. His smile is his answer: He's not going to say more.

"All right, then. Who's Gabriel Perea?"

"Oh, he's a prophet. *The* prophet, man."

"A seer."

"He knows things. The Virgin tells him."

"The Virgin Mary?" Your disbelief is all too plain.

The first fireman nods and flicks away his cigarette butt, the gesture transforming into a cross—"Bless me, father . . ."

"Does he work for Chevron?"

The firemen look at each other and laugh. "You kidding, man? They'd never hire him, even if he made it across the Rio Bravo with a green card between his teeth."

Rio Bravo is what they call the Rio Grande. You turn and look, out past the refinery towers, past the scrub and sand and the Whataburger stand, out across the river banks to the brown speckled bluffs, the shapes that glitter and ripple like a mirage in the distance.

Juarez.

"He's over there?"

"*Un esclavo de la maquiladora.*"

A factory slave. Already you're imagining the photo essay. "The Man Who Speaks to the Virgin," imagining it in *The Smithsonian*, *The National Geographic*. An essay on Juarez, hell on Earth, and smack in the middle of hell, the Virgin Mary and her disciple. It assembles as if it's been waiting for you to find it.

"How about," you say, "I buy you guys a few beers when you're finished and you tell me more about him."

The second guy stands up, grinning. "Hey, we're finished now, amigo."

"Yeah, that fire's drowning. Nothing gonna blow today. The Virgin said so."

You follow them, then, with a sky black and roiling on all sides like a Biblical plague settling in for a prolonged stay.

*   *   *

You don't believe in her. You haven't since long ago, decades, childhood. Lapsed Catholics adopt the faith of opposition. The Church lied to you all the time you were growing up. Manipulated your fears and guilts. You don't plan to forgive them for this. The ones who stay believers are the ones who didn't ask questions, who accepted the rules, the restrictions, on faith. Faith, you contend, is all about not asking the most important questions. Most people don't think; most people follow in their hymnals. It takes no more than a fingernail to scrape the gilt from the statues and see the rot below. Virgin Mary didn't exist for hundreds of years after the death of Jesus. She was fashioned by an edict, by a not very bright emperor. She had a cult following and they gained influence and the ear of Constantine. It was all politics. *Quid pro quo.* Bullshit. This is not what you tell the firemen, but it does make the Virgin the perfect queen for Juarez: that place is all politics and bullshit, too. Reality wrapped in a shroud of the fantastic and the grotesque. Just like the Church itself.

You went across the first time two years ago, right after arriving. The managing editor, a burly, bearded radical in a sportcoat and tie named Joe Baum took you in. He knew how you felt about the power of photography, and after all you're the deputy art director. One afternoon he just walked over to your desk and said, "Come on, we're gonna take the afternoon, go visit some people you need to see." You didn't understand until later that he was talking about the ones on film. Most of them were dead.

Baum covered El Paso cultural events, which meant he mingled with managers and owners of the *maquiladoras.* "We'll have to get you into the loop. Always need pictures of the overlords in their tuxes to biff up the society pages." He didn't like them too much.

In his green Ford you crossed over on the Puente Libre, all concrete and barbed wire. He talked the whole time he drove. "What you're gonna see here is George Bush's New World Order, and don't kid yourself that it isn't. Probably you won't want to see it. Hell, I don't want to see it, and America doesn't want to see it with a *vengeance.*"

He took you to the apartment of a man named Jaime Pollamano. Baum calls him the Chicken Man. Mustache, dark hair, tattoos. A face like a young Charles Bronson. Chicken Man is a street photographer. "We buy some of his photos, and we buy some from the others." There were six or seven in the little apartment that day, one of them, unexpectedly, a woman. The windows were covered, and an old sheet had been stuck up on the wall. They'd

been expecting you. Baum had arranged in advance for your edifi-
cation. "What you're gonna see today," he promised, "is the photos
we *don't* buy."

The slide show began. Pictures splashed across the sheet on the
wall.

First there were the female corpses, all in various states of decay
and decomposition. Most were nude, but they weren't really bodies
as much as sculptures now in leather and wood. The photographers
had made them strange and haunting and terrifying, all at the
same time. In the projector light you can see their eyes—squinting,
hard, glancing down, here and there a look of pride, something
almost feral. The woman is different. She stares straight at death.

"Teenage girls," Baum told you while the images kept coming.
"They get up at like 4 A.M. to walk for miles to catch a bus to take
them to a factory by six. They live in *colonias*, little squatter villages
made of pallet wood and trash. Most of these girls here were kidnapped on the way to work. Tortured, raped, murdered. Nobody
goes looking for them much. Employee turnover in the *maquiladoras* is between fifty and a hundred and fifty percent annually, so
they're viewed as just another runaway *chica* who has to be
replaced. The *pandillas*, the local gangs, get them, or *federales* on
patrol, or even the occasional serial murderer. Who knows who?
No one's looking for her anyway, save maybe her family."

All you could think to say was, "They've lost their breadwinner."

Baum snorted. "That's right. She worked a forty-eight hour
week, six days, for about twenty-five dollars."

"A day?"

"A *week*. Per day they make about four dollars and fifty cents.
Not just these girls, you understand. All of 'em. All the workers."

You tried to work that out, how they live on so little money.
Finally you suggested, "The cost of living here is cheaper?" The
handsome woman photographer's eyes shifted to you, cold with disgust.

The pictures never stopped coming. You finally passed the
gauntlet of dead women. Now it was a man dangling like a *piñata*
from a power line. He'd been electrocuted while trying to run a
line from a transformer to his home. Then other dead men. Some
dying in the street with people all around them. Others dead like
the women, executed, tortured, burned alive. You tried to look
elsewhere as the images just kept slamming the wall. How many
deaths could there be? Baum suddenly said, "Let me put the cost of
living thing in perspective for you. You're seventeen, you live in El

Paso, you work six days a week all day and you buy your groceries
and pay your bills on your thirty-five dollar paycheck. That's adjusted gross to compensate for the differences in cost on our side of
the river.

"On this side along the river there are over three hundred factories. Big names you know: RCA, Motorola, Westinghouse, GE.
We use their products, we all do. They employ almost 200,000
workers, mostly female, living crammed in the *colonias*, altogether
about two million people. That's eighty percent unemployment, by
the way."

Between the images and the facts, you're lost and grasping
for some sort of reality. This is what a series of smiling presidents
promised the world? Even as you flounder, the photos change
course. A severed arm dangles from the big face of Mickey Mouse,
both nailed to a wall; a clown head tops a barbed wire fence post,
with laundry drying on the wire; a six-year-old holds a Coca-Cola
can, only the straw's going up his nose, and you can tell by his slack
face that whatever's in that can is fucking him up severely. The
power of these images is in their simplicity: This isn't art, it just
is. All you could do was repeat the mantra that this is what art is
supposed to do—shake you up, make you think differently. Make
you sweat. Doing its job. God, yes.

Afterward Baum introduced you to the photographers but the
room stayed dark. You walked through the line, shaking hands,
nodding, dazed. One man was drunk. Another, the feral one, had
the jittery sheen of an addict. The woman hung back. Reality after
that onslaught barely touched you.

Baum bought some of the pictures in spite of what he'd told
you, paying far too much for them. Maybe he collected them—
you were sure they weren't going to get into the paper. You know
what the paper will print. He walked you out, across the street, past
his car and through the Plaza de Armas, the main square. It was a
Friday night and there must have been a thousand people milling
about. The ghosts of all those photos tagged along, bleeding into
the world. The cathedral across the plaza was lit in neon reds,
greens, and golds, looking more like a casino than a church.
Everywhere, people were selling something. Most of it was trash
collected and reassembled into trinkets, earrings, belts, whatever
their skill allowed. There were clowns on stilts wandering around.
A man selling flavored ice chips. Baum bought two. Others sold
tortillas, drugs, themselves. All of it smelled desperate. A lot of the
crowd, Baum told you as you drove home after, were actually

Americans. "They come across the border on Friday nights for a little action. The factory girls sell themselves for whatever extra dollars they can get from the party boys."

You remember at some point in the drive asking him why the workers don't unionize, and provoking the biggest laugh of all. "No union organizer would have a job by day's end, is why. Some of them don't make it home alive, either, although you can't tie anything to the corporations that fire them. Just as likely they pissed off their co-workers by threatening the status quo. It's happened before—whole shifts have been fired, everyone blamed for the actions of one or two. When you're an ant, it doesn't take a very big rock to squash you. My, what a glorious testament to American greed—and we've even kept it from crossing the border, too. So far."

That conversation comes back to you now, driving away from your drinks with the firemen. Gabriel Perea was an activist. In Baum's terms, he was a dangerous man to himself and anyone who knew him. The Virgin turned him, saved him. She's protecting him for something important. The firemen expect something between Armageddon and Rapture. Transcendence. All you know is that you want to get there before the Kingdom of Heaven opens for business.

"*Pura guasa*," Baum says when you tell him what you want to do. "Just a lot of superstitious chatter. Nonsense. I've heard about this guy before. He's like an urban legend over there. They need for him to exist, just like her."

Nevertheless, you say, it's a great story—the kind of thing that could garner attention. Awards. The human spirit finding the means to survive in the *maquiladora* even if that means is a fantasy. Baum concedes it could be terrific.

"*If* there's anything to it."

There's only one way to find that out. In *c. de Juarez*, all roads lead to the Chicken Man.

On the outside of his apartment someone has sprayed the words "Dios Está Aquí." Chicken Man has moved three times since you first met him. Most of the street photographers move routinely, just to stay alive, to stay ahead of the *narcotraficante*, or the cops or anyone else they've pissed off with their pictures. Of the six you met that first day, only five are still living. Now Pollamano's holed up just off the Pasea Triunfa de la Republica. And holed up is the right term. The cinder block building has chicken wire over the windows and black plastic trash bags on the inside of them. You knock once and slide your business card under the door. After a while the door opens slightly and you go in. It's hot inside, and the air smells like chemicals, like fixer and developer. The only light on is a single red bulb. Chicken Man wears a Los Lobos tank top, shorts, and sandals. He's been breathing this air forever. He should have mutated by now. "¿*Quiubo*, Deputy?" *Deputy* is the street photographers' name for you. Titles are better than names here anyway. They call Joe Baum "La Bamba."

He invites you to sit. You tell him what the firemen told you. What you want to do with it.

"*El Hombre de la Madona*. I know the stories. A lot of 'em circulating round."

"So, what's the truth? He isn't real? Doesn't see her?"

"Oh, he's real. And he maybe sees her." He crosses to the shelves made of cinder blocks and boards, rummages around in one of thirty or so cardboard boxes, returns with a 4x5 print. In the red light, it's difficult to see. Chicken Man turns on a maglight and hands it to you.

You're looking at a man in dark coveralls. He's standing at a crazy, Elvis Presley kind of angle, feet splayed and legs twisted. His hands are up in front of him, the fingers curled. There are big protective goggles over his eyes. He has a long square jaw and a mustache. Behind him other figures in goggles and coveralls stand, out of focus. They're co-workers and this is inside a factory somewhere. Fluorescent lights overhead are just greenish smears. The expression on his face is fierce — wide-eyed, damn near cross-eyed.

"He was seein' her right then," says the Chicken Man.

"You took this?"

"Me? I don't set foot in the *maquilas*. Factory owners don't like us, don't want us taking pictures in there. Some of the young ones get in for a day, shoot, and get out. I'm too old to try that kind of crap."

"Who, then?"

"*Doncella loca*."

He holds out his hand, takes the photo back. When he hands it back, there's writing on it in grease pencil. A name, Margarita Espinada, and the words "*Colonia Universidad*." He describes how to drive there. "You met her," he says, "the very first time La Bamba brought you over. She lives in her car mostly. *Auto loco*. I let her use my chemicals when she needs to. And the sink. She's shooting the Tarahumara kids now. Indians. They don't trust nobody, but they trust her. Same with the *maquilas*. Most of the workers are women. She gets in where I can't. She's kinda like you, Deputy. Only smart." He grins.

You grin back and hand him a twenty and three rolls of film. He slides the money into his pocket but kisses the plastic canisters. "*Gracias, amigo.*"

Colonia Universidad is easy to find because half of it has just burned to the ground and the remains are still smoking. Blackened oil drums, charcoal that had defined shacks the day before, naked bedsprings, and a few bicycle frames twisted into Salvador Dali forms. Margarita Espinada is easy to find, too. She wears a camera around her neck, and black jeans, boots, and a blue work shirt. The jeans are dirty, the shirt stained dark under the arms and down the back. Her black hair is short. The other women around her are wearing dresses and have long hair, and scarves on their heads. At a quick glance you might mistake her for a man.

They're all watching you before the car even stops. When you stride toward them, the women all back up, spread apart, move away. Margarita stands her ground. She raises her camera and takes your picture, as though in an act of defiance. From a distance she looks to be about twenty, but up close you can see the lines around the eyes and mouth. More like early thirties. Lean. There's a thin scar across the bridge of her nose and one cheek.

If she remembers you from the Chicken Man's, there's no sign of it in her eyes. You hand her the photo. She looks at it, at her name on the back, then wipes it down her thigh. "You want a drink, Deputy?" There's the tiniest suggestion of amusement in the question.

"I'm not really a deputy, you know. It's just a nickname."

"Hey, at least they don't call you *pendejo*."

"I don't know that they don't."

She laughs, and for a moment that resolute, defiant face becomes just beautiful.

The shack she takes you to is barely outside the fire line. The frame is held together by nails driven through bottle caps. The walls are cut-up shipping cartons for Three Musketeers candy bars. No floor, only dirt. There's an old, rust-stained mattress and a couple of beat-up suitcases. She comes up with a bottle of tequila from God knows where, apologizes for the lack of ice and glasses. Then she takes a long swig from the mouth of the bottle. Her eyes are watering as she passes it to you. You smell her then, the odor of a woman mixed in with the smoke smell, sweat and flesh and dirt. You almost want to ask her why she does this, lives this way, but you haven't any right. Instead you say his name as a question.

She lays down the photo. "Gabriel Perea is real, he exists. He's what they call an assembler, on a production line. The *maquila* is about twenty miles from here. The story of him grows as it travels. All around."

You recite the firemen's version: great prophet, seer who will lead them into the kingdom of Heaven.

"*Pura guasa*," is her answer. Pure foolishness—exactly what Baum said.

"But the picture. He *is* seeing the Virgin?"

She shrugs. "Yes, I know. From your eyes—how could I take the picture and not say it's true?" She pushes her thumb against the image, covering the face. "This says it's real. Not true. I know that he tells everyone what the Virgin wants them to know."

"And what's that?"

"To be patient. To wait. To endure their hardships. To remember that they will all find Grace in Heaven more beautiful than anything they can imagine."

"That wouldn't take much of a heaven. Has anyone else seen her?"

"No one in the factory now."

"But someone else?"

Again, she shrugs. "Maybe. There are stories. Someone saw her in a bathroom. In a mirror. There are always stories once it starts. People who don't want to be left out, who need to hear from her. That can be a lot of people.

"In *Colonia El Mirador*, a Sacred Heart shrine begins to bleed. It's a cheap, little cardboard picture, and they say it bleeds, so I go and take its picture."

"Does it? Does it bleed?"

"I look in the picture I take, at how this piece of cardboard is nailed up, and I think, ah, the nailhead has rusted, the rust has run down the picture. That's all. But I don't say so."

"So, you lied to them, the people who made the claims about it?"

She snatches back the bottle. Her nostrils are flared in defiance, anger; but she laughs at your judgment, dismissing it. "I take the picture and it says what is what. If you don't see, then what good is there in telling you *how* to see?"

The anger, contained, burns off her like radiation. You flip open your Minox and take her picture. She stares at you in the aftermath of the flash, as if in disbelief.

Breaking the tension, you ask, "Is he crazy?"

She squats down in the dirt, her back pressed against the far wall, takes off the camera and sets it on the mattress. "Listen, I got a job in a factory because I heard there was a dangerous man there. A Zapatista brother, someone of the Reality. He had workers stirred up.

"And I thought, I want to be there when they have him killed. I want to document it. The bosses there will pay workers to turn in their co-workers. Pay them more money than they can earn in a month, so it's for sure someone will turn him in. But this Perea, he sought out those people and he convinced them not to do this. He offered hope. 'The Dream we can all dream, so that when we awaken it will remain with us.' That's what he promised. When I learned that, then I knew I had to photograph him. And his murder."

"Except the Virgin showed up."

She grins. "I hadn't even gotten my first exciting twenty dollar paycheck. The rumor circulated that he was going to confront the managers. Everyone was breathing this air of excitement. And I have my camera, I'm ready. Only all of a sudden, right on the factory floor, Gabriel Perea has a vision. He points and he cries, 'Oh, Mother of God! See her? Can you see her? Can you hear her, good people?' Of course we can't. No one can. They try, they look all around, but you know they don't see. He has to tell it. She says, 'Wait.' She says, 'There will be a sign.' She'll come again and talk to us."

"Did she? Did she come back?"

"About once every week. She came in and spoke to him when he was working. People started crowding around him, waiting for the moment. It's always when he doesn't expect. Pretty soon there are people clustering outside the factory and following Gabriel Perea home. The managers in their glass booths just watch and watch."

"They didn't try to stop it?"

"No. And no one got into trouble for leaving their position, or for trespassing. Trying to see him. To hear his message. And I begin to think, these men are at least afraid of God. There is something greater and more powerful than these *Norte Americanos*."

"Yet you don't believe it?"

In answer, she gets up and takes the larger suitcase and throws it open on the mattress. Inside are photos, some in sleeves, some loose, some in folders. You see a color shot of a mural of a Mayan head surrounded by temples, photos of women like those you scared off outside, one of a man lying peacefully sleeping on a mattress in a shack like this one. She glances at it and says, "He's dead. His heater malfunctioned and carbon monoxide killed him. Or maybe he did it on purpose."

She pulls out a manila folder and opens it. There's a picture of an assembly line—a dozen women in hairnets and surgical gowns and rubber gloves, seated along an assembly line.

"What's this place make?"

"Motion controller systems." You stare at a photo sticking out from the pack, of Gabriel Perea head-on, preaching, in that twisted martial arts pose of his. This time she has crouched behind equipment to get this shot, but in the background you can see the managers all gathered. Most of them are grainy shadows, but the three faces that are visible are clearly not frightened of what's happening here.

"They look almost bored."

She nods.

"You think he's a fake. Comes in as an agitator to catch workers who'd be inclined to organize, and then he catches them in a big net, a phony appearance by the Virgin Mary, promising them a wonderful afterlife if they just grind themselves down like good little girls and boys in this one."

She glances at you oddly, then says, "Maybe they *don't* call you names, Deputy."

You meet her eyes, smile, thinking that you'd be willing to fall in love with this other photographer; but the idea fades almost as fast as it arrives. She lives with nothing and takes all the risks while you have everything and take no risks at all. Her dreams are all of her people. Yours are of awards and recognition.

She offers you the bottle again and you drink and wheeze and wonder why it is you can't have both dreams. Why yours seems petty and cheap. You don't believe in the Virgin, either. The two of you should be able to support each other. Ignoring the delusions of a few people over their rusting shrine is a far cry from ignoring this kind of scam.

She agrees to get you an interview with Gabriel Perea. It will take some days. He is a very reluctant holy man, more shy than the Tarahumara.

"Come back in three days." To this *colonia*, to this shack, to wait for her. All right, you think, that's good. It gives you time to get information.

You give her five film canisters and she kisses you on the cheek for it. You can feel her lips all the way home.

When you tell Baum what you've found, he sends you down to see Andy Jardin. Andy's a walking encyclopedia of corporate factology —if it's listed on the DJI, Nasdaq, or the S&P 500, he's got a profile in his computer if not in his head.

He barely acknowledges you when you show up. The two of you had one conversation on the day you were hired—Baum introduced you. Andy said, "Hey." You take pictures, he babbles in stocks—two languages that don't recognize each other without a translator. He has carrot-colored hair that might have been in dreadlocks the last time it was mowed, and wears black plastic frame glasses through which he peers myopically at his computer screen.

You clear your throat, ask him if he knows of the company. Immediately you get his undivided attention. He reels off everything—no one has ever accused this kid of trying to hold back.

They manufacture control systems, have government contracts, probably fall into someone's black budget, like most of the military manufacturers. Their stock is hot, a good investment, sound and steady. They don't actually manufacture anything in the *maquiladora*, which is a common story. They just assemble parts, which are shipped up to Iowa, where the company's based. That's where the controllers are made. He says they're developing what are called genetic algorithms. When you look blank, he happily sketches in the details: genetic algorithms are the basis for lots of artificial intelligence research. Of course, he adds, there is no such thing currently as AI—not in the evil computer mind bent on world domination sense. It's all about learning circuits, routines that adjust when conditions change, that can refine themselves based on past experience. Not brains, not thinking—a kind of mathematical awareness.

Before you leave, he invites you to buy some of their stock. This is a really good time for them, he says.

Later on, Baum tells you that Andy's never invested a cent in his life, he just loves to watch, the ultimate investment voyeur. "And you can expect to get every article that even mentions your company from now on. He'll probably forward you their S&P daily, too. "You're into something here?" he asks, as if that's the last thing that concerned him. The real question he's asking is "How long is this going to take?"

All you can do is shrug and say, "I really don't know. This woman—this photographer—she has a notion he's a ringer, someone the company threw in to manipulate the workers, keep them docile. I want to interview him, take his picture, get inside the factory and get some pictures there, too. You know, get what I can before they know that I'm looking at him specifically."

"Is it a Catholic thing—I mean, your interest?"

"It's not about me."

Whether or not he believes you, he doesn't say.

As you're leaving he adds, "You've seen enough to know that weird and bizarre are the norms over there, right?" Again, he's not saying it outright. Beneath his camaraderie lies the real edginess: He's worried about you and this story—how you fit together.

"I won't forget. *Hecho* in Mexico is *Hecho* in Hell."

Baum laughs. It's his saying, after all.

Perea speaks so quietly and so fast that you can't catch half of it. He sits in the corner away from the lantern, on the ground. He bows his head when he speaks as if he's ashamed to admit what's happening to him. This is not, to your thinking, the behavior of a man who is playing a role. Still, how could anyone be certain? You take pictures of him bathed in lantern light, looking like a medieval pilgrim who has made his journey, found his God.

Margarita kneels beside you, leaning forward to hear clearly, translating his murmured Spanish. "'I don't know why the Virgin picked me. I'm just a *Chamula.*' That's an Indian from Chiapas, Deputy," she explains. "'I believe that things need to change. People need their dignity as much as their income. I thought I could do this on my own—change things in this factory, I mean. The other workers would trust me and together we would break the cycle in which the neoliberals keep us.'"

"What does she look like?"

"'She has blue robes, a cloth over her head. I can sort of see through her, too. And her voice, it fills my head like a bell ringing. But it's soft, like she's whispering to me. No one else sees her. No one else hears her.'" He looks up at you, his eyes pleading for understanding. "'She stopped me from doing a terrible thing. If we had protested as I planned, many people would have been killed. They would bring in the *federales* and the *federales* would beat us. There would be people waiting for us when we got home

—people the *federales* won't see. Some of us would have been tortured and killed. It might have been me. But I was willing to take that risk, to make this change.' "

"She stopped you."

He nods. " 'Someone said my very first day that the factory is built on a sacred place. In the San Cristóbals we have these places. Maybe she heard our fear. There is a shrine nearby there where a picture of Jesus weeps. And another with tears of blood.' " Margarita glances sharply at you as she repeats this. You nod.

" 'She tells us to live. To endure what life gives us, no matter how hard. She knew what was in my heart. She said that the greatest dignity could be found in the grace of God. To us finally the kingdom will be opened for all we suffer. It will be closed to those who oppress us.' " He is seeing her again as he speaks, his eyes looking at a memory instead of at you.

Afterward, you ride in your car alone—Margarita insists on driving her own, an old Chevy Impala that rumbles without a muffler. She won't ride with anyone; it's one of those things about her that makes it clear she's crazy. Your tape recorder plays, Margarita's translation fills the night.

Perea's telling the truth so far as he knows it. In a moment of extreme danger, the Virgin appeared. That's happened before—in fact, she usually manifests where the climate's explosive, people are strained, fragmented, minds desperate for escape. It's religion to some, mental meltdown to you. So why do you resist even that explanation now? "A Catholic thing?" Baum asked. That's not it, though. You recollect something you once heard Carl Sagan say in an interview: Extraordinary events require extraordinary proof. "So, Carl," you ask the dark interior, "how do you pull proof out of a funhouse mirror?"

By the time Margarita returns, you know what you're going to do. You tell her to see what she thinks. She sits back on the mattress. You can hear her pulling off her boots. "You might get away with it," she answers, and there's anger in her voice. "If they don't pay too much attention to your very Castilian Español. You still talk like a *gringo*. And you still think like one, too. You listen to what he says, and you see it all in black and white, *Norte Americano* versus us. La Bamba's the same way. You guys see what most of your people won't, but you see it with old eyes."

"How are we—I don't understand. The Zapatistas you mean? What—?"

She makes a noise to dismiss you, and there's the sound of the bottle being opened. Not sharing. Then suddenly she's talking, close enough now you can almost feel the heat of her breath.

"It's not north against south anymore, rich whites against poor Mexicans. That's only a thing, a speck. It's the whole world, Deputy. The *maquiladora* is the whole world now. Japan is here, Korea is here, anyone who wants to make things without being watched, without having to answer to anyone, without having to pay fairly. They're here and everywhere else, too. ¡Ya, basta! You understand? Enough! It's not about NAFTA, about whose treaty promises what. Whoever's treaty, it will be just the same. Here right now in Mexico the drug dealers invest, buy factories, take their money and grind their own people to make more money, *clean* money. Clean! And it's no different here than anywhere else, it's even, *dios mio, better* here than some places. It's a new century and the countries bleed together, and the only borders, the only fences, are all made of bodies. All the pictures you've seen, but if you don't see this in all of them, then you're seeing nothing!"

Clearly it's time to leave. "I'm sorry," is all you can think to say, and you turn to go. And suddenly she's blocking your way. Her hands close on your arms. For all your fantasies you didn't see this coming. Here in a shack with a cardboard door is not where you'd have chosen. Only this isn't your choice, it's entirely hers. Anybody could come by, but no one does. She works your clothes off, at the same time tugging at her own in hasty, angry, near-violent action. Sex out of anger. You keep thinking, she's as crazy as they said she was, she's furious with you for your stupidity, how can she possibly want to fuck you, too? For all of which, you don't fight, of course you don't, it's your fantasy however unexpected and inexplicable.

You fall asleep with your arms around her, her breasts warm against you, almost unsure that any of it happened.

The Virgin only visits Perea in the factory. That's where you get a job. Driving a forklift. It's something you used to do, so at least you don't look like an idiot even if they're suspicious of your accent. If they are, they say nothing. They're hiring—from what Baum said, they're always hiring.

You get assigned a small locker. In it are your work things—coveralls and safety glasses. There are signs up in every room in bright red Spanish: "Protective Gear Must Be Worn At All Times!" and "Wear Your Goggles. Protect Your Eyes." Your guide points to one of these and says, "Don't think they're kidding. They'll fire you on the spot if they catch you not wearing the correct apparel."

The lift is articulated. It can take you almost to the ceiling with a full pallet. It has control buttons for your left hand like those found on computer game devices. Working it is actually a pleasure at first.

The day is long and dull. Breaks are almost non-existent. One in the morning, one in the afternoon, both about as long as it takes to smoke a cigarette. The other workers ask where you're from, how you got here. Margarita helped you work out a semi-plausible story about being fired from dock work in Veracruz when you got caught drunk. At least you've been to Veracruz. A few people laugh at the story and commiserate. Drunk, yeah. Nobody pries—there's hardly time for questions, even over lunch, which is the only place you get to take off the safety glasses and relax—but you see suspicion in a few eyes. You can tell any story you want, but you can't hide the way you tell it. Your *voice* isn't from Veracruz. Nevertheless, no one challenges you. Maybe they think you're a company ringer, a spy. That would give them good reason to steer clear of you. Whatever you are, they don't want trouble—that's what Baum said. This job is all they've got. And at week's end, just like them, you'll collect your $22.50, too.

The second day you're there, the Virgin appears to Gabriel Perea.

You're unloading a shipment of circuit boards and components off the back of a semi, when suddenly you find yourself all alone. It's too strange. You climb down and wander out of the loading bay and into the warehouse itself. Everyone's gathered there. A circle of hundreds. Right in the middle Perea stands at that crazy angle like a man with displaced hips. His hands are out, palms wide, and he's repeating her words for everyone: "She loves us all. We are all her children. We are all of us saved and our children are saved. Our blood is *His* blood!" The atmosphere practically crackles. Every eye is riveted to him. You move around the outside perimeter, looking for the masters. There are two up on a catwalk. One looks at you as if you're a bigger spectacle than Perea. You turn away quickly and stare like the others are doing, trying to make like you were looking for a better view of the event. From somewhere in the crowd comes the clicking of a shutter. Someone is taking shots. You could take out your tiny Minox now and shoot a couple yourself, but there's nothing to see that Margarita didn't capture already. Nothing worth drawing any more attention to yourself. *Nada que ver*, the words echo in your head.

For a long time you stare at him. "The *niño* loves us all. His is the pure love of a child. Care for Him, for it's all He asks of you." People murmur, "Amen," and "Yes."

Eventually you chance another look at the two on the catwalk. One of them seems to be talking, but not to the other. You think: *He's either schizophrenic or he's got a microphone.*

In a matter of minutes the spectacle is over. She had nothing remarkable to say; she was just dropping in to remind everyone of her love for them and theirs for her. Now she won't come again for days, another week.

Except for the first two nights you eat alone in the shack. Margarita is somewhere else, living out of her car, photographing things, capturing moments. How does she do this? How does she live forever on the edge, capturing death, surrounded, drenched in it? How can anybody live this way? It's hopeless. The end of the world.

You lay alone in the shack, as cold at night as you are scalding in the afternoon when you walk down the dirt path from the bus drop. You'd like to fall into a swimming pool and just float. The closest you can come is communal rain barrels outside—which were once chemical barrels and God knows whether there's benzene or something worse floating in them, death in the water. Little kids are splashing it over themselves, drinking from it. Watching makes you yearn for a cold drink but you wouldn't dare. Margarita's friends there cook you dinner on their makeshift stoves, for which you gladly pay. By week's end, they've made more from the dinners than you'll take home from the factory.

Friday you drive home for the weekend, exhausted.

You flop down on your bed, so tired that your eyes ache. All you can think about is Margarita. Gabriel Perea's Virgin has melted into a mad photographer who is using you for sex. That's how it feels, that's how it is, too. A part of her clings to you, drowns with you in that dark and dirty shack, at the same time as she dismisses your simplistic comprehension of the complexities of life where she lives. A week now and you've begun maybe to understand it better—at least, you've begun taking pictures around the *colonia* —it's as though she's given you permission to participate. It would be hard not to find strange images: the dead ground outside a shack where someone has stuck one little, pathetic plant in a coffee can; another plywood shack with a sign dangling beside the door proclaiming "*¡Siempre* Coke!" The factory, too. A couple of rolls of film so far, as surreptitiously as possible. The machinery is too interesting not to photograph, even though you feel somehow complicitous in making it seem beautiful and exotic. Even in ugliness and cruelty, there is beauty. Even in the words of an apparition there are lies and deceit. You finally drift off on the thought that the reason you despise the Virgin is that she sells accommodation. It's always been her message and it's the message of the elite, the rich, a recommendation that no one who actually endures the misery would make.

The phone wakes you at noon. Baum has an invitation to a reception for a Republican Senator on the stump. "All our best people will be there. I could use a good photographer and you can use the contacts."

"Sure," you say.

"You'll need a tux."

"Got one."

"You'll need a shower, too."

How he figured that out over the phone, you can't imagine; but he's right, you do smell bad, and it's only been a week. When you get up, your whole body seems to be knitted of broken joints. It's a test of will to stand up to the spray. Being pummeled by water feels like the Rapture, pleasure meeting pain.

It's an outdoor patio party with three Weber Platinum grills big enough to feed the Dallas Cowboys, half a dozen chefs and one waiter for every three people. Everybody wants to have their picture taken with the Senator, who is wearing tan makeup to cover the fact that he looks like he's been stumping for two weeks without sleep, much less sunlight, and you're glad it's not your job to make him look good.

As it is, you end up taking dozens of pictures anyway. Baum calls most of the shots, who he wants with the Senator, whose faces will grace the paper in the morning. He introduces you to too many people for you to keep track of them—all the corporate executives and spouses have turned out for this gala event. When he introduces you to the head of the Texas Republican Party, just the way he says it makes it sound as if you are beholding a specifically Texan variety of Republican. For a week you've been living in a shack with dirt floors among people who cook their food on stoves made from bricks and flat hunks of iron, and here you are in a bow tie and cummerbund, hobnobbing with the richest stratum of society in El Paso and munching on shrimp bigger than your thumb, a spread that would feed an entire *colonia* for days. It's not just the disparity, it's the displacement, the fragmentation of reality into razor-edged jigsaw puzzle pieces.

And then Baum hauls you before a thin, balding man wearing glasses too small for his face, the kind that have no frames, just pins to hold the earpieces on. "This is Stuart Coopersmith." He beams at you—a knowing smile if ever there was one. To Coopersmith, he says, "He's the guy I told you about who's into image manipulation." He withdraws before he has to explain anything to either of you.

"So, you're Joe's new photo essayist," he says.

A smile to hide your panic. "I like that title better than the one they gave me at the paper. Mind if I use it?"

"Be my guest." If he recognizes you, he shows no indication.

"So, what do you do that I should consider taking *your* picture, Mr. Coopersmith?"

He touches his tie as he names his company. It seems to be a habit. "Across the river?"

"*La maquiladora.* You guys make what—"

"Control devices. We're all about control." There's a nice, harmless word for someone in the big black budget of government bureaucracy, flying under the public radar.

"It's more than that, though, right? Someone told me, your devices actually learn."

"Pattern recognition is not quite learning, not like most people think of it. Something occurs, our circuit notices, and predicts the likelihood of it recurring, and then if it does as predicted, the circuit loops, and the more often the event occurs when it's supposed to, the more certain the circuit becomes, the more reliable the information and, ah, the more it seems like there's an intelligence at work. What we know to be feedback *looks* like behavior, which is where people start saying that the things are alive and thinking."

"I'm not sure I—"

"Well, it's no matter, is it? You can still take pictures without understanding something this complex." Coopersmith says this so offhandedly, you can't be certain whether you've been put down. He flutters his hand through the air as if brushing the subject away. "We just manufacture parts down here. We do employ lots of people—we're very popular in the *maquiladora*. Like to help out the folks over there."

You nod. "So, what's on deck now?"

He looks at his champagne glass, then glances sidelong, like

Cassius conspiring to kill Caesar. "Oh, some work for NASA. For a Mars flight they're talking about. Using GAs to predict stress, breakdown—things they can't afford in the middle of the solar system. The software will actually measure the individual's stress from moment to moment, and weigh in with a protective environment if that stress jumps at all. It's still pattern recognition, you know, but not the same as on an assembly line. I suppose it's really very exciting."

"Amazing." It's probably even important work.

"In fact you all should do a story on it—I mean, not right this second, but in a few months, maybe, when the program's a little further along and NASA's happy, you and Joe should come over to the factory, shoot some pictures. Write this thing up. I'd give you the exclusive. You guys beat out all the other papers, get a little glory. We'd sure love the PR. That never hurts. You come and I'll give you the guided tour of the place, how's that?"

He adjusts his tie again on the way to reaching into his coat and coming up with a business card. The card has a spinning globe on it, with tiny lights flashing here and there as the world spins. Coopersmith smiles. "Cool, isn't it? The engine's embedded in the card. Doesn't take much to drive a little animation. You be sure and have Joe give me a call real soon."

He turns his back, striking up another conversation almost immediately. You've been dismissed. Heading over to where Joe stands balancing a plate of ribs, you glance back.

Coopersmith with eyes downcast listens to another man talk, his hand fiddling with the knot on his tie again.

You might not have been sure at first, but you are now: He was the one on the catwalk, watching as you edged around the factory floor while the Virgin paid her visit.

Joe says, "So?"

"He offered us the exclusive on their new program for NASA."

"You have been blessed, my son. An overlord has smiled upon you." He tips his glass.

When you tell Margarita what you suspected, she isn't surprised so much as hurt. Even though she'd been certain of the fraud, the fact of it stings her. By association, you're part of her pain. Although she welcomed you back with a kiss, after the news she doesn't want to touch at all. She withdraws into smoke and drink, and finally wanders off with her cold, black camera into the *colonia*, disgusted, she says, with the human race and God himself. You begin to realize that despite her tough, cynical skin, there's at least a kernel of Margarita that wanted the miracle in all its glory. Beneath your rejection, does some part of you want it, too? Once in a while in seeking for truth it would be nice to find something better than truth.

Later, in the dark, she comes back, slides down beside you on the mattress and starts to cry. From her that's an impossible sound, so terrifying that it paralyzes you. It's the sound of betrayal, the very last crumb of purity floating away.

You reach over to hold her, and she pushes your hand away. So you lie there, unable to take back the knowledge, the doubt, the truth, and knowing that the betrayal will always be tied to you. There's nothing you can do.

The first opportunity you have, you swap your goggles with Gabriel Perea. The only place you can do this is at lunch. You have to wait for a day when he carries the goggles off the assembly line straight to the lunch area. You sit with him, listening to other workers ask him things about the Virgin. He looks at you edgily. He knows he's supposed to pretend that you've never met, but you're making this impossible by sitting there beside him. Making the switch is child's play. Everyone's staring at him, hanging on his every word. You set your goggles beside his, and then pick up the wrong pair a minute later and walk away.

Close up, you can see that his goggles have a slight refractive coating. He's going to know immediately what's happened, but with luck he won't be able to do anything about it. He won't want to be seen talking to you in the middle of the factory.

If Perea remotely shares your suspicions, he hasn't admitted it even to himself. This makes you think of Margarita, and your face burns with still more betrayal. It's too late, you tell yourself. This is what you came here to do.

Two days later, ten feet up in the forklift, you get what you wanted: The Virgin Mary appears to you.

It's a bare wall, concrete brick and metal conduits, and suddenly there she is. She floats in the air and when you look through the cage front of the forklift she is floating beyond it. The cage actually cuts her off. It's incredible. Wherever you look, she has a fixed location, an anchored spot in space. If you look up, her image remains fixed, sliding down the glasses. Somehow the circuit monitors your vision, tracks the turn of your head. "Feedback loops"— wasn't that what Coopersmith said? It must be automatic, though.

She may recognize the geometry, but not the receiver, because the first thing out of her mouth is: *"Te amo, Gabriel, mi profeta."* So much for divinity. She doesn't know you've swapped goggles even if the goggles themselves do.

She is beautiful. Her hair, peeking out beneath a white wimple, is black. The blue of her robes is almost painful to see. No sky could match it. Her oval face is serene, a distillation of a million tender mothers. Oh, they're good, whoever created her. Who *wouldn't* want to believe in this Mary? Gabriel couldn't help but succumb.

The camera in your pocket is useless.

She reminds you of your duty to your flock. She promises that you will all live in glory and comfort in Heaven after this life of misery and toil, and not to blame—

In the middle of her speech, she vanishes.

It's so quick that you almost keel forward out of your seat, thank God for the harness.

You can guess what happened. Management came out for their afternoon show, and things were wrong. Gabriel Perea, the poor bastard, didn't respond. He's still somewhere, attaching diodes to little green boards, unaware that divinity has dropped by to see him again.

You lower the forklift, and get out, unable to help one last glance up into the air, looking for her. A mere scintilla, a Tinker-bell of light would do, but there is nothing. Nothing.

The last hour and a half you go about your business as usual. Nothing has changed, nothing can have changed. Your hope is they think their circuits or the goggles malfunctioned, something failed to project. Who knows what sort of feedback system was at work there—it has to be sophisticated to have dodged every solid shape in front of you. They'll want to see his goggles at the end of his shift. No one seems to be watching you yet. No one calls you in off the floor. So at the end of the day you drop the goggles in the trash and leave with the others in your shift. Everyone's talking about going home, how hot it is, how much they'd like a bath or a beer. Everything's so normal it sets your teeth on edge. You ride the bus down the highway and get off with a dozen others at your *colo-nia* and head for home.

It's on the dusty cowpath of a road, on foot, that they grab you. Three of them. They know who they're looking for, and everyone else knows to stay out of it. These guys are *las pandillas*, the kind who'd kill someone for standing too close to you. A dozen people are all moving away, down the road, and the looks they give you are looks of farewell. *Adios, amigo.* Won't be seeing you again. They know it and so do you. You've seen the photos. The thousand merciless ways people don't come home, and you're about to become one.

The first guy walks straight up as if he's going to walk by, but suddenly his elbow swings right up into your nose, and the sky goes black and shiny at the same time, and time must have jumped because you're on your knees, blood flowing out between your fingers, but you don't remember getting there. And then you're on your back, looking at the sky, and still it seems no one's said a word to you, but your head is ringing, blood roaring like a waterfall. Someone laid you out. Each pose is a snapshot of pain. Each time there's less of you to shoot. They'll compress you, maybe for hours, maybe for days—that's how it works, isn't it? How long before gasoline and a match? Will you feel anything by then?

You stare up at the sky, at the first few stars, and wait for the inevitable continuation. The bodies get buried in the Lote Bravo. At least you know where you're going. In a couple of months someone might find you. Will Joe come looking?

Someone yells, "*¡Aguila!*" and a door slams. Or is that in your head, too?

Footsteps approach. Here it comes, you think. Is there anything you can do to prepare for the pain? Probably not, no.

The face that peers down at you doesn't help. Hispanic, handsome, well-groomed. This could be any business man in Mexico, but you know it isn't, and you remember someone telling you about the *narcotraficantes* investing in the *maquiladora*, taking their drug money and buying into international trade. Silent partners.

"Not going to hurt you, *keemo sabe*," he's saying with a sly grin, as though your broken nose and battered skull don't exist. "Couldn't do that. No, no. Questions would be asked about you— you're not just some factory cunt, are you?" His grin becomes a sneer—you've never actually seen anyone sneer before. This guy hates women for a hobby. "No, no," he says again, "you're a second rate wedding photographer who thought he was Dick fucking Tracy. What did you do, hang out with the Juarez photo-locos and get all righteous? Sure, of course you did." He kneels, clucking his tongue. You notice that he's holding your Minox. "Listen, *cholo*, you print what you've uncovered, and Señor Perea will die. You think that's a threat, hey? But it's not. You'll make him out a fool to his own people. They trust him, you know? It's all they got, so you go ahead and take it from them and see what you get. *We* care so much, we're lettin' you go home. Here." He tosses the camera into the dirt. "You're only a threat to the people who think like you do, man." Now he grabs your arm and pulls you upright. The world threatens to flip on you, and your stomach promises to go with it if it does. Close up, he smells of citrus cologne. He whispers to you, "Go home, *cholo*, go take pictures of little kids in swimming pools and cats caught in trees and armadillos squashed on the highway. Amateurs don't survive. Neither do the professionals, here. Next time, you gonna meet some of them." Then he just walks away. You're left wobbling on the road. The gang of three is gone, too. Nobody's around. Behind you, you hear a car door and the rev of an engine. A silver SUV shoots off down the dirt road, back to the pavement and away.

You stumble along the path to the *colonia*. Your head feels as tender as the skin of a plum. Your sinuses are clogged with blood and your nose creaks when you inhale. People watch in awe as you approach your shack. In that moment you're as much a miracle to them as Gabriel Perea. They probably think they're seeing a ghost. And they're right, aren't they? You aren't here any longer.

Margarita's not inside. Her camera's gone. There's no one to comfort you, no one to hear how you were written off. The heat inside is like the core of the sun. Back outside you walk to the water barrel, no longer concerned with what contaminants float in the water. You splash it on your face, over your head. Benzene? Who cares? You're dead anyway. You touch your nose and it's swollen up the size of a saguaro. Embarrassing how easily you've been persuaded to leave. It didn't take anything at all, did it? One whack and a simple "Go away, Señor, you're a fool." What, did you think you could change the world? Make a difference? Not a second rate wedding photographer like you. Not someone with an apartment and a bed and an office and a car. Compromised by the good life. Nobody who leads your life is going to make the difference over here. It takes a breed of insanity you can't even approach.

Baum was dead wrong about everything. He simplified the problems to fit, but they aren't simple. Answers aren't simple. You, you're simple.

Two little girls kneel not far from the barrel, cooking their meal in tin pans on top of an iron plate mounted over an open flame. There's a rusted electrical box beside them, with outlet holes like eyes and a wide slit for a switch. It's a robot face silently screaming. The girls watch you even when they're not looking.

Long after it gets dark you're still alone inside. Margarita must be off on some adventure, doing what she does best, what you can't do. You've had hours to build upon your inadequacy. Run your story and they'll tear Perea apart. He was doomed the moment he believed in the possibility of her. Just like the Church and the little Catholic boy you were once. When you see that, you don't want to see Margarita. You don't want to have to explain why you aren't going any further. All you can do is hurt her. Only a threat.

You pack up your few things, leaving the dozen film canisters you didn't use. Let the real photojournalist have them. "*Nada que ver,*" you tell the empty room.

Back across the border before midnight, before your life turns back into a pumpkin—better she *should* think you're lying under three feet of dirt.

A month rolls by in a sort of fog. Booze, painkillers, and the hell-bent desire to forget your own name. Your nose is healing. It's a little crooked, has a bluish bump in the middle. Baum keeps his distance and doesn't ask you anything about your story, though at first you're too busy to notice. Then one day you find out from the sports editor that Joe got a package while you were gone, and although nobody knows what was in it, when he opened it, he turned white as a ghost and just packed up his office and went home. Called in sick the next three days.

When you do try and talk to him about what happened, he interrupts with an angry "Don't think you're the first person who's been smashed on the rocks of old Juarez." Then he walks away. They got to him somehow. If they wanted to, they could get to both of you. Like the wind, this can blow across the river. That message was for you.

Then one day while you're placing ad graphics, Joe Baum comes over and sits beside you. He won't look you in the eye. Very softly he says, "Got a call from Chicken Man. Margarita Espinada's dead."

You stare at the page on the monitor so hard you're seeing the pixels. Finally, you ask him, "What happened?"

"Don't know. Don't know who did it. She's been gone for weeks and weeks, but he said that wasn't unusual. She lived mostly in her car."

"*Auto loco.*"

"Yeah." He starts to get up, but as if his weight is too much for him, he drops back onto the chair. "Um, he says she left a package for you. Addressed to him, so maybe whatever happened, she had some warning." With every word he puts more distance between himself and her death. "There's gonna be a funeral tomorrow."

"So soon?"

Baum makes a face, lips pressed tight. Defiantly he meets your gaze. "She was dumped in the Lote Bravo a while ago."

Pollamano nods sadly as he lets you in. "¿Quiubo, Deputy?" he asks, but not with any interest. His eyes are bloodshot, drunk or crying, maybe both. Some others are there inside. A few nod—some you remember. Most of them pretend you aren't there. Her body lies in la Catedral, three blocks from Chicken Man's current abode. You shouldn't see it. Their newest member took pictures. Ernesto. He was there, following the cops with his police band radio the way he always does, always trying to get to the scene before they do. He'd taken half a dozen shots before he saw the black boots and realized whose body he was photographing. They'd torn off most of her clothes but left the boots. You remember the one who warned you off. The boots were left on so everyone would know who she was.

Everyone drinks, toasting her memory. One of them begins weeping and someone else throws an arm around him and mutters. One of the others spits. None of them seems to suspect that you and she spent time together. In any case, you're an interloper on their private grief. Not one of them.

Margarita must have known you weren't dead—otherwise, why send a package for you?

Late in the afternoon, everyone has shown up, almost two dozen photographers, and some unseen sign passes among you all, and everyone rises up and goes out together. You move in a line through the crowds, between white buses in a traffic snarl and across the square to the neon cathedral. Orange lights bathe you all. Ernesto with his nothing mustache runs up to the door and snaps a picture. Even in this solemn moment, his instinct is for the image. A few glare at him, but no one chastises him. You gather in the front pews, kneel, pray, go up one by one and light your candles for her soul. Your hand is shaking so hard you can hardly ignite the wick.

After everyone else has left he gives you the package. It's nearly the size of a suitcase. He says, "She left it for you, and I don't violate her wishes. She was here a couple times when I wasn't around. Using the darkroom."

You pull out a folder of photos. On top is the picture of you she took the first day you arrived in *Colonia Universidad*. You look like you could take on anything. Just looking at it is humiliating. Underneath is her collection of shots inside the factory. The top photo is Gabriel Perea standing all twisted and pointing. Foam on his mouth, eyes bugging out. The image is spoiled because of some fogging on the left side of it as if there was a light leak. Whatever caused it lit up Perea, too.

You almost miss the thing that's different: He's not wearing his goggles.

You go on to the next shot, but it's a picture of the crowd behind him, all staring, wide-eyed. She's not using a flash, but there's some kind of light source. In the third, fourth, and fifth shots you see it. It shines straight at Perea. There are lens flares in each image. The light is peculiar, diffuse, as if a collection of small bulbs is firing off, making a sort of ring. The middle is hard to make out until the sixth picture. She must have slid on her knees between all the onlookers to get it. Perea's feet are close by and out of focus. The light is the center of the image, the light that is different in each shot.

"Jaime," you say, "do you have a loupe?"

"Of course." He gives it to you. You hold it over the image, over the light. Back in the lab at the *Herald*, you'll blow the image up poster size to see the detail without the lens—the outline, and at the top of it a bunch of smudges, a hint of eye sockets and mouth, a trace of nose and cheek. Can an AI break loose from its handlers? you wonder. Does it have a will? Or is this the next step in their plan?

You give the loupe back.

He says, "That Perea is gone. Disappeared. People are looking all over for him. They say he was called up to heaven."

One way or another, that's probably true. If the Virgin can float on the air now, then they don't need an interpreter. Belief itself will do the work hereafter, hope used as a halter.

"That crazy girl, she went right back into that factory even after he was gone."

You wipe at your eyes, and a half-laugh escapes you. *That crazy girl.*

You close the folder. You can't let anyone have these. That's the ultimate, wrenching realization. Margarita died because of this and no one can see it. The story can't be told, because it's a lie. She knew it, too, but she went ahead.

This is your Sacred Heart. Your rusting nail. Gabriel Perea was called up to heaven or killed—for you it doesn't matter which. By revealing nothing you let him go on living.

Under the top folder there are others full of negatives, hundreds of inverted images of the world—black teeth and faces, black suns and black clouds. The world made new. Made hers. There is a way you can keep her alive.

Jaime pats you on the shoulder as you leave with your burden. "You go home, Deputy," he tells you. "Even the devil won't live here."

—for Sycamore Hill 1999

Afterword

Madonna of the Maquiladora

Second person is a strange viewpoint. I did not start out intending to use it for this story. But nothing else felt right. I had read a novella called "Aura" by Carlos Fuentes some years ago, and was struck by the wonderful, jagged dreamlike quality he evoked by using that POV. The more I learned about Juarez and the plight of the women who work in the factories along the border, the more that kind of disorienting perspective seemed necessary.

Writing is to a great extent working very hard to make something look as if it was easy to create. This story, once written, had to walk a gauntlet where fourteen other, astonishingly fine writers pummeled and lashed it. Then the blood was rinsed off and it was patched up. Because of their combined critical skills, every break was stronger after it healed . . . which is why it's dedicated to all of them.

Collecting Dust

I.

IN THE MORNING, WHEN HE WENT DOWNSTAIRS FOR breakfast, Thomas found new dust on the table. It lay between the folded newspaper and Dad's half-finished cup of cold coffee, in two small heaps. He'd brought his jar with him—a plastic peanut butter jar rescued from the recycling bin—and he carefully brushed the dust with the edge of his hand into the jar. It was getting pretty full. Then he went back upstairs and put it away.

Mom had left him a granola bar and his vitamins, one glass of orange juice and another of milk. The juice had gone watery because the ice she insisted on putting in it had melted. The milk was tepid. It was breakfast like any other weekday morning.

He heard his sister moving around upstairs as she got ready for school. Una was three years older. She had a silver ring through one eyebrow, smoked cigarettes, was having sex with Kevin Blodgett, a senior like her, and called Thomas a *dick* every chance she got. He had seen her naked more than once since he'd turned fourteen. He'd heard her fucking, smelled her smoking, and knew that he could threaten her whenever he chose just by mentioning the skull tattoo that resided above her pubes. Of course it was a double-edged threat, in that knowing of the tattoo's existence meant he *had* seen her naked.

She was either unaware of or ignored Dad's condition, the same as Mom.

He saw that he had time before setting off for school to check his e-mail. Norman was supposed to have sent him the secret shortcut code for *Devilry*, which would let him jump five levels, collect extra lifepoints, and become invisible to all opposition. But Norman had forgotten, and there was nothing in his mailbox. He was a little annoyed; but it wasn't as though he could have played before going. Norman had better have the code written down for him in homeroom, though.

Thomas shut down the computer to keep Una from being able to access any of his stuff. Fortunately she had neither interest nor aptitude for it.

As he was pulling on his backpack in the foyer, he heard her moving in the kitchen. "Bye, Tuna!" he called.

She answered by calling him a "weasel." He left, satisfied to have provoked her.

II.

At the end of the school day he was the first one home. Una would be off with the mall zombies—the five or six girls with whom she did absolutely everything. She couldn't make a move without them. They were stupid without exception, and he was glad they kept her away. It was really hideous when they came here in the afternoon. This way he had the house to himself.

He'd copied Norman's shortcut codes, and instructions. The secret exit to the extra levels was through one of the six canopic urns in the burial chamber of the game temple. He had to collect enough lifepoints before that, but once he had them, he could play extra *Devilry* for hours. Norman swore it would be cool.

Predicting when Mom came home was tricky. She'd already lost one job so far this year. When they ordered her to stay late now, she didn't dare refuse. She was lucky to have found other work. Unlike Dad, she didn't show any signs of the condition yet; but he had a jar rinsed out for her, just in case. The way he figured, it was just a matter of time.

By six o'clock he'd grown weary of the game and its constant, droning soundtrack; and he still lacked enough lifepoints to jump to the extra levels. He shut it off and retreated into the closet with his comics.

He lay on his sleeping bag and, lost in adventures, pored over the graphic panels and superhero physiques—the women's smooth, nippleless breasts, shiny as the lines of a new car; and all of the bulges. Every impossible muscle, flexed or not, bulged, rigid, the bodies like roped cables under balloon rubber.

Una came home while one of his favorite heroes, The Schizoid, was splitting in two to take on multiple street gangs. He heard the sounds she made as she moved through the house; heard her mutter curses in the kitchen, slam cupboards, and then retreat to the den. The TV blared to life. Distantly, he knew she hadn't started the dinner. He could have done it, could have rescued his sister; he knew how to nuke things in a microwave; but he remained in the closet with his heroes.

By the time Mom came in, he'd had to turn on his portable reading light to see the pages of the comics. His watch showed it to be after eight. A fairly long day for Mom; she'd been as late as ten before, but not very often. Not yet.

This time when he heard the angry cursing, he sat up, slid off the bag and tiptoed to the door.

"Una!" Mom was shouting. Her footsteps hammered through the house. The door to the den squeaked. "Una, why is the dinner still in the refrigerator?"

Una's reply was low, sullen, dark, and unfriendly.

Mom snarled, "You self-centered—"

Una yelled back in shrill defense: "Who cares what I do?"

"It's your *responsibility*, damn you. I can't be here to watch either of you, to feed you. You're part of this family—you have to do your *part!*"

Una mumbled something again that he couldn't catch.

"What do you think I'm doing 'til eight at night? Hanging out at the mall, smoking with my friends? Don't look all innocent. You reek of it. Well, I've had it with your attitude, young lady. Had all I'm going to take. You're going to pull your weight around here or else."

Una shrieked the word "Bitch!"—punctuated a second later by a slap, loud and sharp as breaking glass. Before he could think to move, his sister was charging down the hall, right at him. Her narrow eyes brimmed with tears and her cheek glowed where she'd been hit. He slid back into his doorway, and she swung at him anyway. She would have stopped to hit him, but her momentum pitched full-tilt toward her room. The door slammed behind her. A moment later she let loose an unfettered scream of rage, and Thomas smiled with contentment.

His mother went into the kitchen. He listened to her murmurs, her occasional sniffles, which made him wonder if the two of them had slapped each other—but probably not. Una had yet to go that far.

After a while the microwave beeped and Mom called out, "Thomas, your dinner's ready."

His sister's room was dark and silent as he passed it. He abandoned his post, and headed down the hall and down the stairs to eat.

It was a small meal of tortillas with chicken, beans, and rice. His mother, red-eyed, smiled at him when she caught him looking at her, but mostly sat in her private misery. She asked a few cursory questions about school and homework. He answered in quick, practiced lies, not wishing to encourage discourse in this territory.

Throughout the meal, Una's voice yowled in the distance, an off-key banshee, singing along with silent headphone music. He figured she knew exactly how annoying she was.

When the food was gone, he volunteered to clean up. His mother beamed at him from a thousand-year-worn face. "My angel," she whispered, and brushed her bony hand across his cheek. "Why can't your sister be like you?"

He knew it for a rhetorical question and said nothing, but let her get to her feet and leave. He didn't look straight at her.

Much later, while he sat in darkness lit only by the glow of his computer terminal, he heard the front door open and close. Dad was home.

Tomorrow was Saturday. Maybe this weekend Dad would stay home the way he used to.

Thomas hadn't seen his father in two weeks. Only his dust.

III.

He nearly didn't recognize the man seated at the breakfast table. He'd always thought of Dad as imposing—a man who filled a suit the way Clark Kent did. Here instead was a man who might have collapsed and blown away in a good wind: hair receding, a face so sharp it might have belonged in a comic. He could almost see the penciller's work.

As though he hadn't had the energy to undress last night, Dad wore a stiff white shirt and a tie.

"Hi, Tommy," he said. "How's my boy?"

"You're dressed."

"Well, your mother doesn't like it when I come naked to breakfast." He winked, as if a joke could smooth everything.

"No, you're dressed for *work*."

"I have to go in. Finish what I couldn't yesterday."

"But you didn't get home 'til eleven!"

Mom interjected, "What were you doing awake at eleven, young man?"

"No, it's all right, it's okay," said Dad. "He doesn't understand. See, son, it's almost time for the quarterly report. And even though it's sure to show a profit—it always does—there are bound to be some cutbacks. Layoffs. Got to *increase* those profits any way we can. You don't want me to lose *my* job, do you?" The way he emphasized "my" made Mom blush and turn away.

Thomas barely withheld his response. They'd been down this road before. If he said what he felt—that it would be an excellent thing for his father to lose his job—he would just suffer the longer version of the "dog-eat-dog, cut-throat-job-market world" report: It was practically all he'd heard while Mom was out of work. Instead, he grabbed the Cheerios box and started pouring.

Dad leaned in closer, touched his hand. He twitched a little, put down the cereal and stared at the light streak of dust leading across the wood veneer tabletop; at the trace of it like baby powder on his wrist now. "Tommy, I'm sorry I can't be here for your softball game. I know you'll do fine."

"What are you talking about?"

"Why, your Saturday game. I know that's why you're upset, son."

"There's no game."

"Well, was it cancelled?"

"There wasn't any game."

Dad's mouth worked as if he was trying to get at something caught in his teeth. He looked to Mom for help, then at the calendar on the refrigerator. "But it's scheduled right there." He pointed. Dust sprinkled lightly down from his sleeve.

Thomas didn't even turn around. "The team died," he said. "We all quit. Okay? Nobody was showing up regularly anyway, and the dads who coached kept making excuses why they couldn't come, and everybody kept forfeiting games, so we just quit."

Dad looked at his empty bowl for a moment, then quietly pushed back his chair and walked out.

A few minutes later, with his suit coat hanging loose upon his frame, he slunk past the kitchen and out of the house altogether.

Mom went after him. She came back as the car started up.

Thomas didn't look up at her, but ate his cereal attentively. He could feel the crunch of every bite through his skull. He focused on the fake grain in the table, as if by staring very hard he could blend into it and become invisible.

Mom sat beside him. "Tom, why didn't you tell us?"

He set down his spoon. "Tell you what?"

"About softball?"

"There's nothing to say." He wanted to leave, but she wouldn't let him.

"But why didn't you tell us?" she repeated.

"Why would I? I haven't had a practice or a game in a month. It had nothing to do with you."

She looked like she might start to cry. He almost hoped she would. Finally she got up and left the table.

His sister came down quietly. Her radar attuned to the emotional pitch in the room, she glanced around, trading a portentous look with him, then slipped past the kitchen and was gone. On her way to meet the zombie-herd, he supposed.

He got his jar and swept up the dust Dad had left. He was glad at least that Dad always sat in the same chair at the table. A little order was helpful now and then.

The jar was full. He placed it in the closet, on the shelf beside two others, then pushed his clothes in place to hide them. He had no idea how many jars it would take, or what would happen when he was finished. Somebody had to hold everything together, and nobody else was going to do it.

IV.

Sunday morning he awoke to the smells of bacon and coffee. It had been a long time since Mom had made an old-fashioned family breakfast. It meant they would all be together for a change. But arriving downstairs he found only Una at the table. She was halfway through her pancakes. Anticipating him, she commented, "He's sleeping. And Mom went back to bed, too. Your food's in the microwave." She bobbed her head at the counter without looking up from the fashion pages.

Sullenly, he reheated his breakfast. He was disappointed with himself for allowing such hope to grow. Had he really expected breakfast would bring them together?

Una remained conspicuously isolated behind the newspaper.

After eating, he went into his closet, turned on the light, and pushed the clothes aside. He sat awhile on his sleeping bag, beside the stack of comics, and just stared at his collection. Dad's first jar had started out ocher. But if one tracked the jars in order, the color leached out. The dust in the last peanut butter jar was bone white. Eventually he got up, pushed the hangers together again, and turned off the light.

At eleven, Kevin Blodgett showed up for Una. Like many of the kids at the school, he was tattooed and pierced. A deep indigo tattoo circled his skull in a narrow band. He had slash scars across both forearms, which were supposed to be intimidating but just looked ugly. Thomas had seen cooler scarrings among his own classmates.

It was the two silver balls pinned through the tip of Kevin's tongue that disturbed him; Kevin clicked them against his teeth when he was agitated, like a rattlesnake shaking its tail—a venomous promise. Around Thomas, he was always clicking them. With his lips curled and his tongue protruding, he looked exactly like the gargoyles in *Devilry*. Una, thought Thomas, couldn't have picked a bigger doofus to fuck. Kevin acknowledged him by saying, "See ya, *dick*," as they left. He pretended not to hear.

Mom, back from her nap to clean up the breakfast dishes, muttered, "I don't know if I like that boy."

Without thinking, Thomas answered, "He's an asshole."

She turned around. "What did you say?"

He knew what he'd said very well, and had no hope of recanting. Too late for that—Mom was staring so hard the whites showed around her eyes. "Well, he is," he insisted. "He's always calling me names for no reason, trying to provoke me so he can beat me up in front of her. She gets him to do it."

Somehow that seemed to shift the focus away from his tactical mistake. Mom replied, "Maybe if you were nicer to your sister—"

"She'd have to be somebody else."

Mom seemed dispirited. "Why do you hate her so much?"

He almost said "For the same reason you do," but checked himself. " 'Cause she gets away with things."

"For instance?"

He paused. He had to consider how far he dared take this. "She smokes," he said.

"Yes, I know that. I've found her cigarettes. I've smelled her. She's really not getting away with anything."

"But you don't do anything about it."

"What do you think we should do?"

"Ground her. Don't let her go off with her mall zombies."

Mom smiled and nodded sagely. "And who's going to make sure she comes straight home. Are you going to? And when you come and tell me she didn't do as she was told, what privilege do we take away next?"

"I don't know."

She toweled off her hands and sat with him. "That's a relief." She patted his hand. "See, there are good children like you and difficult ones like Una. We try to give them the best sense of right and wrong we can and then they have to decide what they want to do with that, because we can't be here to supervise. It's their decision. Look at you—you come home, you do your homework. You don't get into trouble."

She was right—he didn't get into trouble. He was careful.

"I wish Una were more like you. I watch her. I try to talk to her. But, you know, she isn't very interested in what I have to say. I wish I had time to find out what she *is* interested in."

"Is this how grandma raised you?"

Mom shook her head. "It was a different time, you can't compare things one to one that way. Look at your educations—four years of college is going to cost hundreds of thousands of dollars. We want you to be in the best schools. You *have* to get into the best schools for your futures."

He refrained from asking the burning question of what future they thought they were providing. A lot of his time was spent not asking controversial questions. But he didn't have to ask about his father's work. He wanted nothing to do with it.

Dad didn't get up until after four that afternoon. Mom was in the den, working on her laptop, surrounded by all the paperwork she'd brought home. Thomas sat reading a comic at the kitchen table, pretending to take a break from his homework.

Dad emerged from the dark bedroom, his eyes encrusted, his chin stubbled. The sleeves on his pajamas almost reached his fingertips; the legs were folded over his feet. He stood in the kitchen, with his fingers entwined around a coffee cup.

It was pure coincidence that Una showed up then. She made a noisy, clumsy entrance. She came up behind her groggy father, her head topping his. Her face was slack, drunken. Her eyes focused slowly on her father's shriveled form, then widened with cruel delight. She began to laugh. Dad turned about like a lost and confused lunatic, and she laughed into his face.

Thomas lunged past Dad and slugged her in the belly. She screamed and folded up. Dad dropped his coffee, clutching at his ears, then yelped as the coffee scalded his feet. Behind him, Thomas hit his sister again as she tried to rise. Her shrieking, like a siren, never let up. Mom came running in, yelling, "Stop it!" but not loudly enough to drown out the shrill screams. Dad reached out ineffectually to pry the two children apart, but Una scrabbled back, shouting, "You little fucker, you'll pay for that!" at Thomas. Dad began to quiver. He yelled, "I can't stand it! Can't I have one day of solitude? One place to go?" He started to cry — an act so unthinkable that both children gaped at him. He looked at Mom. "Can't you control them even for an *hour?*" Then he turned and dove for the bedroom.

Una swore quietly to her brother, "You'll be sorry."

"That's enough!" Mom stepped in between them. "How could you behave that way to your father? After all he does for you. You go to your room right now. We'll — we'll *see* what we do with you."

Una sneered as she stood up. Mom accepted the look for only a second. Then she slapped her face so hard that Una's head thudded against the wall. "You filthy, drunken little . . . If I ever see that look on your face again, you'll *wish* I hadn't."

Pain sobered Una. She sped, wailing, up the stairs. But not before Thomas saw the dusty handprint splayed across her cheek. His heart ceased to beat. He stared at Mom, and all he could do was wonder how many jars she would fill.

She faced him and said, "You cannot go around hitting your sister."

The proclamation freed him from the moment's spell. He shook his head. Nothing was going to happen to Una. Mom couldn't even *formulate* a punishment. They all knew it.

"What's happening to Dad?" he asked.

Mom seemed to cringe away from the question. "He's fine, he's just over-stressed."

He hadn't really expected a satisfactory answer. He had hoped to divert her attention, but this time it didn't work. "I'm sorry, Tommy, but you have to go to your room, too. I can't get my work done and have you two fighting."

She seemed resolved, but even before he was halfway up the stairs he heard her first sob. The sound moved off, away into the bedroom.

Una's door was shut.

In his closet he lay on the sleeping bag, with jars of Dad towering in the shadows above him. Drifting into the membrane of sleep he heard a distant susurration like the voices of ancestors embedded in the walls, bleeding through time. All of them talking at once; he understood nothing until one voice shouted his name and he jerked awake to find himself still alone and undiscovered.

Later Mom ordered a pizza. The two of them ate in silence.

V.

In the morning there was more dust than ever. Both parents had gone. He filled his jars before eating. When it was time to leave, he called up the stairs for Una, but received no answer. The house was silent. He hesitated to go up and wake her; if she wanted to skip school, it didn't matter to him. Let her get in more trouble—not that it would change anything.

As he was putting his lunch in his backpack, the front door opened. He went into the front hall and there was Una, a cigarette poking between her lips. She gave him a smoldering look. Behind her, Kevin eased into sight in his leather jacket and black pants. His look was as unfriendly as hers. He began clicking his tongue against his teeth.

"See, I told you he'd still be here," Una said, "Mom's little angel." She walked into the living room and opened the liquor cabinet. A stack of Mom's papers on top fell off the moment the doors opened. Una ignored them. She took out a vodka bottle, then held it up, daring Thomas to say something. He wasn't about to provoke her, and tried to edge to the front door.

Kevin turned suddenly and caught him by the shoulder. "Hold it, dick," he said. "We have a thing to discuss. You beat her up yesterday."

"She was laughing at my dad."

"Wow. A serious offense—laughing at the parental unit." He pulled a black utility knife out of his jacket and pushed the blade up with his thumb. Una's gaze shifted between it and her brother with awful fascination. Then she turned her back and pretended to dig through Mom's papers with her toe.

"Hey!" Thomas protested and tried to pull away.

"Like I said, serious." He swiftly slashed the top of Thomas's wrist.

Thomas clutched the cut. It wasn't deep but it stung and blood spilled between his fingers. He looked for his sister to step in and protect him. Una had gone to ground behind the liquor cabinet.

Kevin said, "Hey, what do you know, we match." Grinning, he stretched out his scarred wrist. "That's only a taste, dickboy. You ever punch her again, it's death by a *thousand* cuts for you. Get me?" He let go. Thomas ran to the bathroom. He poured cold water over the cut. He didn't know where the gauze was, so he taped two Band-Aids across his wrist to hold the cut together. Then he sat on the toilet lid and waited.

The cut stopped bleeding shortly. The house fell quiet.

He crept through the hallway to the front door. Una had poured vodka in tall glasses of ice. She and Kevin were on the couch, kissing; he had her shirt pushed up and her bra off while he kneaded her right breast. She opened her eyes and stared fiercely at Thomas. He threw open the door and ran.

All the way to school he thought of things he was going to do to Kevin, and things he wanted to believe he could have done. He hoped Mom would come home early and find the two of them fucking on the couch. But he knew that if he told, there would be retribution for that, too. He was alone and defenseless. Kevin could get to him any day, anywhere.

He was late arriving at home room, and made up a story about hurting himself with a broken bottle and having to stop to bandage the wound. The story was awfully lame, but the substitute believed the cut when he showed it to her. The Band-Aids were splotched with blood, and she sent him to the nurse to have it bandaged properly. The nurse was out: she traveled between half a dozen schools every week. The attendance secretary attempted to bandage him, but she moved clumsily, as if fearful to touch him, touch the wound, and Thomas finally taped the gauze pad in place himself.

After school he went straight home. He was tired and his arm ached.

As he approached the house he thought his prayers had been answered. Dad's car was parked in the driveway. The driver's door hung open. He imagined that his mother had found Una and Kevin and had called Dad to come home and deal with his daughter. Some things were so bad they had to be confronted. At the same time he knew how implausible this was. Dad wouldn't come home for that.

He went to close the car door and saw the dust in the crevices of the front seat. There was more on the pavement, like a thin trail of ashes.

He followed the trail along the walk and into the house.

The vodka bottle was gone but the glasses were still on the coffee table, standing in little puddles of water. The couch cushions were on the floor.

In the hallway, Dad's clothes were strewn as if he'd undressed feverishly on his way through the house. His leather briefcase lay on its side, his silk tie beside it. The dust led to the back den. There, in the recliner as if watching the giant TV, sat a small, dried husk. It was barely identifiable, like a frog that had withered on the pavement in summer heat, shriveled by the sun. Sockets empty of eyes, the mouth twisted back around blackened gums.

He knew what he was seeing, but its identity seemed distant and unaffecting, like something in a video. Like porn on the net. It didn't really register. It wasn't real.

Thomas backed out of the room. With supernatural calm he went to get his jar. His sister's door was open and he looked around the corner. She lay face down, naked, asleep, the empty vodka bottle and a crumpled cigarette pack beside her, the glass ashtray overturned. He contemplated setting fire to the bed.

He supposed he should call Mom, but she would only rush home and lose her job as a result, and that wouldn't help. It was odd how objective he could be in a real crisis. He swept up all the dust he could gather—everything out of the car, on the walk, down the hall.

There was too much of it for one jar. He had to use a whole relish jar for everything around and under the recliner.

Dad's empty eyes pleaded with him to do something. He decided he should call the family doctor, Dr. Gilbeck; Dad must have gone to him.

The doctor was thin, and younger than Dad, but he looked just as harried. He arrived with a cellular phone in one hand, assuring someone that this would only take a few minutes and to line up the next patient. He set down his bag beside the recliner. He only looked the corpse over cursorily. "You found him?" he asked Thomas, who nodded and began to explain the circumstances. Dr. Gilbeck cut him off. "We'll have to call your mother. Think they'll let her come home early?"

Thomas shrugged doubtfully.

"Well, I can't stay." He checked his own pulse, then nodded to himself, tore open a small foil packet and took two tablets. "Patients won't wait more than three or four hours before getting irate." Thomas gave him Mom's number at work. The doctor called out on his cellular phone again, but turned and walked into the hallway for privacy.

Thomas stared after him, mutely hostile to be cut off from the events. What was the doctor doing that was half so critical as Thomas's own work? He was nothing more than a policeman — someone who couldn't act until it was too late to save anyone. But then neither could Thomas. Dad was dead and what had he done to prevent it?

The doctor came back in. He folded and pocketed the phone. "That's that. They'll be by on Tuesday afternoon between twelve and three to pick him up."

Thomas asked, "What was wrong with him?"

"Wrong?" Gilbeck tapped the back of the recliner. "Well, you can't burn the candle at both ends and not fizzle out in the middle sooner or later." He seemed to wake up suddenly to what he was saying, and quickly added, "But I'm sure he was a dutiful father. Right?"

Thomas couldn't explain why the bland sentiment sent a knot to his throat. "I didn't . . . I wanted to—"

"Look, son." The doctor squeezed his shoulder. "Don't start blaming yourself. You didn't cause this, you kids. You're just stuck with it."

Mom arrived twenty minutes later, looking wretched and a little resentful. She set her laptop and a stack of papers on the footstool just inside the den, and walked past Thomas as if she didn't see him. The doctor ushered him gently but firmly out the door and closed it.

The crying began softly but built to a wail. It even woke Una, who stumbled blearily down the stairs wearing only a large T-shirt. The doctor's presence surprised her. She sat in the kitchen and lit a cigarette. "What's goin' on?"

Thomas told her. She hissed a cloud of cigarette smoke. Only the shifting of her eyes betrayed her deeper terror.

The doctor emerged from the den and came out to the kitchen. He gave his watch a glance. "She'll sleep awhile. Listen now, you kids," he said. "You're going to have to pull together."

Una looked from her brother to the doctor. Thomas saw the queasiness that had been in her eyes when Kevin flicked his razor. "No way do I pull anything together with *him*. I'd rather die." Trembling, she sucked on her cigarette.

Dr. Gilbeck eyed her with apparent distaste. He addressed

Thomas. "You and your mother—well, she'll need your support. You two have after-school jobs yet?"

"What?" Una snarled.

"Well, you should think about after-school jobs." He made a gesture in the direction of the den, the meaning of which eluded Thomas.

"This is *not* what I'm—" Una shook her head violently; she floundered for words, but they eluded her and she finally just blurted, "I'll, like, *leave*, okay? I'm old enough."

The doctor's eyes narrowed but his face remained slack. "Your mother—"

"What about her? The last thing she did for me was name me!" Her voice broke and she grit her teeth together and marched out of the room.

The doctor watched her retreat with opiated calm. He glanced around the room at the microwave, the food processor, the blender and the rest, as if adding up the value of each. "Everything's going to change," he said. "I'm sorry." He squeezed Thomas's shoulder. "I have to get going," he added, then went back to check on Mom.

As soon as he left, Una returned to the kitchen, but maintained a wary distance from her brother. At the sound of his car starting, Una muttered, "Fuck him." She stubbed out her cigarette in the butter dish, then hurried up the stairs. Her door slammed.

Thomas got up and wandered to the den. Through the crack in the open door he saw that the husk in the chair had a bar code sticker on its skull. Tagged and identified like something out of the produce section.

Mom had been moved to the bedroom. The curtains were drawn. He switched on the small table lamp on the dresser. Mom was asleep and there was a syringe in the wastebasket. He crept beside her to watch her breathe in shallow, rhythmic, drugged breaths. Her slack features looked like someone else. Someone he'd never seen. He couldn't remember when her face hadn't been taut, strained, worried.

He patted her arm and dust puffed up. He drew back instinctively. The dust settled like insects on a corpse. He glanced across the bed, at the depression where Dad had slept. How much dust lay there? How much had washed down the shower drain?

He accepted then that he could never get it all—not Dad's, not Mom's. And if he did, what then? What if Dad, like the Schizoid, could be reassembled again? He'd have *Dad* again: the same over-worked and dedicated-to-the-murderous-system Dad. Not a defiant superhero, not a comic book champion. It would only begin all over again. They couldn't help themselves. None of them.

He went upstairs. He switched on his computer, but then sat and did nothing.

The front door thumped. The sound woke him from his thoughtless torpor. He got up and went to the dormer window to watch his sister leaving. She'd pulled on a backpack, probably stuffed with clothes and cigarettes. She strode down the driveway, past both cars and into the street. On her way to Kevin. She was doomed, too, one way or another.

He watched her climb the hill into a late-afternoon haze thick as incense—an ocher pall smearing the sky. Una simply, steadily, evaporated.

Thomas drew the blind on the window. He returned to the computer and opened *Devilry*. Soon he'd accumulated the necessary lifepoints and made it to the tiny vault where Norman had directed him. He knew what he had to do next: take the lid off the jackal-headed canopic jar in the corner. That was all he had to do to skip to the extra levels, but he couldn't do it. He understood now about the jars, about what they were and what they contained. He could feel their pull.

He stood up on tired legs and, with a last look around, went into the closet and closed the door on his world.

Afterword

Collecting Dust

I teach writing. For years in writing classes that touched upon fantasy and science fiction, I explained that one way of discussing the difference between realistic fiction and fantastic or speculative fiction is by considering how they address topics. I said: for instance, a work of contemporary fiction about the disintegration of the traditional American family might show us a family where everyone's alienated, the children are all latchkey kids, parents barely communicate, no one knows what's going on in anyone else's life, etc. In a work of fantasy, on the other hand, the writer might get at this point by making the metaphor real: The family is actually disintegrating. Fantasy allows you a certain freedom to express things, to subvert or at the very least reroute the limits imposed by realistic story-telling. This is why fairy tales can shoot straight for the heart while being impossibly fantastic at every turn.

I like that.

The Bus

THE DOORS OPENED.
Driskel awoke on his back inside a cloud of hot steam. A stretch limo was pulled up at the curb beside his vent, one window cracked slightly. Music poured out of the window, and its bass beat pounded through the pavement, punching at his spine.

The light turned green. The limo thumped on into the night, but Driskel, the derelict, knew he could not go back to sleep.

He didn't stir or try to sit up on his soggy cardboard pallet but lay there, passively, blinking like a lizard. The residue of numerous siphoned cheap wines still floated his brain, and he could not think clearly enough to piece together his surroundings right away. Off in the distance, there was a different music than the thunder from the limo. Then came a sharp hiss, and the music stopped. None of this made the slightest impression upon Driskel. He was an unpunched ticket, a steaming heap of rags.

He heard footsteps approaching and slowly, instinctively glanced in their direction. He glimpsed a face—a woman's eyes beneath a hat, a fleeting sideways glance. Disgust and fear stared down at him, but he was inured to such looks. He pawed loosely at the crust on his eyelids while the footsteps moved away.

The stoplight changed again, from green to red, drawing his attention. He saw the woman. Her back to him, she had crossed the street and was walking straight along the sidewalk toward—he lowered his hand from in front of his face—toward a big bus. Its orange running lights, low and wide apart, glowed like two predatory eyes, but the interior through the windshield appeared to be dark. Further back, a few cars whizzed by on the Franklin Parkway, meaning as little to him as had the limo and the woman; he'd mislaid the memory of the last time he had been in a car.

Driskel snerked deeply at the back of his nose, then raised his head and spat at the street. His head weighed a ton. He lay back down, rolled off his side, face-down. His blood moved like clotted oil through a rustbucket pickup truck. His blankets and coat had kept him warm while he slept, but the vent really made all the difference, heating the cardboard beneath him enough to keep him toasty. He guessed that he probably stank, since he couldn't recall his last appearance before a sink, but it was an acridness he could not say he noticed. It was the smell of humanity without their tubs and soaps, and it had been around longer than toilet paper.

His fingers had gone numb. He tried first flexing them inside his raggedy gloves and then hanging them out past the edge of cardboard, where the steam could heat them.

He recalled that he had been dreaming about a lost tooth. Somebody—the specific memory was gone—had told him once that dreams about teeth were actually sexual in nature. Driskel had never really understood that; besides, he knew without any doubt that his dream about the tooth was about a tooth. He'd lost three in the past month. He was going to lose the rest. His gums were all inflamed. *Periodontal*—the word came unbidden out of the miasma of his brain, some word his dentist had once used. His dentist. One memory had a way of triggering another, releasing buried treasure. He thought about that for a while, then about suits and ties and razor cuts blotted with dots of tissue on his neck. For a second he could smell the tang of witch hazel upon the breeze.

The bus hissed. Driskel looked its way.

A line of light cut across the sidewalk, up the side of the building beside the bus. The door had opened and, as he watched, two people climbed aboard. A black woman and her little boy—he could see them brightly detailed. For a moment, he watched their shadows moving, blocking most of the light; then the door hissed again and swung shut.

Driskel yawned. Some poor fucking woman, he thought, dragging her kid with her to Atlantic City so she could play the slots. She would come home tired, broke, and nasty, beat the kid for making her lose, and then have to borrow from somebody to buy food, and maybe fuck the landlord in order not to have to make the rent right away. Jesus, how many of them just like her had he encountered in the shelters? Used to be it was mostly men like him who lined up for soup and beds; nowadays it was whole damn families, broken pieces of families. Whole fucking world in the soup kitchen. "Vote Republican," he croaked, then began to cough. He spat again and had to sit up. His lungs ached when he inhaled. They were wet from the steam, full of fluid; but so long as he could stay full of fluid himself, that'd be okay. What he needed was to get some booze. He looked the other way down the sidewalk, past the "St. George" restaurant, but nobody was on the street tonight. The cold had driven them all away while he slept. Everybody had gone to a shelter except him. Driskel felt a distant pang of emptiness at being closed out of even this withered society. In truth he chose his solitude, but sometimes he wished he was like the others.

Behind him, the bus hissed again, and he twisted around to see a short guy standing in the strip of light. The short guy was wearing an old pea coat and a watch cap; he barked a couple of words and gestured at the air once before lurching up into the bus. The door closed.

Driskel knew the guy vaguely—had encountered him in the shelters once or twice. His name was Eddie and he was a schizo, one of the ones the city of Philadelphia had released on their own recognizance some years back. Trying to cut costs by shutting down asylums. Driskel chuckled, and coughed again. Even he was smart enough to know that if you put crazy people on the street they only got crazier and soon couldn't recall when to come in or when to take their medicine. The junkies had beat Eddie up a few times when they knew he had his medicine on him; they never hurt him much because they wanted him to get more medicine. Driskel had seen it happen a couple of times. Poor bastard Eddie lying in the alley outside St. Anthony's Hospice, spitting up blood and shouting his stupid, disconnected swear words at anyone who approached him.

Driskel stared hard at the bus. What the fuck was a guy like Eddie doing getting on a bus to the casinos? He expected to see the door roll back and Eddie emerge in a bum's rush skid across the walk, but it didn't happen, and he couldn't figure out how.

Another figure came weaving along the sidewalk. Somebody in a nice, heavy coat. Somebody with money. Driskel waited as the figure passed the bus and crossed the street, then he said as clearly as he could, "Sir, pardon me, but can you help me get something to eat? I'm freezing here."

Most of the time it didn't work, but every now and then, as in this instance, the mark didn't immediately dismiss him. Close up, the man in the coat was nicely dressed, with a gray scarf and ear muffs. His mustache was crusted with ice, and his cheeks were deeply flushed. But his eyes didn't focus so well, and Driskel realized enviously that he was drunk.

"Shit," the mark said. "Freeze your nuts off tonight, buddy. Here." He had dug under his coat and come up with a five-dollar bill; for a second he looked as if he hadn't planned to produce that much money and might take it back. Then he resigned himself to the act and laid the bill across Driskel's hand. "Get some soup, hey." He straightened unsteadily and plunged on along the sidewalk.

"God bless you, sir, thank you!" Driskel called to him. He kissed the five-spot, crumpled it in his dirty hand. He dragged the blankets off his legs, then spent a moment scratching at his ankles. Under the old wool socks, they were scabby. He dragged his fingers through his hair. Then came the hard part—getting to his feet. His knees were stiff and needed coaxing. He knelt for a time, while he coughed and wheezed and spat out more clog from his lungs. He needed badly to piss. There was an alley on the way to the St. George that would serve, and Driskel got to his feet, proud in the knowledge that he was formulating a plan with rare clarity and foresight, all the actions coming together. With one glance back at the bus, he headed away.

The counter girls at the restaurant knew him. He never made trouble for them, behaving with what passed for civility in his realm. He stayed away from the other customers, too—the late-night diners, the teenagers munching pizzas—because he knew they would complain about him and get him tossed out. But this time he had money. He went to the cooler and took out two beers. He'd have preferred his wine but the liquor store was too far away and probably closed. He was afraid to stray very far from his vent for fear that somebody mean would settle there in his absence. Sally, the sweet, black woman behind the counter, sold him the beers, then stuffed a pepper-cheesesteak into the bag with them for his five dollars. She told him, "Go get your ass warm someplace. You gonna *die* on that street." He thanked her, promised he'd obey. A final glance up at the clock told him it was after eleven. No liquor store tonight; no more money, anyway. He went back out.

A few minutes in the warmth of the restaurant made the return outside a shock as powerful as diving into a pond. He shook uncontrollably, humming beneath his breath as his fingers fumbled with the foil around the steak. Steam rose out of the bag like out of his vent.

Driskel bit off a huge chunk of meat and bread, and chewed, savoring the sweetness of the peppers and the solid taste of beef. He'd plodded all the way down the block before his stomach rebelled and he doubled over and threw up. Cheesesteak and gray wine mixed with blood from his gums. A dozen knives stabbed him in the belly and he had to lean on a railing in front of a rowhouse to keep from falling on his face. He spat to clear his mouth, and slid down on the house steps while he tremblingly opened one of the beers and drank it. He gasped between gulps, his system pumped up, his body clammy. The cold brick step stung his ass, and he wriggled his coat down under him. Once the beer was empty he took a chance and tried some more of the sandwich, just a little bread and meat. A minute passed and, when the first bite did not threaten to come back up, he ate some more, then started on the second beer. Looking around he saw, on the far side of the bus, light knife across the darkness, detailing the stone face of a building. A shadow moved across the light, climbing aboard, blotting it out.

Driskel took a half-smoked cigarette from his shirt pocket and lit it up. The first inhalation made him cough again till his sides hurt. He spat into the darkness, then leaned back and took another drag.

Complacently, he started wondering about the bus. How was it that he couldn't see lights through the windows? And what was a casino bus doing picking people up after eleven o'clock in the p.m.? It should have been in Atlantic City hours ago.

Driskel took the second beer and hung it into his coat pocket, forgetting that the pocket was torn through. He got up off the stoop. The can dropped to the sidewalk, spraying a jet of foam across his feet.

He yelped. By instinct, he swooped down, snatched up the can and held it over his mouth while he sucked lovingly at the foam. He shuffled on in some haste, leaving the trash from his meal on the steps.

By the time he had reached the corner, the beer can was empty. He tossed it aside as he belched in deep satisfaction.

Through the cloud of steam, the bus glistened in the streetlights. The strip of four "Michigan" lights on top of it winked on and off as if signaling to him.

Driskel waited but nobody else approached. The winter cold was keeping people home. His stomach rumbled and he knew he would need to find a toilet of some kind soon. On the bus they would have a toilet. Maybe they would let him use it. If they let Eddie on, why not him, too?

He nudged his blankets into a heap with his foot to make it look like he was still sleeping there on top of the cardboard, then crossed the street and started toward the bus. Drawing closer, he noticed that the sidewalk practically vibrated under his feet—the bus engine was running.

The window glass was smoked all around, but the driver's windshield—a clear square embedded in the larger smoked panel—revealed darkness, too. He could just make out the steering wheel and the line of the single seat. No light. Above, no destination sign. This bus wasn't going to Atlantic City. Driskel scratched his ass and began his circuit around, streetside. The lights from the parkway burned balls of halogen fire in the dark windows. Beneath them, a swirled insignia read simply "Worldwide" all the way to the rear. There, exhaust smoke fanned lazily out, drawing his attention.

He wandered around to the back and looked it up and down. He saw himself reflected, a shadow in the metal. There was no rear window. The bus exhaust stank worse than he did, and he got back up on the sidewalk.

For a while he leaned upon a parking meter there and tried to sort through what he had discovered. A taxi buzzed past.

With a slow, confused shake of his head, he headed back toward the front of the bus. Approaching the door, he slowed up, watchful. The bus continued to thrum its subterranean power, down into the depths beneath the sidewalk and rising up into him, binding him to the spot. Transfixed, he became aware of his fingertips beginning to smart from the cold. Down the block, the insubstantial steam promised immediate warmth and security. Driskel wrestled against the pull of two gravities. He took a faltering step toward his vent.

The door of the bus opened.

A stream of bright light flooded over him, and more than light, for it seemed that the light contained particles of warmth; an envelope of heated air enclosed him as if he were standing before an oil drum fire. Inevitably, he edged over to peer up the stairs; he had to hold up his hand to see clearly. There was noise, some kind of celebration going on, further inside. The driver's area was curtained off from the rest of the bus, but light was shining through a crack in the curtain and into the driver's mirror, which had been twisted to reflect out the door. Nobody sat in the seat to watch the dashboard lights.

Driskel put one foot on the stairs. A strong smell poured forth —of cooked meat and good cigars and all kinds of perfumery; there was food inside there, where Eddie and the others had gone. The smell tempted him like a woman's polished fingers stroking his chin, drawing him up one step and then another and finally up a third. The door panels closed smoothly together behind him without a sound, like the blades of a flytrap.

He lingered in the ruddy dimness at the top of the steps. He peered through the narrow slit in the curtain, which showed him movement, glimpses of well-dressed bodies, bottles and glasses of cut crystal. The noise seemed to swell as he stood there. He heard music that he could not quite pin down—some kind of fox trot maybe—more voices, cheering and crazy laughter. He finally extended one grubby hand and peeled back the edge of the curtain.

A man in a tuxedo bent straight at him. The grinning face filled up the opening. "Well, all right, another one! How do you do? Come in, the water is *fine*." The man took hold of his hand and dragged Driskel out of the darkness. The nearer celebrants turned, smiling warmly; the noise damped for a second. Driskel's eyes were watering from the light.

The front ranks of people surrounded him. They handed him a drink, slapped him on the back and on the shoulder. One woman kissed his hairy cheek, and he knew she'd left lipstick there. As though parched, he drank his drink, and the glass was taken from him. A Japanese man offered him a cigarette and he accepted it—a straight, foreign, gold-labeled cigarette, unsmoked. The luxury of it awed him.

Driskel let a woman light the cigarette. She was wearing a black sequined gown, very low cut. She snapped the lighter shut and gave him a brief sultry look before turning away. "Are you hungry?" asked a handsome blond gentleman in a white tux, and he nodded. He let himself be led forward into the throng.

Somebody said, "Here, let me take that," and grabbed hold of his coat from behind, dragging it from his shoulders. He let it go. The interior of the bus was so warm it made him sleepy. Another person offered him a tuxedo jacket in place of the coat, and he put it on over his stained flannel. The jacket was much too large for him but no one seemed to notice. Then the crowd—all of whom said hello to him as he passed—opened up, and Driskel found himself confronting a wide table covered in food. Cuts of meat, cheeses, bread surrounded a row of silver tureens and warm chafing dishes. "Help yourself, old man," said his guide. "The bar's back there." Driskel glanced around to see a carved mahogany bar beyond the crowd. He had circled the bus and knew its exterior was nowhere near as large, but the proximity of food and drink blotted out his doubts entirely.

He snatched a piece of bread and began to construct a sandwich of skyscraper proportions (everything looked too good to pass up), until a slinky woman with the most heady perfume leaned against him and said, "You don't have to do that, you know, my dear. There's no limit. You can always make another."

Driskel stared into her smiling, black eyes, and all at once he found himself weeping. Disquieted, the woman drew back and his guide stepped in again. "Here, fella," handing him a glass of port, "you look like you could use this. Be good for you."

Driskel slurped it, then blubbed, "What's going on? Why are you doing this?"

"Why, it's a celebration. You've moved up in society tonight. Up from the depths, straight to the heights."

"And Eddie—"

"Who might Eddie be?"

"I saw him get on before me."

"Ah," the man in white grinned, "yes, well, you're not the only one ascending around here. It's a *big* bus, now, isn't it?"

"I suppose."

"Well, you just eat and drink your fill, mingle all you want. I'll keep an eye on you."

"Bathroom, I need—"

"Right there, the far side of the bar." The guide patted him.

"Thank you."

"Nothing of the kind. It's us thanking *you.*" And he merged gracefully back into the crowd. Snuffling, Driskel bit into his sandwich, half of which spilled out onto the table. His mouth full, he set the rest of the sandwich down on a sterling silver tray and stubbed out his cigarette. He kept the half-smoked butt for later. From the table, he wove his way to the bar and from there made a beeline to the men's room.

It was deserted except for him. The facilities included a corner shower stall. Driskel looked at himself in the circular mirror. The squalid image had little impact, more as if he were peering through a window at someone in the next room. He could hardly recall what he had looked like, back when he could con people into believing he was a poor working stiff who'd lost his wallet and needed just a few bucks to get home. Then it had been easy to accumulate enough money to get lost; back then he could still get into washrooms in office buildings and hotels to clean up. For a few weeks, maybe months, he had maintained a false veneer of dignity. It had been a long, liquid journey from that place to the steam vent.

The water in the shower was almost scaldingly hot. It swirled into the drain as a grimy soup. There were white towels on a rack and, even though he had washed well, he still left a dirty smear on them. He slicked back his hair once he had dressed, and emerged out of the bathroom, a new man. The change in his appearance had no effect on the crowd; they treated him as the same old friend as before.

He'd left his drink in the bathroom. He took a bourbon from the bartender and mingled again. Now, pausing beside different clusters of people, he tried to insert himself into the conversations, even when he didn't know what they were talking about. A new play someone was backing or a hostile corporate takeover, the outrageous tuition at Yale being offset by the tax exemption their congressman had written into law for them, the price of a really fine armagnac—he learned that he had nothing to say on their favorite topics. He wandered on. The crowd subtly manipulated him away from the bar, away from the front and further into the depths of the party. Voices seemed to be screaming around him now in a dozen languages, the laughter grew positively maniacal.

He noticed booths ahead and to either side. The crowd here at the back was more congested than ever; he just managed to percolate through. The booths presented an even stranger reality than the party itself. In them, Driskel discovered people copulating openly; a man pouring champagne between a woman's legs and then burying his face in her; a table where a woman wearing only a long string of pearls danced above a group of cigar-chomping CEOs; another where two naked men in neckties were doing things to each other on the cushions before a sinister woman in leather garb. Driskel just gaped. Nobody else seemed remotely interested that this was going on nearby. They continued to chatter away like a horde of enraged baboons, as though they had witnessed these perversions a thousand times. Their faces were all round and red, baby-fat cheeks and thinning, pasted hair. Food dribbled from the corners of mouths, cigars and cigarettes jounced as they spoke. Their shirtfronts were stained with spills of food and drink. He sensed an increasing madness about their eyes, the way they looked at him.

The air had a stench upon it much like he had upon him. He was sweating heavily now as if drawing close to a fire.

He downed the last of the bourbon but it couldn't begin to quench his thirst. Another one was needed, maybe two or three to steady his nerves. There was a reason he shied away from shelters these days, they were like this, packed tight like this. He turned to go back, but the crowd had closed in after him. He couldn't even spot the bar.

"Well, I see you've come through," shouted a voice behind him, and he turned around to find his guide there, a white island of unruffled compassion. "Did you have a good journey? Get all you wanted to eat and drink?"

"I could use another. It's hot, you know? Like a vent in here."

"A vent? All right, if you say so. It's only natural it would be hot this close to the engine." He led Driskel on, ever the reassuring guide. The crowd, suddenly, had thinned to a bare handful, and these few moved aside as the two men approached.

They were nearing what looked like steel freezer unit beneath the dark rear wall of the bus. There still weren't any seats like in a normal bus, but the width of the compartment had returned to something like the right size.

"Now it's time for you to bid us farewell," said the guide.

"It is?" Driskel realized that he had expected no less. It had all been too impossibly good to last, just a bunch of rich people having their big joke with the bum. "Look, I took a shower."

"Yes. You're fairly presentable." He gingerly tugged the tuxedo jacket off Driskel, helping him extract his arms from the sleeves. "But by itself it isn't enough, really, is it? Besides, we can't have that." Someone produced a small silver container out of which he scooped a black paste. With the tenderness of a mother washing her child, he smeared the paste over Driskel's face, obscuring his freshly scrubbed features.

"I'll need my coat back," Driskel complained while this was going on. "It's cold outside."

"Yes, but you aren't going back outside." Two of the revelers turned toward him and took hold of Driskel's arms. They stared straight ahead, not at him. There was no mistaking their firm grip. The top of the steel unit opened up quietly and Driskel was propelled toward it, his guide just behind him. "I told you before, it's a big bus, and big buses have to run on something if we are to stay warm and happy and safe. You can see that."

The two who had hold of him lifted Driskel off his feet. He struggled helplessly, then wedged his feet against the side of the steel "freezer" out of which searing heat emerged. He had strong legs and he held his position while the two of them pushed and bent him back. Upside down he glimpsed the crowd behind him, packed together as far as he could see. On the fringe a few glanced his way with something like rapture on their faces. The naked men in the last booth were standing up like prairie dogs on the cushions to watch, while the dominatrix whipped them from behind. His guide leaned close beside him. "You belonged on this bus once, didn't you? I could tell. You understand how things work in the real world." He squeezed Driskel's shoulder, benign as a priest, a father-confessor. "Don't give us a hard time. You're at our disposal, all of you."

His captors held him steady until Driskel stopped resisting. He lowered his feet from the side of the box.

They lifted him over the opening. Below was a chute, a gullet, into whirling cylindrical gears. Eddie the schizo's watch cap lay snagged in the chute. It had a big button pinned on it: "Don't worry. Be happy." Driskel looked back one final time upon the respectable crowd.

They let him drop as though through a gallows trap. He landed atop the cap, dragging it with him down into the shredder. He bit into it to take the pain; the agony was sharp and brief. Any noise he made was drowned out by the wild celebratory shrieks of the crowd above.

His guide, the man in white, handed the shed tuxedo jacket to someone else in exchange for a handkerchief on which to clean his blackened fingers. He turned and plunged back through the melee as the steel lid clamped down again.

The motor hum picked up, and the lights on the walls burned briefly brighter. At the far end, behind the tantalizingly not-quite-drawn curtain, the entrance doors hissed open again.

Afterword

The Bus

Stories come unbidden. You never know when something—some seemingly random series of events, some color or smell—will kick loose a particle of an idea. I used to work in a bookstore in Center City Philadelphia, and I walked to and from work, often past The Franklin Institute.

One cold winter night I was walking home in the dark on a Friday night. Parked in front of the intitute was a casino bus—a bus that took people to Atlantic City, where they could lose some money playing the slots. There was a steam vent halfway down the street, too, and a man was sleeping there, in a sleeping bag on some cardboard. As I walked along past him, looking at him, I heard the door of the bus open. I looked up to see a couple of people get on.

That's really all there was to the germination of this story. By the time I arrived home some twenty minutes later, I had almost the whole shape of it. Fortunately, I was alone, so that there was no one to distract me, to make me lose the idea.

You never know when you'll get a good idea, and that's why I always tell students in writing classes to carry a notebook of some kind wherever they go . . . exactly the way I didn't.

A Day in the Life of
Justin Argento Morrel

I.

THE STELLAR-WIND SHIP *FLAVUS* ORBITS HIGH above the black hole's maw. Inside the ship live four people: one who likes to dance in the face of black hole gravities; one who can't recall his own name; one who wishes to be known as "the Commander," kept strapped in his bed; and the other one, Justin Morrel.

His official title is "Energy-conversion Engineer," a title that barely hints at the reservoirs of knowledge in the man; but titles have little meaning aboard the *Flavus*. He sits in his workroom—a room that, these days, he rarely leaves—straddling one lowered petal of his bulb chair. His favorite chair. The petal is hinged beneath the "V" of his crotch, with the three remaining petals folded up behind him, surrounding him like an enormous teardrop. Like a womb.

An extender lamp, the sole source of light in the room at present, hovers vulturously above him, creating a corona over his dun-colored hair, highlighting his sharp cheeks, burying his crystal blue eyes in the rough-edged shadows of his dark brows.

In the palm of his hand, Justin cradles a disembodied arm. The fingers of the arm are stiffly splayed and rest on a flat plate at the tip of the curved petal. The arm is almost alabaster, like the arm of a mythic snow princess. It is hairless and the wrist too slender and delicate to be a man's. The arm ends at the elbow—not in bloodied and shredded tissue but in braided wire and translucent tubing.

Justin fits a tiny magnifier into the hollow of his right eye, then sights down one of the translucent tubes as if seeking a parallax. His stomach sighs over the cloth belt of his jumpsuit.

In the darkness on his left, two wide, transparent doors present a view of the lowest corridor of the ship—of shiny, anodized walls and dim, yellow light. Halfway between Justin and the doors a silhouetted figure stands motionless.

The figure is Commander Francis Vomer. He wears only form-fitting briefs over his rippling hard physique. The eyes in his square-set face are hooded, calculating, and insane. He watches raptly Justin's every move, although the scene is as meaningless to him as graffiti in Aramaic. Every few minutes Vomer takes a silent, swift half-step nearer the light. Justin supposes him to be sleeping under sedation, strapped onto his bed where he has been kept for months, ever since he tried to jettison the solar sails.

Unaware of the evil, skulking presence, Justin continues to check each tube assiduously and lets his thoughts wander around the woman he loves: E. B. "Kitty" Strunk. ("I love you Kitty, don't you understand? Let me show you, come to *bed*.") He has tried to win her affections ever since they awoke from cryogenic slumber two years ago, but she has yet to respond with anything more dazzling than a passing buss on the cheek.

Right now she is outside somewhere enjoying her favorite pastime: waltzing to made-up mental tunes in the gravitational fields above the event horizon. Recurring visions of her falling forever into the black hole have plagued Justin since the first time she went out. His rational side knows, however, that she is safe so long as her line remains secured to the ship. In his chair, Justin daydreams of the figure in space, an egg bobbing at the end of an umbilical. His X-ray mind slices away the suit. He pictures her naked body firm and slender. He has a fair idea how large her breasts are. She exercises each day, expressing an inflexible desire to stay fit, though for whom she is exercising is beyond him, seeing as how he never gets to touch her, and Vomer is sedated; the only other member of the crew is Clancey, who is over eighty years old and incapable of any activity more strenuous than a slow drool.

The imagined scene changes. Justin, reclining in a lowered command chair, watches Kitty kneeling above him, her body bathed in the deep red glow of the control console LEDs. She wriggles his mighty erection into her and coos softly. ("I want you, I need you, I love you, oh, *Justin!*")

He sighs, "Ah, Kitty."

"Ah, Kitty," parrots Vomer with nasal emphasis. He sneers.

The magnifier drops from Justin's wide eye and bounces on the floor.

Vomer chuckles. "Hey, Justin," he calls, singsong, and strolls closer. "Guess where I've been."

Justin's thoughts careen. Where's my gun, where's the damn service revolver, how did he get free this time, Christ, what's he destroyed *now?* God *damn* Kitty, she was supposed to put him out for four hours before she went out. Four hours . . .

He glances fleetingly at his bandless watch, sees that four hours passed an entire hour ago.

"Oh, boy," he mutters, calculating the damage Vomer can inflict in a single, unrestrained hour. At the same time he reviews locations, scenes, phantom tabletops in search of the lost gun. Sweat trickles down his ribs. He never knew why guns had been issued to the crew until Vomer went crazy; now that he knows, he can't seem to hang onto the damned thing. His throat is dry, tickling, trying to make him cough. "Where—where have you been, Franci—er, Commander?" Mustn't forget how Vomer feels toward his first name. ("All right everyone, let's understand right off that my first name on the voyage is *Commander.* Got that? Fine. Then, into the cylinders!")

"Guess," Vomer urges.

You stupid sick son of a bitch, how should I know?

Justin doesn't say this. If he had the goddamned gun he would say it, but under present conditions he doesn't dare. What he stiffly says is: "Why, Commander, I really couldn't guess."

Grinning like a rabid wolf, Commander Francis Vomer answers, "I was in the airlock. I released Kitty's line. Zoom." He performs an imbecilic terror-mime and titters at the impression.

A phobic image devours Justin: an elephantine spacesuit dropping down, down, slower, slower, until its albedo and its form are absorbed. Gone. . . .

Justin swings a leg over the lowered petal, pushes off and past Vomer, who is too busy laughing at his Kitty-impersonation to interfere.

The doors open silently and Justin bolts down the anodized corridor, past the rooms of the dead—rooms no one feels the least desire to use. The tumbling Kitty clogs his thoughts; he hears her panic-stricken cry, but it comes from his lips. The faceplate of her suit fogs over with her breath. The last impeding doors slide open, and he hurls into the departure chamber, plunges into the airlock, hits the buttons with his forearm, all the while cursing the slowness of the hissing doors, then realizes he is about to launch into space unprotected.

Vomer, you bastard you—

The door whooshes open. Justin madly wrenches the portable emergency life system from the wall, screams a silent scream, and is sucked out the door. His thumb flicks the switch on the life system, and a glowing oxygen-rich field pops into place around him.

He was in time. He wouldn't even lose a toe. He sighs.

The gravitational havoc of the Schwarzchild radius snatches him, and Justin Darius Argento Morrel, in his sparkling field, becomes a vulcanized Ping-Pong ball. He rebounds against the ship like a monkey on a short rubber band, smacking his head repeatedly on a grill plate. Blood surges from his nose. The world explodes in crackling starbow colors that spin away like dying fireworks. His last thought: She enjoys *this?*

The *Flavus* was sent out from Earth as one of three colonizing ships, each on a hopeful journey to a new world. Three ships were all the Earth could afford, and the majority of the crews were volunteers—Justin Morrel among them—all too happy to escape what appeared to be certain annihilation by starvation and social madness. The crews were placed in cylinders—cryogenic life-support systems, one cylinder per person. There were thirty-two people aboard the *Flavus*. They were asleep through departure and were not to awaken again for sixty-three years.

But somehow the delicate cryogenics controls went awry.

Two years out from Sol, twenty-nine of the thirty-two cylinders suddenly snapped open, filling the room with a hydrogen-nitrogen mist that heated rapidly—a fact later established from traces of ammonia rain in the chamber. Of the twenty-nine people released, eighteen died of embolisms, five died from systemic shock induced by the rude awakening and the unknown source of heat. Six survived.

The three cylinders containing Morrel, Vomer, and Strunk remained sealed and flawlessly functioning—or malfunctioning, depending on how you considered it. The six survivors voted to leave them as they were, unconscious and oblivious, in the hope that these three might yet establish a colony. The six would manually pilot the *Flavus* to its new home, essentially giving their lives to the cause. This information and a recorded distress message sent long before to Earth were the only hard facts the three had when they awoke sixty-one years later. The remainder of the record had been sabotaged. Erased. They found the *Flavus* not orbiting Epsilon Eridani as expected, but hovering instead above a black hole. They found also one old man wandering through the ship; he was filthy, his beard long and tangled, his clothing caked in places with his own excrement. For some inexplicable reason he reeked of garlic. He could barely talk and spoke mostly gibberish when he did have occasion to say anything. When asked his name, he urinated, then replied, "Clancey." No one by that name had ever been part of the crew, but no one knew who he had been, so Clancey he remained.

Vomer cracked after three weeks. He was a born leader with no one to lead and no place to lead them. He lacked the means to determine their coordinates because the computer had, at some point prior to his awakening, been rendered practically useless: two-thirds of its memory cells had been removed and could not be found. Without the computer, only one member of the crew had the technical ability and background to attempt coordinating their location. Justin was thus unwillingly forced into the limelight, into a hated position of command. Vomer became the victim of a mental singularity—like a black hole, insanity sucked away at his mind. He arrived at a state of supreme calmness and presumption —a sort of Zen with the black hole outside.

He attempted suicide. Justin and Kitty found him stuck halfway into a garbage liquidation unit. Vomer fought desperately and powerfully for a man on his side, one-third of the way up a wall and up to his ass in a liquidator. He grabbed Justin's gun and tried to eat the barrel, managing only to put three rounds into the bulkhead. His captors beat him senseless with kitchen utensils, took him to his room, strapped him to his bed, and pumped him full of sedatives. The garbage liquidator never worked properly again.

Justin and Kitty labored together for a week afterward, attempting Euclidean projections to locate themselves. In the end they succeeded, but by that time Justin had fallen hopelessly in love with Kitty. He never got around to plotting a departure route, though he did direct their laser beacon toward Earth. Each time he sat down to work out an escape, he found himself humming and composing sonnets to the woman he loved. It seemed then that she cared for him. The desire to return home dissipated. Yet she repelled his amorous advances and explained that her love was merely platonic. He was hope-dashed. She comforted him with the first of her endless, bright, beaded strings of encouragement: "Justin, poor baby, I, well, need time, just give me time."

Time is all she has ever asked for, and all that he has been allowed to give, although he has a definite goal in mind. But time is not Justin's friend.

Time sits rolling blank, white dice with Vomer.

Red light sprinkles in, illumination's snowflakes melting in the Hades of Justin's closed eyelids. He exposes his eyes a wafer-thin crack; painfully brilliant white light seems to be everywhere. Why doesn't someone shut it off? Hardness presses against his back. Where is he?

A shadow falls across his face, blocking off some of the ceiling lamps, an oasis or dark safety for him to look at, a blurry figure kneeling beside him. He brings into focus an ovoid face with beautifully flushed cheeks, blonde lashes and brows, and waterfall hair that tickles his blood-encrusted nose. The strained expression of tension ages her perfect features.

"Kitty," he says, his voice graveled.

She smiles reassurances and pats his cheek. Her hand is spongy and cold. Justin realizes she is still housed in her environ-suit—all but the helmet.

Kitty's face moves falteringly up and away. He is alive, and can be left for the moment. The painful light floods over him again, but he turns his head and shields his eyes to watch the woman in the Humpty Dumpty-shaped suit. She presses three spots along its equator and the suit pops apart, the bottom held up solely by her wide stance. Her arms withdraw into the suit, then raise the upper half over her head. Her breasts are drawn tightly against her ribs. Tufts of blonde hair glisten in her armpits. Justin's head rises from the floor. He blinks to clear his eyes.

He never knew she went out naked before: his thoughts drift to dreamy visions of Kitty bouncing around in the flow of gravity, laughing, singing, masturbating. ("I'd love to go to bed with you, Justin, I honestly would, but not now because I need my daily exercise, so keep an eye on Vomer while I'm out. All right? Dear Justin, don't be so glum. We've plenty of time, plenty of time.") He is both hurt and angered by what he assumes; how many times has he heard a similar excuse from her? That lingering promise of an imminent rendezvous which never arrives, and why should it? He reaches limply out to her. He wants to take her hand, to sniff, to lick away the essence he's yearned for over the past two years. For all she knows, he knows, he might be dying right now from internal ruptures. A few drops of such elixir could keep him alive, might bring him springing to his feet with new vitality. His fingers strain.

She misinterprets his flailing gesture. Stepping from the lower half of the suit, she goes to him, cups his wrist, then strokes it while saying, "There, there." She kneels beside him.

Justin tugs on her hand, brings it to his lips. Kissing, he inhales deeply. Damn it all, she's right-handed. He tries to grasp her other hand, but it has vanished behind her back, where he can hear the nails scratching. He begins to itch all over. His eyes water.

"Justin, don't cry. Have you . . . oh, no, not you, too? Now I'll never get out of this black hole. I'll kill myself, Justin, I swear it! I *depended* on you! How—oh, how dare you lose your mind!"

Justin groans and lowers his head. "Kitty," he asks, "how did you get back in?"

She drops his wrist as if it is diseased. "My God, you *are* insane."

His nostrils flare. He winces as the blood caked there tugs at the hairs in his nose. "Just answer the question."

"How do you think I got in? I came in on my line. How were *you* planning to get back in?"

"But Vomer got loose, came into my workshop and said he cut your line."

Kitty stares at him blankly. Then her eyes narrow. "Shit." She stands swiftly. "Clancey?" she shouts.

Justin blocks the light and peers between her ankles. He sees that the old man has been sitting against the bulkhead and watching them all this time. Clancey rises as swiftly as bread dough, having to turn around and press himself up the curved wall. He shuffles toward them.

That stupid old fool, what is he going to do? Justin attempts to sit up and immediately flops back. Nausea quilts his body, and the room spins like a tired, old windmill.

Clancey leans over him, giving Justin the horrible impression that the old man is about to vomit on him. Clancey's white hair is shaggy and his beard grows high up on his ragged cheeks; his mouth is a crooked hole within. An enormous wrinkled finger appears between that face and Justin's rolling eyes. The finger waggles at him as Clancey announces, "Fish out of water."

Justin whimpers.

Kitty says, "Keep an eye on him, Clancey, and I'll be back in a little while." The old man nods solemnly, his scrutiny that of a guard over a captured enemy soldier.

Justin weakly calls to Kitty, but she is gone, and he is vaguely aware that she is marching away, her bare feet squeaking down the corridor. The face of Clancey, like a hoary Medusa, glowers down at him. Justin closes his eyes to escape it, then begins to imagine what is taking place elsewhere. He sees Kitty enter his workshop. Vomer's back is to her as he rips wires from the arm Justin has made, popping holes in its flesh with his spatulate thumb. Kitty pauses briefly to look around her; she has never been in the workshop before, allowing Justin his privacy, his island. She glides up behind Vomer and kicks him squarely in the crotch. Vomer bites into the ruined arm to keep from screaming, the extender lamp splitting into colors that swirl like the rings of Saturn around his head. A thousand hands clap for him. Finally, he crumples to the floor, a puddle of his former self. Kitty tumbles him into the bulb chair, folding up his rubbery knees, and slamming the petals into place. Then she looks around her. Will she see what he is designing? Will the arm tip his hand, so to speak? If she does comprehend his project, what then? No, he's safe; she won't know whom he has designed it for.

Justin sighs and picks at the brown blood-crust rimming his nostrils. Silently he curses Vomer. So much hate, it could vaporize his blood cells.

Vomer has broken out of restraints three times before this. On the first, he was seized while setting a cockroach trap using raspberry syrup, a pencil, and one of his shoes. There are no cockroaches on the *Flavus*. On his second escape, Vomer attempted to open all the doors on the ship to, as he put it, "get a little cross-ventilation going." While free the last time, he threw out the ceiling panels in the departure room, then sabotaged the food preparation system. Although there is enough food to last them a lifetime, for the past three months it has been meatloaf every meal. Before that, they endured weeks of frozen gazpacho.

Justin admits to having felt sorry for Vomer at first. He could sympathize with the lost-command syndrome, although deep down inside he despises the stratification of rank and privilege and, so, dislikes Vomer as its representative. But now the situation has changed: Vomer has attempted to kill him. Justin has believed for some time that the commander becomes more dangerous with each passing day, while Kitty—who professes to be a *psychologist!*

—seems unaware of this and refuses to listen when Justin explains what could happen if a rescue party showed up while Vomer was loose. This thought leads Justin to speculate on what may have been damaged before Vomer showed up in his workroom. Did he shut off their Mayday beacon? Did he try and take the ship out of orbit? There is so much for him to ruin; everything will have to be checked.

He knows his best bet is to kill Vomer as soon as possible, but he believes himself incapable of cold-blooded murder. He has tried repeatedly to stare it in the face and has lost his nerve on each occasion. The most he could do would be to humiliate Vomer to death.

That is why he has begun work on his new project. Vomer may have slowed it down, but all such damage can be repaired. The other pieces are safely tucked away, and the assemblage will take no time at all and will take care of Vomer once and for all. The arm, if it's been destroyed, will be a snap to rebuild. The head and torso are complete, as are the logic circuits and allophoder. Hardest of all was the construction of the self-lubricating vagina, which Justin had to build from scratch, androids being generally sexless. But he made do.

Justin had been against the inclusion of android parts aboard the *Flavus*. They have intimidated him ever since they appeared on the market, for reasons that lie too deep in the reptilian core of his mind to be explainable. But, like cars and transistors and nuclear weapons before them, androids were the technical vogue, and no well-dressed ship could be without some. They came to serve.

The irony of this does not escape him.

He rolls onto his hands and knees. His head lolls between his shoulders. His jumpsuit is torn, a hole exposing a chubby dough-nut around his navel.

Clancey sees that he is awake and shuffles from one foot to another, cracking a smile like an old vaudevillian who still thinks he's got it. "Fish out of water?" he asks hopefully.

"Go 'way, go 'way." Justin starts the tortuous climb to his feet.

Clancey stands perfectly still, then executes an abrupt turn and pushes his feet toward the door. He will wander on through the ship until some arbitrary point of destination is reached. Justin has seen him do this hundreds of times. More often than not Clancey ends up in the cryogenics room, plugging his ears and wailing to his dead companions. What does he hear? Do their voices call to him from the other side? Does some essence of them, sustained by the artificial eternity of the nearby singularity, still lurk in the empty cylinders? It is assumed that their bodies were cast into space, one by one, as they died. However, Clancey, in a rare moment of lucidity, once recounted how he had put a few for safekeeping in the food processing units. ("Did anyone else find a belt buckle in their soup besides me?")

Justin regrets having yelled at the old man. Clancey seems to share his dislike for Vomer, even avoided him before Vomer cracked up. After all, Clancey is truly harmless and possessed of the supreme gentleness found only in idiots and prey.

Poor, poor old man, thinks Justin. He staggers away to survey Vomer's havoc.

Vomer destroyed the ship-to-ship communication system and launched a Mayday beacon, their last.

The extender lamp, turned to maximum intensity, spreads an even light that casts sharp, deep shadows across the debris scattered throughout the workroom. Justin has cleared most of this from the far wall. Along that wall a nude female figure walks back and forth at his commands. She is medium height, with long, dark hair, a wig. Her perfect body is hairless, like the body of an over-endowed child. She wears no expression, as if nudity makes her vapid, and she performs each task with mechanical, thoughtless subservience. Justin hopes Vomer will fail to notice this.

In his favorite chair he reclines with his feet propped on the lowered petal. "You can stop now," he tells her. She draws herself up, faces him, stands paralytically. Looking her over, he feels nothing but pride. Vomer can only be delighted. "Hestia," he says to her, pleased with the name, "you remember what you're to say to the commander?"

"Yes, Jus-tin." Her voice is soft and rich, a milk bath.

"Let's go for a walk." He squirms out of the chair as Hestia threads her way to him through the rubble of her creation. Then, with Justin in the lead, they move to the exit doors. He drops back beside her and extends his head to plant a happy kiss on her cheek. At the last moment Hestia faces him and takes the kiss on her lips. Justin stumbles as her hands grip the back of his head and her lips part and her tongue flicks against his teeth.

He wildly forces his head away. "Hestia!" he hisses, and pulls her arms down.

"I was just practicing," she explains.

"Yes, well, well, that's fine. I guess." They walk along the hall again, Justin and his creation. He noticed, among other things, that her tongue is too silky to be real. What will Vomer think? He regards her with apprehension and wonders just what he's created here.

They pass Clancey drifting along. He seems to have hurt himself—walks hunched over, dragging one foot slightly. "Hello, Major," he calls. To Hestia, he smiles and bobs his head. She reaches out as Clancey goes by. Justin slaps down her hand. "No," he commands. Hestia pouts. He didn't program her this way.

They climb the ladder to the next deck, Hestia above, giving Justin an unblushing view that he finds embarrassing, despite the fact that he put everything there. He looks down and thinks of Kitty, recalling his view of her from where he lay on the floor. She isn't built quite as nicely as he had expected. Her stomach is rounder and her breasts not as firm as his fantasies of her. Nevertheless, the memory is getting him horny. He wonders where she has been keeping herself while he toiled in his lab.

Outside Vomer's door Justin stops Hestia from entering. "Not yet. The commander may be sleeping, and I want to set the stage. Everything has to be just right or this won't work. Now, you stay right here until I open the door for you. Okay?"

"O-kay."

Justin touches the doorplate, and the door slides back. He places a chummy grin on his face and strolls in, a casual hipster. "Hey, Vomer, I—" His mouth hangs open without words, and his eyes cannot look away, though they burn at what they see.

Vomer is on his back, on his bed, naked. Kitty sits straddling him the way she straddles Justin in Justin's dreams. Both of them have stopped moving, a frozen scenario in dim lover's light.

Kitty twists around. "Justin," she gasps. "Get out."

"No," Justin says, not answering, but trying to deny it all.

Kitty pulls away from Vomer, jumps down and heads toward him. Her body glistens with sexual sweat, the blonde hair under her arms and on her legs sparkles. She reaches out to comfort him and he backs away. The closed door traps him. Kitty's hands embrace his stubbled cheeks. "Let me explain, Justin, please."

"Kitty," Vomer calls hungrily.

"Get away from me!" Justin snaps, and he shoves her. She comes at him again. He shouts, "You liar! All this time you've been promising, putting me off so you could diddle with that brainless lump."

"Hey," Vomer thunders. He sits up and swings his feet to the floor.

"You've been lying to me for two years, Kitty—sneaking in here to him! Haven't you?"

She tries to smile. "Yes, Justin, but I can explain all that if you'll give me the chance. Francis—"

"Don't call me Francis!"

Kitty cranes her head back. "Will you shut up and let me talk to him, for God's sake?"

"Don't bother," Justin snarls. "I wouldn't want to interrupt your coitus any further." His hand hits the doorplate, and he realizes in horror what he's done, but it's too late to stop that door.

Hestia charges past Justin and flings her arms around Kitty. The two naked bodies press together.

"Darling," coos Hestia. Then she kisses Kitty hard on the mouth.

Kitty twists free and backs up two steps, breasts jiggling. "What the *hell* is going on? God, she's plastic!"

"Hi there," calls Vomer. He waves at Hestia. She stands, momentarily dismayed, shining with Kitty's transferred sweat.

"Oh, God." Justin eyes the ceiling.

"Justin? What have you . . . she's an android!"

He backs toward the nearest corner. "I can explain," he begins, but stops, realizing he sounds just like Kitty. He fumes in the hope of regaining some control. "She's a gift to Vomer. I figured if he had something to occupy his time, then you and I could . . . could be *together*." Almost in tears, he cries out, "If there was something to occupy him, then you and I could find each other without him to get in the way again and again."

"Playing *God*, Justin!"

Hestia says, "Let's go for a walk outside, Commander."

"Playing *Justin*, Kitty. Shut up, Hestia!"

"Sure," says Vomer.

"Just sit down, Francis, you're not going anywhere!" Kitty shouts. She closes on Justin in his corner. "She's supposed to take him outside?" Her hands come up like claws. "God, Justin, how could you even consider such a thing?"

"How could I?" He presses his palms against his forehead. "I hate his guts, that's how. Now more than ever. You've spent half your time out in space and the rest in here with him—with a lunatic—I haven't had ten minutes with you in nearly two years. And on top of that the son of a bitch has tried to kill me! Do you understand? Can you see? You're sleeping with Lizzie Borden's brother!" he roars. "Where's your training? How could I want to kill him? Christ, Kitty, it was the easiest thing in the world."

She cloaks herself in calmness and affects concern. Her claws become hands again, turning up, offering comfort, the hands of Jesus. "Justin, this must be very hard for you, but I know I can make you understand if you'll only relax now and let me—"

"Stop it! This won't work anymore. Do you think me stupid enough to go for your compassionate act now? Have you ever stopped lying to me, manipulating me? Ever?"

A change falls across her like a cloud, darkening her features. The sweetness is cast off, no longer useful. "No," she says. "Never. And I had to do it that way, too. If I hadn't treated you that way, you wouldn't be here now. You would have closed off completely or even committed suicide. What would I have then? Francis? A great conversationalist, Francis."

"Then you do comprehend it."

She laughs. "Back to my training again? You think I have to be a psychologist to see what's wrong with him? Well, I guess one more revelation won't damage you now, so what the hell. I'm not a psychologist, Justin. I never have been. No training at all."

Most terrible of lies! It becomes an actual pain, a stab in the chest. Two years, he has been working with . . . an *amateur*. "What are you, then?"

"You don't know, even now?"

He closes his eyes. "I don't want to know."

"I'm his lover. I was his lover on Earth. He got me here, bought or lied or connived me here, and all I had to do was sleep with him, with his hard, fine body. You think I'm going to switch over to you for physical companionship?" She pokes at his stomach. "Hmm? No way, buster." She realizes then that she has gone too far—it shows in the startled look that comes upon her. This isn't what she wanted to do. Justin seems to be caving in right before her eyes. Can she salvage something? "But I—I needed you, Justin, too. Because you're right: he is crazy. And I need someone to rely on, someone sane and intelligent and . . . wise."

His hand snaps out across her face, slapping her back off her feet. She sprawls across the doorway. The door opens.

Clancey stands outside, looking first at Kitty, then at Justin. He might bolt at any moment. "Major?" he asks timidly.

Justin seems not to recognize him for a minute. Then he shakes his head. "Not now. Clancey, please. Kitty—I'm sorry." He reaches to help her up.

"But Major—"

"I'm not a major, Clancey, and I don't know why you have to call me that. Take my hand, Kitty. Kitty?"

"Justin?" She says his name softly as she looks around the room. "Where's Francis?"

He looks back at the empty room. "Hestia." He straightens up.

An alarm buzzer screams once. An air lock has opened somewhere.

Justin shoves Clancey out of the way. "I'll get him, Kitty, don't worry." He runs down the hall, knowing that it is too late, wondering why he is putting any effort at all into this when it's what he wanted all along. He thinks of slowing down, but can't.

The departure room is empty when he comes pounding in; the doors are sealed, the air lock closed, and no one is about. He runs to the wall, clears a view plate, but cannot see anything except arches of color and the blackness of infinity that waits hungrily below. He dashes back into the hallway, to a ladder, climbs up three decks and rushes into the computer-control room. Lurching into a command chair, he flicks on the overhead viewer. The screen blossoms to life with sunburst starbow streaks punctuating the void. Justin presses a button, panning the camera. A moment later, he locates a figure in space. It is no more than a speck, but he hesitates to zoom in for a confirming close-up, tensing at the thought of seeing that face, of looking that specific death in the eyes. He realizes then that death in space has always frightened him somewhere deep down inside, though he has fantasized both Kitty and Vomer in such situations. He looks at the screen again. Something is wrong.

Why isn't Vomer being tossed around out there? Why is he moving in a reasonably straight line? Moving?

Justin fumbles for the controls, zooms the camera, focuses. The camera begins to track automatically. Vomer wears an environ-suit, possibly even the same one Kitty wore. An isostatic field encases him like a giant soap bubble. A line no bigger than a spider web thread extends behind him. He holds a propulsion gun in each hand and fires bursts in opposing directions every second, moving against the black-hole tide with incredible deftness. One would think he had a reason.

Justin traces the line back to the ship, but Hestia is nowhere to be seen.

Dropping back in the chair, he chews his lip, tangles with blocked rage, hopeful relief, and a ripping desire to scream.

Nothing works, nothing ever goes right. Wasn't there a time when a goal was something he went for in a straight line, just plowed through and reached out and caught? Wasn't there? His lower lip pulls out from between his teeth. With grim finality, he shakes his head. No. Never.

Behind him, from the ladder, he hears a sound. He sits up and swings his legs over the edge of the command chair, then looks back.

Kitty stands, still naked, at the end of a row of blank, dead consoles. Two lights from the opposite side of the cabin bathe her in red. Like a child, she has her feet together and her arms wrapped in a tense hug, shoulders hunched, her face an unnecessary prop above it all—the stance says everything.

Seeing her like that makes Justin tired. He lacks the energy to explain Vomer's survival to her. He sees his life as a smooth plain behind him, the last two years as flat as glass, but with this sudden hilltop where he now stands, he can look to his future. In telling her that Francis is alive he will come down off the hill; his future is yet another flat plain stretching to the horizon. He looks at it sadly, knowing no way of staying on the hill.

He points over his shoulder at the screen, then looks back himself to discover that the screen shows nothing—he was searching for Hestia, and Vomer is out of the picture. He reaches for the knob to retrace the line to Vomer.

Kitty's eyes have stayed on him; she has not looked at the screen and will not. She knows Justin was too late to save Vomer. She knows her lover went out, because the alarm told her as much. She needs no further proof.

Justin glances back at her. Strange, he thinks, that he has no desire for reconciliation with her. Right this moment, if he shuts off the screen, he could probably live out his fantasy with her; he is all she has left—at least that's what she thinks. He checks the screen again, finds Vomer floating down into view. Then he stands. How tired he is suddenly. His body aches like an old man's; he thinks he feels like Clancey.

Without the least change of expression, Kitty uncoils her arms. She has his service revolver in her right hand. Justin's weariness slides away.

"Hey, that's mine. I've been looking for that, where'd you get it?"

"I'm going to kill you, Justin."

"Now . . . look here—"

"Then I'm going to kill myself. We can't go back. They won't be anything like us anymore. They probably won't even want us. I'll go crazy here. I'm going to kill us."

"That's stupid, Kitty. You don't want that, listen."

Her arm comes up.

"Kitty, goddamn it, he's not *dead*. He's fine! Look, look at the screen, he's wearing a suit, he's okay!"

She risks a glance at the screen. Her mouth opens and closes soundlessly, recalling for Justin Clancey's words: "Fish out of water." It makes a frayed kind of sense, as if the old man reacts premonitorily to occurrences that will happen shortly, as if he lives ahead of them but occupies space here. And is he crazy or has Kitty begun to glow?

Justin rubs his eyes. God, he's tired. Kitty has just tried to kill him after Vomer has tried to kill him, and he's daydreaming some argle-bargle about Clancey, who will probably try to kill him soon. How long since he has slept? Days, not even hours, but days. How many is impossible to tell since the corridor lights never shut off, and here he is back at the flat plain theory of his constant life. He frowns.

Kitty is still staring at the screen, her mouth still working, and she still seems to be kind of greenishly bright. Justin says, "It's Vomer out there, Kitty. He's fine, he's wonderful!"—he turns around—"He's . . . holy Christ."

The camera has tracked Vomer's dogged ascent automatically, up and up to the bright object that now fills the screen.

The object is gargantuan, so big that only part of it can be viewed at once. What they see is a globe as bright as a star but contained in a definite shape, and green, vivid green. Three parallel rods, shiny black, run out from it and off the right-hand side of the screen. There seem to be no markings, no windows or external trappings as there are on the *Flavus*. Nothing to identify its point of origin as Earth.

Justin glances at Kitty. His gun still stares him down. He sidles toward her. She takes no notice. He starts to reach for the gun, delicately, casually. A tremor rolls through Kitty. "Annn . . . annnn . . . annn," she says. The gun waves about. Justin hops back to the security of the chair.

"It took him," she cries. "It took him away!"

Justin swings around. The green ball fills the screen. Vomer is missing.

"Major?"

Justin jerks and turns in time to catch his gun as it flies past, Kitty having flung it, startled out of her wits. Clancey stands at rigid attention just behind her. "Major," he says again, "one of the women is sick."

The old man must mean Hestia. "Where is she?"

Kitty grabs onto Clancey, shakes him silly. "It took him, it took him, it took him, it took him! Look!" She sobs, her hair spilling over, sticking to her face. "*Francisss*," she wails. She runs to the ladder and climbs, crying, out of sight.

"Where's Hestia, Clancey?"

But the old man fails to answer. The green globe has captured his mind.

Justin refuses to look back again. The Gorgon isn't going to get him twice. He needs sanity, calmness, time to gather his wits. He has to be prepared. Sure, it could be an Earthship. Probably is. Plenty of time has gone by out there, hundreds of years. Like Kitty said. Everything would be different. Sure.

"Aliens," whispers Clancey. His voice creaks.

"Don't be silly."

"Aliens!" he shouts. He flings himself through an about-face and runs, actually sprinting to the ladder. Down he drops without the use of the rungs, like an old sea dog. "Aliens!" repeats over and over as Clancey zealously carries the warning to all parts of the ship.

Justin's head bangs. Multiple shadows of him extend across the floor in different colors, spectro-analyzing him, breaking him up. The green light burns his back. The gun, heavy—it would be so easy, so quick. No. He can't do that. Not yet. He's sick to death of it all, of every single thing in his life, but he can't apply the last, bright coat of paint. Watch it spill down onto the glass plain.

He stands like a statue for a very long time. "I'm hungry," he tells himself at last. The words, like a magic phrase, release him from the green grip, and he walks away to the ladder.

He descends.

II.

The two other ships were called *Arcus* and *Lividus*; both were launched after the *Flavus*.

Justin dreams himself onto one of them. He walks down an immense, cavernous corridor where everyone seems to be walking away from him. He taps them on the shoulder; they turn with gargoyle faces to him. "What ship is this?" he asks each face. "Take your position," they tell him, then face away. "I don't have a position—it's not my ship," he tries to explain. No one listens or responds. He wonders suddenly why the names of the three ships are in Latin. Who dreamt up such names? Stupid space program, he says to himself. The mass of grotesque faces all turn and glare at him with round, green glowing eyes. They have overheard his thoughts.

He awakens with an after-awareness of a loud noise. Sitting up, he finds that his hand, beneath his pillow, has pulled the trigger on his gun. Brown-black smudges smoke on his pillow. In a panic he rubs his hands all over his head. No blood. No wound. The bullet has seemingly vanished. Leaning back against the bulkhead, he trembles and wipes around his neck. He wants a shower, wants to feel renewed.

Over the past two years he figures he must have awakened every other morning and wondered how long he could stand it here, how long this insanity would last. Two years—and he still wonders, and he's still here.

How long did he sleep? His watch shows 3:30, but what 3:30? Whose reality does time keeping belong in?

Justin's stomach churns, making sounds like a water cooler. That meal he ate before going to sleep (what *was* that brown stuff?) does not set well.

He goes into the bathroom and seats himself. The toilet acts as an inverted thinking cap; sitting here, he recalls the recent past with a sober clarity that escaped him while taking part in the events. The first thing he must do is find Hestia. Where can Clancey have sequestered her? He must have dozens of secret niches around the *Flavus* that no one has seen. He can sometimes vanish for days. Therefore, it is actually Clancey he must find. The old man said Hestia was sick; that means something has broken down, most likely. He ponders what he could have overlooked in her construction.

The door to his room clicks open.

Justin looks up, startled. He can't see the door from the toilet. He starts to stand, but quickly sits back down. The gun is still on the bed where he left it, in plain sight. Is it Kitty out there? If she sees the gun . . . should he call out, hope to distract her, or is it too late, will he only be telling her that he is here like a rabbit in an exotic trap, waiting to die? This is terrific, this is marvelous.

A shadow moves swiftly and silently across the narrow piece of the room he can see. On the back of his neck the hair prickles. The sheets on the bed rustle. Whoever it is, he has found the gun. Now Justin waits, huddled, not daring to breathe, hoping his killer will think he is gone.

The shadow reappears. It grows across the outer floor, and stretches like a gray amoeba into the bathroom, across the tiles. Justin looks up.

Francis Vomer appears in the doorway. How did he survive? How in hell did he get back in? Justin shivers from tension. He sees that his revolver dangles from Vomer's fingers. This just isn't fair.

Vomer walks forward with lithe grace. A big, toothy smile grows on his face and he hands Justin the gun. "You shouldn't leave this lying around, Morrel. You never know what could happen. I keep mine in my locker."

Justin swallows, nods stiffly. "Yeah. Thanks." He lays the gun across his lap, twitches at the coldness.

Vomer crouches back against the opposite wall. "Boy, it's good to be back. I can't tell you."

"That's okay. Really."

"No, Justin, it's just that you have no idea what I've been through."

"That's true. None."

Vomer gets serious. "I'm really sorry about . . . well, you know."

"Okay."

"You're all right, Morrel. You didn't have to say that." Vomer becomes animated, begins using his arms to talk, acting out and emphasizing what he says. "I've been so confused. You know, it's tough being responsible for so many people, having all those separate destinies in your hands. And when you're troubled in your mind, you lose sight of the shape of things."

Justin debates if he should listen to any more of this or shoot Vomer now.

"But," Vomer grins, "there are miracles. I've gotta tell you. I've been lucky enough to experience one. Yessir. The Potos are my miracle."

"The Potos."

"Oh, come on now. Hey, look, Justin, I'm okay, see? I'm—I'm —I'm sane now. The Potos saw that I was unbalanced, my mind had gone off kilter, and they fixed me up. God, they're incredible. Brains are like origami to them. Fold and unfold, heh?"

"It was an alien ship," says Justin, his excitement growing. "You met aliens. Vomer! Did they come back with you, are they here?"

"No, they left."

"Left?"

"Yeah, well, see, they have a deadline, you know, to meet, and they stopped by because of your beacon—that was such a good idea —but they had to go."

"Stopped by? We're an alien race to them, we've never met before, and they just stop by, look at us, and take off like it's nothing?"

Vomer laughs. "See, I'm no good at explaining or you'd understand. I went into their ship, and they fixed me up and sent me out."

Justin has to look away from that constant smile. It's like lobotomized joy. Vomer *sounds* sane enough and calm enough, but his eyes are wide open, jet black pupils totally surrounded by gleaming whites. As if he has been in a thousand-year coma and now can't get enough of being awake.

"But they're coming back," he says hopefully. "You explained our situation to them."

"Oh, sure. They'll be back in a couple of years."

"Years!" He squeezes back a sob.

"Well, we're not exactly on their route, you see. Black holes are kind of like collapsing bridges to them, like places you don't want to travel."

"I don't understand. You mean, they go someplace, black holes?"

"I didn't say that."

Vomer is lying, Justin knows it. His hand closes tighter around the gun butt. "The Potos," he begins, "what did they look like?"

"I never saw them."

"But they fixed you. You said."

The commander shifts uneasily. "Yeah, but I didn't see. . . ." His mouth pouts for a moment. The air around him seems to thicken, and colors emerge in smoky veils. Justin blinks and moves his head back. The colors are gone. More hairs stiffen on his head. His bowels want to empty.

"Uh, listen, Francis—" he pauses, expecting a reaction, but Vomer only stares wide-eyed back at him "—um, you must be hungry and all, and I know Kitty wants to see you."

"Kitty." His smile stretches into a vile scythe. "Yeah." He stands. "We'll talk more later, Morrel. And I want to see that woman you . . . I want to apologize to her."

This is what Justin has been waiting for—for Vomer's back. But as Vomer turns away, Justin sees on the back of his head a square patch where the hair has been removed. A shiny knot of flesh protrudes from it, perfectly smooth, like one end of a marble egg embedded in his head. Justin hesitates. Vomer starts away.

Now! cries the voice in his head. Now, or it will be too late. Justin lifts the gun from his naked lap.

Vomer stops mid-stride and turns. "No, Justin. You can't—you don't know how. It's not as easy as you think it is." He waits. Then, satisfied, he nods and walks out of Justin's range of sight. His voice echoes back. "They fixed me. I told them what was wrong."

The door clicks shut.

Justin sights down the barrel for a long time after that. His face is ashen. Sweat runs down his wrist, drips from his elbow. Finally, he lowers the gun, setting it on the tiles.

His body shudders.

As it turns out, the toilet is the best place he could be.

"Kitty!" "Clancey!" "Hestia, for god's sake!" "Where the hell are you people?"

The corridor snakes off to the left. Dark noises—mechanical gurgles, grunts, and sighs—resound from distant points. Justin stands as if in an elaborate steel colon, on the verge of being ejected. He can sense imaginatively a traction tugging him back down the hallway toward the airlock, toward the grim, black sphincter below.

Where's everybody gone? Have they been pulled down, stood here wondering as he does until some hidden force whipped them off their feet? The ship as enemy. Just the last survivor, one man against the forces of the infinite. Sounds pretty awe-inspiring all right, but it isn't the right battle.

He has climbed up and down every ladder to every level of the ship, shouting their names, even crying out, "Aliens!" at one point near the cryogenics chamber but getting no response. He knows, deep down, where he has to go; the options have run out.

So ends the life of Justin Morrel. A man who went aboard a ship, who tried to be a pioneer and a hope for humankind, and who never gave it a second thought.

A fine epitaph. He hopes Clancey won't put him in the food processor.

The ship rumbles like a mountain king.

Justin fingers the gun in the belt of his jumpsuit, then starts down the corridor.

The *Flavus* creaks like an ancient galleon as he climbs the ladder up two decks. He calls out again and gets no answer again. No, there can be no reprieve. What he at first joked about, then promised as a veiled threat, and then attempted by remote control, he must now perform himself. His love for Kitty has nothing to do with it now; in fact, seen in this light, he knows he never loved her at all. What he felt was too perverted to qualify as true affection. At last he can accept that; and if he can face that, he can face Vomer. Sure, it'll be simple.

He glances behind himself. Someone was there, watching him; he could feel it. But no one is there now.

He continues along the corridor, rounding a corner. Ahead, the lights have been put out for a ten-meter stretch. But Justin keeps going, though his steps are smaller and his sweaty palm is sealed against the gun butt.

Kitty suddenly emerges from the wall on his left. There is no door, no niche where she could have hidden. She has simply appeared. And even in the dim light he can tell that something is horribly wrong with her. Her blue eyes are too large, fingers too long, breasts hanging too low and lopsided. The pale hair on her body moves like cilia around a protozoan, beckoning threads. She grabs for him; simultaneously, he tries to push her back. They meet and pass through one another. Justin stumbles off his feet, lands on his knees in shock, and scrambles up. Kitty has vanished. Justin backs against the wall and begins to slide his way along it. None of the walls reflect him any more, and they seem to have a secret depth all their own, like seaquarium windows. The floor fades from sight slowly as a thick mist swirls up.

When at last he reaches Vomer's door, Justin has concluded that he is mad and lost in the fantastic. The shining door stands, the wall around it gone, like a door in the middle of nowhere, opening onto another world. A looking glass, a wardrobe. It bears the sign COMDR. FRANCIS VOMER. The "Francis" is virtually obscured by crayon black shading. Justin recalls when Vomer did that, and clings to the solidity of this memory, as a signpost to his sanity. So encouraged, he draws the gun from his belt and reaches up to open the door.

"Tea party!" yells a deep, deep voice. It sounds like the ship.

Justin presses the doorplate and directs every bit of his concentration onto that nameboard that slides away into nothingness as the door rolls back.

A landscape stretches like an open palm before him. Small,

wrinkled creatures are everywhere, their seamy skin shining like rotted abalone. Some stand in groups, chattering in indecipherable phrases. Others stand alone, wailing. They all stop and observe him as he waits in the doorway, pistol drawn. A few gesture and a few others titter. The joke is on him.

The ground is like desert, with small lumps and dunes, around which more eyes regard him. Where is Vomer in all of this? The idea leaps into his head: Behind me! He starts to turn; something shoves him from behind, sending him sprawling into the room, onto his face. It may look like sand, but it feels like steel. His chin cracks hard, but he manages to hang onto the gun, rolls over ready to fire.

No one is there. Even the door has vanished.

"Vomer." He climbs to his feet. "Vomer." The ground before him swirls around and around and up into a cylinder that shapes itself into Vomer: incredibly handsome, perfectly trim, and smiling like the devil.

"Hey, Morrel, glad you made it."

The small creatures sidle over and mirror Vomer's grin.

"Potos," Justin guesses. Vomer confirms this, but Justin barely hears him; some notion just out of reach is forming in his mind. He has to put a few more pieces together to make the notion a picture. "They real? Did they board with you?"

"No and yes," answers Vomer, being cryptic. Or is he? "I told you they fixed me," he continues. "We're a unit now."

Justin shakes his head.

"See—I'm still no good at explaining." Vomer begins using his hands again, scooping the air as he talks. "They speak in images, in impressions. They all live inside one another all the time. And they tried to live inside of me, but I couldn't accept them, and we were an unknown species to them, so they needed to communicate. They just had to talk to me. So they did the one thing they could do—they fixed me so we could talk, so they could be in me like they're in each other."

"They're in your mind."

"You betcha. And I'm going to help them out."

"How?"

"I'm to be the first man to enter a black hole."

"You can't do that, that's suicide."

"Naw, naw, I don't mean I'm going to take a walk into it. I mean, we're going to descend into it. We're underway right now, going down at this very moment. And the Potos are in constant contact with me, living inside me. I've got my command back, Justin. I've got a crew again. Isn't it great?"

"Where are the others?"

Vomer's face pinches as if in pain. "We don't need them."

"I didn't ask you that. Where are they?"

"Where are they, what?"

Justin stiffens with anger. "Where are they, *sir?*"

"Major!"

Justin wheels around. Clancey has appeared behind him where a dune used to be. He is lying on his back, surrounded by strange, dark figures that seem to be transparent. The figures turn their heads toward Justin, and he blanches. They are all corpse's faces, in various degrees of decay. "Major!" Clancey cries again. "Help!"

Vomer says, "He never liked me. And he always wanted his old friends back, so now he has them."

"Set him free." Even as he says this, Justin watches Clancey vanish back within the dune.

"Not possible. Soon, though, I'll let him join my crew."

"And Kitty?"

"I'm sorry, Justin. You can't see her." He lowers his head, then glowers at Justin through his eyebrows. "She kept me in this room, kept me sedated a lot, and most of the time I had to break out. She was supposed to be my lover, but she didn't love me. So I'm keeping her in here, too, paying her back. She can't see us or hear us; she's in a whole different place and here at the same time. I'm changing her in accordance with her hubris, punishing her by altering her body. I can do that. I can do that by entering the mind and making the mind do the altering, like a . . . a tailor cutting pants by microwave. That's a good analogy. Isn't it good? Say it's good."

"Vomer, don't. She did—she *does* love you."

"No! She never did. The *Potos* love me."

"Sure, and so they send you to suicide."

"No. The black hole's a doorway to someplace else. They just don't know where, and I wanted to do it. I want a command."

"And me? What about me?"

Vomer laughs lightly. "You? Nothing. You can't kill me. You didn't keep me locked up. You're the only one who ever did anything nice by me."

"How so?"

"Don't be so modest. Hestia. You gave me someone who follows orders. And I know that once you get over this crazy idea of protecting the others that you and I are going to be real close. You like me—I can tell. Besides, I need you to repair her."

As if on command, Hestia appears behind Vomer. Justin gasps at the sight of her. One half of her face is gone. The black fabric that lay beneath the flesh, the fabric that pulls and stretches to create the impression of muscle, is bared as is her left eyeball.

"She wouldn't let me out of the ship," Vomer explains. "I had seen the Poto ship, and I wanted to put on my suit. But she wouldn't let me. She wanted me to go out without it. There are some things about her you need to correct, Justin. You didn't get her just right." He smiles benignly. "But, of course, you didn't appreciate the intricacies of my needs. You'll come to."

"Hestia."

"Justin." She walks forward.

"Wait," says Vomer. Hestia continues to walk forward. "Wait," he growls.

Like a man with a severed corpus callosum, Vomer seems to know and yet not recognize that Hestia is mechanical. He can talk about fixing her, even discuss her machine parts, and he still won't know that she is anything but another being for him to order about. He barks his commands again and again, annoyed at the futility of the act.

Hestia passes around him. He reaches for her.

Justin raises the gun and fires.

Vomer turns back to him slowly, surprised. "Well, I never would have believed it. You're like the others after all. I was giving you a *chance*," he whines. "I was gonna let you help. Now you have to go someplace, too."

Vomer begins to fade.

Justin has just shot at a projection. No wonder Hestia failed to respond to him. She comes to Justin with her arms out to hug him. The ground beneath her starts to swirl. He knows what is going to happen. There isn't much time. "Hestia, here!" He shoves the gun into her hands. "Listen to me."

The wind around her rises to a howling gale; the sand surrounds her. He screams at her, but cannot hear his own voice over the wind, cannot even tell if he has said anything at all. The wind changes tone, becomes the creaking of the ship as it descends, rending, into the hungry, depthless maw.

The false landscape seems to be changing as he looks on. He knows that he is going away, wherever Vomer has chosen to send him. His mind is right at this moment being manipulated and its perceptions altered without his feeling a thing. No nerves to tell him. On his way. It makes him laugh. For whom is he trying to save the ship? Who is left? And for what? Like a big Dixie Cup, the *Flavus* will crumple as it drops into the gravity well. If it is a gravity well; if it isn't the doorway to hell. When all else fails, why isn't there suicide for him? Why?

The screaming sky explodes with triple thunder.

The landscape, and the wrinkled Potos with it, vanish like a broken daydream.

Clancey lies on the floor at Justin's side, twitching. He soon comes to realize that he has been freed, that the visions of his shipmates have fled. He begins to cry, curling up into a ball. Justin pats his shoulder. They are both in the second room, the private rear room of the commander's quarters. Justin wonders how he drifted so far inside the door. He had thought himself standing in place. And he was sitting.

He climbs to his feet now and walks out the door.

In the outer room Hestia stands firing the empty gun at a corpse with a missing face. She shot him from behind and the exit wounds have erased his personality.

Hestia lowers the gun as she sees Justin. "Done," she says.

"Yes. Where's Kitty?"

Hestia points to the door. The ship groans.

Justin's eyes go wide. That was no illusion. The ship is really under stress. He sprints across the room, hammers at the door for being too slow, slips through before it has opened fully, and tears down the hall at full tilt, having a momentary sense of déjà vu. He climbs up to the command room. The screen is already on, and the black hole, outlined by a rim of wild, sparkling colors, fills the entire screen. He notes quickly that there is no magnification, that the *Flavus* has passed the point of no return. They will go down quite quickly now. No reason to watch it. He pans the camera away and up. He would rather see the stars, experience the fading of reality. At the same time, he opens up the intercom to call Kitty, to tell her she is all right, that the horror is truly over, and to invite her up to be with him. Even as he flips the switch, the camera picks up an image not far from the lens. He needs little magnification to raise the lump in his throat, to make his heart pound hard. The figure is nightmarish, and not because it has been crystallized by the void.

Vomer's handiwork is still upon her. His tales were not all lies; she is like a figure of wax sculpted by Jekyll as he turned into Hyde. Beyond the grotesquery of her physique, the void has exploded her eyeballs. It's more awful than he could have imagined. Where else could she have gone, though? Her end will last for an eternity.

He shuts off the camera, growing aware of an utter calmness within himself. As if in sympathy, the ship, too, has stopped its groaning.

"Major?" Clancey's head pokes up out of the manhole. "Ah, there you are. Everything all right here?"

Justin tries to answer, but has to nod.

"Good. I'll send that young woman up here to see you. I hope you can do something for her."

He nods again. Can he get through? he wonders. "Clancey? We're going . . . down into a black hole, Clancey."

The old man stares at him for a long moment. Is he dealing with the probability of death, does he comprehend the enormity? Somehow, it seems to Justin that he understands perfectly.

Clancey's expression clears. He nods soberly. "Well, I'd better go pack." His head vanishes into the hole.

Justin leans back in the large command chair and looks up at the blank screen. He reaches up and turns on the camera once again, quickly readjusting it to peer into the black hole that looms closer every second. Then he shuts down the room lights and adjusts himself comfortably in the chair.

Odd that there should be no noise. Perhaps the Potos were right after all. Perhaps the hole does go somewhere.

A great tranquillity settles over him, mingled in the red glow of the console lights before him. Such peace has never found him before.

He thinks: We'll go in together, Kitty.

They fall.

Afterword

A Day in the Life
of Justin Argento Morrel

"A Day in the Life . . ." was the first story I wrote coming off six weeks of Clarion (the character's name even references the dorm where we Clarion students were housed at Michigan State University; where Damon Knight ran into a door while shooting at us with a squirt gun). It was an attempt to go all metafictional on some science fiction tropes: the macho Heinlein commander; the airheaded bimbo who exists strictly as window dressing; the scientist who can build anything out of spit and a stapler . . . I wanted to place them all in a situation where their normal behaviors in a science fiction story are subverted, corrupted by circumstance. So my commander has lost his command and his mind, the supposed bimbo is fiercely independent and likely the sanest of the group, and probably in command, and the desperately lovesick scientist can't do anything to change his situation except make it worse. It's the closest I've come to performing experiments on lab rats. No doubt this was a response to Clarion.

Divertimento

IN THE CENTER OF A RING OF THIRTY OR MORE tourists, a polished clavichord stood, solitary. Although heavy drapes were drawn across the windows all around the room, dazzlingly bright highlights reflected off the clavichord's surfaces. The tourists cleared their throats, muttered expectantly to one another, and shifted from foot to foot while they waited. They had been told not to sit just yet. Most had little idea of what exactly they were about to see.

Their host—a stocky man with a heavy, black beard just starting to gray, and wearing 18th century dress—entered the room. His name was Peter Tellier. He nodded to them, and took his place in one of two large chairs of walnut and upholstery set up directly behind the performer's bench. At his signal, the tourists sat, too. The Beidermeier armchair beside him remained empty.

A few moments later, directly in front of Peter Tellier, a boy appeared out of thin air and walked toward the keyboard. He seated himself imperiously upon the bench. Like Peter, he wore period clothing. His red coattails dangled lazily over the small bench. He crossed his ankles. Then, with eyes glistening, the boy, Mozart, glanced over his shoulder, directly at Peter.

After the first few times he had seen these actions repeated, Peter Tellier had dragged a chair to the spot, so that their eyes—his and Mozart's—would meet when the young composer looked around. He had hoped they would see each other, and maybe make friends. He would so have liked a playmate but had long since stopped pretending that such a thing could happen. That secret glance did communicate something wonderful, but not to him. Who was this look of pride meant for? Sister? Father? The doddering Archbishop? Peter had come to believe, having looked things up in a decrepit music encyclopedia, that it was Michael Haydn being promised something wonderful. Haydn would have had good cause to hope.

Such heavy eyelids, thought Peter. The eyes seemed too large for Mozart's small face. His little powdered wig curled into a ridge running around the back of his head from ear to ear. Peter thought of him as a little sheep. "Safely grazing," he mumbled, then glanced around self-consciously, but no one had noticed. His sister wasn't going to make this performance; probably she didn't even know what time it was. The other mismatched chairs, gathered from abandoned buildings nearby, were arranged in a half-circle that kept everyone at a distance from Peter and Susanne. "Lamb of God," he said, almost in prayer, "sacrificed upon the altar of Salzburg." It was a line from the crumbling encyclopedia that had stuck in his mind; it might as easily have described him as Mozart.

Mozart began playing. The sound of the clavichord was incredibly piercing. Tellier beamed at the beauty of it. He wished he knew how to play. His parents had lacked the money for lessons, and he had never really thought about it back then. Now, for all his wishing, the matter had been irreversibly resolved.

The piece Mozart played was a practice, a test, though not for him—he had written it and knew it so well that he needed no scrap of music before him. It was a trial run for a female singer. The opening was meant to be sung by a choir, but none existed in this performance. Instead, playing off each other's voices, the singer and Mozart would carry the opening together in a duet. Peter had hired a choral group once to see if he could draw a bigger crowd, but the cluster of singers took up too much space and blocked much of the view of the phenomenon, and he lost money. The crowds had thinned even further. He had come to believe since that the eeriness of the unaccompanied performance was what made it so riveting.

The long introduction, one day to be carried out by a small orchestra, neared its end. Tellier knew it by heart now: *Regina Coeli*, Kochel 127. He sat more stiffly. His hands were sweating.

Mozart turned his eager young face to the side, addressing the woman no one else could see.

She began. She sounded as if she were standing just to the right of the clavichord. Her pure voice echoed like the ringing of a distant bell. Peter was pretty sure the voice belonged to Maria Lipp, wife to Michael Haydn. Haydn, so he believed, was sitting or standing right about where the two chairs were. Peter wished Maria Lipp would manifest there with Mozart, but he doubted that would ever happen. All the resurrections he'd heard of had arrived in single lumps, as finished or unfinished as they could ever be. He wished they would stop arriving altogether. Crowds this size were becoming the exception.

She sang out with Mozart: "*Regina coeli laetare*." They repeated it—all of it, parts of it—weaving around each other until the line ended, as did all the lines of the piece, in an "*alleluia*" meant for the complete chorus.

"Queen of heaven, rejoice," said Peter, sharing what he could. The crowd had fliers, in seven languages, translating the text; they didn't need his help but he couldn't keep it to himself. After so many performances, he had to show off just a little. He lowered his head, pretending to lose himself in the music.

The performance went on for a little over ten minutes, after which, unaware of the audience's applause, an excited Mozart got up and dashed right at Peter. An instant before he reached the big chair, he vanished. The crowd gasped as one—Mozart had become real to them. Peter thought sometimes that he could feel Mozart passing through him on the journey back in time, but knew he was making that all up.

The applause thinned out quickly: With the performer nonexistent, who was there to clap for? Peter, after all, had done nothing more than tell them when to sit.

The crowd rose to leave, mumbling, grabbing their coats, thanking Peter as he held open the door for them, some enthusiastically, but most with an air of doubt, as if suspecting the whole thing to have been a hoax. Did any of them, he wondered, even know the story of this house?

When the last of them was gone, Peter stood briefly at the door, looking down the narrow, slush-covered street toward the snowy heights of Kapuzinerberg for a sign of Susanne; but she was nowhere to be seen. She'd be out there somewhere, not very far away. Her playtime wanderings always worried him. If something should happen while she was out there, he might never know about it. He searched for her footprints but the tourists had stamped out all traces. His breath steamed. The cold stung his face. He closed the door and headed back inside. On the way down the hall, he dimmed the lights, then drifted back to his chair. Such weariness overcame him that he thought, with a spark of fear, he might be wearing out.

In the empty circle another performance would soon begin, but no more audiences were scheduled for today. He'd had them all week, five times a day, and that was enough. Too much. But the take had been exceptional. Enough to buy more medical help for Susanne. He looked at the dark space where the clavichord would shortly reappear.

He sat awhile in the dark, his thoughts going nowhere in particular. The smell coming from the kitchen was of warm chocolate. Behind him, the door banged open and his sister shuffled in. Filthy snow slid from her black boots; snow spackled her thermal-weave pantlegs. Peter tried not to show his great relief, because it would have revealed his concern at her absence. He thought she might have grown tired of the music. But of course that was absurd —Susanne had no idea how long she had been gone. One performance was any performance to her.

She had been making chocolate lace by pouring hot caramel into snowbanks. Undoubtedly she had wandered off with her pan of caramel to find just the right pile of snow. She had forgotten the pan outside somewhere in order to carry the product in—a pile of fragile, amber sheets, crisscrossed patterns lying like pages of an open hymnal on her mittened palms. The whole world for Susanne at present consisted of getting the hardened caramel to the kitchen, where melted chocolate waited to receive each layer, thereby creating the time-honored confectionery wonder.

Susanne was younger than Peter by a year and a half, but she could easily have been his mother, even his grandmother. The device that had torn Mozart out of antiquity had detonated much nearer Susanne than her brother. The particles that had passed through her had slowed and lost energy by the time they reached Peter. As a result, her genetic material had received much higher exposure. She would have been dead, a memory, except that their parents—the first ones struck—had inadvertently shielded her somewhat with their bodies. Both parents turned from tissue to dust almost instantly. Cheeks caved in, eyes crackled back into the wrinkling lids, bodies doubled over, folding like accordions to the ground, where they puffed up a cloud of brown smoke. All of this

in a second or two while their children writhed in a torment of stretching bones, growing teeth, sprouting hair—human ecosystems wildly out of control. Peter could still hear his parents' cries go creaking into oblivion and remember how in agony he thought his fingertips would pop open to let his skeleton expand.

He understood little about the "time bombs," as the press had dubbed them. The bombs had exploded in a few places around the world, but mostly here in Salzburg. No one knew why, just as no one knew for certain their source. Experts from Boston to Beijing speculated that the creators of the bombs, themselves from the future, had no idea of the destructive capacity of these devices. They might, in fact, be early experiments in time travel, the first unmanned capsules, inadvertently creating catastrophe by hauling a bit of future matter into the present. There was talk of proto-tachyonic pulses, of bombardment and loops, of matter and antimatter, of fission. None of it meant much to Peter. What no one talked about was the horrible pain of being eleven years old and watching your parents molder in front of your eyes. No one had ever consoled him over that. They were afraid of him and Susanne—absurdly afraid that what had happened might be contagious.

Though his hair and beard showed patches of gray and his eyes were dry and pouchy, Peter Tellier had only recently turned fifteen. Susanne, with her trembling, arthritic hands, was thirteen but as a result of the time bomb had jumped all of adulthood to an immediate, doddering second childhood of perhaps eighty, perhaps more. Her deterioration seemed daily more evident to her helpless brother. Her body was racing to its end. Mozart—the sole means of support for the two children—was both the eldest and the youngest in the room at sixteen.

While her brother looked on, Susanne hobbled out of the kitchen. Chocolate stained her mouth and fingers. Tucked up under her like a football, she carried a feather duster.

The clavichord sat glowing in the center of the room, having reappeared for another performance, and Susanne intended to clean it. Peter sighed, inwardly aching on her behalf. She had been to so many specialists but no one had helped her. They probed her, studied her, probably wore her out faster with their poking and prodding than if he'd just let her deteriorate in peace, but he still sought for some cure. He recalled the way they had looked at him the last time, unable to cope with the idea of a little boy who was in appearance their senior. They often spoke to him about his sister as they might have spoken to his father, and for brief periods he became his father, acted the way his father might have done.

A scary kind of fame surrounded the time bombs; less respectable journals wrote outrageous things regarding them. The attention brought the crowds, certainly. They had to pay a lot to get in here, and they paid it without a whimper, because nowhere else would they ever see the real live Mozart . . . unless, of course, another bomb released another segment of the composer's life. Peter refused anyone the chance to record the event, although a few had initially offered him substantial money to do so. What he couldn't understand was why some world network hadn't come forward with millions for exclusive rights. It was what he'd dreamt of, but no one had fulfilled that dream. There were other places he might have taken Susanne, with that kind of money.

As she neared the keyboard, Susanne disrupted the image. Static sparks danced on the feather duster, traveled up her arm. The clavichord rippled. Heedless, Susanne went right on dusting. Peter could read pain in every tiny movement that she made. She was, he conceded, getting much worse.

Peter suddenly found that he couldn't stand it any longer. "It's time," he called to her to let her know that Mozart would be coming out in a moment.

She turned around, shifting her weight from one hip to the other, wincing but denying it, too. She smiled at him. Half her teeth had dissolved. "What will he play for us today?"

"I don't know. Why don't you come and sit, and find out."

"He likes my cleaning up. He always gives me such a look before he starts, just to tell me that he's pleased."

"Yes, he does, doesn't he?" They'd had almost this same conversation a hundred times. Each repetition weighed him down more; he'd end up stoop-shouldered the way his father had always said he would if he didn't stand up straight.

He got up and helped his sister to her chair. He took an Afghan from the back of the chair, unfolded it and laid it across her lap. She leaned around him to watch Mozart emerge on his way to the clavichord. "Look, he's going to nod to me, Petey," she said. Peter looked down at her eyes full of delight and his face grew hot. He dodged around his own chair and walked off quickly, hoping to escape before the playing started.

At the door he snatched his coat from a peg, hastily wrestled his way into it on the way out the door.

The cold sliced under his skin. Outside, the orange haze of the sky framed baroque shadows and bombed-out buildings. In the further depths behind him, the keys of the clavichord "spanged" under Mozart's fingers, the introduction moving into the first verse of the *Regina Coeli*. How lonely the tiny voice sounded. It seemed to echo through the austere environment. Where had all the tourists gone? To the hotels, no doubt, on the other side of Kapuzinerburg, the living side. No bombs had gone off there as of the last Peter had heard. Smoke and lights sparkled in the early twilight over across the river. Hardly any showed down the street here. Or maybe the tourists had gone to the Cathedral Square. He had read about a time bomb there, that killed twenty and brought to life a piece of the "Everyman" play that long ago had been performed there every year. No doubt he'd lost paying customers to that event. To him that was the real cruelty of the bombs—that they wrought their damage without purpose or plan, robbing a life and then robbing the chance to rebuild that life.

The spirit woman sang, "*Quia quem meruisti portare . . .*"

Peter walked away from the sound. The snow crunched beneath his feet. He pretended to be his father, engaged in conversation with him. "You are fifteen now," the father said, "too old to play make-believe games anymore. You and your sister can hardly get along now. Where will you go when the money is gone? When the tourists stop coming altogether? You haven't saved enough, Peter. You're living like sick people. You have your food delivered, and you never leave the house except to take your sister out sometimes. You've grown up afraid. Afraid of the world."

"I have Mozart," Peter replied, a little scared by what he was revealing from within. "Maybe we could go with him."

"Does your Mozart know that he's here? Does he know that you're here? Or Susie? No. You're playing games, Peter. Mozart's dead, and you and your sister are catching up with him."

"Stop it," Peter said. He stopped walking. The "voice" went away. It hadn't been his father at all. He turned and saw how far from the house he had gone in just a few minutes. He had nearly reached the other end of the street and the arrow sign he had put up. From there, the house looked no different than any of the other uninhabited dwellings surrounding it. Hurriedly, he walked back toward it. Look at the place. Without the sign how could the tourists know in which house Mozart played? No wonder the crowds had thinned out. He'd been so busy with Susanne's care that he had let the house rot around him.

As he neared, he could hear Maria Lipp singing repeatedly, *"Resurrexit,"* then both she and Mozart launched into a series of joyous *"Alleluias."*

Peter closed the door, then stood leaning against it, as if to keep something evil out. His breathing wheezed and little sparkles danced in the air. He couldn't believe such a short run had drained him so much.

The beautiful voice floated through *"Ora pro nobis Deum."* Peter thought, *please, yes, pray for us to God.*

He hung on there until the last *"alleluia"* was sung. Susanne began clapping gaily. Peter peered through the doorway at her, as Mozart came running only to vanish just before reaching her. He wondered, did Mozart know she was there? Could he, from his side of time, see a bit of the present?

Seeming to sense his presence, Susanne glanced back at him. "Hello, Petey," she said. "Would you like some of my chocolate lace? It ought to be hard now."

He nodded. His face had gone dull with dissembling to hide from all the fears that churned inside him. He watched her climb up to shuffle across to the kitchen, obviously in great pain. The feather duster fell from her lap but she made no attempt to pick it up. She looked more withered than when she had sat down, only minutes before. When she was out of sight, he took off his coat and hung it back in the hallway.

"We can share it with Mozart, okay?" she called out to him.

"Fine." The word squeaked out of his knotted throat.

Susanne came shambling out of the kitchen, nearly doubled over with the effort of supporting her treat. It lay, a dark doily across her hands. Delight glistened in her cataracted eyes, senility blocking pain. "Lookit, isn't it nice?"

Peter stared at her and saw no one that he recognized. The sister he knew had gone into the kitchen; this creature had emerged, cut loose finally from his memories of her. What had happened to his sister? "Susie," he lamented. He walked swiftly forward, reaching out to take the chocolate.

Susanne's brows knitted. She glanced down at her breastbone. "Bee bite," she said. Uncomprehending, Peter drew up for a moment. Then Susanne swayed and her head went back with a look like that of ecstasy on her face.

Peter cried out and rushed forward. The chocolate lace slid off her hand and dropped. The fragile, woven strands shattered as they hit the floor, scattering fragments in every direction. Peter clutched her to him, his feet crunching on the glassy bits of caramel. "No, Susanne."

"Petey, I'm funny," she said. Tellier dragged her to her chair and set her down in it. "Where's momma, she here?" Her voice had gone thick. One side of her mouth twisted up as if trying to grin.

"She's coming," he answered quickly, searching her softening face for a hint of the little sister he could barely remember. "Be here in a minute."

For all the death he'd experienced, for all that he knew this would come, Peter Tellier retained a childlike incomprehension of how someone so close could slip away while he watched, while he held her.

She was only dozing between performances, he told himself. She often did that. She would be all right. He straightened her up, tucked the Afghan across her lap. He found a few large pieces of the chocolate lace and placed them on her lap, too.

Behind him, the clavichord fluttered into being. He turned and stared at it as at some horrible and totally alien object. He could not stand to hear that music again. Not ever again.

He forgot his jacket but climbed down into the snow like a figure out of history himself, in lace and velvet and trousers that buttoned just below the knee. The lights of civilization lay across the water, down the hill. He wondered if he would survive the walk.

Within, the house stood silent for a time.

Dust motes dancing in the sunbeams settled on the clavichord. The girl with the feather duster skipped over to it and began whisking at the surfaces, the keys, the bench, until young Mozart in a red waistcoat came marching out and angrily ordered her away. Mozart shooed her along as if herding a cow. She pranced ahead of him, smiling blissfully as if he were proclaiming undying love. Mozart vanished as she settled into the Beidermeier chair with coquettish grace. In the other chair, the ghost of Michael Haydn glanced reprovingly her way.

Mozart returned from behind the chair and headed for the clavichord. To the right of it, with both hands clasped beneath her bosom, Maria Lipp watched him for her cue to begin.

Susanne heard a little noise behind her and looked around to find her older brother closing the doors with great care. He was dressed in a wonderful costume just like Mozart's, but he put one finger to his lips to silence any outburst she might have had, then tiptoed into the shadows. She glanced surreptitiously at Haydn but he hadn't noticed Peter's arrival.

Susanne leaned down and placed her feather duster on the floor. Her feet dangled above it. She gripped the arms of her chair tightly, as if the chair were about to soar into the sky and carry her away to fabulous lands. *"Regina coeli,"* she named herself, then closed her eyes as Mozart's slender hands descended upon the keys.

—for Sycamore Hill, 1987

Afterword

Divertimento

Synchronicity looks like this:

I have had one session in a flotation—a.k.a. "sensory deprivation"—tank. I did this on a fall day and on the way to the tank session, I stopped into a used bookstore and purchased a copy of the complete poems of Wallace Stevens. I bought the collection because another writer had told me that whenever he needed a title for a story he could always find one hidden in Stevens's poems. The bookstore happened to have a copy in very good condition.

The tank session? I was in it for an hour but felt as if I were there for three times that long. When I emerged, it was as if I had never seen or heard anything before. The red and orange leaves seemed to explode off the trees. The hiss of cars passing on rain-drenched streets dopplered all around me. The air was of wet earth, exhaust fumes, and rotting leaves, and the smells of sultry food leaked out of every restaurant on South Street. It was glorious.

I eventually caught a bus home, across Philadelphia. On the way, I opened the Stevens collection randomly to various poems and read them. Then I got to "Mozart, 1935." This short story is encapsulated in that poem as I read it that day on that bus after that hour in a flotation tank. Had I done anything else on that particular day, this story would not exist.

Attack of the Jazz Giants

1.
Precipitating Events

IN THE GRAIN MILL OUTSIDE MOUND CITY, DOC Lewis and the boys had themselves four scared black men to burn. Doc, the officiating Grand Cyclops of the Klan hereabouts, sat way back on a cracked cane chair, two legs off the ground and daring the other two to snap. The dare had weight to it because, like his daddy before him, Doc had the heft of a hogshead keg. He'd lost all but a few strands of hair in the past few years as well, and the baldness bothered him much more than his increasing girth. In his youth, he'd gloried in his golden hair. In any case, the niggers couldn't see his features because Doc wore a flour bag over his head. His boy, Bubba, had charge of the actual branding. It was one of very few events in which the squat, pug-faced boy showed anything at all like industry.

Before he reached for the hot iron, Bubba took a tin scoop, filled it from a sack of buckwheat flour, and then slapped it over his victim. An explosion as from a colossal powder puff, and the tremulous naked man became a blinking ghost, a non-entity, and was thereby reduced further from any kinship with his tormentors. The flour was Bubba's little joke.

Curly and Ed Rose, holding the victim by his upper arms, got powdered, too. But, half-drunk on 'shine, Doc's two assistant Night Hawks only laughed themselves silly and staggered a bit—two demented and pointy-headed art thieves trying to make off with a copy of Michaelangelo's *David*. They did not appreciate as did Doc the gravity of their efforts here. It was sport to them, that's all.

It was four men set to branding eight. They'd brought guns but didn't have to brandish them. Fear, solid as the chains 'round their victims' legs, kept the disguised foursome in power. They could do anything they liked, with impunity. Their victims prayed to survive or else die swiftly.

Bubba drew the iron out of the bread-oven coals, turned slowly, then drove the brand home. The flour puffed up, the black skin hissed. The man kicked and screamed and wrestled but Curly and Ed Rose had braced for that. Flour melted in a stream down a powdered thigh. By the time Bubba pulled the iron away, his victim had passed out. A fresh pink eye within a triangle adorned his left pectoral—a symbol of the magical forces he now lived under.

Bubba was a third-generation nigger-brander. He ought to have had some sense of the history behind his actions.

His grandaddy, the Captain, had maintained this tradition well after slaves had ceased to be property. At a time when carpetbaggers crawled over the body of the South like worms and the Black Codes kept shifting in their proscriptions, the identifying mark was for the black man's own good. First, the branding reminded him how easily the world could turn over on him. Second, it ensured that he knew he had a home, a place where he belonged. Back in the days of Reconstruction, Grandaddy had been a Grand Dragon.

Since then, the family had branded maybe five hundred. There were men and women in Chicago, New York, St. Louis, and Kansas City who bore the cicatrix of the Lewis family plantation. No matter where they went, if things turned around, Doc would send out his Night Hawks to round them up. Many of those branded hadn't even been his workers. They'd been drifters, the homeless and directionless, passing through Mound City on their way to perdition. In other towns all across the south, they hanged those niggers. But his brand was known widely, so in a sense he was protecting them. He had worked this out long ago. Daddy was a man of vision, of foresight. Even those he'd branded couldn't have foretold otherwise.

2.
The Homestead

How Doc got his name was a mystery that went to the grave with his father. Daddy Lewis had been a young captain in the Confederacy and so naturally they'd all called him Captain out of respect. Doc wasn't a medical practitioner, nor a vet, nor even a snake-oil salesman. Somewhere before he turned ten, he got called Doc by the Captain and the name stuck. Maybe Daddy Lewis had had the percipience to know that his successor would need a *nom de guerre* to set him above the rest. Mystical power in names—a fact to which Doc could well attest.

He would happily have conjured something similar for Bubba, but that childish label had already malformed the boy's behavior well past the threshold of manhood. In fact, in moments of reflection Doc wondered if Bubba had ever really crossed that threshold. His desire to take pride in his son's actions had been endlessly frustrated, mostly by his wife, Sally.

Doc and she had two daughters as well: Debra and Psalmody. This latter name was the least likely thing Doc had ever heard, but the indomitable Sally had thought it a "beautiful, delicate, liquid word" and would not bend. Like the Captain, perhaps, she'd sensed something metaphysical about her child. At the same time, she couldn't tell you where she'd heard or what exactly was meant by the word, although it obviously referred to the Psalms. The solid biblical link carried the day. Sally could work Doc like a pump handle back then. Even now she could get under his skin with three or four well-placed words. She ought to—she was his cousin, had known him since childhood. This might also have accounted for a good deal regarding Bubba. His given name was Ezekiel. Biblically, he resembled the wheel, maybe a small ark or the fish that ate Jonah. Nobody was looking for anything metaphysical from him.

Psalmody had revealed her uniqueness early. At five, she'd asked her daddy what radiography was. Dutifully, Doc had looked the word up in a book and still didn't know to this day what it had told him. At six, Psalmody had wanted to know about positive rays, and at seven it had been genetics, but Doc had stopped researching by then. He didn't know what a father was supposed to do who couldn't offer his child the answers she sought. And, besides, he'd had a plantation to run.

It was 1925 now and Doc employed near eighty "workers." Curly and Ed Rose watched over the work force, same as they did everything else for him. He couldn't have imagined how he'd have gotten along without them.

Doc sensed that Curly had become enamored of Debra, his quieter daughter, his pale and delicate angel. Curly was a respectful young man, maybe a bit too fond of his sour mash but not so's it interfered with his work. Doc hoped they would marry and take over the farm. As for Psalmody, it was Bubba who seemed to have designs on her. Just looking at her, he could break out in a lustful sweat. The boy was troubling in his unceasing obtuseness. How could the two girls be such smart and lovely pastries and Bubba such a lump of dough? Surely never before in the family's long and proud history had there been so utterly beef-witted a child.

3.
Intimations of Doom

The morning after the branding, Doc heaved himself out of bed, and went shuffling down the hall, scratching at his butt, toward the back stairs and the door leading to the outhouse. But, halfway down, he found his way blocked.

Sticking up from the first floor stood the enormous lower joint from an impossibly larger clarinet. It looked like some sort of black sarcophagus and it jammed the entire stairwell. The banister below had popped off a couple of its balusters where the clarinet piece exceeded the stairs' width. Doc glanced instinctively up at the ceiling but found no corresponding hole to explain the presence of the thing. The chrome pads and finger plates reflected him in his utter dismay, each one as big as his head. Who in his employ would have carted the infernal thing along the hall and down the stairs? In the middle of the night no less, and without waking him? Who would do it? An' what kind of a joke was it supposed to be? He didn't immediately recognize its musical disposition. All he cared was that, as incommodious as a kidney stone, it blocked his route to pee. The urgency of that need cut through his confusion, and he climbed quickly, ape-like, back upstairs to the bedroom. One of the young maids, named Lizzie, had already arrived and was making up the bed. Somehow she'd known he was up—probably heard him clomping across the floor.

Doc hadn't the time to be shy. He snatched the chamber pot from under the bed, stuck his swollen member into it and glared defiantly at the girl while the echo of his release pinged off the pot. She openly observed his tool as she might have done a passing cockroach, too disinterested to reach over and squash it. With the pressure off, Doc's tool receded and he furiously tucked it back into his skivvies, blotching the flannel with the last remaining drops.

"Lizzie, what's that goddamn thing on the back stairs?" he demanded. Doc never cursed in the house, so he knew that she knew how mad he was.

"Thing?" she asked. Never heard of it.

"Well, never you mind, girl, you go get me Carpy, right now. Don't say anything but that I want to see him pronto."

She nodded dimly and escaped, the bed half-made. Doc put down the brass pot. While he waited for the household retainer, he sat back on the bed. The matter on the back stairs was too perplexing to dwell upon, and his thoughts drifted.

Outside, the field workers were singing a "holler" about not goin' down to the well no more. Doc smiled vaguely at their singing, which brought back memories of other times on the bed: Sally on their wedding night, drunk and catty; Carpy's mother, laid back on it, willing to let him fuck her. The halcyon days of youth — it had all been ahead of him then.

4.
The Homestead-II

Carpy was six years older than Bubba. Not nearly so dark as his mother, he neither much resembled his squat father. Muscular, yes, but long-muscled and trim. The only obvious trait of Doc's he'd acquired was the tendency toward baldness. Carpy's mother died shortly after his birth. His true parentage was kept from him, from the workers, and from Sally (who found out anyway and promptly stopped sleeping with her husband). She mistreated Carpy wickedly, never with any explanation or any apparent cause.

The most Doc dared for his eldest son was to teach him to read so that he could be promoted to the highest household position, that of overseer. It paid a tiny wage, but Doc had secretly hidden funds in a bank account for Carpy. He had rationalized this to himself over the years, so as not to have to face the obvious conflict with his duties as a Cyclops. Unlike his old man, Carpy treated those dozens beneath his command with utmost kindness and compassion — a gentle foreman, fond of Lizzie, but secretly, hopelessly, in love with Psalmody. She was built like a goddess. Her breasts alone stuffed his brain full of immoderate thoughts, and thank God for that or he might have zeroed in on the rest of her.

Psalmody liked to run, decades before jogging would come of age. She refused to ride in the family Ford, preferring to race it along the dirt roads, barefoot, in loose-fitting boy's clothing. The sweat on her upper lip did things to Carpy that he couldn't explain. Certainly he had seen enough sweat in his life. Even Bubba registered her exudence of sexuality, but his elder half-brother was way ahead of him. Rarely, after all, were women excited by the vision of a loved one picking his nose. Carpy, a man of position and responsibility, never would do such a thing publicly; whereas Bubba's excavated mucous adorned chair arms, walls, and the undersides of tables throughout the house. The thought of his hands on her would have made Psalmody faint. She was looking for someone of intelligence, of original thought, and pretty soon, too, or she would go crazy in this prison-farm. Everything that mattered to her existed somewhere else other than Mound City and its predatory environs. Although she didn't realize it, Carpy's gentle nature had already played upon the strings of her heart. History has a way of swinging around for another looksee.

5.
Prelude to War

Carpy had no idea what the monstrosity confronting him might be, nor how it might have arrived. "It's like a big arrow was shot through the roof. Impossible stuff," he called it. "Mr. Doc, nobody in this house can be responsible. Fact, I don' know anybody who could. My word on that."

Of course Doc ought to have guessed that no servant had hauled the thing in here. His mind tried to put together an explanation: Too large to have been dragged and lacking a corresponding hole in the ceiling for Carpy's "arrow," the odd cylinder must have been assembled in place, brought in through the back door. The cause for this blasphemy remained an enigma, but the method at least he could resolve to his own satisfaction. He ordered that the thing be removed. "Break it into little bitty bits if you have to."

Carpy pushed hard against a polished finger plate, which raised one of the connected pads a little ways. Deep below them, the earth seemed to belch out a flat, sonorous note. Carpy backed up against the wall. He and Doc traded worried looks. "Gonna take all the hands," he said, "everybody from the fields just to nudge this thing."

"Then, we gonna deal with it later," replied Doc. "Not messing about the workday over this little damn problem."

"Yes, sir, that seems best." Carpy withdrew past him, back up the steps. He peered down into the sarcophagal blackness of the instrument. Was that the top of a pale head way down inside there? The thing was some kind of sign, like chicken blood or a hanged man. This was a blight upon the family.

Halfway up the stairs, Doc found himself confronted by his wife. Sally had a way of looking at him that reduced his stature. That he was standing on a lower step of the stairs didn't help, either. He tried to take control of the situation quickly. "Damnedest thing I ever seed," he said as he leaned back over the rail. Sally gave the thing a quick look. "Clarinet," she said sagely, "but you'd have to stand on the roof to play it."

"What the hell kind of clarinet is that?"

Sally replied, "A big clarinet." She moved to let him up.

Muttering, Doc stepped around her and headed for his room at full tilt. There, Lizzie had already removed the chamber pot and finished making the bed. The child did look after him well. He thought again of Carpy's mother, but dismissed the memory as both provocative and immaterial. Sally trod solemnly along the hall. He sensed her lingering in the doorway, and he turned around. He walked over and started to close the door. "I have to git dressed if you don't mind."

"You've dripped on yourself," she indicated, staring at his crotch.

Doc shut the door. He listened to her move off. "Sally," he said softly, "you are workin' my last nerve."

Once he had finished dressing, Doc went down to breakfast. He had barely scooped up his first forkful when a cry from outside stopped him. His name upon the air brought Doc running out to the porch. Sausage in his mouth and a checkered napkin bibbing his neck, he towered over Ed Rose, who stood in a panic on the ground. Ed blurted, "You gotta come quick, Doc. You gotta see this thing."

Doc told him to calm down. He threw off the napkin and followed his foreman into the fields. The steamy Mississippi morning pumped the sweat out of him as he waded through waist-high cotton plants. Branded workers had stopped their business to watch as the man himself strode past them. Ahead, a cluster of them surrounded "the thing."

It had crushed rows of plants but no one had been hurt. It was a thin, gold tube, far longer than the thing inside the house, and it had spread a blue stain in a band over some of the cotton. The tube stretched out twenty yards before curving back—a piece from something much larger and more grotesque. In the flattened cotton the shape of the whole instrument could be discerned, as if it had slept there overnight and then moved on at daybreak, leaving the sloughed hand slide behind. Doc walked in its rut while trying to formulate an identity for the thing. He had trouble.

"Hell," he said, "looks like . . . looks like . . ."

One of the field hands spoke up. "Like God's trombone."

Doc whirled around angrily but as quickly realized that was exactly what it looked like. "That's right. A big trombone." And the thing in the house—it, too, was some sort of instrument. What had passed across his land during the night? "This don't make no kind of sense." While he wore a consternated smile, he marked the worker who had spoken—a young man. A smart, clever, and unbranded young man. Wouldn't do to have a smart satchel-mouthed nigger roaming in their midst. Liable to foment all sorts of trouble. He would have to sublease Spangler's Mill again. Soon. As for the mystery trombone, it was so great a mystery that he saw no point in trying to wrestle it to earth. "Drag this curlicue outten here now, and you all get back to work," he told them. "And don't be worrying yourselves over what it portends. It don't portend shit."

They continued staring at the trombone shape for a while before moving off; all save the satchel-mouthed boy. He caught Doc in his stare, and it penetrated and drew fear like a venom from the white man's heart.

Doc retreated from the field. Back on the lawn beside his house, he grabbed Ed Rose by the arm and asked him, "Who is that boy?"

"A-which?" Ed answered.

Doc turned him around and pointed. The workers had all returned to their labors. He knew them, knew their shapes, but he could not pick out the one who had stared at him. "Where the hell'd he get to?" The cotton grew waist-high. Doc convinced himself that the boy was crouched down, hiding, afraid. He wanted very much for that particular bastard to be afraid. Ed interrupted his search. "By the way, Doc, you seen Curly this morning? He ain't around. Nobody's seen him since last night, when he went out after our little business. Said he couldn't sleep, had some kinda tune in his head."

"Too much booze in his head, you mean. He gets back, you send him to see me. I'm not in a tolerating mood this morning." Curly did not reappear all day. Doc's mood developed a razor edge.

That night, alone in his bed, he heard distant thunder, rhythmic and incessant. Jungle drumming derived from a jungle band whose members existed solely in the æther; travelers in the air, ghosts as surely as a skeleton scuffling on his grave.

The image jolted him awake. The sound of jungle thumping diminished. It rounded into words or something like words, briefly: "Juba, juba, juba," a droned spell, which pressed the consciousness out of him. He lacked the means to fight its power, but prayed to keep the evil music far out in the bush. "Don' ever let 'em in," he muttered, then faded away himself like a lost radio signal.

6.
First Blood

Screaming woke Doc. Unmistakably Sally's voice, it sawed through the ceiling below. He wrestled his pants over his long johns, snapping up his suspenders while he ran along the hall. As he pivoted around the newel post, the screaming subsided into blubbering hysteria, and he followed it to the first floor. Such a sprawling God-damned house, this antebellum layer cake of his.

He stormed along the hall, cursing "God damn you, Sally, shut up," but his anger couldn't hold in the face of the new anomaly. It overwhelmed him—as big and broad as a church steeple. This time he knew what he looked at: He had forged the musical link. It was the bell of a trumpet, and for absolute sure it had dropped from out of the sky, because it had pinned somebody beneath it. One arm protruded, nearly severed by the swept gold rim. One arm, a white arm. A familiar white arm. Bubba's arm. His cold hand gripped tightly an equally cold branding iron. The dead idiot, what was he doing parading through the house with the fucking eye of God on a stick? Somebody would see, and some of them had surely been on the wrong end of it. A crawdad could have figured it out and put a name to it: Grand Cyclops and Son.

Doc got down on his knees to pry back the fingers. He drew the iron out of his son's hand. Sally continued her bubbly whining. He would've liked to have smacked her with the iron. Instead, he struck the trumpet bell. It clanged loudly. He thought, "Music destroyed my son." More than that, the trumpet like the clarinet was hollow.

Tossing down the bent brand, he tried to move the bell. He shoved it, grabbed onto the top and tried to tilt it up, he pushed it, climbed up the side and tried to pull it over. His bare feet squealed as they slid down the curved surface. He hung from the lip, his head back. He mewled to God, noticing abstractly that the ceiling remained intact. Yet the thing had passed right through it, must have done—the whole floor had buckled when it hit. He wiped the spittle off his lips and backed up into the counter. Lizzie stood there, struck stupid in her horror. She didn't even notice him.

What plague had been visited upon him? For what? He went to church like clockwork, prayed to and payed the Lord. He knew about original sin, the flood of Noah and the plague of locusts, about coveting your neighbor's wife, about the exodus. How could a man who comprehended those things be thus cursed?

He noticed his wife on her knees behind the bell. She had torn out some of her hair, and saliva foamed on her lips. Her anguish came in great heaves. Doc rushed over to her and tugged her hands down to her sides. "Calm," he said, "Calm now, honey. Easy does it." As if subduing a horse, he spoke. It worked for him but not for her. The strain of all she'd kept inside had broken Sally at last.

Eventually her daughters arrived at the scene. Debra re-enacted her mother's squall, but Psalmody looked on with strange contentment, like Cassandra watching as the wooden horse birthed inside her walls. Debra's screams galvanized Lizzie, and she snapped her skirts at and shooed both girls from the room, at which moment Carpy pushed his way in. He tripped over the bent iron and stopped still. Behind him came Ed Rose and a dozen field hands, but Carpy hardly noticed them. Ed ran over to Doc. The party had been on its way to move the thing in back, but trumpet or clarinet, it made little difference. Now they circled the bell. Silently, together, they bent down. They had no trouble grabbing hold of the rim; and, uttering a sharp "holler" as they often did in the fields, they lifted it all at once. Doc elbowed between them on his hands and knees to see if his son was all right. Probably the boy would have survived had it not been for the mute stuffed into the bell. It had acted as a hydraulic press, splitting the floor. Most of Bubba had been integrated with the boards.

The dark men set the bell down across the kitchen. They gathered around the depressed circle that contained Bubba's stain and Doc. They were silent. Their faces betrayed nothing. Doc found himself trapped like a sacrifice within them. One by one, they raised their fingers to their sweaty shirts as if to pledge allegiance, and each set of fingers carefully traced the hidden shapes of heterotopic eyes.

7.
The Homestead-III

After the funeral, nothing was the same. The workers began to migrate, drifting away on the dry winds of August, but not before a group of them finally hefted the clarinet on the stairs and solved the mystery of Curly. Curiously, he had mummified inside the cramped space. The enormous black joint had hardly touched him. Why he had died at all became the new mystery. Ed Rose read the signs plainly enough and deserted before the sun came up on another day. The Cyclops should have mustered some terror then, but he had no Night Hawks left and his iron had disappeared. He needed guidance from a higher authority. Curly and the others had betrayed him, he felt.

Sally was locked away over in Vicksburg and not likely to be returning any time soon. Debra had taken the household helm. She intended to redecorate the whole place, telling her father, "I want to strip away the old life, Daddy. It's surely gone." Already, in the parlor she had installed one of those nice, big Victrola humpbacks with the crank handle on the side.

Some weeks later, Doc awakened one sweltering night to the recurring thump of the jungle band. He got dressed and sneaked out the back door, careful of the crushed landing lest history repeat itself. The sound had grown in heat and intensity. It throbbed like the blood in his overworked arteries. Music. The battle hymn of a guerrilla war that had already claimed his former lieutenants.

"Oh, jass," cried a voice. "Jass, jass, I *love* it." The music slid around a wailing cornet. He knew already what that sound was—the workhouse radio, a device Carpy had brought in, arguably to keep the rest of the workers content enough to remain. But what was this hopped-up shit they were playing? "Juba," came a reply to chill his blood.

He peered around the edge of the open door. The whole of his depleted workforce sat grouped around the big wooden box. Some of them swayed in the rhythm. Their lidded eyes rolled loosely in their sockets. He might as well have been a ghost: they had no sense of him. A frenzied announcer broke in, babbling mythopœic names—Chippie, Bix, Kid Ory, the Duke, and the King. Names of power, and maybe capable of standing up to Ghouls and Dragons? And Cyclopes?

He wanted to go in there and rip apart that radio but was frightened by the energy pulsing through the room; scared rigid by the presence of Debra, like a ghost herself, cozy in their midst. He swallowed and drew back. This must be a nightmare from which he would shortly awaken. Even the crickets chirped with the beat.

Doc withdrew around the side of his house. Awhile on the steps, he breathed in the muggy night air. Jasmine mist hung thickly about him. There was enough pressure inside his skull to blow out a suture. He stared over toward the field where the trombone had lain but could see nothing. Finally, he climbed for the security of his own house.

Inside, someone had put on the parlor Victrola. The tune sounded like a washboard and banjo accompanied by a kazoo in a tub—just more of the insane noise that was pouring out of the workhouse. Drawn fearfully by it, Doc crept into the parlor, to find Carpy and Psalmody naked on the floor between the sofa and center table. He stared, brain on hold. He couldn't remember how to run away. The impassioned lovers didn't notice him but the eye in Carpy's shoulder rolled open and viewed him harshly. Doc stumbled back into the hall, his teeth clamped on the edge of his hand.

Slowly, an irrational anger took hold of him. Outmoded desire resurged in him against the invisible, the preternatural, which dwarfed him in its freedom. By God he wouldn't just stand here quivering. He'd whip this thing. Doc charged along the hall and down into the cellar. His secret identity hung hidden there—the white linen shroud and flour-sack hood of office. And there, across a keg of nails, lay a new branding iron. Its mark was new to him: a cross with extra arms. He didn't understand it exactly but the iron had a real heft that he liked.

Once in his guise of Cyclops, he took up his sceptre and rebounded up the stairs. At the top stood Lizzie in her nightdress. She seemed drunk or entranced. "Mr. Doc," she said gently, with acute sadness, but he would not be undone by so obvious a ploy. He struck her with the iron and, when she withstood the blow, struck her again. Hadn't he cared for her, hadn't he treated her justly?

The music seemed to race; someone had cranked up the Victrola. Its noise drowned out the thunder of his passing. He would descend upon the workers, scare them into their graves, and only then punish Carpy. Oh, that thankless task would be hardest of all. He had given that boy more than anyone could ask.

Doc stumbled, half-blind within his hood, down the porch steps, music the scent he followed through the night. He'd smash the radio first. "If thine eye offend thee," he recited triumphantly.

In the darkness, something struck him on the head. He paused. Another stinging tap—this one on the shoulder—made him spin about. What was it? Chestnuts dropping out of season? Then another, harder blow caught him over one eye. Defiant, he raised the iron, and a dozen of the pesky things hammered into him. With a grunt, he collapsed onto one knee. He snatched at one of the objects as it tumbled in the grass. He thought he had hold of a chunk of hail for a moment but it was long and smooth and carefully finished. It was, dear God, a piano key. Alert to his folly, Doc tried to get up to retreat and found that a pile of the keys had amassed around him, the hem of his robe snagged beneath them. He whacked away as the wall grew up. He whipped the iron desperately, until exhaustion and a thousand blows made him reel.

The keys showered down, hard as buckshot. Black and white, they pummeled like fists, spreading dark stains across the shroud, until all that remained was the iron, stuck out like a lightning rod with a good-luck sign at the tip. The heaped keys glistened as bright moonlight reappeared, and the music tinkled artlessly away.

Afterword

Attack of the Jazz Giants

Nobody really ever knows when they're going to chance upon an idea for a story (see afterwords to "The Bus" and "Divertimento" for more extreme examples). In the case of this story, I was attending a poetry reading in Philadelphia. A friend and terrific poet, Leonard Gontarek, was one of the participants. His poems are always full of odd observations and the sorts of turns of phrase that catch you off guard or tip you off balance. Such was the case here. His poem has nothing whatsoever to do with the subject or the nature of this story. That's not how the process works. A line in a poem produced a spark. The spark for whatever obscure reason ignited my fondness for early jazz music and then opted to mix it with a recollection of Horace Walpole's "Castle of Otranto." Why on Earth did those two things merge? Well, it's fiction. You get to make up your own explanation . . . which is just another way of my saying that I haven't a clue, either.

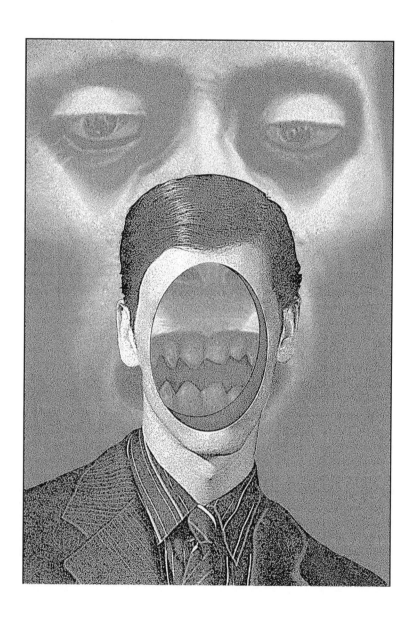

Some Things Are Better Left

"**S**O, WHAT D'YA THINK OF OLD HERBERT HOOVER High?" Toby Eccles asked Deak, which forced consideration of how politic an answer to give in reply. Eccles, after all, had headed up the 30th Anniversary Reunion committee and, according to Mary Jo Hanlon, at least, he'd personally taken credit for the "Elvis" reunion theme. The sequined strings of blinking, pastel lights, the movie posters of *Blue Hawaii* and *Spinout* and *Viva Las Vegas*—these things had emerged from Eccles's brain full-blown. Deak had participated in none of it. In fact he had only come home because of death. Appearing at his high school class reunion had been a last-minute and maybe not-so-hot decision.

Then there was Eccles, with three colorful crepe leis hung over his powder blue tux. He still awaited an opinion. Deak stared down into that hopeful, cherubic face and had a sudden recollection of PhysEd classes in this very gym—specifically of a fat bully-Eccles pinning him to a mat, dimpled knees digging into his shoulders, while another little bastard delivered unto him a stinging, humiliating "pink-belly" till he screamed.

Do we ever truly forgive cruel treatment at the hands of fools? Deak decided we do not.

"Eccles," he said, "the gym looks like you blew up your sister in her prom dress."

"What?" Eccles's mouth pinched. Deak could virtually read his mind: Could he possibly have heard right? Maybe he'd misunderstood because of the music.

"And the band," said Deak, "that's supposed to be 'Louie, Louie,' am I right? The Holiday Inn must be redecorating or I don't know how you'd have gotten these bozos. It's not even 'our' music. If I had a class reunion nightmare, it would sound like this. In fact I do, and it does." Eccles floundered as to what to do, then desperately tried to laugh it all away—Mike Deak's big joke.

Deak took a sip from his whiskey. Still maintaining an air of camaraderie, he squeezed Eccles's shoulder. It came up to the middle of his chest. "You know what dazzles me the most, though, about our class?"

Reluctantly, Eccles said, "No. What?"

"How many dentists it produced." He pulled out from his inside coat pocket the little pamphlet that listed every class member dead or alive: Where are they now? "There must be two dozen of 'em in here. Out of two hundred and six students, we've got an amazing two dozen tooth cappers."

The ribbing had gone too far. Eccles's fleshy chins quivered. "Yeah, an' I happen to be one."

He did a smart about-face as Deak replied, "Well, I *thought* you were the local Indian agent—the one who sold the liquor and smallpox blankets!" he hollered. The nearer faces in the crowd were now looking him over as they might have done a hair in their soup. The nearest tried to read his name tag. "Hi," he said and the fellow lurched back.

Deak stuffed the pamphlet inside his coat, then nudged his way around the perimeter of the polished gym-and-dance floor toward the open bar. Out of the throng a few voices called to him. In response to one of them—that of Mary Jo Hanlon hallooing like a loon—he nodded and waved broadly without turning to look, and pushed more urgently through the crowd. One conversation with her had more than made up for the past thirty years of prudent dissociation.

Reaching the bar, he ordered a Coke. He'd had his one and only whiskey for the night. Some years earlier he had discovered this simple formula kept him from becoming a spectacular asshole and getting either walloped or sued or jailed. And after forty-eight years, most of them unsupervised, his body didn't much care for booze, either: One good whiskey sufficed, for the sheer ecstasy of that first burnt taste on the tongue and palate.

The band had launched into their lounge-singer's medley of

Rolling Stones numbers. Deak found himself laughing as a feeble facsimile of "Under My Thumb" rebounded off the walls. "I used to scream along to this in my car," he told the twenty-year-old bartender, who smiled indulgently in response.

"Sound crew," a woman behind him said, as if it were his name. Deak looked around, fearfully expecting to see Mary Jo hovering there. A slightly plump brunette was beaming up at him, her face vaguely familiar. She had taken off her name.

"Okay, I give up," he said. "Sound crew."

"God, you're tall."

"I was supposed to get shorter?"

"People do, actually, as they get older."

"I have a painting at home that gets shorter so I don't have to. Who are you?"

Exasperated, she replied, "God, Deak, have I changed that much?"

It was the hair color, he realized all at once. She used to be a redhead. "Grezinski?" In one sweep, he set down his soda, wrapped his arms around her, and lifted her off the floor. "Jesus, Pam, how are you?"

"Different, I guess."

"No, no, it's this stupid light show. I don't know if I'm meeting somebody or having an acid flashback."

"That's a joke, isn't it?"

"Part of it is." He let her finish her laugh. "Normally, I'd ask you what you're doing here, but we know that already. So I'll jump to timeworn pickup line number two. You look terrific. You really do—never mind I didn't know you."

Pam said, "You lie very well." She glanced past his shoulder. "Although, if you want to see somebody who *really* looks terrific, look at that." She indicated the direction with a bob of her head.

He expected she was referring to a woman, but even in the dimness and the shifting lights, Deak could tell who she meant. He had noticed earlier that the man seemed an anomaly. Of medium height, he was dancing a basic rock and roll step with a beautiful woman who could have been the daughter of an alumnus, and he was by far the better dancer. While those around him were wheezing through their steps, he danced carelessly, as inexhaustible as the sun. His gray suit—visible when he stepped away to spin the woman—had the double-breasted cut of Italian elegance. It was neither the sartorial splendor of a poor man nor of one who had dressed up just to impress the folks hereabouts.

"He looks like about a hundred high-priced New York lawyers I can think of," commented Deak. "So, who is he? Our chaperone?"

Pam Grezinski was smiling puckishly. "Do you remember the name Barry Kinder?"

The name immediately sparked the nasty memory he'd begun moments before with Eccles, stirring up a deep-seated hostility that dismayed Deak. The rage was short-lived; it gave way almost immediately to utter disbelief. The well-dressed dancer couldn't have been more than thirty years old. Deak glanced evenly at Pam. Calmly, he said, "I remember, sure. He was a swimmer, wasn't he? A smart little prick, too."

"Ooh. Right so far."

"Sorry, that's all, Grezinski," he lied. "It was a big class. He wasn't someone I hung out with ever. So, he decided to play a joke and sent his son in his place, huh? The kid looks thirty, tops."

"I'll add your name to the list who've noticed."

"Okay, it's not his son, I got you. Money doesn't buy happiness but it pays for *lots* of face lifts and injections. I think the whole fucking class has had them. On him it worked."

Pam still seemed puzzled. "But you're sure you don't recognize him, he doesn't call up any special memories."

"I gather you think he ought to."

"I don't know. Earlier in the evening, I overheard him asking about you—if you were coming back for this. I was wondering, too. And here you are."

"He asked about me?" That didn't add up. Deak took out the reunion pamphlet. After a moment of thumbing through it, he exclaimed, "Christ, he's another dentist. Says here he runs his own clinic on Walnut. He sure doesn't dress like a dentist."

"How do dentists dress?"

"Mine always wears this kind of blue smock thing, and rubber gloves."

"Very funny. And what's wrong with dentists?"

Deak asked warily, "You aren't one, are you?" She shook her head. "You didn't marry one, did you?" Again she shook her head. "Are you married at all?"

"I am, and I was going to invite you to come meet him—"

"But now you've changed your mind."

"No, but because of this thing about dentists I think you should be kept under observation."

"Pay no attention—it's left over from a run-in I had with Eccles about thirty-one years ago. Is that too long, you think, to hold a grudge?" He glanced again narrowly at Kinder and picked up his soda from the bar. "So, lay on, Macduff," he said, and then followed her trail to the bleachers. She introduced her husband, Bill, who had a graying Vandyke beard and a face that seemed squeezed of its natural juices. Deak shook hands, then sat down beside him on the polished board. He discovered quickly that Bill never cracked a smile, not even at his own wry comments. He owned a stereo and video shop in the Northgate mall. "My mother had a small component system I picked out for her about five years ago," Deak said. "It's not worth a lot, but I'm going to have to get rid of it. You buy used equipment?"

"I'd probably sell it for you on consignment," Bill replied.

"Your mother?" Pam asked.

"Yeah." He sighed. "That's the real reason you see me here tonight. She died ten days ago. She had a seizure while sitting in her car at a stop sign. She wasn't even in town at the time, but here's where her condo is and where dad bought the family plot, so I've been hanging around town a few days."

"Oh, Mike. The funeral?"

"Over. Don't worry about it. She had friends show up, and my aunt. And, hell, I don't know anybody here anymore, so I didn't make phone calls. I don't even know your last name, Grezinski."

"Forbes."

"See?"

Bill said directly, "You look like you've had a rough couple of weeks."

"Maybe." Deak had decided by then that he did not care to unburden his soul in the gymnasium of his former high school; nor did he want to describe the ups and downs of his career as a journalist, having erringly done so already for Mary Jo. His gaze locked on the youthful dancing figure on the floor below. "*He* sure doesn't, though," he said, and directed the conversation back at Kinder.

Pam leaned past him to explain their previous discussion to Bill. "Yes," her husband said. "Not a very friendly guy, but he's had a less than happy life."

"Him? You have to be kidding. From the expression on his pretty face, he thinks we're his guests and this is *his* gym. What happened to him so terrible?"

At Pam's urging, Bill elaborated. He explained how Kinder started a clinic but had by now almost stopped practicing altogether. "Just acts as an administrator. He's pretty reclusive. After college, he married a girl I guess he'd met there. Elizabeth. She came from a well-to-do family on the East Coast. For a while she was in Pam's circle at the country club."

On cue, Pam said, "Boy, she was a ditz. Neurotic, crazy. Really unstable. One time, she threw her tennis racquet at a guy who was carrying towels, because he was late."

"Charming. Wealth breeds nutballs, though. Our whole generation turned into egotistical jerks, it's our contribution to American society, along with five-figure shopping sprees as a form of psychotherapy. So, little miss too-much-money made his life a living hell, right? This is supposed to buy him sympathy? You're not going to tell me that's her out there."

"No. Elizabeth killed herself about a year after the tennis incident," Pam explained. "She cut her wrists in the bathtub. He came home and found her."

"Oops," Deak muttered. His worst enemy would have gotten some compassion under those circumstances. He let his ire cool down for a minute.

Bill said, "Kinder became a complete hermit for quite a few years. He fobbed off most of his practice to Eccles and some others, I think. Old school chums. That's how his clinic got started. He had the money by then to do it. After a while, he started traveling."

Pam added, "He's dated some of the girls I know at the club. They all say he's charming but really sad. He refuses to consider anything like a serious relationship. Tends to be good for only a few dates . . . and, well, he's a little flaky. He's got this thing set up in his house—"

"An alembic," interjected Bill.

"Yes, and sometimes he gets drunk and starts babbling about rituals and stuff."

"Great, a dentist with delusions of alchemy. You're not going to tell me he maintains his looks with a Philosopher's Stone, I hope."

"No." She huffed. "Honestly, Deak. About every three years—right, honey, three years?—he goes off somewhere in Europe and gets a treatment. He's really overdue for one in fact but his clinic's had some problems this year, so I guess he hasn't had the chance to get away."

"They treat him pretty well in Europe." Rhetorically, he asked, "Has anybody ever seen him in daylight?" For a moment longer, he stared into the crowd. He turned away all at once and said, "In the face of tragedy, the man became a narcissistic nut, so who cares?"

He set down his drink and abruptly asked Bill, "You mind if I take your wife out on the dance floor for a turn?"

Bill Forbes seemed lost in his own revery. He glanced up as the request sank in. "To tell you the truth, you'd be doing us a favor, Mike. Pam likes to dance and I can't because of my damn hip. Going to have surgery on it in the fall."

Deak stood up and extended his hand. Coquettishly, Pam took it. She told her husband, "You know, there were a couple of dances my junior and senior years I remember where I hoped he'd ask me."

"No, there weren't," Deak replied. "Come on, let's get down there before this excuse for a song ends." Even as he spoke, the tune died its unnatural death; the band jumped straight into a rendition of "Good Lovin'," and Barry Kinder stayed on the dance floor. The cheering crowd hopped about furiously, only a few still clinging together. Deak used the opportunity to sidle nearer Kinder.

Close up, he was phenomenal. Virtually no lines etched his face, and it lacked the artificial tautness that repeated face lifts could bring. His tanned skin shone only lightly with sweat. Kinder's date looked more exhausted than he did; and, watching his ecstatically closed eyes, Deak got the impression he would have been as content dancing without her. Then Kinder's eyes opened halfway and stared back at him in lizardly fashion, the look casually dismissive as though his thoughts had been read as of no consequence. Galled into action, Deak grinned back, bounced over and said, "Hiya, Mike Deak." He stuck out his hand. "Aren't you Barry Kinder, the dentist?"

Kinder shook his hand politely, then with more enthusiasm. "Wait a second, I know you—you write for—"

"I freelance actually."

"Okay. But I've read your stuff. Your investigation of serial killers. What a fascinating *piece* that was." He had stopped dancing altogether, his partner entirely forgotten. "You delved pretty deeply into the social matrix that creates them *and* their ritualistic behavior."

Deak brushed back a forelock of thinning hair. "Nimbly put. Uh—you remember Pam Grezinski?"

Kinder hardly glanced her way. "Of course, Mrs. Forbes. We've met a few times over the years," he commented. "Look, do you have a drink?"

"Not on me. It's sitting with Pam's husband, down the end of the second row there."

"Miriam and I could probably use one ourselves. Why don't we join you?"

Deak looked delightedly at Pam. "Great," he said. Kinder took his Miriam by the elbow and led her away.

Pam complained, "The shortest dance I've ever had."

"Yeah, but think how much farther this'll go at the club than telling the girls you were on the floor with me." They started back to the bleachers. "He buys his cologne by the quart, doesn't he?"

Pam ignored the jibe. "I didn't know you were a reporter," she said. "What was that article he was asking about?"

"Something I did that came out earlier this year. I'm surprised he knew about it. It was for kind of a specialized magazine. Dentists aren't police psychiatrists, are they?"

"He's amazing, isn't he?" She sounded strangely captivated.

"He's already charmed my pants off."

"Really?" She craned her head back and looked down at his legs.

"With advanced age," he remarked, "has not come subtlety, I see."

"Advanced!"

"It's a fact we all have to live with. At least, most of us do." He climbed up the first row.

Kinder arrived almost as quickly as they did. Miriam hung back with her drink after being introduced all around. Since it was immediately apparent that Kinder wanted to talk to Deak, Pam moved over and chatted with Miriam. Kinder took out a cigarette and, without begging indulgence, lit up. He inhaled like a man who couldn't drag the smoke deep enough, and Deak noticed for the first time a hint of something like strain worked into his expression—the result of all he'd suffered? Somehow, that didn't fit. "Deak and I were absolute enemies in high school," Kinder immediately confessed to Bill. "Yes, somebody once dropped a chemistry textbook down a stairwell onto my head. I had to have traction, and wear a neck brace for a month. I always suspected it was Deak. I had my reasons, believe me. Ah, well, childhood pranks, right? We all played them. Still, I'd hardly expect somebody like you to come back for this desperate affair, Michael. I can't imagine it's your scene."

"You're right about that. The only reason I'm here is that my mother died recently—"

"Ah, of course. I believe I did see something in the paper, or was it the radio? It was sudden, wasn't it? I didn't mean to touch a nerve." He lowered his eyes.

The whole act riled Deak. Kinder was so transparently disdainful of them all. "You didn't touch a nerve," he replied. "It *was* sudden but it'd been a long time coming. An invitation turned up in her mail is all, and I had to be here—you know, taking care of estate business, putting her condo up for sale. I figured this might be diverting at least."

"And?"

"It's turning out to be."

Kinder tossed an amused look at Bill. "Give us some examples, Michael."

"It's Mike. Well, Barry, let's see, our homecoming queen is now into channeling and claims to have been a princess in Atlantis."

"The continent or the casino?" Bill remarked.

"That's not so surprising is it?" asked Kinder. "Everyone who channels thinks they've been to Atlantis."

"Does seem so."

"What else?"

"Two women I dated in my junior year admit to having had liposuction, and Mary Jo Hanlon even confessed that she had the fat re-injected to enlarge her breasts. With her renovations came divorce—she made a point of letting me know that. A lot. Divorce in letters like the 'Hollywood' sign. And then there's you, Barry."

Kinder smiled indulgently.

Deak continued, "You look like an ad for every hopeful health spa on Earth."

"Well, thank you." He tugged at the edge of one eyelid.

"What's your secret?"

"I have a painting that ages while I don't."

Deak laughed and winked at Pam's startled expression. Above her own conversation, she had been monitoring everything Kinder said.

"Dorian Gray, huh?" said Bill.

"Now tell us the truth. How do we late-forties derelicts get in on this rejuvenation?"

Kinder exhaled smoke. "You pay an enormous sum of money to a Swiss clinic every few years and they tighten your jaw, fill up your creases, and put you on a proper, regimented diet according to body type."

"I should tell Mary Jo about it. She looked loaded."

"She does tend to drink too much," Bill chimed in as if deadly serious.

Deak refused to let go. "What's the place called? Might be worth a story to me. They use alembics?"

Kinder's smile evaporated. His hard eyes flicked across Pam and Bill. "I'm afraid I couldn't let you write about them. They're very private, the Swiss. They'd not care for the publicity."

They'd not care? "Catering strictly to the rich and sagging?"

Kinder laughed stiffly as he ground out his cigarette.

The band took a break to a round of applause. Eccles climbed up on the small stage to announce that the main event—that of pointing everyone out to everyone—would shortly begin. As he spoke, the overhead lights came up. Kinder winced at the glare. He turned to his date and said, "I think I would prefer to miss this. Let's call it an evening, Miriam, what do you say?" She answered that she wasn't certain she wanted to leave. He reached over and squeezed her hand. "The champagne's on ice, darling, waiting for us," he coaxed. "We can dance there, much more intimately." His perfect teeth gleamed. She folded her fingers in between his, her affirmative reply. He turned to Deak and Bill then and said, "I'm sorry, but we've been here for hours already, and this whole business of getting up in front of the crowd is thoroughly obnoxious. It's time to go. Not that you aren't pleasant company, you understand, just that Miriam and I have a private celebration of our own yet to come."

"You conjured it up pretty well. I can see the champagne bucket right next to the loveseat."

"Exactly. Please excuse us. Bill, Pam." He paused, as if to place them properly in the background. "I do hope to see *you* another time, Mike." He led Miriam to the floor.

Deak hesitated a moment, then climbed down and caught up with him. "Barry," he said confidentially, "in all seriousness, I would like the name of your clinic or the doctor at least. Hell, man, I'd love to look as good as you." He hoped he sounded genuinely envious enough to push Kinder's buttons.

Kinder seemed to size him up for a moment. "All right," he answered, "the clinic is in Bern. It's called the Bodelier Clinic. The doctor's name you want to speak to is Gruben, Sepp Gruben. A very nice man—something of a pioneer in his field—but I can promise that you won't get an interview." He seemed to have shed his earlier enthusiasm over Deak's work.

"Swear to God, I'm not going to write about him. Thanks for

telling me, Barry. I really do appreciate it. Goodnight, Miriam. It was nice to meet you." He turned away. Then, putting on a hang-dog expression, he went back up and sat between Pam and Bill.

Pam said, "Jesus, he was extra snooty tonight, wasn't he? And I sat here feeling sorry for him, too."

"You got the name of the clinic?" Bill asked Deak.

"Hmm? Ah, no. No, he wouldn't give." He didn't want to lie, but a lifetime habit of guarding sources of information kicked in automatically. After that, the reunion seemed less tolerable to him. He promised to get in touch Pam and Bill before he left town—the kind of promise that no one believes—then hastily left the gym as Eccles, on stage, was worriedly calling his name.

Later, alone on his mother's couch, surrounded by cardboard boxes, Deak lay awake. In the darkness over his head, he pasted up his motives as he replayed the events of the reunion. Every time Barry Kinder loomed into sight, Deak's heartbeat sped up and his jaw tightened, which happened often enough to keep him from falling asleep. He had re-invented his memory of humiliation at Kinder's hands, turned it into a memory from hell, attaching Kinder's perfect face to the body of the seventeen-year-old who yanked up his shirt and then battered his soft belly till he thought he would choke on his own vomit; Eccles grinding his elbows into the blue mat and spitting laughter on him somehow made him despise Kinder more. All around stood other kids in orange and white gym clothes, jeering his name. *No*, he thought, *we do not truly forgive, ever.* Kinder and Eccles—he wanted to dig up enough dirt to make banner headlines across the country, ruin them both. Most of all he wanted to wipe that fucking smirk off Kinder's face. Permanently. He had the ability to do it, and Kinder had handed him the lead. Whatever he found, he would donate to the *Tribune*; let them run his byline for the sheer pleasure.

Then, when the images faded and his anger cooled to where he could see reason again, there remained the matter of Kinder's hands. He was surprised that Pam and Bill hadn't noticed them; but, then, they weren't outsiders, they were used to seeing Kinder as he was. Deak had spent more than an hour last night with a group of women who had confessed their cosmetic surgery sins to him. They all looked tremendous—even Mary Jo Hanlon when he ignored the side of her that was reptilian manhunter. Nevertheless, he could still tell she and the others were older—mature and hand-some, the kind of beauty that came with middle-age. Not so with

Kinder. There was not a hint of the fix-up shop hung about him. Probably he just paid for better work, and no doubt that would turn out to be the explanation once Deak had spoken to his doctor . . . except for his damned hands. Faces got lifted and creases filled in all the time; hands were another matter. Kinder's hands were as smooth and tanned as his face. Deak, plagued in recent years by minor arthritic cramps, hated him even more for such luck.

Kinder had been perversely smug in giving up the information about the clinic—he had all but outright dared Deak to pry. Maybe he had cheated on his taxes. He must have done *something* illegal sometime. Deak couldn't wait to see the look on Grezinski's face when he finally found whatever he was going to find. She might be mad at him for pretending to leave town and for keeping all his inquiries to himself, but she would love to hear about Kinder.

Instinctively, he knew he had let a little incident from his childhood get out of hand, but he didn't care. He never did get to sleep.

At four he finally picked up the phone and placed a call overseas.

Outside, in the dark, paperboys were heading off for their various routes. Deak could remember what that was like—drinking a glass of milk because his mother insisted he have some, and then as a result farting through his deliveries. She'd never understood the problem he had with milk. She would have been upset with him right now if he'd told her he never drank it anymore.

First he had to get an overseas operator to connect him with a Bern operator to give him the number of the clinic. He knew already they weren't going to reveal anything about their patients. Instead, he hoped to play upon the vanity of Doctor Gruben to ferret out whatever facts he could about the egotistical patient; surely any surgeon would be proud of his accomplishments. The hands, for instance, maybe he'd actually worked on them.

While the connections were being made, Deak had another idea. He got up and carried the phone across the room. On a shelf there stood a line of his mother's trophies—she'd won a dozen of them for her shooting skills with handguns. Deak had never understood her hobby; guns bothered him. Under the trophy shelf lay a pile of papers and books that belonged to him. He rooted through the pile until he found a large vinyl-bound book in the school colors of blue and white. Grinning, he flipped to the back of the book.

Kinder was listed in the index, two photos of him: a class photo and one with the swim team. The portrait showed a blond kid overdressed and trying to look angelically serious for the camera. The swim-team photo proved more interesting. Here was the real Barry Kinder standing at poolside, his hair slick with water, a cavalier smirk upon his face. The close resemblance to his thirty-years-older flesh-and-blood counterpart was chilling. Deak closed the book as the connection went through.

A woman answered in German. She might have been next door.

"Yes, hello," he said. "I'm calling overseas, *über Meer*, yes? My name is Mike Deak. A friend of mine who has used your clinic recommended you to me. My friend's practically a walking ad— um, *Anzeige*—for you."

"Yes, sir," the receptionist replied. She sounded bemused, like someone who knew he had made a joke but who couldn't understand the context. "Did your friend name his doctor? You would have to speak to the individual doctor. Our specialists are diverse, you understand."

"As a matter of fact he did. It's a Doctor Gruben."

There was a silence on the line, a hiss like ocean spray. Deak thought for a moment that he had lost the connection.

The woman asked, "That is Doctor Gruben, you say?"

Deak's scalp began to tingle. "Doctor Sepp Gruben. Is there more than one?"

"*Nein*, no. I wanted to be certain."

"Then there is a Sepp Gruben."

"Yes, he was one of the founders of Bodelier. However, he has been dead for nearly ten years. Your friend has been a patient here a long time ago I think."

Deak sat up. "No, he comes there every three years."

Her perplexity sounded in every word. "Why would he do that?"

"For rejuvenation. Face lifts, mineral baths. Whatever you do that makes him look that way."

"This much confuses me. We are not such a spa. Bodelier specializes in urinary disorders, how do you say, *Geschlechtskrankeit?* Sexual diseases?"

"And Sepp Gruben's specialty?"

"Dr. Gruben's specialty was gonococcus infection."

Deak pinched the bridge of his nose, his eyes squeezed shut. What direction did he go in now? How could that tie in with Kinder? Why had the bastard given him *this* name, *this* specific lead? Some other question needed asking, some other direction.

Think, he told himself. "Doctor Gruben—how did he die? Old age?"

"Oh, I should not be—"

"Look, I know this sounds crazy, but I'm calling a long way. His death must have been in the papers there. It's not like it's secret knowledge, is it?" He pictured her—young, uncertain, maybe seated within earshot of some older matron.

"I suppose."

"Please?"

"Yes, all right. It was by accident, in his laboratory. There was a terrible storm. The lights—the power, you know—went off. Dr. Gruben fell and cut himself badly in the dark. He injected a serum he was testing. Through his wound. What is called an anti-coagulant agent. All of his blood escaped and he could not stop it, and he could not call for help because of the phones."

"In a lab, surrounded by all that equipment, he bled to death?"

"Yes, a horrible accident. The storm was what you would say a 'freak.' The Doctor was alone, or was there a patient? I forget."

"Sure," Deak muttered. He was envisioning the beakers and ring stands and vacuum jars from the chemistry class of his youth, and the way the chemistry book had dropped in the stairwell when he let go of it. He continued quickly, "You said that was nearly ten years ago. How do you know the details so well?"

"They refer to it in the college, to remind us how careful we must be always in laboratory work. It was a very infamous accident here, that a founder should die of such ridiculous carelessness."

He could assume that the local police had made inquiries but had turned up nothing. And neither had he, he reminded himself. Nothing but speculation. "Well, I'm sorry to have taken up your time."

"Perhaps it's another clinic, with a name similar to ours."

"That doesn't seem very likely, does it? Thanks. I'll look you up next time I'm in town." He added in thought, *Which might be sooner than you think.*

Deak got up and poured himself a glass of orange juice. He wandered the small rooms, surrounded by the remnants of a life that had been close to him but utterly separate, almost a mystery. He could sort through the piles and reassemble pieces of that life if he wanted to, probably discover things about his mother that he hadn't known. He preferred not to; whenever he went digging, what he most often found was cruelty, torment, ugliness. He believed that he had, in the process of overturning so many stones, lost the sense for sharing gentler things. It was one of the reasons he was alone—that and a Pyrrhonic regard of permanency.

He glanced at the clock. It was not even six yet—certainly too damned early to go hunting a depression.

He tried to assemble the new bits of information he had into the picture of Barry Kinder. Kinder's wife had cut her wrists. He had gone into mourning and then retreated for years, then one day ten years later had taken a voyage overseas. Maybe he'd fooled around in Europe the way he did here; he had the money.

Say that he contracts gonorrhea, Deak surmised. He finds a doctor, who treats him and then who dies by bleeding to death while Kinder is coincidentally on the scene—if in fact that's true. There is no way to be certain without the aforementioned visit to the clinic. But at the reunion, Kinder drops this doctor's name, and in such a way as to guarantee not only that he'll be caught in an absurd lie but that both deaths will thereby appear linked. Had he said *anything* else—if he had refused to submit—there wouldn't be questions. I would be packing and on my way. Why, then, did Kinder toss out Gruben's name?

A trip to the library was required—and possibly to the cops. He wondered whether his journalistic credentials would get him a look at a closed case twenty years old. Twenty years old: a German urologist and Mrs. Kinder. Those two pieces fit together somehow.

"All right," he said to the empty room, "but where's the connection, Mom?" Kinder—here and in Europe. Every three years, someplace. Every three years . . . He wondered how he was going to sit still until the library opened.

Five hours later, Deak sat in a gray vinyl dentist's chair, a paper towel alligator clipped round his neck. The door opened and Toby Eccles walked in, his eyes cast down as he read the fake medical biography Deak had filled out. "Mr. Milburn," he said, coming around the chair.

"It's, ah, Deak, actually. Mike Deak."

"Holy Christ." Eccles bumped against the bracket tray beside him.

Deak swung into an upright position, feet dangling over the side of the chair. He picked up an oral explorer. "Been admiring your tools, Toby. Are Kinder's this shiny? Yeah, his are probably gold."

"What are you doing here, you asshole."

"Doctor, your language. I dropped in because I need some

information, and I figure you owe me a few minutes for all the times I let you beat me up."

Eccles's multi-chinned face went through three or four emotional change-ups before settling on bewilderment. "I've got a patient getting fitted for porcelain in the next room." He looked at his watch. "I'll give you five minutes and that's it."

"Fine. All I want is for you to confirm a couple of things for me about Barry Kinder. Then I'll go away forever."

The doctor looked doubtful.

"Tell me about his wife."

"Liz? Why?"

"I'm thinking about doing a story on him—you know, success, looks, money, this clinic, but behind it all a tragic life, et cetera. You know. Sunday morning magazine exposé."

"No kidding." He shook his head. "Liz'll bring in the readers. An absolute loon. She had a few affairs, even hit on me once." He quickly added, "I didn't go for it, of course."

"Sure. I read all the articles on her from ten years back. They claim she'd had an abortion because she'd gotten pregnant by somebody other than her husband. They blamed the suicide on her state of mind."

"Absolutely true," he said, nodding vigorously. "After she died, Barry hid out awhile. He called me out of the blue one day and said he was going to travel around and try to forget what had happened. We—that is, me and a few other guys—we were already handling his patients from when she died, so we just kept them. Hey, we were all making money off him. It was a good deal."

"And when he came back?"

"Gangbusters. He looked twenty-five. Tanned and healthy. Not a line on him. The women—did they flock to him. It was incredible," he said with obvious envy.

"Then, three years later he took off again."

"Right. And every third summer since, like clockwork. I've got his patients again now."

Deak pursed his lips. "So he's taking off soon."

"Tomorrow. Why?"

Now he had to decide whether or not to explain what he'd found to Toby Eccles. He doubted the pudgy dentist was going to believe him, then decided he didn't care. "I've found a pattern in my researches to do with this ritual vacationing."

"Well, sure, every three—"

"No, Eccles, I don't mean that. That's a blind, a front. There is *no* procedure of cosmetic surgery that has to be performed every three years. You're a D.M.D., look it up. And the clinic he told me he went to—it specializes in VD."

Eccles's eyes widened. "What are you saying?"

"Well, it isn't AIDS. From here on, things get a lot stranger. You want to hear?"

He didn't reply, but pulled at his lower lip with his rubber-sheathed fingers. All at once he realized what he was doing and wiped his hands against the front of his smock.

Deak said, "You can date for yourself when he took off on his so-called vacations. In all likelihood he *was* a patient in that clinic once. At least he pretended to be. And while he was there, one of the doctors—the one he claims treated him—died under very remarkable circumstances. He lost all of his blood."

"Aw, c'mon—Barry the vampire?"

"No, no. Nothing so obvious. That would be silly. Bear with me. Barry comes back, takes up his practice, and starts fucking like a bunny rabbit."

Eccles nodded in a wistful way.

"Three years later, less a few weeks, a dead woman turns up down on Fourteenth Street here in town. One of those little dive hotels the hookers work out of. I drove past it on the way here. Very tawdry. Once again our local paper made a big deal out of it." He took out his notebook, and flipped through a couple of pages. "Headline: 'Police Suspect Satanist Cult in Death of Prostitute.' She'd been battered unconscious, then drained of all her blood. They suspected Satanists because they found charred remains of some sort of ritual circle adorning the carpet. Blood—hers—bits of bone, and some sort of godawful-smelling paste, unidentified. They went out and arrested a local biker, but turned him loose after two days. No one's ever been charged. It's still unsolved."

Eccles laughed. "Look, Mike, Barry was out of the country. You just said so."

"Uh-huh. You took over his practice—*you* just said so. Give me the date he left. If it doesn't fit, then I'm out of here, like I said—pink belly and all."

Eccles slid off his stool. "It'll take a few minutes to look that up. That's a while ago, six years."

"While you're at it, check three years back. I maybe need that one, too."

"I'm only doing this," Eccles said dourly at the door, "because of school, I want you to know."

A few minutes later the dental assistant who'd ushered Deak in showed up and insisted that she needed the room. She led him down the hall to Eccles's office, no larger than a small washroom with a desk in it. The walls were hung with honorary plaques next to charts depicting plaque, jokey posters about Mr. Root Canal and the Gingivitis Gang, a bunch of tooth decaying rustlers. Photos on the desk showed a skinny woman and a couple of dumpling-shaped teenagers with acne but great teeth. There was even a photo of a young sausage of an Eccles wrestling in a state tournament. Nowhere was there a picture of Barry Kinder. Deak relaxed a little. Eccles had said that he owed Barry a lot. Deak was willing to bet that Kinder never let him forget it. He sat down behind the desk and waited.

When Eccles returned, his smock was stained with something pink. "I had to finish up the impression for that crown, sorry. Okay, we got the dates off the floppy disks for you." Deak took out his notebook and pen; Eccles unfolded a yellow Post-it note. He said, "Six years ago, he took off on the twenty-second of June. Okay? You need the other one, or does that get rid of you?"

Deak shook his head. "Mimi Caudel died the night of June twenty-first." He stared sharply up at Eccles. "And three years ago?"

Eccles stared sourly at him for a moment. "July," he said finally. "Seventeenth."

Deak nodded, flipping back two pages. "Three years ago, the third of August, the body of a paperboy was discovered under the Second Avenue bridge."

"That's it, then. Barry was out of the country."

Deak read from his notes, "The boy had been missing for three weeks. Forensics experts placed death sometime during the week of July fourteen. The boy'd been strangled. No blood in him or at the scene. Assume he was killed elsewhere and dumped there." He closed the notebook. "Getting the idea?"

Crumpling the note in his hand, Eccles tossed it at his desk. "No. You're impugning the reputation of a good dentist." He paused, his mouth open, as if he wanted to testify in Kinder's defense but could think of nothing to add. He switched gears. "Besides, if he murders people here, then why does he bother leaving town?"

Deak shrugged. "Because he's going to get younger and has to make an excuse for it?"

"Come on. He gets a makeover. That's a hell of a lot easier to swallow than this ritual crap."

Deak nodded. "I agree. All right, let's try it your way. Say he has the best God damned plastic surgeon in the world. One who does hands and everything, who takes every little crease out of every little cell like he's ironing the body. In that case, he's a serial killing loon who's compelled to make believe his ritual works. Can you handle that?" When Eccles said nothing, he pressed on. "Look, I didn't start this. Barry did. *He* dropped the name of the doctor and the clinic on *me.*"

"Why would he do that? Why would he tell you that?"

Deak smiled. "Pam Grezinski overheard him asking someone about me before I turned up at the reunion. He wanted to make sure I showed. When I did, he pretended he hadn't been expecting me; and then right away for no reason at all he brought up this article I wrote on serial killers."

"So?"

"One of the elements I described was how a serial killer will often leave clues to his identity in his slayings. He's sociopathic—he believes in some way that he's the superior man, so he taunts people with what he feels are obvious leads to himself. Sometimes they are, if you know how to read them."

Eccles sagged back against the wall. "My God. Then he's asking you to catch him." He shook his head. "What about Liz? He murdered her, too?"

"I don't know. I'm guessing this ritual of his required an initial sacrifice to get things rolling and she was not only convenient, she was asking for it. Everybody says so. You say so."

"But, Jesus H. Christ, Mike—you think this ritual of his *works!*"

"Believe me," Deak said, rising to his feet, "I have *exactly* as much trouble with that as you do." He walked up to Eccles and patted him on the shoulder. "Don't worry, Tobe—if it was me in your place, I wouldn't believe me, either."

He went out, leaving Eccles to wrestle with the facts, and before having to explain what he felt he had to do next.

The house lay in an exclusive area of town bordered by a city park. As a kid walking home from school, Deak had cut across many of the broad yards of these same homes. A couple had their own tennis courts.

A brick wall bordered the road. It opened into an arch over a gravel driveway. The VW's engine sounded like a jack-hammer in the enclosed yard. Kinder's house stood back from the road, behind a lawn of stately oaks and walnut trees. The drive led around to the rear. Tall hedges surrounded the parking space, which lay empty.

Deak hesitated a moment, testing his resolve, deciding he had to do this. As he climbed out, he wondered if the enemy had skipped the country already. Turning, he got his answer.

Kinder stood at the top of the steps. He wore dark jeans and a turtleneck—"sleek," as the society pages had described him. "Well, Eccles, you were right about the vampire," Deak muttered.

In his hands Kinder held two brandy snifters. He pressed a new screen door open against his back. It was a pose of nonchalance. Nothing could touch him.

He thinks he's the superior man.

More intensely than ever he had as a boy, Deak hated Kinder. As he walked up, he asked, "You always a two-fisted drinker so early in the day, Barry?"

"Let's say I anticipated your arrival," Kinder explained. He handed one of the snifters to Deak at the bottom of the steps.

Deak studied the outstretched hand, the face above him. Had Eccles been dumb enough to call and tip him off? He said, "I suppose you have friends at the library," but accepted the drink. He inhaled, then sipped it. The flavor of an ancient, perfectly smooth cognac lit a delicious fire in his mouth. He swirled the glass, staring into it uncertainly.

"Not at all. I simply make sure to know everything. It's a way I amuse myself. From your comment I know that you went hunting bright and early this morning. I'll bet you haven't even slept."

"No, Barry, but I know a lot about you now, although I'd never pretend to know *every*thing, Barry."

"Of course not—that's the thrill of the work you do. You've gathered all you can, and you hope now to hear my confession, because the story is too implausible, too outrageous. And I do want to confess.

"Why don't you come into my parlor and you can tell me what you've learned. I'll show you some wonderful ancient books I've collected and tell you about my researches. More than that, I'll tell you all that I know about *you*."

Looking dismayed, Deak asked, "What's to know?" but he continued up the steps, compelled by the process he had put in motion—that one of them had put in motion. He noticed for the first time a dozen or so flies swarming on the screen behind Kinder.

His host moved aside, pushing the inner door further open to let Deak enter the house. At the same time, casually, as if accidentally, Kinder tipped his own glass so that its contents poured down past the landing. The flies dove after it. "You'd be surprised how much I know about you, Mike. I sent you the invitation to the reunion; I knew you couldn't pass it up, as I knew you couldn't pass up a chance at me even thirty years later. That's the kind of person you are. I know." He glanced thoughtfully across at the parked Volkswagen, then turned. The screen door banged like a clap of thunder. He said, "I even know your blood type." Beneath his perfectly smooth hand, the big brass knob rattled in its collar as he swung shut the second door.

Afterword

Some Things Are Better Left

It has been established by no less a personage than Karen Joy Fowler that the vast majority of fantasy and science fiction authors did not attend their high school proms. I've gone a bit further determining that most of us avoided the reunions, too.

When my high school class's 20th reunion was approaching, I decided rather than attending I would write a story about reunions. An *acte gratuit*, in that I had no idea of a plot or direction when I started.

In my opinion there is no vampire in this story, either. Nevertheless, a couple years after its original publication, it ended up in the anthology *Isaac Asimov's Vampires*. When an editor tells you they want your story for their anthology and they're going to pay you, it's best to smile nicely and say, "Okay."

Lizaveta

AS HE STROLLED WITH HIS COMRADES ALONG THE fog-bound, filthy walk, Sergei Zarubkin wondered if the war with the Japanese were to blame for the eruptions of violence spreading through Moscow. The war had become a travesty in the failure of so vast a nation as Russia to devastate the upstart Orientals. Added to that, the hot August temperatures this year had inflamed tempers, fueled fights, even murders . . . as for instance last night in the Yama.

The Yama: the Pit, Moscow's Red Light District. Three blocks of ornate houses, with windows trimmed in carved scrollwork and lace curtains; where a woman cost three rubles for one hour of her time, ten rubles for a night; where boys of high-standing became men. But that quiet tradition had been suspended—because this night the Yama lay in darkness, in absolute stillness, with the houses all looted, their bright scrollwork smashed, lace curtains charred and hanging in tatters. All the whores had been beaten, killed, or driven out. And that was why four soldiers had to come here to the cesspool called Khitrovka Market, in search of women for the night.

Zarubkin took a swig from the bottle of Smirnov's he carried, then passed it to Gladykin on his right, who lifted it, hailed it as a national treasure, and drank his fill before passing it on to Getz.

From Zarubkin's left, Vanya handed him another bottle—he must have had it hidden inside his greatcoat. Zarubkin smiled to him, but recalled for an instant Vanya's despairing face, lit by the fires all around, last night in the Yama. Dragoons not unlike him had initiated the destruction: Two fools who decided they had been cheated out of three rubles by some madam; two men who had, because of tension and heat, impotency and drink, managed to stir a civilian army into looting and killing. Tonight those same civilians ran amok somewhere in Moscow, violence begetting violence. The disease of the mob had turned away from the whores, reshaping into something with a more sinister purpose: *Zhidov*, the new target. Jews.

Zarubkin, a captain in the Czar's guards, looked past his friends and into the fog. Why, he wondered, hadn't the zealots burned this pestilential place instead of the Yama? Even the police tended to avoid Khitrovka Market. The thick blanket of fog tonight hid much of the district's rot, but it carried the intense stench of the place, so that Zarubkin felt smeared with rheum. He took a hard pull from Vanya's bottle, then snarled, "To hell with the righteous citizens." It was they, after all, who had forced him and his friends to come here. Anywhere but where the mob was on this night off. Let those on duty look into the face of Hell. Not him, not two nights in a row.

Gladykin laughed and slapped his shoulder. "To hell with the righteous," he agreed, then added, "May they all burn for every one of us who carries crabs out of here tonight." And "Crabs!" cried Vanya, "To the crabs!"

They all drank to the health of lice and strode on. Their boots clopped like horses' hooves on the cobblestones in the dark.

Whatever evil had really dwelled in "The Pit," it hardly compared with Khitrovka. Here, as Zarubkin had learned from the heartfelt writings of Gilyarovski, the young girls were called *tyetki* when they advanced, at the age of ten or eleven, from begging to prostitution. Many had become alcoholics by that point, although their pimps—their "cats"—generally watered down the vodka. Few survived past their fourteenth year. Gilyarovski had found none in his search through the rubble. Because of two uniformed idiots, those hapless children would now have to match their indecent skills against professional prostitutes—the desperate survivors of last night's conflagration. How many of each, Zarubkin wondered, lurked in the fog ahead?

As the four men neared the heart of Khitrovka, beggars began to emerge from the darkness. The beggars choked the houses round about—thousands of soiled bodies wedged into a few blocks of space. Some were mutilated or deformed, unable to work. Some carried the corpses of babies in their arms as an appeal for sympathy in the form of coins even though with the child dead they had one less problem in their lives. Often the dead babies weren't even their own.

The sight of four large, well-fed guards in uniform sent most of the beggars scurrying back into shadow, the fog swirling after them. The four men walked on toward the building called Peresylny where the prostitutes had most likely found a haven. As he passed a curbstone fire, Zarubkin sensed someone watching him. The watcher turned out to be a scrawny creature warming its hands over the fire where another wretch, oblivious of him, cooked up a "dog's mess" of sausage and onions in a rusty iron pot. The creature staring so boldly was by appearances an ancient dwarf. The fire between his fingers revealed skin like parchment and a nearly hairless head that looked to have been smashed in on one side. The dwarf sneered at him, revealing brown and broken stubs, and gaps in the gums, like a child in the process of losing his baby teeth. His nose looked like a rotting carrot. By a trick of sound, the sizzle of the "dog's mess" seemed to emanate from the dwarf. Zarubkin looked away. He made himself relax, and discovered that his hand had closed over the butt of his revolver.

At that moment Gladykin announced, "I think it's time we separated, gentlemen. Together, we're going to scare off our nightingales. After last night the *tyetki*, I'm sure, expect us to burn their little world to the ground." He gestured at the fog, laughing as if to say that no sane man would waste his energy on such a task.

"All right," Getz agreed, "see you all inside Peresylny." Abruptly, he broke away from them and went up another street. They heard him walking long after he was lost to sight. Gladykin gave Zarubkin a wink, then turned and followed Getz like a bird in formation. "Later, my friend," his voice carried back. Zarubkin was going to share a humorous reply with Vanya, but he found that Vanya had quietly taken his leave, too. Zarubkin slowed and glanced around. Of the four of them, he had least wanted to venture on his own in this place, though soldiers would be quite safe. Especially, as Gladykin had said, after last night.

Pinpoints of light here and there revealed clusters of people, but the fog drank their voices and turned them into primeval lumps. The dwarf at curbside had vanished. Maybe the fog had swallowed him, too.

Zarubkin turned toward Peresylny, and a tall figure rushed toward him from a doorway on his left. He leaned away, his bottle held at the ready to smash down. Hands in fingerless lace gloves reached out for him. Delicate fingers closed on his wrist, over the neck of the bottle, pulling with the weight of a single body. The darkness swished. To his surprise, a woman pushed herself up against him. She stared into his face for a moment, her terror quite naked; then she glanced past him, all around, nervously.

Zarubkin guessed her age to be twenty-five. Vodka had puffed the skin beneath her eyes, adding some premature years there, but had not yet swelled her body or burst the capillaries in her nose. She was lean, her cheeks prominent and proud, her body like a whip in the dark decolleté dress that had blended with the fog. Her hair—it looked perhaps auburn—hung in disarray at her throat but also bore the signs of a coiffure not many days earlier.

When her attention returned to him he saw again the unrestrained terror in her dark eyes. What was after her in the fog? He could not help glancing around himself. Whoever wanted her, they would doubtless be less inclined to trouble one of the Czar's guard. Had she recognized that as he passed by? Was that why she had scurried to him? He smiled reassuringly, said, "Would you care for some vodka? It's not watered down—it's good Smirnov."

A smile trembled desperately on her lips, made little creases in her cheeks and revealed good, white teeth. Of course, he realized then, this girl was from the Yama. No wonder she was terrified: in this place she played the part of the lamb in a field packed with wolves.

She drew nearer, like an intimate companion. "You're very kind, thank you." She took his bottle and drank deeply. He saw her looking over it into the fog once more, eyes searching, always moving.

Vodka glistened on her lips as she returned the bottle to him. Then she asked, "Would you stay the night with me, soldier?"

This nonplused him: It was supposed to be his question to her, after all. As a Yama whore, she ought to have recognized the proprieties of their encounter. He politely took back his vodka.

She seemed to sense his withdrawal from the proposal. "Look," she said and dug fervidly into a small purse. "I have a ticket." She held up a yellow card. "Government approval."

He hesitated, but there was something about her, about her predicament, that he wanted to know. "Yes, all right," he said, found her staring out into the night again. She had made enemies here — probably, he thought, by trying to push her polished manners on the denizens. In Khitrovka she might disappear and no one ever look for her. What was one whore more or less afloat in the stinking Yauza? She had to be scared to be so forward as to express *her* wants. The problem, as he saw it, lay in the fact that he had only enough money for an hour of her time if he was going to rejoin his friends for more drinking. In some embarrassment, he explained this. The woman started to laugh, very near hysteria. "Three rubles?" she said and pressed tightly against him. "My darling captain, with three rubles you can have me for life."

Zarubkin merely gaped. He had paid for a woman twice before, and he knew enough to know that this was not the way it was supposed to go. Then she buried her face against his collar and whispered, "Please stay with me this night, fair captain. Don't leave me to this . . . this horror."

She smelled of soap, and perfumed French soap at that. He wondered how so delicate a scent had survived a day amidst the ordure of the Market. The whore's breast rubbed against the back of his hand where he held the bottle to his chest. Her scent, her looks, her mystery aroused him. "Of course," he lied. "Of course I'll stay. Where do you live?"

The small room contained three beds wedged in around a scarred and warped washstand displaying a cracked ceramic pitcher and a brass oil lamp. Two of the beds had been stripped, and the whore assured him the other occupants would not be returning. "They fled the city this morning, Neva and Olenka. The landlords don't know that yet. I would have gone with them . . . they didn't wait." She hid her face where she could regain her composure. "I'm sorry. You delight that we're alone of course." She drew back the covers. Blotches and smears the color of rust stained the sheets but she swore that no vermin hid in the bedding. The business side of her came out as she undressed, her manner mechanical, any hints of nervous tension coming only at the end, as she removed the last of her shiny underclothes. Next she helped him remove his own clothing, her fingers quick but twitchy.

They lay down together. Her thin body shivered, but she smiled bravely, prepared to endure anything to have him. He found her peculiar forlornness arousing, and he pulled her to him. She stopped him briefly.

"My name is Lizaveta Ostrov," she said.

"I'm Zarubkin."

She looked questioningly into his eyes.

"Sergei," he added in compliance.

"Sergei," she replied flatly, and opened to him at last.

The warmth of the vodka seemed to shoot through him. Her lovemaking had urgency, as if she must race to the end before the whole world burst apart. It defied Zarubkin's prior experience with whores: usually, they feigned vague interest in their partner, and some not even that. He had always seen through the shallow facade and not cared. This woman treated him like a drink of water in the desert, or a last meal before execution. They made love three times in as many hours and polished off Vanya's bottle of vodka as well. She retrieved a bottle of her own from a small cupboard beneath the crooked window, crawling across the two other beds to get it. As she climbed back into bed and handed it to him, she apologized, "It's not as strong as yours. In the house in the Yama, the madam didn't wish for us to get so drunk as to forget to collect our fees."

"You'd prefer I paid you now, I understand."

The fright reappeared in her eyes. "Don't—don't pay until you leave. Not before day."

"What is it, is your 'cat' looking for you?"

She shook her head. "I represent myself here. Now that so many others have come, it's become more difficult. I'm . . ."

He had to ponder that before the astonishing meaning became clear. "You came here *before* the Yama burned? Dear God, why? A beautiful woman like you, with your manners, your grace—"

"Oh, I did well. I learned very quickly, even though I'd arrived upon it so late, as a trade. You enjoy me?"

"Very much—I mean, three times is . . ." He looked around to cover his embarrassment. Her boldness in asking—that was like the whores he had known. "You became a prostitute recently then. Why did you choose—I mean, of all the things to do with your life?"

"You're beside your whore this very minute—don't make it sound so foul, captain."

"I didn't mean—all right, yes, I suppose I did." He studied the creases in the sheet between his elbows.

Softly, Lizaveta said, "I was a teacher," and he glanced up. Her gaze had become distant. She drank long from the bottle of weak Smirnov. "I loved children. I did." Slowly, she lay back beside him with her head against his shoulder. Her toes rested on the tops of his feet. She was nearly his height.

Zarubkin had intended to leave shortly, certain that his friends would tire of waiting and go off without him. Now he realized he would not be with them. He had asked his other whores to tell him about their lives, mildly curious. But the woman Lizaveta Ostrov did not act like any whore he had known. Her pose—if it was a pose—had him desiring the explication of her life as much as he had desired the union with her body. He really did want to know what had driven her here. What lay in the fog.

At first, when he asked, he thought she would not say anything. Then she sighed, leaned up and kissed him. "You'll stay with me, then?" There was, implicit in the question, the revelation that she had known his earlier lie for what it was.

"I'll stay. This time I swear I will, till light."

She covered her eyes with one hand, beneath which her lips trembled. The glistening of a tear crawled out into sight.

Unwilling to commit himself to her further, Zarubkin waited and drank, drank and waited. When she began to speak, it was so soft that she caught him completely off guard. She was telling him her story, and he had to ask her to begin again.

"When I graduated from the university," she said, "I was equipped to teach but could find no jobs in Moscow, so I returned to the university in the hope of inquiring after a job there. I should have done that at first, right away, because by then I think I must have been the last person in all the city to ask. What they gave me instead of a job was a list of places that needed teachers, and it wasn't a large list. A handful of jobs, all in distant places, too. Only one of them lay in the south, near the Kazakh border, in the foothills of the Urals. It sounded very lovely—warm and inviting—compared to the chill of Moscow, or of such places as Zhigansk and Obdorosk, which were among the remaining choices. I have always desired warmth, probably from having lived a cold child-hood. We always want the other thing, the thing we don't have—don't you find people to be very polar in this way? I wrote a letter to the people petitioning, saying that I would take the job of teacher in their village, called Devashgorod. Next I waited—almost a month before the village replied. They sent back a letter of acceptance with directions on how to reach there.

"I left right away. A train took me to Orenburg, which was the closest civilized place to my new home, and that nearly a hundred kilometers away. I located a troika going into the Urals from there, a coach of odd travelers, and I secured a place on board, next to a man, a Persian I believe, just arrived from the Caspian Sea. He smelled of an alien sweetness and his Russian was terrible, but he smiled broadly, openly, with huge, white teeth, whenever I looked his way. The others in the troika seemed to take offense at his presence and scorned me for befriending him even that little bit. No one spoke to me really the whole first day of the journey. I didn't care. I leaned back and watched the incredible scenery float by—the rolling steppes, whole hillsides covered in flowers, the mountains growing always larger and more distinct. By that second day the majority of the passengers had reached their various destinations or had gotten off at a crossroads to take a different path. Only three people remained: myself, the Persian, and a man who was going with the driver to some place on the Tobol River. 'This is old country,' he said to me. Left alone with us, I suppose he no longer felt the need to pretend indifference. He claimed this place we traveled through belonged to the oldest civilizations in the world. Time, he said, had hardly touched the land there. He could not understand why someone such as I traveled alone in such a place. So I told him about my teaching position, my first one. Where? In Devashgorod.

"The traveler to Tobol hadn't heard of it but the Persian beside me was plainly disturbed by the name. His face pinched, and it furrowed like a plowed field, and he clutched my hand, saying, 'Must you go? Lady, must you go?' I answered that I had to, yes, or have no employment and a bad record. From that moment on, I became the outcast and he, the dark man, avoided me while the other man laughed contemptuously and called him a 'superstitious peasant,' but also quickly turned to revery. Shortly after that he feigned sleep. Eventually, the wagon deposited me and my trunk at the intersection with the Devashgorod road.

"A one-horse cart arrived. The driver greeted me with a great wave. He stood up in the cart, a huge man with long, shiny black hair and a heavy mustache. He had the cheeks of a Kazakh that looked set in place with a trowel. He wore a bright peasant shirt and rough trousers tucked into high boots, very worn. His name was Trifon, a curious name, I thought. As we drove to his village, he explained that he was the *ataman*, which is the chieftain of sorts, but with religious as well as judiciary duties. Every Kazaki village had an *ataman* he informed me.

"The road took us up into the true foothills of the Urals. Peaks still had snow on them in May. The road became a trail, barely more than two ruts in the high grass. I experienced the moment that comes upon the threshold of a new life—of fear and doubt and a tingling excitement.

"The wagon bounced over the top of a ridge and there below

me lay Devashgorod. Like a collection of dollhouses, quite lovely, colorful, it was a scene of utter serenity—or very nearly so. At the edge of the village nearest the road below us there was a great pit grown over by grass and flowers. From above I could look right down into that pit, and I found myself staring at the peaked roof of a house. It looked not very old, and I was amazed. 'What happened there?' I asked. Trifon replied quickly, 'Terrible. An earthquake, the ground opened up, the house was simply devoured by the earth. Most terrible day for our village. But here, look,' he said and pointed to a grove of fir trees nearby, where they had built their schoolhouse—no more than a shack really. 'That is where you will teach.' Trifon clapped his hands, just like a chieftain denying further discussion, and down into the valley we went."

Lizaveta paused to take a long pull from her watered vodka.

Puzzled somewhat, Zarubkin asked her, "But how did this drive you into whoring? Did Trifon rape—attack you?"

She laughed, dribbling a little vodka. "Oh, dear captain, no. As if such a thing would make you want more of it! I will tell you, it's coming, but let me do it naturally, please." She hugged against him to win his patience. Outside, someone shouted an angry string of invectives and someone else told him to shut up. Lizaveta ignored the noise and said, "Listen now. I began my teaching the next day. A local family called Shaldin took me in. They had a farm and a big house, and Trifon had prearranged everything with them. They had a son and a daughter who had been schooled for some years. From them I learned of how my predecessor had approached teaching and some of the names of the students, the ones who were their friends. The daughter, Larissa, warned me to watch out for a boy named Akaky. He was apparently the ringleader for trouble. In all, only twenty-two of them attended, a fact which hinted that there must be families who chose not to send their children, who taught them at home if at all, but who did not want them to know of the 'other world.'

"Early in the morning, before the children would arrive, I went to the schoolhouse. There I found stacks of papers and notebooks left by my predecessor. Dust coated the stacks and the desktop. I wondered how long the children had been without a teacher.

"While I finished cleaning off this area, the children began to file in. Most of them were shy, a bit afraid of me. Then, from outside, there came loud jeering, a teasing chorus of voices. I went to the doorway. At my appearance, they all fell silent and moved off— a dozen or so children. At first I thought they had been picking on an old man, but in a moment I saw that the old man was in fact a child, a victim of a terrible, withering disease that had made him age prematurely. I had heard of this, but never had I seen so pitiable a sight.

"He stood in a sort of hunch, as if the disease were pulling his body in upon itself. His head seemed too heavy for his neck. The purple veins showed under his skull, which was almost hairless. His skin had that quality of transparency that an onion has. Awful. His cold, birdlike eyes glared at me, and he hobbled past, still staring at me, wheezing as he climbed through the door, his right hand crippled up and pressed against his side. I could not believe the cruelty of these children, that they could openly taunt such an unfortunate. I resolved to change that if I accomplished nothing else. Children afflicted by this disease rarely live more than ten years, and I wanted above all to let this boy enjoy what time he had left.

"Once the children had taken their seats, I asked them each to tell me their names and how far they had advanced in their learning. When the time came for the wizened little boy, he refused to speak and just stared with his hard eyes straight ahead, as if he were deaf. I thought here was a poor victim, so harassed that he distrusted even me. I asked that someone tell me about him. Larissa Shaldin stood up. She made no sound, but the boy seemed to sense where she stood behind him. 'That is Akaky,' she told me in an incomprehensibly bitter tone. 'He rejects what you teach him and will continue to, no matter how hard you try. His family even despises him for—' she stopped and looked around herself—'for shunning everything.'

" 'Why do you despise him, though?' And, though I addressed her, it was a question to the whole classroom. Larissa became dismayed by the question and sat down. Someone more daring called out from the back, 'You can see why—just look at him!' This engendered snickers from around the room. I saw that I couldn't carry the argument further without terribly embarrassing the child, so I left it at that and turned to instruction, working on their alphabets and handwriting skills. They knew barely half their letters. My predecessor had not been very qualified for her duties it seemed.

"That evening I knocked on Larissa's door and went in to apologize for singling her out, which I hadn't meant to do. She sat on her bed in her undergarments and wouldn't look at me until I sat beside her. 'Child,' I said to her, 'you can't treat an unfortunate that way. It's morally wrong.'

" 'An unfortunate?' she replied. Again virulence shot through her words. 'Akaky? He's everything he deserves to be, everything. Death would do us a service to take him.' She stopped speaking but her face expressed how much more she could have said. Her eyes moistened from this contained anger and she jerked her head away. 'You're just the same as the other one. You come here with your ideas about how things are. Everywhere is not like here. Please, I'm warning you now—let Akaky alone. Don't try to help him.'

"'But that's ridiculous, child. Why shouldn't—'

"'Do houses sink into the ground in your Moscow? Does the earth open up and devour people?' After that outburst she refused to say anything further. Her cheeks burned as if she were ashamed to have said any of this. I squeezed her hand quite uncomprehendingly and then left, thinking that her family must have put such ideas into her head. I could not imagine why. Had they branded him an outcast because of his disease? Did they think him contagious? Or were these people so backward in their thinking that they saw such physical calamity as a curse from God, a mark of evil? Questions such as that kept me awake a long time.

"The next morning, Larissa's father reinforced them for me. He confronted me in the hallway, blocking my way to the door. He said that, while he prided himself on doing his part for the village, there were rules in his house and one of these was that I was never to enter the children's bedrooms. I didn't know what to say. He went on, asking rhetorically, 'How would it have seemed if you had gone into my son's room last night to speak with him?'

"I answered that such a thing would have been unseemly without a doubt, but I added, 'Nevertheless, your son is but thirteen, sir.'

"'Well, and just so,' was his reply as though I had agreed with him. 'An impressionable age. And he is already infatuated with you. You didn't know? He's a romantic boy, my little Vald. He would mistake your attentions. Or he might think that he, too, had the right to pass into other people's bedrooms at night—his sister's for instance.'

"I could not believe this argument. Nevertheless, I deferred. I was, after all, a guest. But Shaldin could not leave the matter there. He went on, 'Just remember, madam, you may be the teacher in the school, but here I make the rules and it is only proper that you adjust to them. After all, what do we know of you, or you know of any of us?'

"'Very little,' I replied, 'but I know enough to see now that this is in some way connected to the incident with the child, Akaky.'

"I had known nothing of the sort, but the urge to say that seized me. Shaldin actually blanched as if I had uttered blasphemy. Then he pushed past me and went out of the house, slamming the door. The entire family must have heard the argument. The echo of the closing door banged all around the upstairs.

"I had no doubt now that Shaldin had forbidden any talk of the child in his house. Now I suspected there might be a blood feud between families involved. Everyone knows how strong are blood ties among the Kazaki. I've heard of disputes that lasted through generations, when the actual cause had been forgotten or even repaired. On the weight of that assessment alone, I determined to go see Akaky's family that afternoon.

"When the day's lessons had been completed, the children went off to help with family chores. There is always work in the fields and at home. I kept Akaky after all the others had gone, and I didn't tell him until then what I wanted of him. He did not even blink at my demand to see his family. That wrinkled mask of hatred became, if possible, more disdainful. I was struck with an extraordinary sense that all of this had happened before, that I was repeating the actions of my predecessor. The child climbed off his stool and shuffled out of the schoolhouse. I hurried after him, leaving my papers and things behind.

"I can remember my eyes stinging from the humid heat of the day as I hiked after him. I took to holding my hair off my neck and unbuttoned the collar of my blouse. The light breeze helped somewhat. Keeping up with Akaky proved no trouble despite my lace-up boots, which were hardly designed for rough hills. We passed sheep and goats—the stink of the goats clung with a particular tenacity to the steamy air. It pervaded my clothes."

The captain laughed. "There's surely no stink like it," he agreed, and passed the bottle back to her. She rose up to take a drink, and he saw her profile against the vague light of the window—saw the sparkle of moisture on her lips. She was, he reminded himself, really very lovely. In the street below Peresylny, he heard feet clatter on the cobblestones, and more shouting—spewed cries that sounded like alarms. He climbed past her, across the beds as she had done, and stared down through the grimy window. Fires spotted the night, but except for these small enclaves he could see nothing of Khitrovka no matter how he strained. The footsteps ran on, fading away.

Behind him, Lizaveta said, "It's like this here every night. Sometimes you hear it and you know someone's being murdered."

Zarubkin accepted that he would learn nothing from his watch and crawled back beside her. The bottle touched his hip, cold. He flinched and took it from her, took a drink, then settled back to listen to her. "You were going to his house," he prompted.

"Akaky's house," she said, "it was a hut actually. They had a large pen built on one side of it, but the animals inside were scrawny things. We had reached a rise slightly above the hut and as we descended, four people emerged from the doorway and stood in a row outside, waiting. They must have been watching for us. Akaky went up to his father and stopped. The child shrank into himself more than ever and glanced up at his father without raising his head. Then he pushed past his family and went inside. Only then did they all turn their attention to me—all staring with that same dark malignity the boy had. I tried to excuse their hostility by telling myself they must have felt cursed by his affliction. I told them who I was and that I was offering to help both the boy and them.

"The father snorted at me. 'Help us?' he said. 'You wish to help us, then kill that boy. You'll be helping the whole village *and* yourself, lady teacher.'

"I couldn't believe what I heard. The man saw this, too, but all he did was shake his head sadly. Then he told me I was like the others, and that perhaps the next one would have a chance. 'Maybe by then the boy will use himself up,' he remarked. 'Maybe he'll use himself up on you.' Then he told me to go away. I turned to his wife, but she refused to look at me. His older sister—a girl who should have been married by then in that village—eyed me askance, as if daring me to try and address her. The grandmother beside her was the only one showing any sympathy in her face. Maybe she had traveled or at least understood that a world existed beyond Devashgorod. She said, 'Best you should teach those who need your gifts.' I thought then, my God, she could be Akaky's *wife*, he looks so ancient. The father inserted himself between us and repeated his order that I leave. What choice did I have?

"That evening no one in the Shaldin household said more than a few words to me, and even then they would not meet my eyes. Larissa's brother—the one who supposedly had a fondness for me— actually fled to his room when I encountered him on the stairs.

"I lay in bed that night, finding sleep impossible for hours. When I did finally drift off, I had vivid dreams. The sunken house had been resurrected, and I was walking through it, down wainscoted hallways. Ahead of me, doors on both sides of the halls swung open and closed.

"As I drifted along, I thought I heard a voice softly call my name. Drawn toward it, I waited for that door to open to me, then passed through it into a small room, the walls papered in burgundy, the curtains of white lace.

"A woman stood there. I thought at first that she must be a grandmother, but oddly, she wore clothes not unlike mine, clothes that a young woman would wear. The curtain fluttered around her. 'Don't give in to him,' she said. 'He'll eat your life up to survive. Look at me.' She turned more toward me, and I saw that her blouse below the collar shone with a wet darkness and seemed to be stuffed into a depression between her breasts, a hole. She might have said more, but the curtain came to life like a serpent. It wound around her throat and dragged her off her feet. I took a step toward her, but she held up her hand for me to stay away. Then the curtain snapped and she crashed back through the window. Beams of shadow, like an infernal opposite to sunlight, flooded the room. The floor splintered beneath me, and I dropped down into a pit.

"I awoke in my own room in the Shaldin house. The bedclothes stuck to me as I sat up, and I pushed them aside. My pulse raced like a horse. I threw off a great shiver. With the lamp turned up, I sat against the pillows and thought over the dream. The woman— I knew that she had been my predecessor at the school. What had he done to her, how had she been made to age like that? Akaky's grandmother then came to mind. What if she was no older? The more I thought about this, the less it made sense to me. It was, I reminded myself, no more than a dream, which had conveniently assembled the things that were most unusual about the village into a narrative, but not a coherent reality. Feeling utterly foolish, I crawled back beneath the covers and went back to sleep; but I left the lamp burning brightly. I had no further dreams then that I remember.

"The child did not appear at the school that day, and another of the children informed me that Akaky had been too weak to come in today. The whole of the morning went uneventfully. In the after-noon, as I was returning home, I saw Trifon. He asked me how I found my new job, and I told him that it was going well, that the children needed a great deal of assistance because the last teacher had not done her work properly. 'She was a weaker vessel than you,' he replied, 'but we shouldn't judge her too harshly, should we?' It was as though he could read my doubts, or had shared my night-mare. I agreed with him. He told me, 'What she forgot was that not all children *need* special attention, that some are made to learn, and others not. There are children who will refuse to be helped. Though they are only children. You, I believe, understand not to invite problems.' He bid me a good afternoon and went along the road. My hopes sank with that meeting, for I had expected that Trifon would give me answers where the others would not. Now I felt truly lost and a thousand miles away from the world I knew. I went to my room, closed the door, and began to cry. If anyone there heard me, they did not come to see what was the matter. Eventually, I cried myself to sleep.

"Immediately, a dream overtook me, vivid as the night before. At first I didn't know I was dreaming, because I was in my room still. But then I noticed how dark it was outside. The window across the room was open wide, the curtains drawn back. I could see stars for a moment, but then a shape blotted them out. The me in the dream got up and turned up the lamp, then carried it over to the window. The flame reflected me in the glass, but through myself I could see the child, Akaky, floating beyond, more hideous than ever, more withered and malicious. 'Let me in,' he said, 'you must help me.' I stepped back with the lamp, gesturing him through the window. He slid over the sill and settled on the floor. A mist curled over the ledge at his back. He stood hunched, grimacing in pain. I put the lamp down beside the bed and turned back to help him, remembering that he had been too weak to come to school, but he said, 'Lie down.' I found myself obeying him. A part of my mind watched me performing, but the rest of my will had been left outside the dream. He came to the foot of the bed and began picking up the discarded clothes lying there—the ones from the previous day—and my nightgown. Each item he held to his nose and sniffed, like a dog. Then he dropped each one and took another, until he had soiled everything. All the while, his liquid eyes glistened at me. Finally he came along the side of the bed and stood beside me. His crippled hand that he kept always curled at his side unfolded over my face. The fingers all ended in long, sharp nails like tiny blades. With his other hand he untied the bow at my throat, then grabbed the blouse and pulled it apart, exposing my breastbone. He turned the hand slowly and the nails hung above me. It no longer appeared deformed in any way. He let his hand descend slowly, savoring the moment. The promise of ecstasy gleamed in his cruel eyes—I've seen it in many lovers since. His hand dropped below my view, and I waited, not breathing, not thinking. Waiting. And then those nails sank into my skin. I went rigid. It was like terrible ice inside me. My back arched away from the bed until I thought it would snap, but I couldn't make myself move to stop him. He sighed, and I could feel him wriggling his fingers down into my heart. That pain—how can I explain the sweet edge it had to it, pain that was almost unbearable pleasure. I began to scream and scream, trying to roll away from his clutch. He laughed—not a child at all, but a fiend. He rose up straighter. His eyes swelled, growing closer until they blotted out everything else.

"When I did wake up, the afternoon sun blinded me, coming in the window from just above the horizon. I got up, but rocked back from dizziness and had to catch my breath before I could stand. These nightmares, I thought, were draining my reserves. I went to the washstand to pour some water and cool myself, and I saw myself in the mirror. Between my breasts was a bruised ring of five tiny, white scars. The bruises are gone now, but if I turned the lamp up I could show you the scars. I began to cry when I saw them. A moment later, Shaldin's wife called us all to dinner. I didn't know what to do. Should I tell them? There seemed no point; they would not be more sympathetic now than before. They might drive me from their home. I wiped away my tears and splashed my face, then buttoned and neatened my blouse.

"At dinner, I kept to myself which seemed to satisfy them all. I must have eaten something, but I don't know what it was. The family made countless covert glances at me. Both children showed concern, but the parents had fear in their eyes. I had no energy left to cope with them, and I excused myself and retired.

"In the hallway outside my room, I heard Shaldin's caustic voice. 'I told Trifon I won't bring this on us,' he said. 'Some other house can have her, some other family can suffer on her account.' I had gone from guest to intrusive enemy. The man blamed me, even though he obviously had known of Akaky's powers before-hand. Why had he said nothing? I cursed him for his cowardice then and slammed my door so that he would know that I had heard.

"Once inside, I went to the window and latched the shutters before closing the window. The air would become stuffy. I hoped it would make me uncomfortable, and keep me awake, but it had just the opposite effect, and put me to sleep. But no one came into the room, and no dreams came to trouble me.

"In the morning, I sought out Trifon again. He sat in the corner of the store where they served pastries and tea. When I arrived, he was speaking with some others and his back was to me. I waited a short distance away. The men with Trifon grew uncomfortable and, one by one, they got up and left. He still had not turned to look at me, but he gestured over his shoulder for me to come and join him. I sat down. He took an empty cup and gave me tea. 'What is it?' he asked.

"'I will know all the things that you didn't tell me the other day.' He pursed his lips, then brushed the crumbs from his mustache. 'What would you know?' I said, 'Akaky.' I needed to say no more than that. Trifon was a huge man, but that name seemed to shrink him. He nodded as if he had long expected this, but he did not speak, so I prodded him further. 'Why do you all tolerate him?'

"'You know nothing of us, not even as much as you think you do,' he answered. 'We believe in God, yes, but also we believe that when a person is murdered, that soul enters the heart of the murderer to plague him.' I remarked that this was an interesting belief, but of no relevance I could see. 'Not relevant?' he said. 'It's the reason we've let the monster live. It's the reason he is the way he is. His father killed a neighbor—I'm sure it was an accident of emotion, but it happened. And the boy was born within weeks of that. Born evil, cruel, powerful, and desiring nothing more than to ruin himself and his family. The harm that he has done has been directed at them, at no one else. That is how we know whose soul he has, that's why his family lives in shame.'

"'How can you say he's harmed no one but them? What about the house out there that's sunk in the ground? What about that poor family?'

"Trifon stared at me as if to say I was a fool. 'That was *his* house. That was where *his* family lived. He brought it down.' As if to dismiss me, he shoved his cup away, but I had not finished.

"'What of my predecessor?' I demanded.

"'Her? She witnessed the event and fled from us. Nothing happened to her, just as nothing will happen to you. She lost her position. Akaky withdrew afterward, and no one here saw him. His family keeps away still in shame. They told us he had fallen into a trance and would die. We acted on that, believing—Merciful God, hoping for it. He should have died. We sent for you then. Now you're here and Akaky's weaker than before, so let him be, let him rot. Just don't run away in fright or we'll have to send for another teacher. Evil he is, but he won't do anything except frighten you. Especially at the house of Shaldin, because he fears Larissa—her gifts outshine his, and the rest of us. Oh, yes—you see, I told you that you knew less than you thought. We all have some powers like his. But we take precautions, and we don't use our gifts frivolously.

If we did, we would all look like Akaky. Now you know why we put you there of all places in spite of Shaldin's objections.'

" 'No,' I insisted, 'no, she didn't run away.'

" 'What? Who didn't run away?'

" 'Your last teacher. She's dead. Akaky sucked her life away.'

" 'Rubbish—now you think him too powerful.'

" 'Really?' I said. 'Well, let me tell you, wise *ataman*, the reason I know what Akaky did to the last outsider is that he is doing the same thing to me.' I wanted to show him the marks, the bruises and scars, but the high-necked blouse I had put on to hide them would not let me. He would have denied them, too, I was certain. He had his system of belief, as did the entire village—of witches or devils or whatever they were in Devashgorod. Angrily, I got up and marched out of the shop. I was no demon, nor had my predecessor been. We were something altogether different. We were prey.

"That afternoon I went into the church, as orthodox a church as you'd find in any village. I prayed for my soul, though I feared that I now dwelled somewhere that God did not visit. Afterward I returned to my room in Shaldin's house. My thoughts collided, but as I sat there I spied my trunk at the foot of the bed and I thought that I should obey my instincts and flee. I could steal a cart, but how could I drag the trunk out of here without the whole house knowing of it? The situation had trapped me, do you see, my captain? There was no way to leave and no hope of survival unless I could deal with Akaky. I thought then that perhaps I could make him leave me alone.

"At dinner I said nothing of my intention, but that night I dressed for bed and then opened the window into my room. A cool breeze from off the mountains blew in, and I settled back on the bed to wait. This time I hoped that the cold would keep me awake. For a while I tried to read some Gogol but could not concentrate, so I set it aside, lay back, and waited.

"Even with the cold I eventually drifted to the edge of sleep. I might have dozed but it was at that moment that Akaky thumped against the window. Again a mist trailed in behind him. He was grinning. I sat up and said, 'I'll speak with you,' as harshly as I could muster. My tone dismayed him for a moment, but then he sneered and came forward again. 'Lie back,' he said, 'I've no desire to speak with *you*. It's your life I want, not talk.' I fought his control over me, but my body obeyed against my will. Still, I could talk, and I said, 'You burn your own life up, doing this. Stop before you damn yourself.'

"He laughed, which turned into a cough. 'I burn either way,' he rasped. 'You can help me live a little longer.'

"'Why not stop, why not rest?' I asked him.

"'Because I love it too much. What would life be without the burning inside?' And his eyes rolled up in ecstasy as he lost himself in his own fire. In the room, as he did that, the furniture began to rattle and shift. The bed beneath me trembled, creaking. Then Akaky's rheumy eyes settled on me again. 'You can't imagine it,' he said. 'Or if you did, you'd give in to the pleasure with me—only your kind doesn't have the knowledge we do.'

"'Then why don't the rest burn themselves up, too?' I asked. 'Why aren't all the villagers out devastating their town for the sheer pleasure it brings?'

"'They're afraid. But I'm tired of talking to you. Be quiet now.' He uncurled that deformed hand of his and it was whole again, the nails glinting as if sharpened. The part of me that he controlled ached for him to insert them again. Terrified even of myself, I tried to roll free of him, but I might have been paralyzed. He undid the bow on my gown, exposing the bruise he had made. Then, behind him, a shape emerged from the shadows. Slender hands closed over his wrist above me and yanked him around. I found myself able to move, and I turned my head to see Larissa there. She whispered sharply in the Kazaki tongue, words I didn't know. What she said must have been a curse of some kind, because he reacted by spitting at her. With his free hand he swung at her face and knocked her against the door. Then he didn't touch her, only looked at her, but somehow this seemed to mash her against the wood of the door. She answered his assault, and he stumbled back a foot. She might have superior powers, but Akaky was willing to use his at a murderous level, which Larissa dared not. I thought of her withered and dried out from saving my life, and I couldn't let that happen.

"Akaky's head swiveled and his teeth creaked. He jerked with his neck and Larissa spun away, smashing against a chair and onto the floor. He seemed to expand, to rise almost to the ceiling. The house groaned and snapped. It must have spun somehow, because I was tossed across my bed.

"Larissa climbed up quickly. Blood was running out of her nose. 'Akaky,' she said, but he shook his head and replied, 'It's too late, you waited. I've new strength, from the teacher, and you shouldn't have picked now to try me, you shouldn't.' He closed the distance between them. I sat up, but reeled with dizziness, and I

fell on my side, my face pressed against the cool binding of my book. The house lurched with a bounce. It would sink like the other one, and because of me. I grabbed the volume of Gogol in both hands, and I swung around and smashed it down across the back of his wretched skull. The blow drove him across to the door, and I heard something in him crack when he hit it. I thought I had killed him, but when Larissa and I turned him over we saw that only his nose had been broken. She could hardly stand and I made her sit in the chair she had fallen across, while I wiped the blood from her face. Beneath it, she had lines I'd never seen before—she had aged years from that short confrontation. 'He'll come again for you, night after night,' she assured me. 'In each generation here, there's one like him, who does damage until he perishes from his own obsession. Evil is always consumed by its own heat. But never before have there been outsiders. Now the evil will spread to the outside from us.'

" 'The world has evil in it already, Larissa,' I told her.

"She nodded. 'True, but no evil before had your name on its lips.' I considered then finishing what I had started, killing the child. Larissa sensed this and told me that I would be foolish to do so. She believed the myth of her village. Perhaps I had come to as well.

"Larissa sighed, exhausted. I was surprised that no one else had stirred. She must have seen my distant look, because she said, 'They've been kept asleep. Akaky's magic. He wouldn't want to fight us all—it would drain him utterly.'

" 'But why not destroy him like that?' I asked. Here they had what seemed to me the perfect solution to their problem; but Larissa shook her head. 'You don't understand us,' she said. 'He's evil, but he is of us nevertheless. We must tolerate him though we don't want him. In this way he destroys only himself, nothing else.'

" 'Except me,' I pointed out.

" 'Yes,' she agreed. 'He can destroy you. You should never have been allowed here before the village knew for certain that he had perished. And now you must go. I'll take you to the *ataman*, and he'll send you from here tonight.' She left my room to put on her clothes. I changed mine, stuffing my belongings into the trunk. When I came around the bed, Akaky's hand shot out and grabbed my ankle. 'Larissa!' he wheezed. 'I'll murder you. I'll wear you down till you're a rotting corpse.' He clutched my skirts, and dragged himself up me. Blood covered his lips and outlined the stubs of his teeth. I shoved him away, but he hung onto me with those fingers. I tried to reach the door, but he pulled me off balance. I fell, catching myself against the doorknob. Akaky was on his knees. I whirled around and slammed him against the wall. He growled, and his eyes rolled back, and a horrible pain opened in my breast. Akaky was grinning in pain and pleasure combined, his head back, the blood drawing lines up his face now. Frantically, I tore him from me, peeling his tiny hand away, crushing the fingers. He became weaker and more fragile by the moment. He laughed at me then, as if rejoicing in both our sufferings. I was not of their village; I could not block him out, and I could not endure this any longer. I slapped him as hard as I could. It was like hitting old, thin plaster. His cheekbone shattered under my hand. That whole side of his face caved in. He hissed, his breath foetid; but his hand went limp and he tumbled back across the chair.

"I stood there, shaking, waiting. If he had moved again, I would have taken something and beaten his head into the floor. Instead, he lay unmoving, as repellent a sight as if I had disinterred a corpse and brought it to my room. The stench of him seemed to fill the room.

"Larissa returned and saw him. In a mad rush I explained what had happened. Horrified, she bent over the chair. 'I think you've killed him,' she said. 'Come on, you have to get away now.' She grabbed my arm and pulled me from the room. I wanted to go back for my trunk but she insisted that someone else would get it. I was not to return to that room.

"Trifon listened to her story morosely. Was it me, I wondered, who shadowed the *ataman*'s thoughts? But no, it was Akaky, for Trifon cursed him and spat. He agreed to hitch up his horses. My trunk was loaded on his wagon and I left Devashgorod in the dead of night, like a criminal, a spy. At the edge of town, Shaldin's house now stood canted to the right, as if the pit that had swallowed the neighboring house was growing, unseen.

"On the way along the road, Trifon handed me some money. 'This is payment for as much of the year as I can afford. You won't have a successor. Not till Akaky is taken care of.'

"I thought, *But he's dead, I've killed him, what of me?* I lost myself in gloom until I saw him. He stood beside the road as we went past. Trifon didn't see him, but I did. I saw the moonlight on his wild eyes, and I turned to watch him hobble into the dust after us. In terror I watched him recede into the night. When we reached the main road, Trifon wanted to leave me, but I wouldn't let him go. I pleaded with him to stay, not to leave me where Akaky could prey upon me. Trifon remained until morning, when he assured me in the sunlight that I was safe. Then he would not be kept there and drove off. His village needed him he explained. Larissa Shaldin needed him. The troika was due around midday, or so he had claimed. I sat on the trunk, surveying the landscape for that hunched, repulsive shape. The trunk shifted under me, so gently at first that I didn't understand what was happening. Then it shook violently. I jumped up at the instant that the latch burst. The lid flew open so hard that one hinge tore free. Clothing, all that I owned in the world, went spinning up like a fountain. At the center of it, a shape rose up—Akaky. His bleeding mouth drooled. The indented side of his face was purple and black. He scrabbled at me with those claws, but in his blind lunge he fell over the side of the box. I thought, *Now is the time to finish him.* I took a step. Should I kill him with a rock? Then he sprang from the ground, and his sharp fingers reached for my face. He missed but tangled them in my hair. I grabbed his wrist and tore myself free; his arm snapped and he wailed. I turned and ran.

"The troika picked me up later that day and I rode in the safety of the other passengers, saying nothing to them but protected by their presence, or so I hoped. But on the train to Moscow, I saw him outside the window twice, pressed to the glass like a fly on a wall. Where had he gotten the strength to do this? Had he killed someone else, drained their life to pursue me? I could not—did not want to—imagine it. And each time I saw him, he was more decrepit, more horrible. He looked like a mummified corpse, like nothing living. In Moscow I tried to go back to the university, but he sat on a bench by the door, knowing somehow that I would go there. In my despair I contemplated taking my own life, jumping into the river; but I haven't the courage.

"I don't know when I decided at last to go to the Yama. I think I just found myself there, wandering, and I saw the fine houses and realized that Akaky could never imagine I'd go there. It frightened me at first, but the women were kind, and understanding. Most of them had been through the same initial fears. The madam promised me that I had a cultured look that would appeal to her aristocratic clientele. I used most of my money to bribe an officer into getting me a yellow card, and the rest was, as the girls had assured me, just a matter of playing a role. I came to enjoy it. Hardly ever did I go out, but one man wanted a companion for the opera season, and I knew opera where the others did not, so the madam insisted. As I feared, Akaky found me. I saw him as I came from the opera one night, but he would not approach while the man was with me. Like a gnarled stick creature, he hobbled along behind our carriage, following it all the way back to the Yama house.

"I escaped that night, dressed like a beggar, my clothes in a bag. No one paid me any mind and I saw nothing of Akaky. This became my refuge, a shabby room with two other whores; nights I've always had company, but now they've fled. Now I'm trapped in this pestilent hole. I must go out to work, to protect myself, but to go out is to invite Akaky to find me. I drink vodka and hope it will kill me, but it's too weak. All it can do is keep me from dreaming. He'll find me in my dreams. He'll get inside me again." She shivered. "Safety, I learned long ago, is an illusion. None of us are safe. All Moscow isn't big enough to hide me. He'll find me. The filth here feeds a million rats."

Zarubkin thought of the creatures outside in Khitrovka Market. He recalled the hideous dwarf where the sausage had been cooking. Dwarf! He sat up.

In the street something exploded. The lopsided square of the window lit up and the shutters rattled. Zarubkin jumped from the bed. Screams echoed from below, reports of gunfire. "What's going on?" he cried. He pressed against the glass. A few vague, scurrying silhouettes were all he could glimpse. Then came the rumbling that became hooves clopping on cobbles. Many horses. He could imagine them, the cavalry, like a wave. Shots sounded in a volley, a string of sound; and when that echo died down, it revealed a growing chant: *"Bei zhidov! Bei zhidov!"*

Zarubkin hurried to the bed and pulled on his trousers. He leaned back toward the window. Lizaveta sat up as if spellbound by the chanting. "The Jews," she said. Last night the whores, tonight the Jews. Here in Khitrovka lived all the usurers to whom so many of the soldiers owed money. The city, devolving into chaos, would take her captain from her. "No!" she cried. "You can't go, you promised to stay!" She stretched and grabbed his arm to make him look at her.

Footsteps pounded in the hall. Doors slammed open or closed. Zarubkin drew his pistol. A voice shouted his name—it was Vanya—and he answered, "Here!" by reflex, wishing even as he called out that he had kept silent. Lizaveta's hand slid away and he could not meet her gaze.

The door burst open to the whirlwind Vanya, his pistol also drawn. His wide eyes gleamed in the low light from the oil lamp;

he looked to Zarubkin like a lost child. "It's a pogrom, Sergei! Come on, they're shooting Jews tonight. It's worse than ever." He glanced at Lizaveta with embarrassment. "Gladykin's already out there, 'for target practice,' he said."

Zarubkin had known Gladykin for over a year—how had he tolerated the cruelty of the fellow for so long? Lizaveta rose, naked, from the bed suddenly and charged at Vanya. "You!" she shouted at him. "Here's a Jewess for you. Start with me."

Vanya's mouth hung open.

"Don't," Zarubkin protested in confusion.

"Here, you foul pig, here's all you could possibly want, both a whore and a Jew, one shot gets you double your prize. Where's your guts, oaf?"

Zarubkin said, "Lizaveta," harshly. She ignored him, closing on Vanya, who was trapped confusedly between two cogent thoughts and could not even move. She took his hand, caressing his wrist, the butt of his gun. "Help me with it," she implored him. A moment later the gun fired. It lit up the room for an instant like a sputtering candle. Lizaveta stumbled away from the horrified Vanya. Zarubkin caught her in his arms. Her head slid along his shoulder, into the crook of his elbow. "What did you do?" Her blood darkened his hand. "Why?"

She looked up at him and said, "Vodka's too slow." Her whole weight suddenly sagged against him.

"But—my God, Sergei, *she* did it," Vanya was stammering. This was worse than the deaths of anonymous peasants, this was a woman with a face and a name.

"Yes, Vanya, I know, I know." Zarubkin laid the body on the bed. He knelt beside her and held her hand. "God forgive her this terrible sin," he said finally. "Give her peace."

Outside more shots and cries resounded. The chant bounced from building to building, a cannonade. The air in the room seemed to stir around Zarubkin and he lifted his head. A cool draft brushed his cheek, then passed across the other. It breathed his name. He could barely believe what he understood then. She was with him still. Behind her presence, however, he could feel the smaller one pressing in. She clung to him for a moment, as she had in life. Then he lost the sense of her. He wanted to reach and bring her back. Sadly, he glanced at Vanya. The hairs on his neck crept up.

Vanya's mouth was turned down in a bitter scowl. The gleam in his eyes was no longer that of a scared child. It had become a feverish shine of the most intense hatred Zarubkin had ever seen. Vanya saw him watching and the scowl flattened smugly. Zarubkin had seen that face before. For a moment the pistol wavered in his direction before Vanya reholstered it. Jerkily, he turned away and walked out of the room, leaving the door open.

"Vanya!" Zarubkin cried. A shriek from down the hall answered him. Hastily, he grabbed up the rest of his uniform and charged out. In Khitrovka Market, the horror had barely begun. Bullets filled the air like flies.

Afterword

Lizaveta

Many of the details in this story came from a Harrison Salisbury book on Russia, *Black Night, White Snow*—a wonderful book. I was reading it for pleasure. I had no intention of writing a story because of it, but that's often how things get started. You find the most interesting things when you aren't looking.

This points to another maxim of mine (and of Jack Dann's) that I urge on workshop students. If you're in a bookstore (most likely a seedy, second-hand shop of dubious character) and you find a book that seems to want you to buy it but not for any reason you can fathom, you must buy that book. Later, the need for it will show up. Trust me on this.

In the Sunken Museum

"Yet his stories contain no mystery greater than the one surrounding his untimely death. The fact that he took with him his host's walking stick rather than his own, and that he got on the wrong train for Philadelphia but arrived in Baltimore—these suggest that he was ill or feverish. But even a protracted attack of his disabling headaches does not account for the missing five days before he *was* discovered on the streets of Baltimore. Nor is there any solution to the puzzle of the name he cried out as he died—a name with no known referent in his life. There can be no doubt that the occurrences which befell Edgar Poe during the few days prior to his death will never be known to us. . . ."

Stephen Wyralski, *The Gallows Poe*

HIS EYES OPEN SLOWLY TO TOTAL DARKNESS. THE lids are swollen from fatigue and from a feverous illness that threatens to consume him. Behind his left eyeball is a headache he has endured for weeks.

(Where is this? It cannot be the train to Philadelphia, there is no motion, no noise, have we stopped? But there is no light, it's like a tomb . . .)

The terror of premature interment has haunted him throughout his life. He feels the tickle of sweat on his mustache, attempts to brush it away, but his arms are numb as though he had slept on them. Panic spins in his head, shreds his thoughts; he would kick and claw out of this blackness if only he could move his arms and legs; but, paralyzed, he is incapable of exploiting the surge of adrenaline. The itch of the sweat on his lip is driving him mad. He finds then that he can move his mouth; pushes out his lower lip, huffs and huffs at the irritant mustache, until the sweat blows away. He discovers that his back is arched and that the dullest of sensations has returned to his feet. He begins to feel again. This comforts him and he relaxes.

All he knows is that he is lying on his back on a comfortable, somehow buoyant, surface. Yet, when the lights come up moments later, a scene appears before him that suggests he is defying gravity, standing on his feet. Vertigo whirls him, the contents of his stomach push into his throat, and he looks away from the flickering scene with its clustered figures too quickly to assimilate it. With gritted teeth he represses the surging knot at his throat, though this task swells his headache till it bulges against his eye. He lowers his head, sucking cool, cool breath.

He finds that his coat has been removed and his shirt replaced by a thin shirt of some kind of gauzy material. Despite its thinness, he is hot. Both hands are folded across his chest in imitation of death—

(*They thought, they thought I was dead, beaten? Robbed? Buried, would have been buried, would have been—calm now, be calm, you're alive, yes, yes, alive.*)

—clutching a stick, a walking stick. He can see only the bossed knob—a ring of silver around a black circle in the center of which has been pen-knifed the name CARTER.

(*Carter, Carter, Doctor Carter from Richmond?*)

His hands are tingling now and he can feel his legs to the knees. He watches his left foot move and is comforted by it somewhat. Blinking from sweat, he attempts to confront the bright and seemingly motionless scene again. Squints in preparation, then raises his head, then wishes he hadn't.

The scene is grotesque, culled from a nightmare. A sickly, malignant yellow light is cast by hundreds of misshapen candles spitting hissing animal fat flames. The candles are high up on dozens of circular chandeliers hung from chains that vanish above, where there is no sign of a ceiling. Wax plops onto robed figures who seem oblivious to it, figures who have remained motionless since he began to watch. They are gathered close together, facing away from him, intent on some central object. He thinks he hears, above the candles' sibilance, a hiss of a different kind as of something whipping through the air.

He flutters his hands until the tingling dies away, then pushes away from the surface at his back—

(How can I be standing when I know I'm lying down?)

—takes a first hesitant step, like the first step into Hell, moving slowly, delicately forward. Some enormous machine groans, shaking the floor, and he halts, poised like prey ready to run. He hears squealing, glances down, and sees enormous rats weaving between the legs of the frozen figures. The rats skitter as he draws near.

He stretches on his toes to see over the shoulders of the robes, but they are too tall. He risks reaching out, shoves gently at the two in front of him. They turn away easily, allowing him to slip between them, ignoring him as they ignore the rats. There are three rows of these robed figures. The two at the back close up behind him and he is trapped among them, panicked by closing claustrophobia. Now sweat pours out all over him; he fights through the second row, kicking at the rats that scuttle over his boot. The swishing sound is much louder, and something black and enormous moves steadily in the dimness just ahead.

He glances at the face beside him. It is shadowed by the cowl, a thin face, eaten by disease. The eyes, though narrowed, burn like those of the rats below, tiny jewels blinking at him from the floor. He cries out and shoves through the last row.

The object of their rapt attention is a stone altar. He stands at the foot of it—watching. A single victim is strapped there, head back, neck muscles locked. He rocks desperately from side to side to break the belt across his waist. He wears a coarse parody of the robes around him. A shiny black crescent swings ponderously back and forth, lowering insidiously notch by notch with each pass over the victim's body. It's scant inches above him.

"No!" the watcher shouts, and the victim raises his head to see who has yelled, and the watcher sees himself strapped there, sees the madness of the certainty of death on his own tortured face, and howls with terror. He looks frantically about the scene, sees one robed figure to the side, working a lever. He charges at that figure, who makes no attempt to defend his position. He swats the robed man aside with his stick and pulls the lever back even as the blade splits the first few threads of the coarse gown the victim wears.

Victim and watcher gibber out of control, weeping the same sounds simultaneously.

The watcher drops to his knees, suddenly overcome by his

fever. He vomits up air, then cries out, praying: "God, tell me I'm not in Hell!"—though that is precisely where he knows he is. He crawls toward his shackled double, certain that he must save that figure in order to save himself, not knowing why that should be or why he believes it, not caring, only crawling. His stomach heaves with every movement. He hears footsteps running as if down a mile of stairs, nearer, louder, like the fist pounding behind his eye. He reaches up blindly to unlace the belt but his heavy arm slides away and he falls face down onto the floor, stretched out beside his twin.

When his eyes open, he is again on his back. His head rests on its cheek. He can see beside him a thin line of crimson ruffles between black lapels of a coat, the ruffles shadowed strangely from lighting set below. Painstakingly, he raises his eyes. The red ruffles lead up to a collar open at the throat, this space filled with a golden cravat. Above the shiny gold is a face that is proud, with a stiff jaw, cleft chin, wide friendly mouth, fleshy nose, dark eyes and brows, and a high forehead. The face is smiling, delighted. The coat smells of ghastly French perfume.

Can the Devil look like this? he wonders.

"Who are you?" he asks.

"My name is Reynolds, Mr. Poe. I've given you something for your fever—sorry I failed to do that earlier—and a sedative."

Poe's deep–set gray eyes blink in incomprehension. "Sedative?"

"Sleeping draught."

Poe closes his eyes, feeling the sweat oily on the lids. "Ah, that explains it. The dreams," he says softly, "the horrible dreams I have had. My own words came down to haunt me. Never happened before." He glances again at the proud face lighted so sinisterly from below. "Tell me, Mr. . . . Reynolds . . . am I in Philadelphia?"

"No, sir. You are in Baltimore."

He raises his head. "But I was on the train for Philadelphia! I had already left Baltimore!"

"Yes, of course. But in your fever I presume, you mistakenly caught the train back to Baltimore."

Poe sinks back into the cushion. After a period of deliberation he says: "Then, be so good as to take a letter for me and post it to Mother . . . to my dear . . . Muddy." Reynolds's hand has passed over his head, and in his last moments of consciousness, Poe follows it, seeing for the first time a hairline of silver in the darkness behind Reynolds's head, which can be nothing other than the pendulum itself, and a splinter of terror accompanies him into dreamless sleep.

When Poe awakens, Reynolds is standing in precisely the same position and place. Watchful, imperturbable, so kindly of visage it would be impossible to dislike him, Reynolds exudes trust.

Poe remains doubtful, however, uncertain of the border of reality as he searches in vain for the blade in the darkness above. Nothing is visible there. He refuses to accept the offered assurance in Reynolds's eyes, but says nothing.

(He will think me mad.)

He feels cooler, realizes his fever has broken, and that he seems full as if he had feasted while asleep. And, amazingly, his incessant headache is gone!

"I—I am recovered."

"Yes."

He sits up gingerly, but finds himself feeling vigorous, healthy. "For whatever you have given me, for whatever you've done to aid me, I cannot sufficiently thank you. I am in your debt more than you can know, but I am penniless to repay you. You see, even my coat has been stripped from me, no doubt by villains. My memories are so vague—there are periods when I recall nothing, when I stumble like a madman through the streets, so I am told. Because of my illness. That I have managed to retain this stick of Carter's is miraculous. Again, my thanks upon my rescue, sir."

"Think nothing of it." Reynolds pats him on the shoulder.

"My first thoughts were that I was dead and had been buried. You have no windows."

"Not here, no. But you are hardly dead, Mr. Poe."

"Yes," he agrees and, feeling so much better, cannot help but add one of his habitual mendacious asides. "However, I have been in many countries, sir, including Russia, and nowhere have I seen a place as dark and impenetrable as this." He pauses as if thoughtfully, then adds for effect, "With the possible exception of the Antarctic in summer. Nonetheless, you and I can see one another perfectly. So it comes I must ask you just where it is that I am."

Reynolds claps his hands, cries, "Marvelous!" Laughs. "Of course you want to know. But, please, come with me and let me explain while you see."

"See what, Mr. Reynolds?" His expression hardens. "Is my old rival, Griswold, responsible for my situation? Yes, I believe he is. Only he would be so bold as to—"

"Griswold is dead, Mr. Poe."

He gapes. "What?"

"Please, come with me"—he offers his hand—"and all will be explained."

(I do not care to trust you, yet I must appear to if I am to discover the explanation for this place, what it is and where in Baltimore. There must be a simple solution such as a deep cellar or moonless night, but where then are the windows? Griswold dead, too, dear God.)

He allows Reynolds to help him stand, then follows as the tall man leads. He discovers that the floor, which he could not see while on his back, is the source of the sinister light. A ring around his unusual bed is composed of panels in the shape of stone tiles, but seemingly made of stained glass. Reynolds steps forward and a trail of these colorful gems ignites, extending as far ahead as he can see. He is quite taken with the idea of lamps beneath a glass floor, a twinkling path like stars in the darkness. What a unique effect it conveys upon their features, which seemingly change color with every stride; on either side of the path, the darkness is impenetrable, and reminds him of bottomless chasms. A tiny knot of terror clenches in his stomach, but he turns all of his attention to the trail, concentrating on the sequence of colors, fighting against the frightening conjectures; he wants to understand the truth of this place and concentrates on the more hopeful explanations. The mounting misgivings of his reverie are interrupted as Reynolds begins to speak.

"I am a student of your work. You may not have realized there were such people. Nevertheless, I have read every word you have ever written. I have, in fact, dedicated myself to erecting replicas of your work. I have chosen scenes, poems, tales, sometimes combining them, and modeled them into representations." He grins.

"I am speechless, sir. I don't know what to say." That someone would construct a wax museum in his honor is astonishing. He relaxes, wondering if this accounts for the lack of light—for, surely, sunlight, heat, would melt the wax figures. They must be protected. And a museum dedicated to him is proof of his rightness. Who else could make such claims? Not Hawthorne or Cooper. A museum of his own! And in Baltimore! "A museum," he says quietly, but with a pride so immense it has erased even his memory of being afraid.

Reynolds latches onto the word. "Yes! A museum!"

"And you've peopled it with your own reproductions—"

"Of your work, yes."

He dwells upon the scene he witnessed earlier, depicting "The Pit and the Pendulum."

(It was not a dream!)

Admittedly, it was lifelike, incredibly so. The man, he tells himself, is a genius in wax. Wax also accounts for the apparent intentness of the robed figures and why he was ignored. Of course. But the victim had been himself. And it had moved! Hadn't it? Or had that been illusion?

(Madness, fever.)

He asks about this.

Reynolds replies: "Of course it seemed lifelike. That is the illusion I strive for, and it was, indeed, your face. You were the narrator, your voice was the story, so who better to represent you than . . . you?"

Poe blanches. The thought of his double turning up as the victim in each exhibit is unsettling. He is unsure as to just how much of that he cares to see.

"Let me show you something," Reynolds says, as amiable as ever. He leads the way more quickly, bobbing with each step on the tiles. The clump of footsteps resounds from unseen walls and ceilings; the echoes sound cavernous. Poe reflects on the areas of Baltimore he knows and tries to place a building of this size. Then he recalls the train ride from Richmond, but that memory is ebbing, as vague as the recollection of a former life. He looks again at Reynolds, wonders who this man can be. He has known a good many of the wealthy, the elite. This place would take money to build. Yet, he has never heard of Reynolds. The realization is a discomfiting one.

"Beyond this building—" he begins.

Reynolds, as if finishing his thought, says, "Is a city, yes. There." He grabs Poe's arm and turns him.

Poe gasps into the palms of his hands.

A few feet before him is greenish water glowing like liquid fire, and he seems to stand behind an enormous aquarium partition. The light that kindles the water comes from clustered phosphorescent buildings that squat on the murky ocean bottom; twisted spires thrust between domes; frescoed walls are hidden behind thick vines. The windows in the structure are comparatively dark; but, as he watches, a light appears in one of them, then moves on, carried by some unseen hand.

He draws closer, peering.

A fish swims lazily before him. He reaches out his hand to

touch the glass. There is no glass! And his hand comes back dripping, smelling of brine. His eyes plead to Reynolds, who pulls him back with a casual reply, "Done with mirrors, don't you know?"

He thinks: *(No, I don't know, I don't believe.)*

"You know this place, don't you?"

He looks again at the towers, though without turning his head, without facing it. " 'The Drowned City,' " he answers, horror-struck. He flicks water from his fingertips. "I know it as I know myself."

"Well said, sir," his guide answers, shaking his head, marveling at his own creation. Obviously, his guest is supposed to do likewise. He recites:

" 'Lo! Death has reared himself a throne
In a strange city lying alone
Far down within the dim west
Where the good and the bad and the worst and the best
Have gone to their eternal rest.'
A marvelous verse, sir."

The words attempt to inveigle him; praise has swayed him all his life. Advocates of his work have never been evil, for how could a villain see Truth so well?

But not this time; not this one.

Poe presents a favorable attitude, makes his voice sound joyous. "You have created a wonderful work here, capturing every detail just as I saw it."

(Escape.)

"I had hoped you would come to feel that way, especially after the first scene, which was an enormous error on my part. I had no idea how ill you were, that you would see it as a nightmare, and again I sincerely apologize, Mr. Poe."

"Think nothing of it. The honor you do me here is quite enough recompense."

(How in God's name do I get out?)

Reynolds bows. "There is so much more for you to see."

Poe drops the sham of delight. The additional delay suggested is out of the question. It is important he try to make Reynolds aware of that, despite the risk of offending the man. Warily, he adds, "That is most wonderful." He rubs at his eyelid; the headache, like a hornet, seems to have reclaimed its nest. Ignoring it, he continues, "But, sir, you must understand I have vital appointments in New York. Already, I am days late, no doubt. If you know anything about me, you know how much I want to begin my magazine. And

it has come true. I will have *The Stylus* if I carry through with my
meetings.

"I could return at some future time, of course. To spend a week
here with you. I will advertise your museum for you, let the world
hear about you. They will come in droves and your fame might
well match mine. But I beg you, sir, to let me go!" He watches
attentively for a shift in expression that will reveal the answer, but
Reynolds's face still smiles.

"Nonsense," he says. "I can assure you that you have lost no
time, that not a solitary day will go by while you are here."

Cold sweat beads on Poe's brow, his mouth is drily clogged, as
with paste, his tongue thick. Nausea floods into him again as the
medicine starts to wear off; but he cannot afford to falter now.
"How is that possible? I must be three days late as it is. How can
you say that?"

Reynolds opens his mouth as if to reply but closes it without a
word, as if recognizing that any explanation would be impossible.
Then he laughs and says: "What are a few days to men like you or
me?" He laughs again.

"Then I am your prisoner until such time as you see fit to
release me!" Sweat trickles on his temple. He wipes it away, brushing his hand against his hair. It is matted; he hates being dirty. He
shakes his head gently to clear his thoughts.

"No!" Reynolds shouts, aghast. "I would never dream of such a
thing. Would a host ask a prisoner to dine with him? Would he be
held in a prison designed for his own introspection?"

Poe studies the guileless face.

*(Yes, that is precisely the case when the host is a madman who
thinks time outside has stopped for him. I'm your prisoner because I
understand nothing here, your questions are lies and your answers
say nothing, only confuse me.)*

He says, "I would be delighted to dine with you, but my fever
and sickness are back." It is hardly a lie.

His host waves it off. "I can give you something for your fever
again."

Hesitantly, "Very well. I thank you for that. But I am also tired,
and would prefer to rest first."

"Of course." And he leads the way back along the trail of
gems hanging motionless in space where no stars sparkle. This
place, Poe is certain, can only be underground. There is no place
in Baltimore so gargantuan that it could hold this museum of
unnatural art. He will regain his strength through sleep just as he

did before, and then, somehow, escape. Even if it means clawing his way through sheer rock with his bare hands. He perceives now that the magnanimity his host has shown is that of a lunatic. These tableaux are supremely wrought, but all with that overpowering vision of a lunatic's reality. To Poe they are more horrible than the demented dissection of a cat's eye—a ghastly image from childhood that haunts him.

Trembling, he lies back on the flat, yielding bier, frightened nearly to tears, but fighting to remain outwardly composed. His host must not catch wind of this plan.

Then Reynolds passes something over Poe's head, and he retreats to where the ubiquitous darkness drapes over all his troubles.

His own voice calling for Virginia, his late wife, awakens him. He lies still, seeing her face from the dream; yearns for her. Later, he listens for some sound to suggest that Reynolds is returning, has heard him, knows he is awake. There is no sound beyond the tubercular wheeze of his own breath, still racing from the dream.

His vision rises through the supposed Earth's crust, into the daylight that must be above him—city streets where, even now, people search the alleys and taverns, expending every effort to find the ragged or the drunken Edgar Allan Poe. They might even have come to Reynolds's mansion while he slept. Mansion, he realizes, is a presumption on his part that on the surface is a facade—a structure with windows and curtains and drawing rooms—the falseness of which no person could detect. The thought of such a house redoubles his notion of captivity, ignoring the fact that the structure lives only in his mind. At the moment, his mind is the single reality he can trust.

(*Escape.*)

He sits up quickly. Somewhere there must be stairs, a way out if only he can locate it. The problem is where to look.

Carter's Malacca stick is leaning against his bed, and he picks it up as he slides down onto his feet, pressure lighting the tiles.

(*Which way?*)

A pathway lights, stretching out to a false horizon, as he steps forward and vanishes when he moves on in a circle round his bed. A second one lights, then a third. Completing the circle, he has found eight paths that lead away like the dew-beaded threads of a web.

"Mr. Poe."

He falls stricken against the altar. Reynolds stands beside him, holding a small device that looks like some bizarre, chamberless pistol. It points loosely at his chest. Yet, Reynolds's fixed smile still exudes charm and compassion. Poe is now certain that this is the smile of madness. He grips the cane tighter and raises it defensively.

With heavy disappointment, Reynolds says, "Mr. Poe, you surprise me. This is no weapon." His thumb snaps back the hammer. "It's for your fever. It will alleviate your illness again."

Poe swings the cane against Reynolds's wrist, but falls forward from the force behind the blow. The gun flies into the darkness, clatters somewhere. Reynolds's wrist dangles, broken. Still he smiles. Poe scrambles to gather up the cane, stumbles onto a lighted path, taking it, blind, hoping that it will somehow lead him from the nightmare.

"Mr. Poe! Mr. Poe!"

(Mr. Poe.)

Running, running, aware that the lighted path is nothing other than his own rainbowed spoor, he turns to the darkness, praying to God there is a floor out there.

Soon he has crossed three paths. A corridor flares up before him, a long thin hallway with brick walls and a smoking, burning brazier. The solidity of walls, ceiling, and floor comforts him. The cries of pursuit—

(Mr. Poe!)

—are gone. Only the flutter of the bluish flame is audible. He creeps stealthily into the lighted hallway. The smoke is pungent, and he coughs.

Reaching a bend in the corridor, he discovers, set in the wall on his left, a large, slender blue-stained glass window. Directly opposite it stands another brazier. Poe watches his shadow shrink as he nears the glass. Cupping his hand around his eyes, he peers through the lead-limned plates.

On the other side is a room—an apartment—with polished wood furnishings, gold ornaments dangling from the ceiling, tapestries, carpet, portraits, flagons, and creatures—parodies of human form, some covered in fur, others in feathers, a grotesque gamut of faces, animal travesties. He realizes then with relief that it is a masquerade. More people enter the chamber every moment, there must be hundreds. "Real people," he hears himself say. They are not wax! It is no dream, no fantasy. They move.

He forces himself to leave the window and continue along the corridor, which turns every ten steps, each turn presenting a different window, a different color, the scheme of tiny, leaded panels giving view to another chamber. After the second one, the purple one, he knows where they lead, where he is going, and though he wants to pull away, to retreat the way he has come, the situation is as it was with the Drowned City; he is helpless to resist.

The last window is red: The chamber within is black, and every detail is smothered in a hellish glow. There is the black clock rising out of view; there, the people standing in the doorway, afraid to enter this ghastly travesty of a tomb; there, a tall figure wrapped in a shroud, its cadaverous mask mottled with drops of blood, empty of eyes. Suddenly, the figure turns toward him; the Red Death stalks him through the glass.

The clock strikes once; a tremor runs across the floor, travels up his legs. Dust sprinkles from the ceiling.

He flees up the corridor as the clock strikes again, into darkness as the hollow, dismal note rings again, followed ineluctably by another, on, on, on, changing pitch subtly until it is the reverberating peal of bells, Bells, *Bells*, clapping at his ears, inescapably near, beating in time with his heart.

A rainbow path flashes as he runs across a stone. He stumbles and falls across the top of a flight of stairs. The bells stop.

Scraping, slow footsteps approach. He huddles beside an oaken banister. Out of the darkness a figure with lustrous eyes appears, searching, unaware of his presence, the face scarred by more grief than he has ever seen on one face. The tissue cheeks are collapsed in against the bones. The thin lips quiver, part.

"Madman!" The figure clasps his hands to his ears against his own voice. He removes them only a few inches, fingers spread. "Now hear it?" he asks. As Poe watches, his own double appears again, this time dressed in his usual black habiliments; the double takes the other's arm with care and leads him through an open doorway. The door swings closed.

A moment later he hears a somber voice—Roderick Usher's voice, and yet his own!—begin to read from the "Mad Trist." He flees, leaps the last of the stairs, out of Usher's sinking House and into black limbo.

Sparks of color dance in his eyes. He coughs up something thick from his lungs, spits it out. His head seems light, cloudy, but so very hot.

Another chamber suddenly appears around him, but this one is more ghoulish than any he has entered before. It is a vault. The walls carry inscriptions on plaques behind which, he infers, are the corpses that match the names.

He arrives at the end of the vault.

The plaque reads: MADELAINE. Even as he comprehends it he grows aware of faint scraping sounds, slithering, icy, clutching at his backbone. His body shakes like a hooked fish and he falls against a wall. The scraping is louder. He envisions fingernails digging in death's darkness, and he tilts back his head, eyes bulging, his mustache outlining the scream to come.

The plaque falls and shatters on the floor. Above it, two bricks vanish into the wall, and a set of bloodied, shredded fingers curls over the edge of the hole. Light glints from a single, milky eyeball.

"Roderick," calls the husky voice of the tomb.

He shrieks, runs, plunging away from it all.

"Reynolds! Please, Reynolds, stop this! This is the desolation of my *soul!*" His cries are unanswered. He runs on.

A vague figure looms from out the darkness. He runs toward it. "Reynolds," he sobs, chokes back the last sob. Stopped. He falls slowly to his knees. A few feet in front of him is a woman. She is tall, wrapped in bandages which, even as he scrambles back, biting his hand to keep from screaming, she begins to unravel: from her mouth; from her hair falling thick and glossy black, below her shoulders. Her large eyes open.

"No!" he cries. "No!" and rolls back, his stomach heaving. His head wants to explode. She walks purposefully after him.

She is Ligeia. But she resembles no one in Poe's life so much as his dead and cherished wife, Virginia. His fever alters any differences in her appearance; she is his wife. The frail shell of his sanity slides like the House into the Tarn.

Running is a reflex of panic; figures, rooms, ghosts assail him, but he stops for none of them, responds to none of them. He wants out, only out.

He comes upon a door that's nothing he has ever envisioned— a wide, gleaming door of glass. But there is no handle. He pushes against it; it is immovable. He has no idea how to get through, and he knows, somehow, that he must.

"You mustn't go there," a voice calls.

He recognizes Reynolds moving out of the dimness between paths, and immediately he backs away, raises the stick.

"You could not stand it," the host continues, unmoved. Poe sees the hand he had broken with the stick, sees that it is no longer broken; his lips draw back from his teeth and he stares sidelong like a rabid wolf. "Poe, you should not have run. It was wrong." Reynolds's tone is that of a regretful father speaking to his child. "I'm so sorry, so utterly sorry. Others have come here and enjoyed it. But I didn't know you were ill. No one did for certain. There is no one to blame but myself for this." And that kindly smile goes on forever.

Such kindness is lost on Poe; the sympathy conveyed is buried beneath the jarring beat of his headache. Pink foam bubbles in one corner of his mouth. He screams in pain and rage. Reynolds is taller, heavier, but Poe grabs him and hurls him at the door, smashes Reynolds's head into it again and again with frenzied strength. One side of the proud face cracks, a slice of it flips up, falls onto the glowing tiles, and rocks there like a gutted clamshell. Poe continues to batter Reynolds against the door until the clear wall flexes and shatters. Only then does he release Reynolds and see the destruction he has caused in that proud face. No blood. The wound is razor sharp, a gash in the hollow of the cheek the size of his palm. Within it is a crosswork of woven fiber.

No blood.

Poe squeezes tears of agony and confusion from his eyes. Reynolds says, "Mr. Poe," in a syrupy slow voice.

Poe turns and leaps headlong through the shattered door. As he rolls, dazed, his arm is cut by a jagged shard. A ramp suddenly illuminates, a glowing maroon ramp that leads upward. Someone calls out from behind him. He runs, crying with joy, sucking in hoarse, ripping breaths, pleading to God to save him. The ramp seems to go on as far as heaven. Up, up, until he reaches a plateau and another door. It is solid metal, and hums to life as he touches it. He cowers. It rolls back, buzzing, to let him escape.

He's outside before he comprehends the landscape.

Black trees, bent from the weight of swollen, cystic leaves, surround him and dance in an acid breeze. No grass, but rotted, eroded, gray ground, smelling of centuries of decay.

The sky is red behind brown clouds. The hazy sun hangs like a dead eye. He coughs and closes his hand over his mouth, beginning to choke. A thin trickle of blood escapes between his fingers.

(Hell it is Hell after all like no Hell ever seen, I am doomed by God to live in my own nightmares, and soon they'll come to take me back to my own mind, oh, Virginia, it is! It is! The Haunted Palace is Hell!)

He sees down an embankment a large valley that has once held water but is now dry. Thick smoke rises from it. He cannot run there.

In the other direction, through tears, he beholds twisted towers, some as high as mountains, their surfaces like the scales of serpents—stiff snakes twined against the bloody sky. Small lumpy shapes move on the ground there, and he shudders at seeing them, knows no safety there either. He whirls around. The building he has escaped is a black mound with a small black cupola at the top, glossy, shining, a clean, polished anomaly. He vomits pink foam, leans against one of the spongy trees. The leaves above him spill a thick, yellow fluid on his shoulder. He screams and flings himself away, toward the building, then stops, skids, and falls back.

In the doorway Reynolds stands motionless, his dull smile, as though painted on, curves up to the jagged hole in his cheek. Beside him, moving forward, is a short gargoyle figure. Its flesh is gray and leathery, its torso hangs in doughy folds, flopping like a clotted skirt, just above the ground. It is the image of the creatures Poe has seen below the towers. The feet are in shadow; the arms are short, reedy, fingers grossly extended. And the face—

(The face!)

—is a lump on its neckless shoulders. The eyes are jelly, the nose a single vertical vent, the lips purple and crumpled in an uncordial crescent.

Reynolds, he now perceives, is his only hope for salvation from this purgatory. He would plead and prostrate himself, he would beg his host to take him home, to take him away, to save him, to explain, just to explain!

But the swollen gray monster moves between them with alarming ease, and Poe dares not step forward. "Reynolds!" he shrieks. "Reynolds!"

His host remains seemingly ignorant of him, staring blankly ahead, smiling as before.

The monster moves closer. Poe scrabbles to the crest of the hill. "Reynolds!"

The large purple lips part, and the monster speaks—a raw, bubbling voice not meant for English speech, but conveying a tone of detached annoyance and, somehow, in some vague way, reminiscent of Reynolds's voice. "He does not hear you, Poe. I've shut him off."

"What?!" His head begins to shake, as from chills.

"He's only a mechanism, voice-activated. Oh, stop it!" One of the hands raises, fingers curled, looking like some kind of hide-covered claw. The creature snarls. "I have brought you all this far forward, gone to incalculable expense and trouble to learn your language, build your monument—for you—all for you—and you refuse to take solace. You have not entertained me at all! You are the only—"

"Reynolds!"

"Poe, I am your host. I brought you here from out of your sleeping compartment. You saw Reynolds because you could not have stood the sight of me. Could you? Can you?" The creature appears to have expanded.

Poe's mind spins, dazzled, tumbled, and the creature's words are no more distinguishable than the horrendous roar of breakers on rocks. But he fights off the weight of the fever, refuses to be dragged into unconsciousness; he clamps his hands over his ears as if this will shut out the roar, and shouts, "What are you? Where am I?"

"There is little point in explaining further. You cannot be expected to comprehend the differences in the world eight thousand years have made. You weren't supposed to see it!" The gray face darkens to the color of its lips.

Poe stares blankly. The stick drops from his hand.

(*Is this a man? God, oh God no! How can these things be? That a city and this museum of abominations and he calls me his entertainment?! No no no no, the Bells the Bells, hear it! I grabbed the poor beast by the throat—*)

His hands in loose fists pound at the sides of his head. He falls to his knees. The cane of Doctor Carter lies before him, tangled in threads of mist.

(*—and deliberately cut one of its eyes from the socket, oh the bells, the bells the bells . . .*)

The gray bulk turns. "Reynolds!" it burbles, hawks, and spits out a wad of brown syrup.

Poe's fingers caress the knob of the walking stick. He is not aware of himself rising to his feet.

"Reynolds! Come and collect Mr. Poe."

The stick smashes down upon the back of the lumpy, gray head. Again. Again, Poe batters out the soft brains, breaks the eyeballs like egg yolks that ooze down the face, caves in the ridge around the single nostril, spatters blood from the lips before Reynolds can rip the frail, dying madman off of his bloated, dead host. Reynolds takes away Poe's stick with an ungraceful tug.

Poe looks up at the proud, cracked face. "Reynolds?" he says timidly, like a child. His fist is balled around the tail of Reynolds's coat.

"Yes—yes, Mr. Poe. Ple-please come with me." Reynolds's speech has become flat and disjointed. "It's time I sent you back home. I am . . . really very, very sorry. It's never happened before."

Poe, not listening, looks back at the corpse as Reynolds leads the way into the black mound. Poe tags after, his eyes idiot and childlike, his mind running free through unconnected verse.

(The play is the tragedy man and its hero the conqueror worm, the conqueror worm the conqueror worm . . .)

They shamble, the manic and the mechanism, down a sparkling trail of gems. The colored specks wink out behind them, until the museum is reinstated in its shroud of gloom evermore.

Afterword

In the Sunken Museum

This was my first sale.

You go along writing and submitting fiction for years, and collecting rejection slip after rejection slip. It's terribly frustrating. You keep trying to figure out what is missing, what's wrong, what you should be doing differently in the stories. Then one day you sell one, and you sit back and look at it and ask yourself, "What the heck did I do here that I wasn't doing before?" To this day I still don't know. But some sort of threshold had been crossed, and once this one had sold, I started selling more and more of what I wrote.

As for the story itself, I love Poe, and I loved that there was a mystery at the end of his life that had never been solved. Now there's a pretty fair theory about what happened to him, but I'm not going to tell you what it is though it's probably true. Mine's more fun.

Touring Jesusworld

DR. HANI FOUND ME STANDING AT THE ENTRANCE to his theme park. Piled in front of me, carved from mammoth stones that would have pleased C. B. DeMille, was the fifty-foot park sign, proclaiming for all to see: JESUSWORLD. A crane was at work moving the blocks, although I couldn't see why. They seemed just right to me.

All around the twenty-foot high walls lay desert hills, outcroppings of rock—a landscape as forbidding as you could want.

Hani was a small, wiry man dressed in an ivory linen suit. Such clothing always looks as if the wearer has slept in it—in Hani's case, for days. He extended his hand in welcome and said, "Please, drop the 'Doctor,' it's just plain old Hani the Circle Drawer here."

"Circle Drawer?"

He had heavy-lidded eyes, which he now closed as at some tired joke. "It's an ancient joke that one of the staff hung on me. Hani was a messiah—a *nabi*, a wise man—who predated Yeshu."

I'd made a twenty-hour drive from Cleveland in a car I probably couldn't make the next payment on to get here, and already we were getting our signals crossed. To his credit, Hani recognized this. "Why don't you come around back of the sign and let me take you on an appropriate behind-the-scenes tour. That way I can fill in details for you. Most people, you know, have so little knowledge of the subject on which they place so much hope and dependence."

"Right." I took out my pen and wrote that down, at the same time switching on my buttonhole recorder. I should have done it right away. Hey, twenty hours—I was cooked.

Hani held open an emergency exit door in the "D" of "Jesusworld" and then came up beside me. "Okay, let me get you started, my boy. Even though the park is called 'Jesusworld,' that's mostly to get the public in through the door. If we'd called it the more accurate 'Yeshuworld,' who would make the turn off I-15?" He grinned at the obviousness of that question.

"I see."

"The fact of the matter is this: his contemporary name was Yeshu, which has come down to us, romanized, as Jesus. It was a very common name of the day. There was a Jesus son of Sec, a Jesus son of Gamaliel, and so on. The name is a shortened form of Yehoshua—the Joshua of the Old Testament. Appropriately, it means, 'God Save.' " He stuck his index finger in the air. "Always, you'll note, a Jesus, son of somebody. That's important. Be careful to step over these cables here. Most of them are underground to maintain the air of authenticity."

"Right. So, who is our Jesus the son of?"

"Delighted you asked. This is a point of great speculation. There is a faction that holds he was Yeshu ben Pantera, *ben* meaning son of, Pantera being the name of a Roman Centurion. This was thought to be a total fabrication for a long time until the tombstone of just such a soldier was discovered in Germany. So, it is just possible he was a bastard son of a Roman. That actually is somewhat supported by another faction who say he was called Yeshu ben Miriam—Jesus, son of Mary. You see, sons were always called after their fathers, and if our Yeshu was called ben Miriam it again suggests illegitimacy."

We had been walking for some time behind the various park-building facades. Most were only empty shells, intended to be seen from one side only. I could distinguish the shapes of ziggurats here and there, but mostly from the back the features were unidentifiable. We descended along a rocky slope until Hani raised his hand and glanced back at me. "Now, this is our first stop. This is where the little passenger train comes out and the tour guides meet everyone. We've actually taken a shorter route."

Hani led me around an enormous outcropping of rock that became an overhang beneath which was what looked like three cave entrances. Within the nearest one, a small fire burned. Hay was strewn across the floor and there were some blankets, woven mats that might have been for sleeping. "Mind you, we don't actually hold with this story, which I'll explain in a moment, but this is your manger tale."

"But it's a cave."

"Very incisive of you. It is a cave. The so-called manger of that derived tale would have been like this. We copied these from real caves that probably were used in this manner."

"But you don't hold with them?" I prodded.

"Not really. The 'poor carpenter and family tossed out on their ear' story is unlikely. In the first place, 'carpenter' was the equivalent of 'builder' to us. Do you know any starving builders?"

"Well, no, actually. My brother—"

"Precisely. Most likely, he was a well-to-do kid. Not impoverished at all. Carpentry and rural images run through all his teachings, you know, which indicates he knew how to plant and feed. Only when he got to Jerusalem would he have been regarded as a second-class citizen."

"Why?"

"Well, it was the voice, the accent. He sounded like a hick come to the big town. Jon Voight in *Midnight Cowboy*, that sort of thing."

We walked past the last of the caves and up the hill on the far side while I chewed on that notion—the idea of Jesus the Geek being made fun of by the local toughs. It wasn't too hard to imagine.

Next we descended even further, to the edge of a broad stream. It hooked around a hogback hillside and out of sight, all apparently natural but of course serving Hani's goal of surprise, for when we rounded the bend, the stream broadened into a river. On our side a sandbar hooked out, forming a huge pool. In the center of that pool about twenty naked people stood up to their bellies in the water, their faces turned from us. They were watching a single, bearded figure who stood with his eyes closed, his hands on the head and one shoulder of a dull-looking youth. The bearded man was muttering something, the people hardly moved. Then all at once the baptist shoved the lad underneath the water.

"John the Baptist."

"Jesus' mentor. Many of Jesus' sayings were derived from those of John. He was quite popular—something like five thousand followers, whom Jesus inherited when John was executed."

"Salome?"

"More likely Herod Antipas, who didn't care much for criticism."

I was watching the event in the center of the pool. "He seems to be keeping that kid under for an awfully long time."

Hani's brow furrowed. He watched for a few more seconds, then took out a folding cellular phone and tapped out a code. "Ernie," he said, "get someone to reset John the Baptist's timer, would you? . . . Yes, he's just drowned Jesus." He folded up the phone and slipped it into his pocket.

"They're not real, then."

"Heavens, no. Animatronics. Real actors would be sneezing with pneumonia by the end of the day. However, the crowd is invited to wade in and participate, so getting that timer set is crucial. I should add, the tour guide can stop the performance at any point, so there is no danger."

He turned away while I continued to watch. There were no bubbles coming up. John was still bent to his work. He could keep that kid down for a week. Maybe they had shut him off in order to repair him. I imagined unseen engineers in subterranean vaults beneath the artificial stream. It reminded me too awfully of another park in Florida.

When I looked up, I found Hani ascending the hillside behind us by some mystical force. He beamed at what must have been a look of amazement on my face; no doubt it was the effect he'd hoped for. I strode up below him and saw the real means of his rising. There was an escalator built into the hillside. That made sense, after all—you couldn't ask the public to climb heights such as these. On a really hot day, no one was going to want to walk very far. I said as much.

"Of course," Hani agreed. "And no one will. The temperature here gets to one hundred ten degrees, but the humidity is very low, you hardly notice it. Nevertheless, had we been part of the regular tour, we would have had the option of returning through doors inside the caves back there, traveling on carts through cool, subterranean corridors. There's a refreshment stand and rest rooms, tables to sit at. This journey is for the more adventurous." I had to admit, he seemed to have covered the comfort of his flock. Still, I could see one of his problems right off. He needed to install rides. Where was the sense of fun? Where was the laughing Jesus?

At the top we emerged onto a broad plateau in front of what I can describe only as a true spectacle. A hundred meters away, huge, stone walls stood before us, buttressed randomly, seemingly erected straight up out of the hillside. I could see a few domes and rooftops above the heights, indicating a real city within. It seemed to be the front entrance to an ancient desert city. "Jerusalem?" I guessed.

He nodded vigorously, then leaned closer. He smelled heavily of *Obsession*. He said, "It's really a reproduction of the town of Mar Saba, which is not far from present day Jerusalem, but don't put that in your article. Jerusalem is what it's intended to be, as it might have looked in 15 AD."

"I still have a question about the baptist."

"We'll get him working," he promised.

"No, my question is, why did you devise young Jesus there to look so totally vapid?"

"Ah, well, again, a matter of interpretation. It would seem that John and other *nabi'im* of the time relied heavily on basic hypnotism to transport their followers to ecstatic experiences. The practice was well known even then; there exists written corroboration by the more ancient Egyptians, who apparently practiced it themselves. It is very likely one of the aspects of the art that John would have taught his young apprentice, who in turn taught it to his disciples in order to send them out across the countryside, performing their own cures. I see from your look that you doubt me."

"Not doubt," I replied. "I'm just trying to take all this in. It's not exactly the interpretation of events the church mentions."

"Well, they wouldn't, would they?" He became somber. "Churches are the modern equivalent of the temple that Jesus railed against, and that ultimately crucified him. They have power and political influence. They're full of iconography, never mind that it's Christian in representation—the real Jesus would have loathed it."

We passed through a small doorway in the wall. Within was a vast complex of buildings and streets. Large flagstones the size of human torsos lay beneath our feet—Roman flagstones, according to Hani. We arrived before a pillared building with a vast doorway, surrounded on three sides by crenelated walls, and on the fourth by a large arch, where we stood.

"This is the Temple of Herod as it would have looked then. It's here that he really got into trouble. All of his following, behind a man who entered the city on a donkey during the big feast. That was a real slap in the face at the Sadducean aristocrats who ran the temple. You were supposed to enter on foot, you see. To show up on a *donkey*—well, in the first place it fulfilled an Old Testament prophecy, and that couldn't have sat well. In the second, he was laughing at them. He might as well have dressed a monkey in priest's clothing. To his view, they were defilers of all they believed in—rich priests and their families. Oh, they were the kings of nepotism. Were he alive today, he would no doubt enter Vatican City the same way, and with the same attitude. He would throw out the Pope, I'm quite sure."

"Forgive me, but you seem to have something against the Catholic Church."

Hani shrugged. "Merely its own history of lies, greed, licentiousness, bastardy, defilement, murder, intrigue, and rapine, to name a few items on a still larger list. Where is the truth of their beliefs?"

I stared up past rows of marble benches, to the temple, where animatronic moneylenders sat ready to do business. Were they designed to interact with the public? I could have used a car loan myself. I didn't know my Bible half so well as I should have for this assignment. Mostly I covered the local events calendar—antique shows and circuses and trucks with big tires. "What about Mary?" I tried. "The Virgin?"

"Ha! First of all, the word is misleading. Originally, it was the word '*almah*,' which meant nothing more than 'young woman.' It is through mis-translations that she evolves into an icon of parthenogenesis. For most of what is held as valid today in the way of faith on this subject, we can blame the emperor Constantine. It was through his political meddling and siding with various factions in the nascent church that certain unfounded beliefs gained in power over the truth. Mary became the Mother of God in 431 AD by a *vote* taken by these same greedy priests. How is one to embrace such nonsense? There is *nothing* to it!" He was breathing heavily.

I must have looked bewildered by his outburst. He held up his hand and added, "I'm sorry. I am trying only to educate people. Belief is well and good, but belief in obvious falsehoods is madness, futile. I want to change the belief of the world."

I looked into the temple. Except for the moneylenders, who were like sidewalk vendors in their booths, there was no one around. In fact there wasn't a soul in the place except for us. "I've noticed that you don't seem to be attracting much of a crowd."

His bright expression dimmed. He lowered his head. Finally, he admitted, "No."

"You've been open, what, six months?"

"Go ahead, skewer me the way everyone else has. I've had articles written about Jesusworld in every magazine. Most have mocked me for what I'm doing. They don't understand my purpose."

"Or maybe they do," I proposed. After all, I'd read most of those articles on the way here. I hardly felt he had been misrepresented, except by the more fundamentalist reporters. "It seems to me, Hani, that it's you who've made the error. You assumed that people would want the truth about Jesus. The fact is that faith is itself irrational and therefore not interested in the facts. If someone's got a drug problem, say, they might embrace Jesus as a way out. Now, that person's not going to want to hear about what the real Jesus had to say. He's not going to care that you can point out the Sheep Pool or Golgotha or Pilate's house. He's got a personal Jesus, see. It hasn't got a damn thing to do with the real story, the true events. The only people who're going to care about your little world are people who've already blown off the whole story, and who therefore aren't *going* to travel to a place that offers answers such as yours."

To my surprise, he was nodding and smiling again. "Yes! That's it exactly. The very conclusion I came to, my boy. And that's why we're in the process of adding our very newest exhibit, which you *must* write about. The latest, best, and a sure draw." He ushered me excitedly out of the holy city. We exited through a different door, into a short tunnel to the underground rail line he'd had installed. About a dozen small cars waited to whisk us to the next remarkable location.

I climbed in after him. "Now where?"

He put the car in motion and we whisked along the rail. Recessed lights flashed by overhead. He had his back to me as he watched the rail ahead, but his words whipped over his shoulder, and he gestured broadly as always. "I'm looking to the future now, exactly as you suggest. People personalize Jesus, just so. They mix him up in colors of their own choosing, stretch him and redesign him. So I said to myself, how will they next redefine him? What will his next devolution be? And the answer came to me—you won't believe where from."

"Divine intervention?" I hazarded.

"Supermarket tabloids!"

The car shook and started to slow down. He craned his neck to look at me. "It's really the new folk religion, isn't it? People without a smattering of education embracing all of these ridiculous stories about UFOs and past lives and film stars and diets. That is precisely how we've ended up with the absurdities embraced by the very church itself. The future as I thus perceive it will be the source of the next phase in the growth of our park."

The car came to a stop. We stepped onto a concrete runway. "You must understand, it's not finished yet. I have the backing, though. The money is there."

"Naturally."

"You'll be the first journalist to see it."

We rode up another escalator. At the top of this one was a pink light as bright as anything I'd ever seen. It was like looking into the sun. Squinting, I edged along after him. The light seemed to be tracking me; but it soon dimmed down, and there before me was a sight that riveted me to the spot. It was a cyclorama of a great, curving hillside full of crosses, there must have been hundreds of them. And in the center, right up front, there was one made of gold. On it, dressed in tight, black pants and a red jacket, hung Elvis Presley. His face, tilted and looking up to the sky, wore the same soulful look of a million third-rate portraits of Jesus. Hani had captured him perfectly.

He was watching my face, but this time I knew better than to let my reaction show. Give me some credit as a reporter, for Christ's sake. I said, as noncommittally as possible, "This is different."

"Isn't it? And what a draw it will be. They're changing the sign out front right now—you saw the crane as you came in. From now on, no more Jesusworld. No. From now on, it's *Kingsworld.*"

"Kingsworld."

"I predict, a hundred years from now, it will be the firmly held belief of the majority of America if not the world, that Elvis was the Second Coming. That he, too, returned from the dead. He appeared on refrigerators like little children's finger paintings. He sang from out of cash registers. The myriad stories will all tangle up and a single entity will emerge. We will be there first. Leading the way. If I can do that, I can perhaps lead them all back onto a more reasonable path. Don't you think so?"

I didn't, but I didn't dare say so. He didn't want to hear it. Like everyone else he disdained, he, too, had personalized his Jesus. Jesus was not Yeshu ben Miriam. Jesus was not the Christ. Jesus was certainly not Elvis Aaron Presley. Nope. Jesus was Silly Putty.

"Don't you agree that by adding Elvis we will bring the audience we want? People misled for centuries by absurdities and their own confusion?"

"I've no doubt whatsoever." I was looking for an exit.

Hani was rubbing his hands together. "Wait till you see how I've combined them. We're going to be selling a book that combines the real teachings of Yeshu with some of the more pithy comments of Presley. We're calling it *Wise Men Say*. Recycled paper, naturally. This crucifixion scene I realize is wholly unrealistic, but won't it get them in the door, though? You have to get them through the door."

"Won't it?" I spotted an exit sign next to the men's room and eased in that direction. "Hani, will you excuse me for a minute?"

"But of course." He gestured in that direction as though I weren't heading for the rest room already. "I will be here when you've finished. We'll have some lunch."

"Sure we will."

I made a beeline for the bathroom and only deviated at the very last moment, without a look back. He must not have been watching, because he didn't come screaming after me. I found myself in another hallway. Another sign pointed the way out. I passed a room under construction, the only time I saw other living beings in the whole damned park. Workmen were replacing the robot head of Lazarus with the head of Elvis. I could imagine all too horribly the musical number that might follow his sitting up, and fled before the performance could start.

Finally, I burst through a set of double doors in the outer wall of the park and out into the deserted parking lot. The roar of machinery surrounded me. Off to the left the immense diesel crane swung a giant "J" out over the tarmac to where other letters were piled up. I jumped into my car and looked at the display that remained. "USWORLD" it proclaimed.

"Who's the leader of the club?" I asked it as I backed the car out of its space. The front axle shivered violently. It didn't like to go backward.

Twenty hours back to Cleveland. Maybe, I thought, I should detour south and stop off at Graceland before heading home. I didn't want to waste the trip, and it might prove educational. Jesus knew.

—for Damon Knight

Afterword

Touring Jesusworld

Some years ago, the Clarion Writing Workshop at Michigan State University held a reunion. It took place the final weekend of the workshop program that year. I'd attended in 1975, and so elected to go to the reunion. Three of my friends from that year also showed up, and we had a pretty good time. Harlan Ellison was on hand, as were Damon Knight and Kate Wilhelm, both of whom had been teachers of mine in 1975.

In the airport on the way to the reunion, I'd seen someone wearing a T-shirt that had on the front a surreal image of Christ floating in space while seemingly crucified on large stone blocks. On the back, the shirt read, "I Died for Your Sins and All I Got Was This Lousy T-Shirt." (Please don't write me, I didn't make it up, and I didn't design the T-shirt.) I happened to mention this to Damon. I think if he'd been drinking a Coke, foam would have come out his nose. What I didn't know was that Damon had been invited to guest-edit an issue of a (now-defunct) magazine called *Pulphouse*. I'm not sure if he'd decided on the theme of his issue by then or not, but he contacted me not long after and invited me to submit a story to it—to Issue 18, the all-fiction, and more specifically *all-Jesus* issue of *Pulphouse*.

This is the story I sent to Damon. I think he liked it a lot. But then he had a very puckish sense of humor. He used to shoot his students with squirt guns. Routinely.

Most of the details presented in this story are accurate. That is, they've either been validated historically or else speculated upon as real possibilities. But as is the case in the story, hardly anyone wants to hear that. I'm just mentioning it in a further attempt to get myself in trouble.

The Road To Recovery

I

HARRY, WHO WAS SHORTLY TO CHANGE HIS NAME to Colman, pushed open the lid of the packing crate where he had hidden for protection. Thick plastic padding surrounded him, and he peeled it back as he floated up out of the box. Instantly, the padding began to expand to fill the vacated space. Harry closed the lid before the stuff overflowed. Still holding on to it, he stretched his cramped muscles as much as he could in weightlessness.

Across the room something thumped. "Dover?" he called softly. The cargo bay was full of secured, padded containers similar to the one he had crawled out of. Dover might have been in any of them. "All right," Harry called more loudly, "where've you got to?"

The thumping came again. Harry floated from container to container, drawing himself toward the source of the sound—a door marked "Exopak." Behind it, the thumping grew frantic. He pressed a square switch beside it and the door rose up on levered arms. Out of the dark doorway a foot swung up, nearly connecting with his chin before vanishing back into the darkness.

Light strips finally flickered to life inside, revealing a deep, narrow storage chamber. Recessed sockets in the walls secured a row of jetpaks. The nearest one was occupied: Harnessed to it, a figure wearing a bullet helmet whirled relentlessly. The thrust-tubes of the pak, lodged in wall sockets, acted as a center axis. Harry didn't have to see the face to know that the spinning figure was Dover's.

The helmet came round again, and Harry pushed in and caught it under his arm. The wheeling Dover hauled him up till he smashed into the raised door. Wedged solidly against it, he tore loose the helmet, revealing the swoop-nosed face of his sidekick. Dover's eyes spun like quasars. With his foot Harry managed to kick the release plate for Dover's jetpak. Then he flipped Dover onto his side and pulled. Dover began to float out of the closet. It was at that precise moment that the ship's artificial gravity system kicked in.

Harry felt himself fall. He let go of his partner and caught himself on the door overhead. Helpless, Dover crashed face-down to the floor. The force of the blow triggered the jetpak controls on the front of the harness. A blue flame blasted between Harry's legs, and Dover shot like a bobsled back into the closet. He struck each jetpak in turn, spinning them like wheels. The striplights flickered and went out.

Crashes, yelps, and spots of blue flame filled the closet.

Harry lowered himself to the floor and walked to the nearest soft crate. He sat, then casually picked up the weird, bug-eyed helmet. "The 'exo' in Exopak, Dover," he lectured, "means 'outside'—it's strictly for use *outside* the ship. That is why it's kept in the cargo bay, for emergency exit purposes only." He set the helmet down. "I'm surprised you didn't suit up, too."

"No time," came the shouted reply. Dover lurched out of the closet. He wore a bright, flowery shirt and baggy trousers like Harry's, except that his cuffs were now charred and smoking. He'd escaped from the jetpak harness, but continued to spin in circles as he stumbled past the crate where Harry perched. "Don't just sit there, *stop* me!" he begged.

"Sorry, old man, but my dance card's full. Besides, *you* always want to lead."

Dover clutched onto a strap on the side of a carton and hung on, his eyes closed, until his lower torso stopped trying to twist around. "I feel like the rotor on a vacuum pump."

"I've noted the similarity before. What were you doing in that rig?"

Edgily, Dover approached him, going from crate to crate like a man on a storm-tossed deck. "*You* took the only crate where the packing hadn't expanded. I was just going to hide in the closet, but the harness looked secure, and I figured that would be a lot safer."

Harry nodded sagely. "And then we did the hyperstring snap."

"That's what made me thumb the thruster. Believe me, I didn't intend to do it. Next time, I'm traveling as a passenger. Flying as cargo lacks the necessary class, which you'd recognize if you had any."

"You wound me, boy, you hurt me deeply."

"Give me the chance," Dover muttered. He glanced around, as if for an appropriate utensil. "What do we do now?"

"We're supposed to dress up like stewards and help people with their luggage, for which we'll get tipped—"

"Oh, boy, Terra Firma, here I come. You're going to love Earth."

"—except that I left the uniforms we stole in the head when I used the zero-g toilet. It takes both hands, you know. I consider it a terrific plan except for that."

Crestfallen, Dover asked, "Remind me why I came along with you."

"You were about to be arrested for pickling a certain official's daughter with your so-called butterscotch drops," Harry reminisced. "Karlotta was her name."

"I should have stayed and taken my chances."

"On Momerath the punishment for inducement to intoxication via foreign substances is flogging over slow coals for the three days prior to execution."

Dover considered that for a moment; then he clapped his hands together and said, "At least I'm home."

Harry got up with him. "That's the outlook, old son. We'll find a way out. We're too close to be sent back now."

"Yeah, let's go." As they crossed the room, Dover drew a large bag out of his pocket. "You want one?" Harry stared at him severely. "Sorry. They're sort of addictive. Secret family recipe, in fact. Grandma was a chemist." Dover popped a round, yellow candy in his mouth and his eyes widened. "Anyway, we're home. This is great!" he said, and flung open the bay door. It clanged to an abrupt and premature stop and something behind it thudded to the floor.

Warily, the two stowaways peered around the door. A crew-woman was lying on her back, blood trickling from her nose.

"No time like the present," Dover urged. He turned and fled, with Harry close upon his heels. They ran past rows of cargo doors like their own and dozens of branching halls, every one of which led to a dead end. "We'd better find something soon—she's going to wake up and blow the whistle on us!"

"I know, but we came in the other way," Harry explained. He ran past an airlock, realized what he'd seen, and looped back. Dover circled back to join him. A sign on the far side of the airlock pointed the way to the staterooms.

"That's the way to travel," exclaimed Dover. A klaxon sounded, and lights flashed above the airlock. It began to swing shut. Having no choice, the two men leapt through the opening. "You think that had something to do with us?"

"What doesn't?" Harry ducked through the first hatch he saw.

Inside stood six large, vertical cylinders. The doors into each were transparent, and revealed a solid mass of some viscous purple substance inside. Dover shut the hatch behind him. "G-tanks," Harry said.

"You're welcome," replied Dover.

"No, G-tanks for hypertravel. Look, everybody's still asleep." Harry circled the nearest cylinder. "But the ship's spinning or we wouldn't have gravity, true? Which can only mean that we've docked with a station, which can only mean the people inside these tanks are about to wake up."

"You trying to say this isn't the room we wanted?"

"No, boy, I'm saying 'It's time to hide,' " and he slipped from view behind the cylinders, Dover close at his heels.

Within two minutes the transparent doors on all the cylinders rolled back and the purple gelatin began to withdraw from the openings. It parted with a crackling sound—billions of carefully engineered cells realigning into a new pattern. Embedded deeply within the tanks, people—neatly clothed and clean of gel—gasped their first breaths and opened their eyes. One by one, on shaky legs, they emerged from the tanks. They paused in the open doorways, blinking like babies at the bright colors and lights and shapes.

A woman in a strapless, sequined gown was the first to step out. She remarked, "Oh, it's so startling. Everything's so crisp."

"Rebirth, sweetie," answered a man in evening attire of striped waistcoat and checkered balloon pants. He came up behind her and squeezed her bottom. "The best way to travel, you watch. For the next twenty hours or so you are going to live everything at optimum intensity. That alone makes the trip worth the price." He took her by the arm and walked her away.

Another passenger climbed out of a tank. He was grinning at everything he saw. An older and very portly man joined him unsteadily, saying, "Well, lad, we have arrived."

"I'd sort of expected Cathorius would meet us. He's a shifty bird, isn't he?"

"Probably awaits in the private stateroom. Just let me catch my breath a moment. Gel rides are really for the younger set. *I* always think I'm suffocating. Even in so-called twilight sleep, I have some sense of tendrils seeking purchase in my nose and my mouth. Ugh." Then he smiled in spite of himself. "The colors *are* vibrant."

With obvious awe, the younger man replied, "It's almost like a drug . . . twenty hours of *this*. I could just sing an aria!"

"That's right, this is your first time through the snap, isn't it? Well, with the money from our performance here, Colman, you'll be able to spend the rest of your life traveling and never see the same place twice. Yes, indeed." He wandered around, his pudgy face childlike in beholding the miracles of light and shadow across the room. "All we have to do is placate the bastard a little—you know, negotiate down from Bellicose's ridiculous price to prove our sincerity, say something nice about Columbus and the others, and go home retired. Pretty remarkable luck for my junior partner on his first assignment. You can sing all you like after this."

"Tell me he's really as rich as that," the young man asked.

When he received no answer to the question, he glanced happily back. His senior had vanished. "Alonzo? I say, Mr. Crews?"

"Here," came a reply from in back of the tanks. "Look," said the voice.

Excited at the prospect of something new and wondrous to behold, the young man hastened around the tank and into the shadows. Neither he nor his natty partner reappeared.

"There we go," said Harry. He watched the purple gel fold in and around the unconscious Colman, who now wore Harry's clothes. In moments, the stuff swelled to fill the tank, and the clear doors closed airtight. "Probably nobody'll find them till they get back to where they came from. I wonder where that was." He straightened his new, green waistcoat. "What do you think, Dover? Do I look the proper gentleman?"

Dover, in the process of sealing another tank, nodded without looking. "At least your clothes fit you," he complained. "I'd have to put on ten kilos to fill this." He plucked at the striped waistcoat he had adopted. "Even *I* know better than to wear stripes with a checkered past."

"You're lucky big pants are in style."

"Are you kidding? I look like Snow White wearing the seven dwarves."

"Consider the bright side—you're in rich clothes, you're going to lead a rich life for a while, and down the hall somewhere you've got your own stateroom, which is exactly what you wanted."

"All right, but I don't have to like it." He reached into the pockets of the waistcoat and came up with a packet of business cards. "What do you think of this?" He handed one to Harry. A miniature Parthenon popped up off the surface of the card. Harry peered at the details of the image, smiled, and then struck a smart pose with his nose tilted toward the ceiling. "May I present to you," he announced, "the redoubtable Alonzo Crews, of the famous trio Bellicose, Crews, and Winkie."

"Delighted," said Dover, with a bow.

"Here, let me see," and Harry rooted through his own pockets, coming up with a similar stack of cards. He also held a gleaming fresh credit disk. "Pay dirt, Dover." He put the cards back, then sat down on a large corrugated tube.

"Credit disks are only pay dirt if you have the code. Do you have the code?"

"You know I don't. Our young benefactor has it, in his head."

"Which is now in suspended animation inside a jar of grape jelly. Terrific planning."

Harry nodded sagely. "A triviality. Inconsequential."

For a second, Dover didn't get it. Then his eyes grew large and he grabbed onto Harry. "Oh, now, hold on there, you're not trying that somnambulapathic stuff again."

"And why not? I can stretch out right here behind this tube, won't be but a moment."

"Oh, sure, and when the crew comes to clean up I'll just tell them you pulled a knife and I had to shoot you."

"Thanks, Dover. I appreciate you offering to take the rap for me."

"I get to do it often enough, you'd think I'd be used to it."

Harry lay down on the floor. "You stay by the door, make sure no one interferes."

Dover stepped back reluctantly.

Harry folded his hands across his chest, and a great shudder surged from his feet to his head. He sighed deeply, as if pushing all the air from his body. Then his large, blue eyes rolled back, the lids fluttered for a moment, and he became absolutely still.

Dover closed the hatch. It opened again almost instantly. Four uniformed security people strode into the room. One of them, a woman, wore a broad tape across her recently battered nose. She looked him up and down while he stood rigid with fear, certain that she would comprehend the odd fit of his clothes; then, to his amazement, she ignored him and cast her glance at the tanks. The leader of the foursome, a portly, bearded blond, begged his indulgence. "I'm Guardian Fourth Class Goldstein, and we're searching for a possible stowaway, sir."

Dover floundered for an answer, and blurted, "Only one?"

Goldstein cocked his head. "Hmm, I suppose there could be more than one. Good point. Have you—" he stopped as the woman grabbed him and pointed to where Harry's two feet showed. "Good God, what's happened there?" He and the woman nodded at the other two, who took hold of Dover and dragged him around the tank. "What's going on?" Goldstein asked icily.

Dover glanced abjectly down at Harry. "Oh, him? He's just my sleeping partner. That's the way he gets when he's tanked up," he tried to explain. "The travel, I mean."

"He looks dead." One of the Guardians knelt and gently prodded his cheek.

"No, no. Just severely unconscious. Any minute now he'll come around—won't you, old *thing*?" He gave the body a kick in the ribs. Harry's crossed hands flapped like little wings. "There, what did I tell you?"

"Well, we could send a doctor—"

"No! I mean, there's no need. I've traveled with old, um . . . him a hundred times and he always faints like this. Really, he wouldn't dream of wanting to involve you. And you have so much to do already what with these stowaways."

Goldstein rubbed his chin. "Well, all right. As long as you're sure. If you see anyone suspicious, you will let us know."

"But of course."

"Oh, and Mr. Cathorius, one of our local celebrities, is hosting a reception inside the station. All the passengers are welcome. Your friend might care for a glass of brandy when he comes around."

"What a capital idea. Thank you, Guardian Goldstein."

He maintained a broad smile until the door had closed. Then he sagged against the corrugated tube.

"You kicked me." Harry's blue eyes stared accusingly up at him. "Even in cortical space I could feel it. Right in the ribs."

"I had to prove you were alive before they arrested us."

"Before who arrested us?" Harry asked, sitting up. Dover told him what had happened, to which he remarked, "It was a good thing that crewwoman didn't get a look at us. What about that other name—Cathorius? Isn't that the name our two benefactors mentioned?"

"Sounds like a pharmacist."

"I do believe the team of Crews, Bellicose, and Winkie is not working for a pharmacist. The name sounds vaguely familiar, though."

"Say, that brings up a point. Who are you?"

"According to my card, I'm—let's see—Colman Winkie. Of the Galpathien Winkies, you must have heard of us."

"Sure, the Winkie-dinks. The pleasure's all yours. Let's blow this place, grab some food and drink at this little party, and be on our way to Terra Firma fast."

"I couldn't have put it better myself. Especially now that sleeping beauty has allowed me to wander in and pick up our credit number, we have money to burn, my boy." He laughed. "There, you're forever complaining about my eccentricities, Dover, but how do you feel now?"

"I feel like eating until these clothes fit." He bowed and waved one arm toward the door. "After you, Mr. Winkie."

"Let's stroll."

Four ships had docked at the spinning station. Dover and Harry paused in a deserted debarking lounge long enough to look over the graphics simulation and flight status information. What they learned to their horror was that they were not circling Earth, not even close. They had arrived aboard a twin-ringed supply station in asynchronous orbit over someplace called "Recovery."

"This is terrific," Dover snarled, "we're not even anywhere *near* Earth. I should have known it when that bozo Goldstein said Cathorius was a local gewgaw." He fell silent for a moment as the two of them entered a corridor that seemed to be a main thoroughfare between the various ports. People traveled in both directions, but vast majority—their de-tanked expressions radiant—were heading up a slight incline to the right. Dover drew Harry aside. "What is Recovery?" he asked. "You think it's the whole planet? I've never even heard of it."

Harry nodded solemnly, unable to make eye-contact. "I've heard of it, I think. Things are starting to clear up, unfortunately. Dover, I'm sorry, but we really are far from home, farther even than when we started out. This place is way out at the Edge."

"Is that so? Well, all I can say to you is . . . where have you been all my life?"

Harry blinked in dismay, glanced at his partner, and found Dover staring past him in profound imbecility. "Oh-oh, *cherche la femme*," Harry said. He followed the mooning gaze to its inevitable object—a dark and doe-eyed beauty. She had noticed Dover watching her and, taking that as some form of invitation, was already making her way to him through the crowd. Heads turned, admiring, as she passed. Her body moved like liquid beneath an open-sided surcoat. A deep blue gorget enwrapped her throat. Harry sensed sexuality radiating from her like heat thrown off by a star. His eyes fluttered, but he fought the urge to drift into languor. Rarely had anyone exhibited such an aura in his presence. He found Dover puckering his lips in response to an invisible kiss.

The woman took Dover by the arm and slipped in between the two men. "Will you help me?" she asked him.

Dover, practically drooling, replied, "Anything."

"It's my husband," she said.

Dover staggered. His mouth firmed up. "You have one?" he asked.

"Oh, yes, but I have to escape him. I must get away, you understand? He *owns* me." Her fingers dug into his biceps. "He's going to take away my mind. My whole personality will slough away and only the bacteria will remain. I don't know how long—even now, my brain aches for activation."

"What's she talking about?" Dover asked Harry.

His partner was not looking at him. "She's brought trouble," he said.

Two sinister figures were snaking through the crowd against the flow, directly toward them. The taller one sidled up against Dover. He was not human, but humanoid, with compound eyes that bulged as if in excited contemplation of a meal, an impression further enhanced by his crazed smile. His straw-colored skin looked as if it were woven about him. Dover gently pressed him back, explaining, "Excuse me, I'm very territorial about my subderma."

"Yaa, yaa, very territory, Al," the alien brayed.

The smaller man—whose heavy-lidded eyes made him appear sleepy—wore a bronze tattoo on his cheek, a mandalla of intricate design. He tended to sneer as he spoke, which he began to do immediately, disregarding Harry. "Azize, lovely flower," he cooed in a thick accent, "you surely haven't tried to run away from your dear husband. And you cannot have desired to entangle these two innocent gentlemen in what is but a family squabble. See what I have?"

He opened his hand. On his palm sat a tiny pyramid glowing so blue that even a moment's view of it made Harry wince. Beside him, the darkly beautiful Azize strained against its gravity. Her body stiffened for an instant, then relaxed. Her sexual radiance evaporated. Harry cleared his throat. "Now, just hold on, gentlemen," he tried to protest, but the woman closed her hands over the folded palm of the little man and cut Harry dead with a strangely vacant backward glance. "Please get away from me," she said to him.

The little man backed away, with Azize pressed to him.

Unaware of what was happening, Dover took a step toward her. The alien blocked his way. "Take it under advisement, 'reet," he urged loudly, "the lady doth protest too much."

"Maybe, but she's not for burning."

"Ooh, a scholar, Lee. Here—" he slapped two shiny credit disks into Dover's hand "—unlimited drink chits. Why not use them right away? Remember her as your mountain flower, yes, yes, ephemeral and gone." He turned smartly and sprang after his companion, who had vanished around a bend in the corridor.

"Thanks for the memory." Dover rubbed the two disks between his finger and thumb. "But I just ate my heart, and I don't know if there's room left for a drink."

"Dover, whatever our business is here, I think we'd best wrap it up post-haste and get gone."

"What *is* our business?"

"I might know the answer if someone hadn't kicked me before I found out."

Ignoring the dig, Dover inquired, "What was that blue thing in Slimy's hand?"

He snatched one of the drink disks. "It looked like living death, and I'm not in the market," he said, then headed for the party before Dover could ask what he meant.

The reception was unfolding in a cargo deck that had been decorated at great expense. A sheet of monoglass had been laid in under the ceiling and formatted into an expanse of cracked emeralds that threw off light in faceted bursts of green. A curved bar filled one side of the deck, with a dance floor in the middle and rows of small dining tables studding the rest of the room like mushrooms. No one was dancing and no music was playing as Harry and Dover entered. The crowd was watching the entry hatch opposite in some anticipation. They were all kinds of people, both human and not—some dressed formally, even ostentatiously; others, unshaven or unshowered, in greasy jumpsuits, appeared to have rushed in straight off a work shift.

The two stowaways made a slow, uneventful circuit to the bar, ever vigilant for a meaningful glance of which they wouldn't know the meaning. The dark woman, Azize, and her abductors, had disappeared. Harry watched Dover straining for a glimpse of her in the crowd.

At the bar, he tried Winkie's credit out and watched cautiously as the code he entered cleared the system without a hitch. The bartender brought him two large drinks made from some exotic fruit. "I don't know what this guy likes to drink," he told Dover as he handed him one of them, "but it looks too sweet. Next time, I use *your* drink chit and get what I want." They clinked glasses and drank. Harry sighed, then suddenly bugged out his eyes and shook his head. "Whoa," he said, "Forget what I said." He drank again, deeply. "Why, I feel like singing. Ba-ba-ba—"

"Hey, ixnay on the ingsay."

A sweaty man with a teeny mustache came over and stood beside them. A sad, gaunt alien of the same race as the one who had abducted Azize was leaning against the rail behind Dover. He wore evening clothes not unlike Dover's. "Everyone's debarked," the sweaty man announced to the alien. "What are we going to do, Gilbert? It's sheer luck that Cathorius has been so far delayed. That won't matter if the two of them don't show up immediately."

Harry and Dover glanced at each other.

"You should have gotten their pictures," Gilbert complained.

"Garbled transmissions. In a week they'll turn up, like always, apologizing about getting on the wrong shuttle or some other feeble excuse. I just assumed—that's always a mistake, isn't it, Gilbert?—I mean, they want to get *paid*, don't they? Musicians! You can't trust them. And singers are the worst." He tried to tug at his mustache but there wasn't enough of it to get hold of.

"Singers," Harry mouthed excitedly.

Dover leaned closer to Harry. "Hey, you think Winkie and Crews are headliners? The kid *was* talking about singing right before you clobbered him."

"We dare speculate."

"At least we can sing."

"At least *I* can. If we had Bellicose, we could do that Nairobi trio number." Harry leaned past Dover to the two men. "Excuse me, I hope we didn't keep you waiting, Gilbert?" he said.

"You're—"

"One of your headliners. Sorry to be late, but we needed a drink first after our journey."

"Your partner?"

"Right here." He dragged a reluctant Dover from behind him.

The little man slid a forefinger over his mustache. "I thought your partner was a woman."

Harry froze—long enough for Dover to dive in. "Well, that was last week, but he changed his mind at the last minute. One look at him and you can see he made the right decision." He gave Harry a kiss on the cheek. "Of course, it doesn't change how I feel about him."

"Say," Harry interjected before the tale went further, "your club doesn't have temp-scan orchestration, does it?"

"Of course it does. Gilbert, the orchestra, please."

Gilbert, still frowning, dug around in his baggy trousers and came up with an envelope containing three iridescent squares, each no larger than a fingernail. He held them out on his three fingers.

Harry snatched them before Dover could. "I think I'd better handle this end of things. The last time he did, his thoughts wandered, and we ended up with a medley of Karlheinz Stockhausen's greatest hits, which nothing human can sing or dance to, in case you've ever wondered."

Gilbert shrugged.

"I was feeling mechanical," Dover said. "I think I'd better have some of that drink of yours, myself."

While Gilbert climbed up on the stage to silence the crowd, Harry attached two squares to his temples; he held the third at the ready on his index finger.

Dover set down his drink. He shivered from its effects. "You could resurrect Wagner with two of those. What number are we going to do?"

"I was thinking about a fast samba," said Harry, "one we both know."

"The faster the better."

"Adapt."

Gilbert announced, "Ladies and gentlemen." Hidden microphones amplified his voice.

Dover nudged Harry and gestured toward the back of the room.

Azize was just entering, in the company of the two abductors and a third man—a large, mustachioed figure in immaculate evening wear, his long hair worked into a single braid. He burned the room with his black glare as the crowd surged toward him.

"Adapt, huh? Maybe we should do a whole set."

Gilbert announced, "May I present to you—" then spread his hands toward them. Harry declared, "Ah, Colman Winkie and Alonzo Crews. Thank you very much." The man with Azize stared their way, one eyebrow raised quizzically. Harry stuck the third square onto his forehead. Music began to play, rising like a wind out of nowhere into a percussive Brazilian rhythm.

"Harry, they've seen us," Dover warned.

"We *are* on stage, my boy." Harry danced lightly up the steps to the center that Gilbert had vacated. Quietly, he added, "I think I better start, give you time to catch up." Then, as the music swelled under his guidance, he began to sing.

(Harry)   "We're on the Road to Recovery
           They told us it's lovely,
           But so far it's not.
           We're on the Road—could I have another please?
           This one is way too dry
           And way too hot.
Take it, Dover."

(Dover, stealing the square from Harry's forehead, applied it to his own, then found himself desperately improvising a hula.)
           "I wanna go back
           To my little grass shack
           In Minneapolis, Minnesota—"

(Harry)   "Hold on, boy, that's another song."
(Dover)   "Maybe that's so, but that's a fact."

(Dover pressed the disk back onto Harry)

(Both)   "We just bid adios to the worlds we knew
           On a stringshot through the great glowing cosmos we
              flew,
           As for what lies ahead we haven't got a clue,
           Nevertheless, we want to impart to you, that—

(Harry)   "We're back on the Road to Recovery
           Filled with discovery
           And a little champagne.
           We're going down that Road to see what we see
           Please tell my family
           Where to collect my remains."

The music continued, and the two men danced in precision side by side to the samba beat, Dover looking doubtful.

(Dover)   "I'm not too crazy about that verse."

(Harry)   "Then, try it again. Just don't make it worse."

(Dover)   "He said—

> We're on the Road to Recovery.
> I'll go if you cover me,
> Who knows what we'll find?
> We might as well hie ourselves to a nunnery,
> I know what you're thinking,"

(Both)   "You're right! We're out of our *minds*."

As the samba faded out, Harry shrugged. "I can live with it." He quickly plucked the squares from his head as the crowd began applauding, politely, no more than was necessary—save for the big man with Azize, who was grinning and clapping furiously as he approached the stage. The crowd, noticing his zeal, increased in enthusiasm.

"Oh, oh, here comes trouble in the convenient family pack," Dover said. "Let's scram."

He turned, and bumped into the ever-frowning Gilbert, who had just slithered up beside them. The large man and his entourage arrived. "Mr. Cathorius," said Gilbert. "How nice to see you again, sir."

"Thank you, Gilbert, but I wish to talk to you about these two. I'm afraid you have been misled."

"The jig is up," Dover muttered.

"Best to come clean then," Harry replied.

"Where do I start? It's such a long list."

"Skip your childhood—just talk about today."

"Mr. Crews and Mr. Winkie, so at last we meet. I had no idea you were so multi-talented, gentlemen."

"He can't mean us."

"Steady, son."

"Which of you is Alonzo Crews?"

Dover twitched, recalling that it was he. "You win, I give up. I didn't know she was behind the door, honest."

Cathorius stood perplexed, then smiled away his confusion. "It was you I most wanted to meet, and here you've exceeded all expectations—a singer as well."

"As well as what?" asked Dover cautiously.

"Why, as well as being the designer of my Memory Palace, what else?"

"Oh, that. You know, I got so excited, I forgot all about it."

Again, Cathorius seemed at a brief loss, then burst out laughing. "A sense of humor—so important in both our vocations, I venture. You're a marvel of a man, if I may say so."

"I come from a long line of them," Dover explained. "Dad was a captain."

"Thus you, sir, must be the renowned Colman Winkie."

"Happy to make your acquaintance," Harry said. Cathorius reached out to shake hands, but Harry pressed his fingertips together and bowed ever so slightly in a gesture of formal respect. Mildly surprised, Cathorius touched his own hands together.

He said, "I understand you've already met the other members of my household. My companions. Bragone." He gestured to the little sleepy-eyed man with the tattooed cheek. "And Irge, who is a native of the planet below us. They are with me always."

"Must be a big bed," Dover muttered to Harry.

"Irge, bring her forward. This, gentlemen, is my wife, Azize. I'm worried about your first impressions. Her instability is my misfortune, but it has inconvenienced you, for which I cannot apologize enough."

"Forget it," Dover said. Harry observed Azize's vacant stare; and a blush on her cheek that was either too much rouge or the burn from a few hard slaps. One thing he knew for certain—she hadn't noticed any of it. Irge's blue pyramid had fixed that.

"I apologize for troubling you earlier," she said flatly.

"Trouble us later and we'll do better," Dover said. Harry kicked him.

Cathorius had Bragone lead Azize out of the room. "She gets out so rarely," he said, "that she has learned, really, few social graces."

"Trust me, we forgive her," Harry replied earnestly.

"Mr. Winkie, you are too kind. I know we will all enjoy one another's company greatly, eh? You will be pleased to know that the Palace is complete; however, that can keep until tomorrow. I don't want to mar this celebration with the clutter of details. For now, please amuse yourselves as you wish. You can even—" he allowed himself chuckle "—you can even sing again if you're so inclined."

Harry patted Dover's shoulder. "I think we'll *decline*—one rash act per adventure is enough."

Cathorius beamed. "Oh, yes, no rash acts on Recovery, please. Isn't that right, Irge?"

"A rash hand in evil hour," he stated.

"Thank you, Milton," said Dover.

Grinning at the recognition, Irge bowed before turning to follow Cathorius, who departed while in conversation with Gilbert.

Harry tapped Dover, who blinked as though coming out of a trance. "Did you see the way she looked at me as she was leaving?" he asked. "Have you ever seen a more beautiful woman?"

"Nope, but I've seen plenty of less dangerous ones."

"Dangerous?"

"Well, for one thing, her husband gives the impression of someone who takes marriage very seriously, exactly the way you don't. For another, she's completely under his control."

"Her? A 'Trilby'?"

"Didn't you see her expression?"

"That's what I was talking about—the way she looked at me."

"The way she looked at *everything*. Dover, you poor sap, why do you think Laurel and Hardy there stick to her wherever she goes?"

"She's in trouble, and we've got to save her."

"*Save's* a little strong. How about 'get to know' first?"

Not wishing to tamper with his romantic ideal, Dover diverted the conversation, asking, "What was that malarkey about a Memory Palace?"

"I'll tell you what it means to me. Before the advent of the printing press, there was a popular practice among scholars to memorize massive amounts of knowledge. You mentally fabricated a building and gave yourself a tour of it, populating the rooms with images—statues and paintings and things—that connected to specific memories. Sometimes whole strings of memories with mnemonic titles so that you could remember them at will. By which process you could learn all sorts of things associatively and keep them in your head. From the sound of it, however, Mr. Cathorius has taken his memory out for a walk."

"And without a leash," Dover replied. "He's going to find out I don't know the first thing about his memories!"

"Maybe not. We may be able to bluff our way through. In any case, Dover—or should I say, Alonzo—we don't have a choice." Harry stared narrowly at Cathorius's broad back. "I'm not sure we could get far enough away to be safe."

Dover swallowed. "I hope you're saying that just to make me feel better."

II

A shuttle carried them down the elongated greenish-gray oval area on an otherwise barren, brown landmass. The oval defined itself as they descended, becoming a lush target, an oasis city smothered in vegetation. This, Cathorius explained to Harry, was a resort he had created.

"It's called Macerata, which means 'thing of beauty.' You'd have heard of it—what men of influence haven't?—even without knowing me. I revolutionized the economies of dozens of warring peoples who gave up their petty squabbles to enjoy the riches they can make here. My power shapes their own.

"Thousands of years ago on Earth, people not unlike Irge's race created deserts in the Mediterranean and Indus areas by overgrazing their livestock. The same thing happened here. I've convinced them that I can return life to their dead territories. Macerata and my own estate stand as proof of this. In time—in perhaps a century—the rest of civilization will have spread to this little system, by which time Macerata will have consumed the entire landmass, a tropical paradise covering a whole continent. And it won't need a mono-molecular film over it any longer because the planet's biosphere will have adjusted."

"Whereby comes 'Recovery,' " Harry commented. "I've noticed that terraformers keep themselves at a distance from civilization. There's something in the blood, isn't there?"

Cathorius looked at him curiously. "We have no use for regulations and restrictions."

"Well, who does?"

"Most of the human race. Both of you do, if you forgive my saying so."

"Codes of behavior do make it easier to remember how to behave."

Cathorius said nothing to that, but turned away and began speaking quietly with Bragone.

Dover leaned in beside Harry and remarked, "You want to go a little lighter on the great thinker pose before you poach our eggs?"

A flashing cross that hung magically in the sky marked the landing window through which they passed. The film encapsulating Macerata was all but invisible. A few minutes later, the shuttle touched down on a scorched plateau in the heart of the lush city. The buildings seemed to protrude through a network of vines and trees. And everywhere there were towers—tall cylinders with open cupolas, like bulbs, at the top.

Harry looked down upon a multitude that waited not far from where they landed. As the passengers emerged from the shuttle, the mob closed in; before they had reached Cathorius's party, a dozen natives in white uniforms appeared from somewhere and circled the passengers. The approaching mob didn't seem hostile, more like a flock of fans straining to touch a celebrity. The uniformed guards cleared a path through them. To Harry's surprise, he noted that most weren't natives—or at least weren't of Irge's race. They appeared to be guests of the resort. They looked wealthy and well cared for—members of the class of people who could afford repeated bioengineering.

People wore bright clothing, mostly gauzy robes or saris, and Harry understood why: already, he was soaking in his formal wear, and Dover looked similarly uncomfortable. The air was thick as water.

Suddenly, the crowd pushed past two of the guards. Hands clutched at Harry, faces circled him. He read a strange forlornness in the black, faceted eyes. One of the crowd grabbed hold of his wrist and pushed something into his palm just before the guards, wielding sticks, shoved them back to a respectful distance. Harry surreptitiously opened his hand to find a small, glazed tile there. He quickly closed his fingers around it and stuffed it in his pocket.

They reached the edge of the plateau. Broad steps led down to an open mall full of market stalls, empty platforms, and fountains, all surrounded by more areas of dense foliage. It was the cluster of platforms that caught Harry's eye. The pillars on them sported lengths of chain. He didn't care particularly for what they suggested; but all at once he realized who Cathorius was. If he hadn't been sweating already, he would have started then.

The white-clad guards came to attention at the top of the steps. The mob hung back. In the lead, Dover went down four or five steps before discovering that he was no longer protected. He turned back in a panic.

"I think I left something on the shuttle," he told Harry.

"What?"

"My mind."

"No, you don't." He nudged him around. "Don't worry, I'm right behind you."

"Where have I heard that before?"

At the bottom of the steps a peculiar vehicle awaited them. It ran on crawler tracks. A large dome topped the middle of it, with two smaller domes at each end. A narrow doorway in its side led under the center dome.

Before going in, Dover glanced back. Harry craned his neck, too.

Coming down the steps, Bragone led a figure swaddled in indigo robes. Not a bit of her was visible, but Dover was certain it must be Azize. Near the top, Cathorius had paused to wave to the crowd like some benevolent dictator. He shook hands with an honored few. The white-uniformed staff abruptly closed in behind him, building a wall that cut off any further invasion of his territory. Only then did he descend.

The interior of the vehicle consisted of a cushioned ring on which to sit. Harry and Dover settled across from the door, then watched Bragone and his charge come in and take a place as far from them as possible. Even close up, nothing of the woman was visible. Beneath the hood her face had been masked by an impenetrable mesh veil.

Irge dropped down beside Dover. "What do you think of our architecture, Mr. Crews? Phallic enough for you?"

"Oh, extremely phal," Dover quickly replied.

"You haven't seen anything yet," Irge promised madly.

"And at these prices you'd expect to, wouldn't you?"

For once Irge seemed at a loss for a response.

Their transportation rolled through the city and then out into a desert of orange sand.

Harry knelt on the cushion as if to get a better look of the barren landscape rolling by, but he looked in fact at the tile. On one side of it was a simple line drawing of one of the tall towers that dominated Macerata. On the other side someone had scratched the words "Your friend changed. Beware."

Cathorius's desert estate, when it appeared on the horizon, looked like a mirage of Eden. The land had grown rocky, the barchan dunes giving way to a broken surface of scrub and outcroppings. If the reclamation of Macerata had been impressive, the private world Cathorius had built robbed the two men of their speech. A dozen more large towers with the characteristic bulbous tops stood near the edge of the estate. Although the curve of skin above it was invisible, the line of demarcation between floral estate and trackless desert was sharply defined. A glowing crosshair image not unlike the landing window signaled the entrance to a solitary road through the thick jungle. Branches scraped against the dome of the vehicle. Here and there birds darted into view, and the sound of their songs never stopped. At one point, something large and reptilian lumbered into view but vanished in the undergrowth.

The flora exploded with color. Out of it the house emerged like a clap of thunder.

Cathorius's home had been carved from natural rock, with roughly edged and seemingly unsupported wings jutting from the central bulwark. Waterfalls spilled out at various points up the sides, which their host admitted was an unforgivable extravagance on his part. He pointed out that all of the water was carefully channeled back into an underground network that recycled it, and the evaporated moisture captured and returned through the osmotic properties of the mono-molecular film.

As they emerged from the vehicle and walked around, stretching after the journey, Harry murmured to Dover, "I've figured it out. Those are cooling towers. The desert winds blow into the openings at the top and are channeled underground, where the air naturally cools. It's a passive air conditioning system for the house."

Dover asked, "Why are you behaving like an encyclopedia all the sudden?"

"Because, old son, it's just conceivable *we* designed them."

"But I don't know anything about them."

"You do now, don't you?"

Dover grabbed his wrist. "Let's not get separated anytime soon."

"Just be careful what you ask about. I'll explain later."

They entered the house. It could have accommodated dozens of guests with ease. Cathorius led them through the main salon. A hanging garden enclosed the three-story-high room. The opposite end of it opened onto a balcony running the length of the house. Below, pools and fountains and well-tended gardens dazzled them wherever they looked; but all that was dwarfed into insignificance by the thing they had come there to see: the Memory Palace.

Set upon an artificial hilltop across from the salon, the palace jutted above the trees like some vast mastaba for an ancient king. The basic edifice facing them had then been decorated in cathedral style with flying buttresses, running ornaments, and thousands of intricate, spindly crockets. Between the spires, dome-shaped pavilions topped off tiny, pent-roofed towers—more than could be counted in a single glance. Harry looked at Dover who stood in complete awe of the thing. "Make sure you've stopped drooling," he whispered, "before you look at our host again. That's *our* building."

Dover swallowed. "I had no idea I was so talented."

"So," Cathorius said, loud enough to make him jump. "It's colossal, isn't it? Tomorrow, we'll tour it, and you can see how your designs have been executed. Bellicose and I did make a few minor changes, but you won't mind."

"Mind?" Dover asked nervously. "Why should we mind? It's your mind we mined."

"I appreciate your flexibility, Mr. Crews."

"Elastic's my middle name."

Harry leaned on the balcony rail and sighed.

Cathorius ushered them back inside, promising a tour of the building in the morning. Bragone ordered another servant to escort them to their quarters, two bedrooms sharing an outer room and bath. Their luggage cases had already been delivered. As soon as they were alone, Harry dragged Dover back onto the balcony.

"You have to stop being so jumpy around him."

"I couldn't help it. He's going to figure us out."

"Not if we're careful."

"We've never been *that* careful."

"Just follow my lead."

"That's how I got here in the first place," Dover complained. "'I'll just run along to the head,' he said. 'Find a place to hide, and don't worry,' he said. 'I've got our uniforms,' he said."

"At least I got you out of trouble."

"This is what you call out of trouble?"

They had a few minutes to wash up and change clothes before they were called to dinner. Dover did his best to conceal the excess girth of his shirt.

The dinner was served in the large salon overlooking a series of stepped fountains. The table was a low, circular slab of stone encircled by thick pillows on which they sat. Five servants in white stood back in the shadows, ready to come forward to pour drinks or serve food. Otherwise they were as motionless as statues. Azize was conspicuously absent.

Bragone and Irge sat protectively on either side of Cathorius. They did not eat, nor seem to notice the presence of food. On the table in front of Bragone sat five tiny pyramids, each a different color and to which Bragone paid no attention at all. He stared—as did Irge—at the two "architects." This combined lunatic vigilance put little dent in the appetites of Harry and Dover, however, who knew that you ate when you had the chance because you never knew when the chance would come again. They devoured and had seconds of a chilled berry soup.

The bowls and tureen were removed by two of the servants.

One of them seemed to be trembling, although her blank expression suggested nothing of a cause. As she picked up Cathorius's bowl, her fingers slipped. The bowl bounced off the edge of the table and shattered. Harry watched as the muscles in her neck tautened, as though she were straining against some invisible cord, but she did not move away.

For a moment Cathorius looked as if he would explode, but he held his temper, calmly picked the pieces of the bowl from the pillows and offered them to the serving girl. He dabbed the drops of soup off his clothes, and commented humorously, "Better the host than one of his guests."

Between courses, he asked them politely about the method they'd used for their mnemonic representations. "I've been so impressed by the many pieces of sculpture and architecture," he said, "the pottery as well—elements in which I can so readily see my own ego shaped. I cannot believe that the brief biographical information I supplied could have engendered all of it. How did you accomplish so much, when we had never met?"

Dover would gladly have stuffed his face with food had there been any left within reach. "Well, method implies system, doesn't it?" he replied, while he fumbled for the rest of an answer. "And system suggests—how can I put this?—something misleading, because, you see, there wasn't anything like a consistent pattern. You have your matrices and you have your shapes—your shape is certainly different than mine. And of course, there's intuition. An awful lot of intuition. And let's not forget Bellicose."

"What Mr. Crews is saying, I believe," Harry interjected, "is that things are a good deal subtler and thereby more complex than they were for the likes of Simonides, or Giotto, if you wish to bring artistic values into it."

Dover nodded in silence. He didn't dare pretend any familiarity with the names. Cathorius obviously knew them.

"Well, and of course," he said, beaming. "This was obvious even to someone as unsubtle as myself. I'm impressed by the degree of your research, Mr. Winkie."

"We build anything for anybody," he replied, adding quickly, "Our presence here signifies our concern, after all. It's not every day we design a building out of the Arabian Nights."

"'In Xanadu did Kubla Khan a stately pleasure dome decree,'" his host quoted, and Irge smiled blissfully, as if the mere breath of poetry transported him to rapture.

"A fitting comparison," Harry said.

Cathorius thoughtfully twirled one end of his mustache for a moment. Then he said, "What impresses me the most is how you worked the theme of water into so many of the exhibits. Water is wealth to these people. That was something I recognized immediately, because water—the release and capture of water—plays so pivotal a role in *my* life. With the gentle, cyclonic rainfall I brought them came a rebirth and peace they had not known in living memory. A common marketplace. Unification. They saw the furnace they live in turned into a fruitful Eden.

"In return for their salvation, they grant me broad freedoms. As you said, terraformers don't care much for society and its restrictions. Well, neither do I. A lot of little people leading little lives, doing little jobs and watching little entertainments in their little homes. I shape whole worlds. I have no desire to stay and watch the little people move in and debase the places where I've been."

"Naturally," agreed Harry. All of his doubts had been removed.

Cathorius studied him a moment. "You do understand, I can see."

"As to the question of water, you said it just now—that it plays a pivotal role in your work. We didn't need to know anything about matters in Macerata to comprehend that."

"Ah, Mr. Winkie, what a pleasure it is to have company such as you. Both of you." His smile, directed toward Dover, was positively predatory.

After that they managed to coast through the meal without much trouble. Dover sat hunched over his food, hoping not to be noticed, while the other two threw terms such as "kusabi" and "shimagi" and "riwaq" and "spandrel" at each other. He tried to look bored with the whole terrifying, alien dialogue.

As the dessert arrived, he felt he ought to say something, yet didn't dare tread in the territory where his partner and Cathorius had gone. There was only one thing he could think of to talk about. "It's a shame," he said, "your wife couldn't join us for this terrific meal."

Bragone and Irge stared at him with something like horror, then glanced toward Cathorius as if they expected to be punished for this blasphemy.

Cathorius did not even blink. "Yes. I confess to you that she's been a problem for me. The first time I laid eyes on her I was smitten, much as you were I think, Mr. Crews. Normally, you know, I'd have nothing to do with the merchandise. She had run away from one of those little families I despise. I won't tell you what trivial place she came from or how she ended up on the market here. I've forgiven her for many indiscretions, before and since. She was headstrong. I fell in love with her fierceness, her spirit."

"And she fell for your power, your influence," Dover suggested. "Your indomitable will."

"I accept the compliment. Regrettably, not so, though I've rescued her from a fate more horrible than she can imagine. I know she would do herself harm, and I protect her from herself by what limited means I have. I fear that she's quite insane—multiple personalities. She deceived me for years. Madness, addiction . . . so sordid." He covered his eyes.

Harry shook his head at Dover. "We're sorry to have mentioned it," he said.

Cathorius took his hand away, and brightened as if nothing had happened. "Oh, good. Coffee, then? I have beans originally from New Kenya that are cultivated here. Very dark. Very strong."

"How can we say no?"

"Exactly."

When Cathorius finally ended the dinner, Bragone got up to usher them to their room. Seemingly by accident, he knocked one of the little pyramids off the edge of the table. Harry alone saw this, but before he could say anything, the little man took a step and crushed it underfoot. In the shadows, where the five servants stood, the girl who had dropped the soup bowl suddenly spun in a drunken spiral. She tore at her head and made a squealing noise in her throat. The seizure lasted no more than a few seconds. And then she was dead. The remaining servants stood their ground and coolly overlooked her as they might have done a bit of dirt that hadn't been swept up.

Bragone reached her just before Harry did. "Oh, dear," he said. "I'm afraid I've killed her, Cathorius."

"Then you'll have to train another, Bragone. It's your responsibility for being clumsy. I'm sorry, gentlemen—a perfect dinner ruined by my incompetent servant." He did not elaborate as to which servant he meant.

Harry tossed away the pillow he'd grabbed to place under her head. He stared at the other four servants but they wouldn't or could not meet his gaze.

Irge led the two of them solemnly to their adjoining quarters.

Dover immediately went into Harry's room. Harry led him out to the balcony. "All right," he said, "if it were up to me, I'd be packing my bag and catching the next camel out of here. They just murdered somebody and treated it as if they'd sneezed. And meanwhile you've developed a new lobe to your brain marked 'architecture.' What are you, a Mason? And what's a 'kusabi' anyway? I thought it was a melon."

"In my misspent youth, Dover, I was sent to a trade school back on Earth. Architecture got sandwiched in between economic theory and the history of torture."

"Oh, a Catholic school. You know, sooner or later he's going to ask me questions that you can't answer."

"I know, and I have a solution."

"You've got a way to make me look smarter?"

"Let's not presume too much on my abilities—a way to make you appear to be Alonzo Crews is the most I'm willing to promise."

Dover stroked his chin. "Would this plan involve a little dreamwalking?" he asked.

"Possibly."

Dover grabbed his arm. "Then you can hunt for Azize, too. She has to be around someplace. I'm sure that was her on the shuttle with us."

"I agree, but—"

"Go into her dreams, tell her how I feel about her."

"I'm not about to play Cyrano for you—besides, *you're* the one with the nose. Leave her be, Dover. Forget about her. We have enough problems."

"But look what they did to that *girl.*"

"Azize is in worse trouble than you've ever been in." He stared out at the jungle for a moment. "Do you know what Libitina is?"

"I had a doctor once, told me I had an uncontrolled one of those."

"Your doctor was right, even if you aren't. Libitina's a bacterium, usually kept inert, in cube form. The cube separates naturally along a central seam into twin polyhedrons—one contains the bacteria. The other contains some form of activator. The idea is you feed the one half to somebody and the little bacteria nestle into certain receptor sites of the brain; in the presence of the activator, they perform a little mating dance that alters neural transmission, and the victim follows you anywhere, utterly without will. I can't believe you've never heard of it."

"Well, I've never been very psychoactive. Okay, once, but only because I had a head cold."

"With that proboscis, I'm not surprised."

"Don't go all rhinal on me, what's the polyhedron have to do with Azize?"

"The thing that Bragone held out to her in the way-station and the thing he stepped on at dinner were Libitina activators."

Dover became agitated. "Then they gave it to her against her will!"

"Sure," he replied grudgingly. "You should know, though, the longer she's exposed to it, the more gray matter gets new wallpaper. Eventually, she'll have no personality at all, exactly as she said. Like Cathorius's servants. They didn't blink when that girl died."

"Yeah, well, Azize still talked okay. She didn't twitch or bark or anything like that."

Harry said, "All right, then there's still hope."

"Right. And where there's hope, there's, uh—"

"Crosby?"

Dover looked disgusted. "Never speak that name in my presence. Now, give me the lowdown on Cathorius."

"I made a mistake with him. I thought he was a terraformer, but he's not. He's an entropicaster. Where terraformers bring them to life, Cathorius kills whole worlds and then offers them up to developers, along with a blueprint for re-engineering the destroyed biosphere. By then, he's sold off any useful indigenous population to colonies looking for cheap labor. There are plenty of places where slavery's tolerated. Look at Momerath—that's where I heard his name before. That's where I learned about Libitina. He introduces the victims to Libitina and they don't even complain: they can't remember how. Cathorius stays two jumps ahead of civilization, and gets whatever he wants."

"Like glowing polyhedrons?"

"More than that. You heard him refer to Azize as part of the merchandise. That market in Macerata was a slave market. He saw Azize go up for sale and bought her, himself. I'd wager the tourists who turned out to see us arrive were mostly prospective buyers."

Dover asked, "But why didn't he wipe out Recovery?"

"Because he's settled here. He's far enough away from the thrust of civilization that colonizing won't reach here in our lifetime. Plus, this way he gets to come down out of the sky like a benevolent god."

"I noticed. How do we get out of here?"

"My guess is, one of two ways: We either keep up the facade and go home rich or we screw up and end up on the block."

"Tremendous. A vacation on Zombieworld."

"You wanted to rescue the fair damsel." He handed the tile from his pocket to Dover. "Look at this."

"What's this mean — 'your friend changed'?"

"I don't know. I thought it meant you but that doesn't make sense." He explained briefly how it had been given to him. "It seems there are some people in Macerata who don't care for what Cathorius has done."

"How's that going to help us?"

"I don't know that yet either. We'll have to wait and see." He turned to go inside. "It's time we slept."

"You've got to be kidding. After all this?"

"Well, I have to sleep if I'm going to learn anything."

"Not me, brother," said Dover. "I'm psychoactive for the night."

Harry was about to argue, but shook his head. He said, "Goodnight, Dover," then walked off.

Dover returned to his room. For a time he paced, then he drank some water. A cool breeze blew through the room. He closed the door, but the breeze was coming from a vent in the floor — one of Harry's wind tunnels. Dover tired of pacing. He sat down in a hard cane chair and propped his feet on the bed. He crossed his arms, began whistling a tune under his breath, then sang the chorus: "Polly-wolly-hedron all the day." After two verses he yawned deeply. "Oh, no you don't. Wake up, you. Let's waltz the rumba." He got up and performed a series of frenetic dance steps more or less in place. He went into a hula like the one he'd performed on stage with Harry, but finished by banging his toe against the bed. He hobbled back to the chair and sat down again; rubbed his toe awhile, muttering, "At least the pain'll keep me alert." Then he stretched out.

A minute later his eyelids fluttered closed and he nodded off.

III

Cathorius had untied the braid in his hair. It hung like a black fan down his back. While Dover and Harry drank the coffee he was so proud of, he said, "This morning we tour the Palace. I think you should see for yourselves how matters stand."

Harry caught a hint of underlying menace. "How do they stand?" he asked.

Cathorius ignored the question. "Tomorrow night," he said, "I'm opening the Memory Palace to the world. Many of the people who greeted us in Macerata will be attending. I want to complete

all business before then so that nothing will interfere with our pleasure."

"That sounds good," Dover agreed. "Let's go."

Outside, a hot, dry wind made the tall palms hiss and pushed
ripples across the pools, sprinkling the men with prismatic spray.

Harry took hold of Dover, slowing him, allowing the other three
to extend the distance. He said, "Listen to me. Our entropicaster
has bad dreams and we're in them. Crews, Bellicose, & Winkie
tried to halt work on this place for a change of terms. Bellicose was
supervising construction, representing the firm. Cathorius didn't
respond kindly to being squeezed. Something happened to
Bellicose and you and I are here to try to re-negotiate. Whenever I
tried to get specifics—"

Dover stopped dead. "Bellicose is *here?*"

"Shh." Harry beamed at Bragone, who was scowling back in
their direction. When the little man looked away, he continued,
"He could still be around, so be prepared for the worst."

"But he'll know we're not us."

"Maybe we can get him to play along if we can talk to him first.
If you find him—"

"What are we going to do—go off for a picnic together?"

"Hush. We've been in worse scrapes. Accentuate the positive,
Dover."

"Oh, sure." Nervously, he took out a candy and began sucking
on it. He asked, "Did you find Azize?"

Bragone suddenly turned to them. "Why do you both hang
back, hmm? I don't like for people to hang back. It makes me
nervous. I hear plots in the wind. You don't want me to hear plots,
do you, boys?"

Harry plunged ahead. "Furthest thing from our minds," he said.

"Mr. Cathorius, he's very lenient. He tolerates obverse opinions.
I have never learned such patience. Besides, there are things in the
jungle you do not care to meet." He laughed once, as if he had
made a joke. The tattoo on his cheek glistened like copper. He
stayed at their side, urging them forward by his sneering presence
alone.

"Has anyone ever told you that you have remarkable eyes?"
asked Dover. "I haven't seen eyes like yours since the last time I ate
lobster."

They climbed up the portal steps.

Irge reached the top first. He surveyed the estate until
Cathorius caught up with him.

Cathorius patted him on the shoulder. He told them as they climbed, "Irge was an outcast among his own kind because of certain . . . preferences of lifestyle. I took him in. Many of his loudest detractors worked for us, under his command, in building this monument to me. Sweet revenge for Irge." He made a circle with his hand. "The wheel turns. But he knows it can turn again, and so he's ever-vigilant. He protects himself by protecting me."

Two tiers of columns fronted the palace, creating a narrow, shadowed arcade. Cathorius hesitated beneath the nearest, allowing his two "architects" to pass him; but he stopped Dover with a touch on the shoulder. "I'm reminded of something you said in one of your early communications. It was: 'Memory has no doors and windows, it opens as you choose.' And so it should, I agree."

"Did I say that?" Dover asked cautiously.

"Come to think of it, I believe that was your Mr. Bellicose, yes."

"A regular Zen master, that Bellicose," Dover replied.

This seemed funnier than it should have to Cathorius. His head bobbed as he laughed. Abruptly, he stopped and said, "We'll go in now."

Harry and Dover exchanged a look of agreement that all three of their companions were barking mad; both sensed that something unpleasant awaited inside. Dover hurried around in front of the group. "Can we wait a minute?" he asked. "The view from here is so terrific, I want to absorb it all. You know, being here is very different from imagining being here."

"I'm sure," Cathorius replied, slightly bemused.

"Yes," Dover said, "this is really something." He picked a blank space of wall between two of the cinquefoil arches and leaned back to take a long, leisurely look. He fell through the wall into the building. It absorbed him. In desperation, he twisted, stumbled, grasping for purchase. Around him, the air had become thick as paste or G-tank gel. He had to strain to draw a breath. He knew he was suffocating. Sparks danced before his eyes—they played on the standing hairs of his arms and defined the shapes of his empty, groping hands. He crashed down in submarine darkness inside the palace.

Outside, Cathorius and his two bodyguards were laughing. "Is he always such a joker?" Cathorius asked.

Harry tried to mask his own shock at Dover's disappearance and replied, smiling, "Non-stop."

Bragone turned and passed into the wall. Cathorius followed.

Irge grinned maniacally; his furfuraceous skin crackled. "Once more into the breech, Winkie," he said.

"Isn't that followed by a line about closing the wall up with our dead?"

"And more fun that you can shake a spear at. Go in." He gestured toward the wall.

There was no fighting it; Harry took a deep breath and plunged into the illusive barrier.

Emerging on the inside, he stepped through a small entrance and found himself beside Bragone. Dover had regained his feet and was feigning equanimity but Harry could tell that he would have fled already if it hadn't meant passing through the trick wall again. He turned around. The entrance he had come through was the open interior of a standing sarcophagus.

They were, it seemed, inside an Egyptian tomb, in a chamber containing a second, horizontal sarcophagus, in the shape of a scarab. Beautifully outlined, graved, and colored glyphs decorated all the walls. The colors vibrated against the orange stone surfaces. Many of the figures represented had the heads of birds and other animals. One, however, repeated many times, was a green god, seated on what appeared to be a woven box. The god had a familiar, easily identifiable, profile; stylized as it was, the face belonged to Cathorius.

"So appropriate," he said. "The chamber leading into the next life in a real tomb becomes the chamber leading to the inner life of my palace. What a wonderfully clever design."

"You're too kind," quipped Dover.

He led them around the sarcophagus and through the tiny doorway on the opposite side of the room. They had to duck to get out; straightening up, they found themselves confronted with a maze of hallways. By some trick of lighting, the halls were splashed in colors as if a thousand stained-glass rose windows were lighting them. The towers and pavilions overhead contained no such windows, which made the effect all the more astonishing, but once again they couldn't ask how it was done. The Egyptian tomb was one among hundreds of small galleries. The layout had been arranged in such a way that hallways appeared to radiate from every gallery. It was, Harry thought, a perfect labyrinth. It *was* Memory.

Columns lined the aisle down which they went. Occasionally, Harry glimpsed into a chamber—many of them directly inaccessible from the aisle. Some contained sculptures, others mosaics and statues. Part of a mobile was briefly visible inside another. The clever lighting seemed to erupt from within them, giving the impression that each work had been scooped out of the air itself, imagination made solid.

In the next gallery they entered, the floor had been paved with huge stones like an ancient roadbed. Tall trees swayed in a breeze and sunlight glinted through the branches. Along the road, soldiers in Roman uniforms and helmets, carrying small shields, swords, and javelins, stood frozen as if in the midst of a march. A solitary figure held the lead. His face was clean-shaven, and his hair had been cut differently, but he was all too real and identifiable: Cathorius again.

Harry noticed a small plaque in the wall beside the door. "Caesar at the head of Roman Infantry, Ulixes Superbis." He shook his head at the incredible hubris of the man.

Cathorius said, "I *was* that man in another life. He rewrote the rules. He defied the odds. I am still he."

The next gallery appeared to be a tropical scene—a beach of sand and clumps of reeds. In the background, out in the natural harbor, an ancient Spanish ship rocked at anchor. A group of men—some stripped to the waist, others in doublets and trunk hose—encircled two brown natives. One of the natives was kneeling in terror. The other, held in place by two of the men, had just had his left hand severed. His gushing blood glistened wetly.

"Columbus's Azores, the hyperbolical Orient—reluctant Indian's ulna severed," read the monstrous little plaque.

"You were Columbus, too," Harry said.

"I've been so many," Cathorius replied. "Yes, as Columbus, I wanted to find the Emperor of China, to teach him Christian ways. That was my calling. But I also had to have gold to take back to the Spanish court. The natives had so little of it on their naked islands. When they failed to satisfy me, naturally I expressed my displeasure. Ultimately, I shipped most of them back as slaves, anyway. I was venerated for it. Conquest courses through my veins like an extra ingredient in my blood." He turned and paraded out of the gallery, his guards in tow.

Dover read the plaque. "I don't get it," he said.

"Mnemonics," whispered Harry. "Very single-minded mnemonics."

Dover read the plaque again. "It spells his name."

"So did the other one about Caesar."

"Every room spells his name?"

"Or makes reference to an event in his life—make that lives.

He's perverted the whole concept of the Memory Palace. Be very careful in here, Dover. And if you see anything that looks like a waterspout, it's an image from his childhood. I picked that out of his dream—it was important to him in some manner. Now, after you, Mr. Crews."

"I feel like Madame Tussaud, Mr. Winkie."

Cathorius said, "Mustn't dawdle. I've one or two others among my favorites for you to see. Then I'm afraid I have to leave you, to transact some business. You may stay on with Bragone, however."

In a nearby gallery hung the mobile Harry had glimpsed earlier. Harry would have sworn they'd left it far behind. The mobile was as delicate as breath, composed of glass and iridescent, metallic threads, at once abstract and unified. Harry covered his awe by saying, "It seems so different here."

"I have wondered, since I figured out its significance, where you acquired the formula."

"We have to have our little secrets," he answered.

Cathorius nodded sagely. "Secrets are so important. Now let me show you my favorite."

They followed him from one aisle to the next, and somewhere along the way Bragone disappeared. From time to time, as they walked, they could see an immense dome overhead where a celestial map whirled. Dover paused to stare at it, and in a matter of moments he became dizzy. He shook his head and fumblingly hurried on.

They came to a wide staircase built in a double spiral. On the landing halfway up, a broad niche contained another scene, this one clearly of statuary. A naked man ran ahead of a string of beasts—many of them from other worlds than Earth and all with vaguely familiar anthropomorphic faces, one of which resembled Irge. The arrangement was called "Man Alone Can Enter Race Against Tremendous Animals." Dover muttered, "Macerata."

Cathorius said, "I think the faces successfully evoke them all. *I* recognized them in any case, which is what you wanted." They could not ask him whose faces were evoked. He insisted they hurry, then lingered at the top to lean upon the railing and look out across the building that lay beneath the dome. "Pause a moment, enjoy the view," he said.

Below them stretched a cross-section of chambers, all separate but looking as if they might easily be fit together to complete a puzzle. "Memory has no exit," Cathorius quoted again. "How true." The lights of the galleries imitated a city.

They passed a working astrolabe. A gold model of the world Cathorius called Recovery was connected by a spinning, bejeweled spiral of hyperspace to a whole revolving universe.

Ahead of them now, emerging from the darkness as if flung up against the sky, a huge waterspout ascended out of a storm-tossed sea. Where the illusion of the sea was an image frozen in time and space, the waterspout was alive, spinning, whirling up onto purple clouds.

Cathorius had two people with him. One was Bragone; but the other wore a hooded cloak and seemed to be stooping. Dover feared that it would be Azize. He glanced over and caught Harry's urgent nod toward the waterspout. "Oh," Dover said. "Your childhood . . . certainly makes for great art."

Cathorius twisted around, his look fierce. "It does," he said triumphantly. "I've named it 'Chaos.' Appropriately, I think. Now, before you go further in your attempt to convince me of the depth to which I ought to be grateful for this marvel, I want you to consider something. Bragone."

Dover took a step, certain now that some horror had been performed upon Azize. Sleepy-eyed Bragone pulled back the hood and nudged the figure forward, and Dover stopped dead in his tracks. It was not she.

A bent and twisted old man stood there, his gaze both sharp and deranged in its sharpness. The watery blue eyes fixed on Dover, and the dry lips opened. "Ahm," the old man made a rheumy noise.

"Do you suppose he recognizes you?" Bragone asked tauntingly. "We can't be certain, can we? Let's try Mr. Winkie." He prodded his charge across to Harry. "Here's another face. Look and see. Who is it? Oh, but he doesn't seem to be aware of you at all, Mr. Winkie."

Harry experienced a premonition that he was seeing himself in the parchment skin and lost gaze. He wanted urgently to flee. "What's wrong with him?"

"Unfamiliar to you?" Cathorius asked. Behind them all, Irge tittered fiendishly.

"I'd say so," he answered warily.

"Your own partner and you don't know him any better than he knows you." His sarcasm told them everything.

"Bellicose?" Dover exclaimed. The old man gibbered a bit. "He's completely demented."

"Not quite," Cathorius said. "Just this morning, Bragone tells me, he had a few minutes of lucidity. He knew who everybody was. He even remembered his own age. Twenty-nine. He's so looking forward to being thirty. Aren't you, Mr. Bellicose?"

"What is this, Cathorius?" Harry asked.

"You require explanation? You shouldn't. It's simple. When Bellicose delivered his ultimatum on behalf of Crews, Bellicose, & Winkie as regards what I would call an unreasonable adjustment in your fees, I was not very amused. We had an agreement. Halfway across a galaxy I do not care to hear about cost overruns and other such nonsense. Politics and shifting prices on Earth do not concern me in the least. A figure was named, and that is the figure to be paid."

"And very generous it is, too," Dover agreed.

"I think so. Mr. Bellicose argued otherwise. Am I to assume, then, that he was acting on his own initiative?"

"Is that so surprising," asked Harry, "given the distances involved? What happened to him?"

"Let me tell you something you may have suspected about me. I never do favors; I collect debts. I've unmade dozens of worlds and sold them to the richest people, the wealthiest societies. I can buy anything, and the universe is full of substances and elixirs. Some alter the mind, others the body. Some are natural forms discovered on planets I myself have un-shaped, and I control the supply; others are manufactured where there are no worlds, and no prying eyes. No restrictions. If I remained in among mankind, I would certainly and ultimately violate too many laws to be tolerated. But out here who is there to object to my whimsical excesses? You built this palace; you studied my history as few have done. You ought to know that I have come a long, long way."

"So has Bellicose," Dover noted ruefully.

"Yes. Too far, I'm afraid, to return."

"And if we retreat to our original agreement?" Harry asked.

"A bit late for that I think. I was considering, all in all, that you will settle for less."

"Less!" cried Dover.

"Take the difference out of Bellicose's salary. He won't be spending much of it in the time left to him."

Harry said resignedly, "I don't see that we're really offered a choice. Alonzo?"

"I'm not crazy about being my own grandfather. Whatever Mr. Waterspout suggests sounds fine with me."

"Then it's settled. The new agreement will be ready for your signatures in the morning. Business will be concluded then. Now you must excuse me, I've other matters. Please let Bragone show you anything else you wish to see." He walked past them. "Irge," he commanded. The alien turned and accompanied him.

Dover smiled uncomfortably at sleepy-eyed Bragone, who asked, "*Is* there something you'd care to see?"

"I'd like to see a stateroom back to Earth."

"Naturally," Bragone sneered.

Bellicose edged over and grabbed hold of Dover's hand. "Go walkies, Pop-pop," he urged.

The remainder of the day they spent by themselves. The domed vehicle was gone. Cathorius and Irge had driven to Macerata. Bragone was never far away, so that any hope Dover had of finding Azize was all but squelched. In his frustration he began chain-sucking his supply of candies. He convinced Harry to take a stroll with him, in the hope that they could lose their guard in the foliage.

They had nearly arrived where the road entered the jungle when a huge lizard suddenly clambered out of the trees ahead and blocked their way. Dover's reaction was to spit out his candy. He pressed against Harry. "We just stumbled into a remake of 'The Lost World,' right?" The lizard had spikes along its tail and up its back. It regarded them balefully.

The two men waited, and so did the lizard. Finally, it lowered its head to where Dover's candy lay in the dirt, sniffed and then bit at the ground, capturing the butterscotch between its bladelike teeth. The nictating membranes over its eyes fluttered and it snorted. Then the lizard started for Dover. He backed away and ran right into Bragone.

"Gentlemen, you should not have wandered off so far. I told you there were things in the jungle," said Bragone. "This one is Deplida. See the purple spot on her head? She doesn't care for me. Do you, Deplida?" He walked right at her; as he did, he withdrew a small box from his clothing and pointed it her way. The lizard staggered as if he had struck her a blow. Her sullen eyes rolled up. When Bragone continued forward, she turned and crashed unsteadily into the underbrush to escape him.

Bragone smiled broadly, tucking the little box away. "If I hadn't been here, she would have made a meal of one of you. You couldn't run fast enough. Now, where would you like to go?"

They opted to head back to the house. Clearly they could not use the jungle for cover.

"Whatever he wants us to sign, I'm signing," Dover told Harry.

"If I end up with just enough money to get back to Earth, I'll be happy—so long as I get there intact."

Harry asked, "What about your heated passion for Azize?"

"Oh, it's still hot, but I can't even find her. Even if I did, I can't help her unless I can get my hands on the blue activator that little toad back there keeps. And even if, by some miracle, I got my hands on *that* and could get her to the road, all I can look forward to is feeding her to Mrs. Repticulus on the way out. What sort of a life is that to offer someone?"

"None at all. I'm glad you've come around."

"Oh, no. I haven't come around. I still feel the same way about Azize. I'm sick at the thought of abandoning her. But I'd be sicker if my arms and legs went home in separate compartments."

"I confess I was worried about you, Dover. I thought you might be experiencing an unselfish urge."

Dover frowned at him. "Well, perish the thought. You know what? From now on, you stay away from me, too. Once we're off this backwater planet, we part company, you and me." He set off at a quick-march pace. Harry watched him go.

Momentarily, Bragone caught up. "Your partner disagreed with you about something?" he asked.

"He doesn't enjoy associating with reptiles," said Harry. "Frankly, old man, neither do I." He walked away, leaving Bragone to stare daggers after him.

By the time the dinner gong sounded, Cathorius and Irge had still not returned. "They've been detained awhile yet," Bragone explained, "but your food is prepared. You'll forgive me if I don't join you."

"That's okay," Dover said, "I don't think I'd want to see you eat."

With a slight, confused laugh, Bragone bowed to Harry and then walked away. The four native servers remained, at a distance, as they had on the previous evening. The low table was set with red linen and an array of exotic, fleshy flowers.

"How do you suppose they decide who clears the plates?" Dover asked.

"After last night, they probably draw lots."

"Think they understand what we're saying?"

"Irge does."

"Yeah, that's different, though—he's sociopathic."

Harry smiled. "But literate."

"Remind me to throw the book at him."

"What are you trying not to say, Dover?" Harry asked.

Dover set down his fork and took a deep breath. "Look, I'm sorry about this afternoon," he explained. "That's all. I wasn't myself." Harry studied him doubtfully. "Okay, I *was* myself."

"Listen, old stick, you haven't anything to apologize for. I wasn't sure how deep your feelings ran for Azize, and now I am."

"Let's forget the conversation ever happened."

"Capital idea." He opened his mouth to say more, but glanced at the servants and thought better of it.

After the meal, Dover went directly to bed. He had slept so badly the previous night that he was exhausted.

Harry stayed at the table, alone, sipping sweet liqueur and puzzling over the tile. It frustrated him. The message had become clearer—no doubt Bellicose was the friend who had changed—but that only opened up more questions. Who in the city knew about him? And why had they sent a warning?

Harry was more disturbed by the fact that he could not locate Azize's presence anywhere in the house. Either she was no longer there or else the Libitina sealed off her thoughts from his kind of prying. Also, she might be dead. He didn't want to confess any of this to Dover.

Finally, he tired of playing with the tile, and set it on the table. He nursed his drink awhile longer, staring into it, rolling the stem in his fingers. He shifted his position on the pillows, and gradually became aware of another presence in the shadows nearby.

Glancing up, Harry found one of the female servants approaching. She pointed at the tile. He realized what a fool he'd been to lay it down in full view, even with Cathorius and crew absent. He quickly placed his hand over it.

The serving girl stepped over the pillows and said something in her raspy native tongue. When Harry shook his head that he didn't understand, she took hold of his wrist, gently uncovered the tile, then pointed at it. When Harry continued to display his ignorance of its meaning, she glanced about, then leaned forward and carefully put a second tile beside the first.

"Well, well. Something new has been added. All right, m'lady, what do we do now?"

At that moment, Bragone walked into the room. Harry turned, shoving the tiles off the table and dragging the girl down under him. He kissed her passionately, pretending to be too lost in the kiss to notice as Bragone came up beside him.

"Mr. Winkie, I had no idea," said Bragone.

Harry jumped off the girl as if embarrassed to be caught in the act. "I, that is, I found her —"

"Yes, yes, I understand everything. I must tell you, they're not very compatible with us sexually. However—" he opened his hand, revealing a small, grainy pyramid, this one glowing green—"if you want her, she's yours." Harry held out his hand. Bragone dropped the pyramid into it, then walked away. "Mr. Cathorius should be returning momentarily," he called over his shoulder as he left.

Harry picked up the two tiles. He leaned down to hand the new one back to the serving girl. "I do apologize for taking advantage, but it was the only thing—" Before he'd finished, she yanked him back onto the pillows and climbed on top of him. Her lips burned against his. The kiss seemed to last an eternity. When she finally withdrew, Harry was a moment opening his eyes. They'd crossed. He swallowed and craned his head as if drunk. "Not compatible?" he said.

She stood and tugged on Harry's hand. He opened it, revealing the little pyramid. It glowed with a pulsing light. "I thought you were immobilized by this." She smiled slyly and shook her head. Then she pointed to herself and said, "Geela." He nodded, repeated her name.

She drew him to his feet, then pulled him along after her toward the door through which the meals had been served. "Ah, I was wondering what the kitchen looked like here."

But they didn't go to the kitchen. She led him to a concealed doorway out of which a chill breeze was blowing, and indicated that he should enter it. Clearly, he was going on from that point alone. He wished he could get Dover but sensed that he wouldn't be offered another look at this—whatever it was—if he did. Geela stepped back to let him pass.

"Call me Orpheus," he said, then descended into the darkness.

He knew he had to be dreaming. Azize, dark beauty, hot number, stood at Dover's bedside. Moonlight from the balcony windows spilled in stripes across her. She was thin, wan, no more than a spirit. Her wide eyes gleamed, two pearls. "Whatever you do," Dover muttered, more to himself than to her, "don't pinch me—I don't want to wake up."

A scent drifted from her, reminding him of some night-blooming flower; it did things to him. He sat up and reached for her.

Azize took his hands in hers and drew him out of the bed. He hadn't expected her to be so strong. Her eyes searched his face as if seeking the answer to life's mysteries. He wanted to have the answer, any answer. He'd have made up an answer.

"Go with me," she said. Her fingers squeezed his own till he thought the knuckles would crack.

"I don't need that much persuading," he complained. She relaxed her grip and he snatched back his hand and shook it. "Look, why don't we go out on the balcony?"

"Yes," she breathed.

"Just let me put on my pants."

"No."

"Listen, if I go out there in my shorts, we're going to re-enact the boxer rebellion. Just give me a second." He wriggled one hand free and made a grab for his trousers at the same moment that she yanked him the other way. Dover flipped and crashed to the floor; the thunder of it shook the walls. Azize dragged him out into the night. "Okay, I get it. *You* Tarzan, me Jane."

Once on the balcony, she released him. Dover scrambled up, then hopped ungracefully into his roomy trousers. "I'll say this much, you don't waste time with courtship." He thumbed his suspenders over his undershirt. He looked both ways along the stretch of balcony. "I think we're alone now. How about we—"

Azize took hold of his face and kissed him. Her tongue pressed his teeth apart and snaked into his mouth. He was glad he'd put on his pants.

By the time she finished kissing him, he'd forgotten he had legs. Her perfume clouded his thoughts like a narcotic. Her lips melted his will. Drawing back from the kiss, she pressed her cheek to his.

"Go with me," she repeated.

"Anywhere," he replied.

"To the palace."

"I always wanted to play the Palace."

Dreamily, he let himself be led along the balcony. He seemed to float down a curving flight of steps and across an open plaza. Water trickled nearby, and he glimpsed flickers of light in the sprays of a dozen fountains.

She led him to another flight of steps carved into a steep hillside. Halfway up the exhausting climb, a shadow rolled across him, and Dover stared up at the spires of the Memory Palace, black against the starry sky, an overwrought Gothic outline. At the top of the steps, he and Azize passed into the deeper shadows of the arcade.

From the exertion of the climb, the erotic charm had begun to wear off, and Dover resisted a little now. "Why do we need to go in *there?* I'll get lost," he said. He forced her to stop. "Look, I'd go anywhere with you, Azize, but this isn't the escape I had in mind. We have to get you away from here."

"Come," she insisted, tugging.

"In a minute." He pulled her to him. "Remind me again why I'm doing this." He closed his eyes and kissed her. He felt a pinch to his left shoulder, and he muttered, "I told you not to pinch me— I don't want to spoil the dream." At least, that was what he intended to say. Somewhere in the middle of it, he found his lips become heavy and the words emerging as, "Og mabr grmol." To his horror, he seemed to be shrinking, falling away. Azize towered above him. And beside her stood Bragone.

Irge moved into his circle of vision a moment later. He glanced at Dover, then slapped Azize. "Oh, what lies there are in kisses. You were to bring *both* of them."

"The other was not in his room," she replied woodenly. She was watching Bragone.

Dover noticed then how clearly he could see them, and realized that the light came not from Recovery's moon but from a bluish glow escaping between Bragone's fingers. He knew it was the blue pyramid; he didn't have to see it to understand how Azize had been driven to deceive him; he forgave her on the spot.

Bragone opened his palm and the blue glow made Azize burn with its light. Bragone brought it near her face. She trembled violently the closer he got. Irge stepped away, as if anticipating a more frenzied reaction, but Azize only collapsed unconscious beside Dover. He tried to console her, and with supreme effort managed to say, "Erk."

Bragone said, "Irge, this foolish one was in love with her, but the other assassin's eluded us."

The notion seemed to excite Irge. "You drag them into the vault. I'll dispense with his partner. Give it me," he said, and Dover saw Bragone pass him a tiny injection gun. Irge turned away. " 'O magic sleep! O comfortable bird!' " he recited. "But Irge murders sleep." He vanished between the columns of the arcade.

Bragone bent over Dover and dragged him into the wall of the Memory Palace. The sparks swirled around his head like a constellation. He followed them down out of the sky and onto the surface of a familiar world, where he settled on a bench inside an enclosed yard.

IV

Dover was reclining on a bench in Karlotta's garden. It looked nothing like her real garden on Momerath—every unearthly plant seemed two-dimensional, nothing but cut-outs stuck in soil—but Dover's dream-self knew where he was no matter how it looked in the dream.

A zephyr spread the arousing scents of nightblooming flowers upon him. He sighed deeply and glanced toward Karlotta's bedroom. Behind the closed screens, she was dressing for him. Her semi-nude silhouette moved across them.

Karlotta's father hated him—that was the real reason she paid Dover any attention at all. Fickle, spoiled, and reliably mean-minded, Karlotta never did anything without first weighing the cost to her father. The curious thing was, Dover and the old man probably shared similar views on what ought to be done with her.

Harry had warned him it would end badly. How else could it end? Harry seemed to recognize the inevitable outcome of situations long before he ever did. Part of Dover's frustration with Harry was how frequently he was right.

The scent upon the air developed like an itch that couldn't be scratched. Unable to sit and wait any longer, he sprang up and found himself before the sliding screens. Karlotta's wonderfully naked shadow turned to face him. He placed his fingers in the handles and pulled the screens apart.

Just inside, in front of a checkered divan, stood Harry, dressed in Karlotta's parti-colored gown. Glancing at himself, he asked, "So, what do you think?"

Dover frowned. "All that's missing is the bag over your head. I suppose this isn't part of my dream and I would have been with Karlotta if you hadn't butted in."

"Sorry if you were expecting someone else."

Dover remembered suddenly how he'd gotten where he was. "Harry, pal, they've killed me and they're coming for you, get out of your room—"

"Relax, my boy, I'm not in my room. By my calculations, I'm almost underneath the Memory Palace. I guess that means you must be, too. Tell me what happened."

Dover described how Azize had awakened him and led him into a trap. "What a chump," he said.

"Dover," Harry spoke the name with a mix of affection and

exasperation, "you're always falling in love and it's always turning out badly. Nothing I do or say ever seems to help, or keeps you from re-enacting disaster the next time."

"I reject the uniformity of nature."

Harry looked skyward. "I tried. All right, for once someone else is in more trouble than you. Azize couldn't help duping you. I already told you they have absolute control over her will. In the grip of that power, she's like a machine."

"She doesn't kiss like one. Anyway, laughing boy thinks we're assassins. Us! We couldn't kill the *lights*. And now I'm dead and they're coming for you next. You know, dead's not much different than being asleep."

"You are asleep."

"Yeah, I knew that. But how do I get out from underneath the Memory Palace?"

"I'm not sure yet. If they've gone looking for me, I guess I can't go back to the house. I wonder what happened. I thought everything was settled. First, let me make good my escape, then I'll come find you. Whatever you do, keep dreaming till I get there."

"I'll try." He sounded as if the effort would be monumental.

"Just stay unconscious—for you it should come naturally."

"At least when I sleep I stay put," Dover said, and slammed the screens together. He stepped back to look at them. The shadow of Karlotta had disappeared, leaving the empty glow of a lamp to light the screens. Try as he might, he could not will the shadow to return. In frustration, he flung the screens apart again.

Karlotta lay upon her side on a low divan. Except for small slippers, she was naked. She stared at him over a rind of speckled fruit on which she was noisily sucking.

"Why, Karlotta," Dover said, "I didn't hear you come in."

By way of reply, she spat a seed toward him.

"And refined as ever. I like your outfit, though—nothing suits you." He turned and closed the screens behind him.

Opening his eyes, Harry experienced brief disorientation; in Dover's dream there had been light and color; in the cold darkness of the wind tunnel there were neither. Currents gusted over him, roared in his ears. His teeth began to chatter, and he rubbed his arms roughly for warmth. Cathorius's cooling system worked exceedingly well. What he had yet to understand was why Geela had sent him down here in the first place. Had she known they were coming for him? She hadn't acted as if he was in peril.

He got up and walked farther along the tunnel. By his estimate, he wasn't under the palace yet. It lay ahead, beyond a patch of absolute darkness. He'd only stepped into it when something stung his shoulder, and a voice whispered, "Irge murders sleep."

He had time to say, "Nuts," before toppling into the dark. It seemed to have no bottom.

Harry didn't dream. He floated in a gauzy cortical space, in which active minds flashed and vanished like fireflies at a distance. If he came near one, the dream leaking from that unconscious mind drew him in, and he became a dream voyeur.

He approached one that seemed nearby. Suddenly, chaotic, distorted creatures surrounded him: Great crowned pavilions and hopping pillars and even a flexing Tower of Pisa that glared with huge, red eyes at another figure, the dreamer. The monstrous architectural forms lumbered after a younger version of Bellicose. No wonder he'd looked insane on the outside. On the inside he was. Whatever they'd done to Bellicose, he was caught in a nightmare where his own expertise became his enemy. Harry called after Bellicose. The dreamer ran right past him, as did the monsters. Bellicose fled toward a distant, charcoaled horizon line. The dream retreated with him.

Harry floated along, drawing near another sleeping entity. He maintained his distance. He needed to find Azize, not try out every dream of every prisoner beneath the palace, and who knew how many might be under here. He had to remind himself that he'd joined their ranks.

Drifting higher, Harry found the dark space overhead glittering with minds. The palace's main floor seemed to be full of them. He concluded it must be the night of the following day, and the party—Cathorius's celebration—was underway. No wonder he couldn't find Azize. She'd be up there among hundreds of minds. He would probably never find her. Just his luck.

Then something shook his real body. The sensation reached his detached spirit like an electric current. Alarmed, he spooled back through the subconscious mists and into his physical shell, then kicked like a swimmer straining to reach the surface.

He opened his eyes to find Dover, upside down, staring at him. "I was about to kick you. It worked so well last time."

Harry cleared his throat. "We're in the same cell?"

"No. I came to get you out."

"You . . . came to get *me*? How?"

"You want the version I'll tell my grandchildren or the truth?"

"The latter if you don't mind."

"Okay. *She* did it." He pointed, and Harry found Azize in the doorway of the cell, leaning on the jamb for support. She raised her dark, tired eyes and said, "It may be the last thing I do, but I won't let him destroy you the way he did Bellicose. The way he did me."

Harry got to his feet and caught her arm to hold her up. "We have to find Geela," he said. "We have to get out of here now."

Dover took Azize's other arm and the three of them moved into the hallway. There was a cell next to Harry's. Irge lay sprawled there, his feet sticking out. Harry pushed his legs inside and closed the door. "Irge murders sleep all right," he muttered. "Is there a way to lock this?"

"Yeah. I took this off him." Dover handed Harry a flat, black keypad with eighteen buttons on it. Harry looked at it for a moment, then intuitively he placed it against the door. The bolt clanked into place. "Too bad I don't know the combination. I'll never get him out now." He turned to his companions. "Azize, how many guests are upstairs?"

"Hundreds. I don't know precisely. I've a cell down here, too. Most everything he wants done out of the way is done beneath the palace. These were dungeons before your structure was built above. The wind tunnels are full of cells and people."

"Everything's stored down here?"

"That's right."

"Then all we have to do is find the right room."

"Find the right room, are you both crazy?" Azize asked. "Bellicose's cell is there. Take him with you if you must, but go now. The tunnels lead back to the house. You can steal a vehicle."

"No way, sugar," Dover interjected. "We don't leave without you."

"Couldn't have said it better myself, Dover," Harry added.

She looked from face to face and saw that they were resolute. Her eyes welled with tears.

"Oh, don't do that or I'll start," said Dover. She hugged him and shook with sobs.

"He'll kill you," she said.

"Nah. Not us." He glanced over her shoulder. "Right, Harry? Not us?"

But Harry was already lying down. "I'll just be gone a minute," he said. "Keep the home fires burning."

Dover led Azize a few meters away. "It's better if we give him

some room," he lied. "And, besides, now I can tell you how much
I—that is, how you—"

She put her fingers on his lips. "I know it already. You've no
idea how terrible it was, betraying you. I wanted to kiss you, but I
had to kiss you for *them*, and the taste of your lips became foul and
corrupt."

"That won't leave an aftertaste, will it?"

She saw him smiling, and flung her arms about him. He bent
his face to hers.

"Okay, Dover, I've got it!" cried Harry, "Let's go!" He sprang up.

Azize's lips were but a millimeter from Dover's when she pulled
back. Dover stared blackly at Harry. "How much is the Hays Office
paying you to do this to me?"

"Not enough." Harry brushed past him. "Come on—no, wait,
Azize should go back to the party before they come down here
looking for her. We'll just have to chance it that no one misses
Irge."

"I know I don't."

Azize started away. Harry said, "Oh, one more thing. Where are
the drinks being served?"

"From the waterspout," she answered. "He's filled the pool
around it with one of his exotic concoctions. People dip their
glasses in when they get thirsty. He's calling it *Chaos*."

"If I have my way, he's going to be more right about that than
he knows."

Azize continued along the tunnel.

"Come on, Dover," said Harry.

"Don't rush me. I want to watch her walk away." Harry waited
impatiently until Dover came to him. "Okay, what are we doing?"

"Opening a treasure trove. I didn't want her along. For all I
know, just being close to the stuff might kill her."

They walked through a maze of wind tunnels until Harry
stopped them at one door. It was a dark, solid alloy, featureless.
Dover rapped on it. The door absorbed the sound. Harry took out
the small keypad he'd used earlier and fit it against the door. "Now,
don't say a thing." He closed his eyes. After a moment he tapped at
the buttons and the door thudded as the tumblers inside shifted,
released. The door began to slide up into the tunnel wall. Harry
took the keypad off and stuck it back in his pocket.

Inside was a large chamber with metal walls. It was filled to
near capacity with modular shipping crates like the ones they'd
hidden among on their journey from Momerath. Harry placed the

keypad on the nearest crate and typed furiously again. The crate hissed open. Inside were stacked cases in silver and black. Harry opened the top one.

Dover leaned around him to stare at the contents: hundreds of small pyramids, all neutral gray in color, dormant and separated from their activators. "Vacuum packed and ready to eat," he commented. "There must be millions of them in here if the rest of the crates are the same."

"Yes. The cases are paired, see? The activators will be in this one." He slapped a hand on the nearest black case.

"So, what do you plan to do with them, Mr. Winkie?"

Harry stuck his hands in his pockets and rocked back on his heels. "Well, I was thinking we should see if they float."

The two men, carrying two cases, emerged from a recessed doorway beneath the double-spiral staircase of the Memory Palace. The doorway had been designed to be unobtrusive, and Dover and Harry went unobserved by the revelers despite the glow escaping from the activators in the crate.

The crowd meandered in and out of the maze of chambers. Some were clearly confounded by the labyrinthine arrangement, others seemed to find great amusement in getting lost. At the base of the steps, tables of exotic foods had been set up, and people stopped on their way up or down for something to nibble upon. Two servers from Cathorius's staff stood there, busily preparing more food. Along the far-left aisle, Azize came strolling beside her husband. She was glancing in every direction. Cathorius paid her no attention. He was chattering blissfully to an obese man in a tuxedo. Dover thought he looked familiar but couldn't place him. Bragone was nowhere in sight, perhaps off looking for Irge.

"How are we going to get up the stairs?" Dover asked.

"We need a little assistance. Don't run away." Harry walked out to the serving table. Two servers were mechanically slicing strange fruits and vegetables, and piling them onto a serving tray. "Pardon me," he said, and the two glanced dully at him but continued their chopping, "Would you help me over here? And bring that covered salver along, would you? It's perfect."

Most people would have asked why, but not Libitinazed slaves. The servers put down their utensils, picked up the covered tray and followed him unquestioningly. They followed Harry under the stairs.

A few minutes later, Dover emerged, wearing a starched white jacket, vest, and red tarboosh, and balancing the covered tray in one hand. Harry followed, pausing to stash the black case beneath the serving table.

They started up the stairs. Bragone was coming down; he was craning his neck, searching everywhere. Harry ducked in close behind Dover, who used the tray to conceal their faces.

No one else paid them any mind, although Harry spotted the alien, Gilbert, and some of the staff people from the orbiting way-station. He followed his partner across the upper floor, straight to the waterspout.

As Azize had said, the base of the illusion had been turned into a refreshment fountain. Dover set the tray on the lip of it and sat down to catch his breath. He flexed his fingers. The heap of little pyramids had proved heavy when held up by one hand. Harry stood in front of him as if admiring the view of the spout and, above it, the whirling celestial forms. "Hurry up, will you?" he whispered.

"All right." Dover got to his feet. He turned, picked up the salver and lifted the lid, then bent over to pour the contents into the fountain. They tumbled in, swirling darkly as they dissolved. At that moment, someone grabbed hold of Harry from behind; instinctively he jumped, crashing into Dover, who went flying over the lip of the containment.

Dover hit with a splash and came up flailing, spewing. His jacket absorbed the liqueur and turned dark blue. The crowd gathered around, laughing and cheering.

Harry tugged free of Geela, who stood horrified at what she'd caused, and strained desperately over the low wall to reach Dover, but couldn't. Some invisible force propelling the waterspout had caught hold of him. It dragged him inescapably under the illusion. In helpless horror Harry watched as Dover spun up into the core of the spout and vanished in the roiling clouds above. He stared expectantly, waiting for the body to come crashing through them, but nothing penetrated the clouds. Who knew what machinery lay behind them.

The crowd jeered and hooted loudly—after all, it was only one of the slaves that had been dispatched. They dipped their cups and toasted the waterspout, shouting, "Here's to chaos! Here's to Cathorius!"

The tarboosh floated, turning a circle in the drink. "Oh, Dover, I'm so sorry," Harry said to it.

Geela tugged urgently on his arm. Before he could react, she dragged him behind the nearest cluster of celebrants. She had only been trying to warn him that Cathorius and his retinue were approaching. Azize was clearly terrified, and Harry saw why almost at once. Bragone, close by her side, was followed by a disheveled Irge, looking insanely angry. His insect eyes scanned the room.

Safely hidden, Harry watched while Cathorius heard what had transpired. Cathorius started laughing. He dragged over another servant and had him fish out the fez and the tray, which came up empty, its contents dissolved. Harry breathed a sigh of relief: at least Dover had not died in vain. Cathorius took a tankard and filled it from the fountain. "A toast," he shouted. The crowd yelled in agreement and pressed in to fill their glasses. Loudly, he proclaimed this night a triumphant success and dedicated his toast to everyone present. "Especially," he said, "the magical firm of Crews, Bellicose, and Winkie."

And there, at the front of the crowd, stood the two architects, the young one who'd wanted to sing, beside his fat mentor. Harry understood now how he and Dover had been discovered. The real Crews and Winkie had been found in the G-tanks. That explained where Cathorius had gone with Irge, and why they thought of him and Dover as assassins.

"All right, Geela," he whispered, "it's important that one of us get out of here and down to the table at the bottom of the stairs. There's a case underneath it filled with Libitina activators, and this entire crowd has just drunk an elephantine dose of the stuff. I'm going to draw their attention."

"No, you can't," she said. Her multifaceted eyes pleaded with him.

"You speak our language. Of *course* you do. You're a spy, you were listening to everything in the house."

"They would kill you. Wait. My people are coming."

"I can't wait. Dover died because of this. I have to see it through. There's no way I can get around them, but Irge probably won't notice you if he's concentrating on me. Take the Libitina and go. Cathorius can be controlled anytime you wish now. They won't realize—they'll think they're just inebriated." He nudged her gently away. "Harry," she said. He smiled as though he weren't going to his own funeral. Then he stepped boldly through the crowd and announced, "I have a toast, too, if you don't mind."

The guests stopped talking and stared at him. What was a server doing offering a toast?

Cathorius's eyes narrowed. Irge and Bragone started to move, but he held up a hand. "And what would that be?" he asked.

Harry took a cup from off a tray and strolled toward Azize as he spoke. "I'd like to toast my good friend, Dover Demerit, who gave his life for the success of this event. Dover, old man, wherever you are, I miss you already. The universe has lost a lot of dark matter in your passing." He lifted the cup. Indulgently, the crowd lifted theirs and drank. Harry smiled.

"He's had his joke. Take him below and kill him," Cathorius told Irge. "I no longer care who sent him—and find the other one."

High overhead, something twanged like a gargantuan guitar string snapping. A tremulous cry preceded a figure in a blue coat, which burst out of the clouds. He clung to a sparkling star—a piece of the galactic display overhead. It was still attached to the rest of the galaxy, and to everyone's horror, the stellar display unthreaded and came zooming along like a tail after a comet. A thousand milky, sparking stars shot out of the clouds. Harry watched in awe as Dover sailed over him, over Cathorius and his henchmen, and crashed into the largest globe of the astrolabe. Stars rained, exploding all through the shrieking crowd. The astrolabe whirled wildly, as if trying to throw Dover. One of the small planets smacked against the head of a guest—a female security guard from the way-station with a tape across her nose. Another planet spun loose and just missed Cathorius, taking out instead the obese architect, the real Alonzo Crews, who stumbled back and crushed a group of four, then flipped into the fountain. The crowd dove for cover. Crews was sucked into the waterspout, but stuck halfway up. The pool began to roil.

Chaos was what they had toasted and what they got. In the melee, Harry eluded Irge, grabbed Azize, shouldering into Bragone and snatching away the glowing blue activator the little man guarded. He ran for the stairs. Dover slid off the astrolabe and dragged himself upright, but he could not stop turning in little circles. "Oh, not this dance again," he protested.

"Are you all right?" Harry called.

"Well, would *you* like to swing on a star?"

Harry grabbed him by the arm, gave him the activator. "I think I'd rather be a pig. Run!"

Behind them, Cathorius was screaming, and they didn't have to look to know who was after them: Everybody. Reaching the landing, they met Geela hauling the second case up the stairs. She had removed the lid. A twinkling rainbow of light poured from the inside as various activators ignited in the presence of the released bacteria.

Harry let go of Dover, who grabbed onto Azize for support. Grabbing a handful of the activators, Harry flung them up the stairs. Guests froze in place. Some, struck by activators, shook violently and fell. One or two simply sat.

Cathorius, at the top of the steps, bellowed, "What is happening here?" He charged down, Bragone and Irge at his side.

"I'll show you," Harry said. He flung a fistful of activators at Cathorius.

The large man batted them aside like insects, or at least tried to. His arms froze, and his feet seemed to anchor on one step. His eyes rounded with panic. He could not stop himself from plunging headfirst down the stairs. He shot along like a torpedo, his skull striking the edge of each step in succession. He skidded across the landing and lay still.

Irge and Bragone glared at Harry. "O conspiracy!" Irge yelled. "I'll carve you as a dish fit for the gods!" He started down the steps. Bragone, too. Harry flung another handful of activators at them to no effect. Bragone tittered, "We never eat and drink with the others, no."

Beside him, Dover said, "There's a small crowd gathering on the first floor, and I don't think they dipped in the magic fountain, either. This is starting to look like the Alamo."

"I remember. Time to go, then." Harry turned. The foursome bounded down the steps. Dover shouted, "Fire!" but it was the explosion of the waterspout above that spurred the crowd away. Bragone and Irge plunged into the melee behind them.

They reached an intersection and Dover cried, "It's *this* way," and split off with Azize down a different corridor. There was no going back. They dashed along from room to room, thwarted by displays that Dover had never encountered, glancing around long enough to see Bragone in hot pursuit, closing the gap. "This is great—a Memory Palace and I can't remember the way out," he told Azize. At least when so ordered she could run.

They dove around a corner, and glimpsed Harry and Geela zipping past in another corridor. Dover tried to reach them but instead strayed deeper into the maze. The only advantage from all the turns was that he briefly confounded Bragone and gained some distance.

Finally, he spotted what he wanted and shoved Azize ahead of him through the small doorway into the Egyptian tomb. He scooped her up and leapt headlong through the standing sarcophagus, battle-crying, "Ankh if you love Imhotep!" The two of them merged into the wall.

Harry and Geela, meanwhile, ran like rats in a maze. Every turn confounded them and Irge clearly knew the arrangement in his sleep.

Harry recognized one aisle and swung suddenly left, catching Geela off-guard. She stumbled but he would not lose her, and pushed her into the nearest—and what he hoped would be the correct—chamber.

They came to a halt before the display, but it wasn't the Egyptian one after all, it was the marching Roman legion, and Harry realized that he had made a dreadful mistake: he had trapped them. He could hear Irge's feet slapping the stones outside. "Ha, ha! The pure fool!" Irge shouted in triumph.

Harry jumped past Caesar and tore a javelin from the nearest soldier's hands, then turned and charged at the door. In the same instant Irge burst into the room. The spear drove straight through his mouth and out the back of his neck. In agony he whipped around, trying to get out again, smacking the long javelin repeatedly against the wall. Dying, he could not understand how to withdraw through the doorway. Finally, he turned upon his prey, stumbling almost blindly at them. They backed away and Irge collapsed on the roadway in front of Caesar. He twitched once and was still. The weight of the shaft dragged his head down as if he were merely dozing, part of the display.

Geela walked over and spat upon the corpse. "He was monster," she said. "He"—she didn't know the word for it, so she raked her fingers across her belly, miming a disemboweling—"to children."

"Well, thanks, that gives me the new title for the exhibit," he said. "'Child Abuser Tackles Harry of Romans—Irge Upchucks Spear.'"

"What?" she asked.

"Just restoring order. We'd better find Dover and Azize." He started to go out past her, but she embraced and then kissed him. Coming up for air, Harry remarked, "Surely, he'll be all right for a few minutes," then plunged back into the kiss without waiting for her reply.

Outside, Dover and Azize were trapped between Bragone, a fountain, and one spotted lizard. The nearness of the activator in Dover's pocket had Azize paralyzed. He could think of no command to give her that might help. Bragone was maneuvering the reptile by use of his little box toward his victims.

"Deplida will make a meal of you both," he said. "A fitting end for what you've done."

"And there I was, hoping for a reward I could survive," Dover said. He watched as the huge beast came nearer. "I'll go first," he told Azize, "Maybe I'll be enough for it. I know you can hear me. I'm taking the activator with me. I hope it'll dissolve inside the beast and free you. Either way, Bragone won't be able to get at it again." He stepped away from her, confronting the lizard. "Okay, Deplida, bring it on."

Hissing, the reptile crawled straight up to him, but then hesitated as if seeking the tenderest spot to begin.

"Go on, you," urged Bragone.

The lizard glanced dismissively his way. Then she lifted her right forefoot and tore off the left half of Dover's trousers. His bag of candies ruptured, scattering butterscotch all around him. The lizard disregarded him entirely. She began devouring the candies. After each one, she raised her head and rolled her red eyes skyward as if in ecstasy.

"What are you doing, you prehistoric blockhead?" Bragone cried. "Kill him!" He shook the little box at her, then hammered at it to shock her into action, striding ever closer to inflict more pain. Deplida's muscles twitched each time he stabbed the box, but she continued grazing, hunting the candies. Bragone screamed at her in frustration. Deplida suddenly raised her head, stared straight at him. Bragone realized his blunder and turned to flee. The spiked tail slammed into him, flinging his body halfway to the fountain. Deplida calmly returned to gobbling up more treats. Dover led Azize out of range. "Nice dinosaur," he said, just in case.

A group of figures burst from the jungle at the end of the path. They raced across the courtyard and up the steps of the palace, ignoring Dover and Azize. That would be Geela's underground army, he thought with a sigh. It was a good thing they hadn't waited to be rescued.

He walked over to Bragone's body and picked up the black box. "You're much too involved in your work," he commented to the deceased before returning to Azize.

"Well, here we are again, you're a zombie and I don't have any pants on." He dug into the ruin of his trouser pocket. "Only two left," he said of the candies he found. "We might as well celebrate, right?"

Mechanically, Azize answered, "Celebrate."

"Great. Open your mouth," he said, and she obeyed.

"Suck on the candy till it's gone," he said. She obeyed. He glanced back at the palace. "Gee, I hope Harry's okay."

"Me, too," she replied.

"Yeah, I— Hey, you talked. On your own."

Azize's eyelids fluttered. "I did, didn't I?" She turned her head back and forth. "I can move, Dover. What have you done? How have you done it?"

"I don't know," he replied. He took the activator from his pocket and held it up to her. Even as they stared at it the glow was dwindling. In seconds it had gone out, and the tiny pyramid was gray and lifeless. Azize began to laugh. She spun about, rapturous in her freedom. "Oh, Dover, it's the candy. It has to be. Something in the candy is blocking the Libitina. Killing it."

"What?" He glanced at the lizard, which uttered a bovine bleat and collapsed in drunken delight upon the road.

"It's *these*," said Azize, and she picked a few of the candies out of the dust. "It's why even though you fell into the fountain, you weren't affected by the drug. You're immune."

"I wonder what we can get for this stuff."

"You can set free all the people Cathorius has imprisoned. Everywhere."

"I can?"

"You'll be a galactic hero."

"I will?"

"And I'll love you for it, dear Dover."

He pressed his hands together. "Baby, that's all I was waiting for. And this time, there's nobody here to stop us."

Azize took his face in her hands, and finally—of her own accord and without interruption from Harry—she kissed him.

Afterword

Road to Recovery

Okay, to recap, at a Sycamore Hill writing workshop one day, I was discussing with Connie Willis the fact that John Kessel had covered the Marx Brothers with his story "Faustfeathers," and that she had put a lock on screwball comedies in "Blue Moon" and various other stories of hers (she later made off with P. G. Wodehouse and Jerome K. Jerome, too, and, really, someone should investigate). So I asked her if I could have dibs on Hope-Crosby "road" pictures. She said, "Sure." If you ever talk to Connie Willis, you will understand immediately that she has the power to grant such wishes. It's why I won't be the one who turns her in.

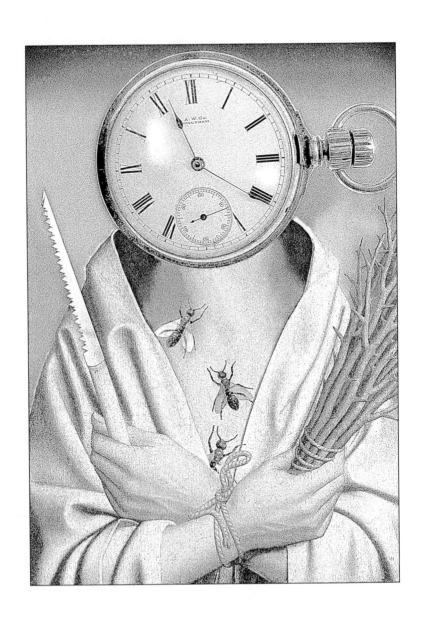

From Hell Again

HE PULLED LIGHTLY UPON THE OARS, STROKE upon stroke, and his boat skimmed the black water of the Thames. Mayhew was a dredger and this his work, but no commission had ever been so strange. He pondered what it could all mean and how it had come to be. In his Peter boat, shallow-bottomed and easy to row, he often forgot himself entirely. Sometimes he sang or hummed a tune. Sometimes his thoughts just strayed, to happier times before his wife had taken to drink and run away, when his daughter had lived with him. But now she was back after all, and things would be better again . . . with this commission.

He remembered Demming. Two nights before, coming out of the fog in a frock coat, a tall toff's hat and shadow for a face, Demming had appeared upon the quay as Mayhew tied up his boat. Gaslight glinted off the gold of Demming's walking stick. He asked after Patrick Mayhew, and feigned surprise when he learned who he was speaking to. "You've a reputation as a dredger," Demming told him. And Demming knew how lean the summer was — so lean that no sane man could have denied his offer: a job of dredging with five hundred guineas paid in advance and a promise of an impossible five hundred more if it proved successful. "Tomorrow night then," Demming said, "I'll meet you here at two."

Mayhew remembered how his footsteps faded in the fog but the sound of the stick tapping went on and on.

It seemed to echo in the slap of the water against his squared bow.

The second meeting. Demming had given him the heavy purse as promised. He hadn't needed to count it to know how much it must contain. But in the interim the questions filled with worry had come to plague him, and these had to be cleared up. "This is criminal, what you want me to do," he said over the purse. "Not at all," Demming replied. "It's dredgework that you've done a thousand times before." "Will I need a net or grappling hooks? What is it you want me to find?" Demming paused before answering. His face was plainly visible now in the light of Mayhew's lantern: a long, proud face, pouchy under the eyes, perhaps from drink. A clean-shaven face, a powdered face. "Hooks or nets is a matter for you—I can't say. What you seek is a body. However, the corpse itself hardly concerns me. The man—for it is a man, Mr. Mayhew—stole from me a watch, a family heirloom that is irreplaceable. The mischief that befell him is of no concern. If you find money on him, you may keep it, but you may *not* turn him in to the police for any finder's fee. I'm paying you quite enough to discourage that. Nor are you to mention him to anyone. Anyone at all." Mayhew thought he understood this: "You kill the fella?" he asked. But Demming hardly balked. "That is none of your business, either. You perform your dredgework, stick to that, and we will get on just fine." This left him believing that Demming had killed a man without knowing that the man carried the stolen watch on his person. An odd oversight, but not an impossible scenario to envision. And it was not much of a crime to refrain from turning the corpse in, not enough of one to overcome a small fortune.

Mayhew listened for a moment to a drunk shouting, somewhere out in the dark, near the passing quay.

Last night on the river. With the half-built Tower Bridge a mangled horror hanging over him, he secured his weighted nets to the boat, then unshipped the oars and began the long, exhausting process. Lights on the ships at dock winked at him. He dragged and hauled nets, dragged and hauled again. His black-tarred sou'wester coat kept the sodden nets from soaking him, but made him sweat twice as hard at the oars so there was hardly a difference. As dawn came up, he called it quits with three shillings worth of coal dredged up but nary a sign of a body.

Then the happiest moment of all in this whole adventure took place. Returning to his house, he found his daughter, Louise, on the stoop. She had come back to him out of the depths of the East End. He listened to the whole sordid story, forgiving her for her sins before he even heard them. She had lived as a whore for nearly a year, keeping with a man in Castle Alley. He had been cruel to her, but she feared, as most of the whores did, the one the papers called "the Ripper," and her hateful prosser was at least protection against that. Soon enough she had turned to drink—ironically, to the same Dutch gin that her mother had loved. She cried as she spoke, and Mayhew held her close; she was his little girl again. He felt the weight of the money in the pocket of his coat, and he dreamed their new life. Soon he would quit the river, carry his daughter away from the squalor of Lambeth. They would take a country house, a small estate—just as soon as he found the body, and the watch.

With renewed vigor at the thought of success, he put his back to it, and the Peter boat skimmed the water like a skater across ice.

At three he was under the Tower Bridge once more, his weighted nets dragging, catching. Ship lights gleamed like will-o'-the-wisps along the banks. The first haul produced a piece of a hansom wheel and an intact lantern, also from a carriage, and Mayhew wondered if an entire cab could lie beneath him in the black depths. The lamp was worth some money to him, and it was a curious enough proposition that he dropped his nets there again to see if he would collect more fragments from a hansom. As he rowed vigorously, the nets caught again, this time holding like an anchor. He tried, but couldn't pull them free. Taking one of his grappling hooks, he stood, removed his coat, and tossed the hook out behind his boat so that it would sink beyond the nets. Down and down the rope played out, until the hook touched bottom. Then he retrieved it, slowly, letting it drag along. The hook, too, caught on something, and Mayhew pulled on that for all he was worth. He strained till his pulse was throbbing in his head. The hook tore free suddenly, sent him sprawling back into the wet bottom of his boat. He reeled in the hook. It brought up a large broken slab of wood caught on one of the spikes. When he tried the nets, he found them freed as well, and drew them in as fast as he could.

The nets brought up more broken wood and what looked to be a piece of iron rail of the sort that might garnish a driver's platform. Then there *was* a hansom on the river bottom, as unbelievable as that seemed. He sat back in wonder at how such a thing could happen, and looked right up at his answer—at the jutting promontory of the Tower Bridge. As Mayhew imagined what had happened, the water behind his boat erupted in a release of bubbles. He scrambled to the rear in time to see a body flung up onto the surface of the Thames, bob there for a moment, then sink out of sight. Hastily, he grabbed his nets and flung them out where the water still rippled. Then he rotated the oars into the water and rowed hard, nearly lifting himself onto his feet. The nets took on weight and dragged. He shipped the oars quickly and started drawing the nets in hand over fist, soaking himself but too single-minded in his purpose to stop and put on the slick sou'wester.

The nets and their tangled capture bumped against the boat. Mayhew grabbed hold and pulled the whole mess in at once. The body rolled beneath the ropes, the head flopped back, and death stared up at Patrick Mayhew.

The man had been in the water much longer than Mayhew had supposed, long enough for the skin to have sloughed away from the sludge-covered bones in most places, to leave a wet, glistening visage, a moulage of mud. As much as a year, Mayhew guessed, pulling back. He had hauled corpses in every horrible state of decay imaginable, most of them obscenely bloated. This eyeless figure ought to have been insignificant by comparison, but it now sent a wave of terror shooting like an electrical discharge through Mayhew. He found himself pressed against the side, gripping one oar as if to crush it. This unreasoned fear lasted only moments and then passed like a breeze continuing on downstream. Mayhew had a vision of the people on the ships at dock waking from their sleep, lifting taut faces from pints of ale, as the cadaverous wind rolled by. He wanted nothing more than to grab the nets and fling this body back into the blackness of the Thames; but he had a purpose here, and he was not finished.

He inched his way to the remains. The body wore a cloak and, beneath this, the remains of a coat, vest, and tie. Mayhew tore the cloak apart when he lifted it—the material shredded with the weight of muck to support. He dug his fingers through the slime and drew back the black coat—which looked to have been a fashionable dinner jacket—to get at the vest. At first he thought there was no watch, because the chain, covered with weedy slime, was as dark as the material. As he shifted the corpse, something in the watch pocket gleamed, and he moved the lantern nearer, then reached in and drew out the watch. Where every other part of the corpse was caked or colored from its long stay in the water, the

watch case glistened as if it had been polished that morning.
Mayhew turned it over, disbelieving that it could be in such condition, but the other side was as shiny and unblemished. He could
make out distinctly the smoothly molded ridges of the case and the
stylized face of a Gorgon in a raised circle, even in the lantern
light. He stood, and the body rolled slightly. One arm was suddenly
flung out. The knuckles clacked against the side; the sharp, blackened fingers began to curl up slowly. He could bear the thing no
longer. He stuffed the watch into his pocket, knelt down, grabbing
the netting, and heaved the body over the side. When it did not
sink right away, he grabbed a short boat hook and stabbed out,
shoving the body under the surface. The hook must have caught on
the corpse's coat because, when he tried to draw it back in, it
snagged, tipping Mayhew off-balance. He twisted around and the
hook caught on the edge of the boat. All of his weight went on it as
he turned, and the hook snapped. The spot was cursed. In a panic,
Mayhew threw down the broken pole, sat and began hauling on
the oars as hard as he could, desperate to escape that haunted
place. Never had the Thames carried any fear for him before this,
but now, even with the body back where it belonged, he could not
get rid of the apprehension that had crawled into his boat with the
corpse. It was as if the fear had slithered off and condensed into the
muck on his clothes, at his feet. His shoulders ached and his lungs
burned at the effort, but Mayhew did not slacken his pace until he
was in sight of his dock. He left hooks and nets in the boat, threw
the tarp hastily over everything, and set off, almost at a dead run,
for home.

Louise was awake, and he could not hide his uneasiness from her.
He had told her of the job, of Demming, and of what he suspected.
Now he showed her the watch as he described in trembling detail
his encounter with the submerged carriage and the passenger he
had released, for that was how he interpreted the events. They sat
at the small dinner table, Louise in her nightclothes and a shawl,
Mayhew still dressed in his checked shirt and smelling of the river,
the watch on display between them. Louise marveled at the etched
Gorgon on the case. She reached out and picked up the watch,
which Mayhew, in his loathing of it, was unable to do. He wanted
to tell her to put it down, but also wanted to see inside it. Louise
pressed the winding stem and the case popped open. She opened
the lid. Mayhew dragged the lamp closer.
   The face of the watch amazed him; whatever he had antici-

pated, this certainly was not it. The watch dial, a simple dial, took up the lower quarter of the face. Around it, the gold had been etched beautifully with trumpet swirls and leaves. Above and to each side of the dial were two oval insets. These contained small photos that appeared to have been stuffed in; one of them was loose along one edge, and Mayhew peeled it down to find a painted design like a piece of foreign calligraphy underneath. The photos themselves were the only parts of the watch that showed damage from being in the river. They had gone dark and gray, and the best that Mayhew and his daughter could make out was that one of the photos was of a woman's face. The features were too vague to hint at more than that. In the top of the watch, filling that quarter, was a circle the same size as the dial below, and containing another etched Gorgon ringed by snakes. Mayhew noticed now that the face was not quite human in that it had two eyes to each side of the nasal fissures where a nose ought to have been. And the teeth came to points, bared, like two rows of daggers. He closed the case to ascertain that the other Gorgon mirrored this image, and it did. He raised his eyes to Louise. She smiled at him, apparently unaffected by the horrible aspects he saw in the watch.

"Let me see something, papa," she said as she spun the watch toward herself. She sprang open the case again, then lightly ran one fingertip around the edge of the Medusa circle. About three-quarters of the way around, she stopped and pressed with her thumb, and the circle popped up. Louise stared with momentary shock, then began to laugh. "Oh, look at this," and she held the watch out to him.

The Medusa circle had hidden a small painting. For a moment, Mayhew did not comprehend the picture, but then he understood and did not know whether to laugh or be disgusted. The painting showed a grinning priest seated on a small padded stool while a demon knelt, its mouth and one claw clamped around his marrow-bone. The demon's body was a dark green, rough with warts, and it had a second lewd face on its arse, yellow teeth and red eyes. That second face finally tipped the scales for Mayhew. "Don't laugh," he ordered Louise, "it's blasphemous. What sort of a gentleman would own a watch like that?"

"You'd be surprised as to what 'gentlemen' carry on them."

"I don't want to know. I found what's wanted and I'll give it away like I'm supposed to, nor do anything but."

"I wonder if it still runs," Louise mused. She closed the case, then began winding the stem. The watch started to tick after a moment, loud and precise.

"Put it down!" Mayhew spluttered. "The man was in the water well onto a *year* by the look of him. There wasn't a part of him that the water hadn't rotted at, and here's his watch that runs like it come from a shop this morning. By what Providence can such a thing be?"

Louise put the watch down. "I don't have an idea. But there it is. Maybe that's as why he wants it back, your Mr. Demming. Maybe he's got the most special watch in the world."

"Maybe so. I don't care nor I get my money, but you leave it be. I'm tired from rowing for my life, so let's get us some sleep, and today I'll take him his watch and buy you something real fine." His head swam for a moment as he stood. He shuffled off and lay down on his small bed, listening to Louise climb into hers, listening to the watch ticking on the table across the room.

The rhythmic ticking washed over him as he fell asleep and followed him down into the landscape of dream. He found himself walking through a darkened Aldgate Street. Gaslight created bubbles of clarity along the murky avenue, which contained shops that he did not recognize, many of them canted forward, looming over him, others stretching high above. Soon, he walked along Whitechapel Road. People began to appear in the pools of flickering light, their faces as distorted as the buildings. They watched him pass; most were grinning like the priest in the little painting, and their sharpened teeth held all of his attention. The rest of their features escaped him. He hastened on, found himself in a darkened lane. Someone spoke close by, and he turned to see Louise's face. At first she was the forlorn child on the doorstep but as she came to him her features distorted, her hair writhing as if alive. He stared into her eyes and found them empty, two great holes through which he could see some other place where the sky was shot through with stars. The ticking of the watch sounded like a scrabbling rat.

A weight in his hand tugged at his awareness like a child pulling on his arm. He looked down, found a huge knife there, a strange knife that looked like an immense carpenter's file. Again he faced Louise, and this time he found the features of her face fallen away, revealing muscle and bone, teeth like daggers. Her mouth hung open and he could see more of that other place between the ivory points. Her jaw clacked shut, the bared grin horrible. "Take me *here*," she said softly. Her fleshless hand slid down across his trousers. He was becoming aroused by his own daughter. The knife pulled at him, begging to be put to use. "*Open the gate*," a cold voice said. Could it have been him? "You don't want to do that, or the coppers will find us," Louise said. *"Open the gate, let them through,"* the voice insisted harshly. He turned, and Louise was a skeleton poised before that other place, which now poured through the alley, suffusing every shadow with a reddish glow. Someone moved into it, and he saw Demming there, behind the living skeleton, looking accusatorily at him. Demming reached out, saying, "Give it to me," and the skeleton begged, "Papa, don't." Demming scowled and slapped the bones aside. They shattered and went tumbling; some clattered on the stones, others landed in the altered shadows without a sound and dropped into the star-shot void. "The watch," Demming demanded. With a scabrous, warty hand, he opened his cloak to attach the gold fob, which now ran from Mayhew to him. The swirling stars played in the shadows beneath his coat, too. "Papa," Louise called. "Papa." The ticking of the watch beat at his brain. He squeezed shut his eyes and tried to cover his ears.

When he opened his eyes, he was standing near the door. Pressed between him and the wall, Louise had her palms up under his jaw as if trying to push him aside. Mayhew backed away. He saw that her nightgown was torn, purple marks on her throat. "Did I—?" he tried to ask. Tears spilled from her eyes. Mayhew could not look at her. He had known other dredgers, other men, who actually boasted of having coupled with their daughters; and once, in a pub years earlier, he had struck a man who grabbed hold of Louise. That *he* had almost done this awful thing, that the desire might live inside him as it did in those other monsters—he could hardly stand to think on it. He went and sat on his bed. Louise covered herself with her shawl and came to sit beside him.

"Papa," she said, "I ain't like that, no matter what you think. I ain't a whore for you, nor any more for anyone else. I wish I'd never told you none of it." He tried to reply, to explain, but beyond her shoulder he saw the lamp on the table and, beside it, the recovered watch. The watch had run down and stopped.

Demming lived in St. James's, a neighborhood far more fashionable than Mayhew's. Both the dredger and his daughter went along to Demming's house; he feared that if he left her home she would not be there when he got back. She had accepted his apology and his explanation, but he could tell that she did not truly believe any of it.

A black iron sign hung on the wall beside the door: WALTER A. DEMMING, DOCTOR OF NEUROSES. A servant answered their knock and escorted them directly to a second floor office. There was a single desk to one side of the room, and behind it a case containing skulls of humans and related mammals. A glass jar on the desk held for viewing a model of the brain. Mayhew went to the case and saw, on the shelf below the prominent skulls, a display of medical tools, most of them scalpels and probes. He understood only that these were tools for cutting into people. Behind him the door opened, and Demming, all in tweed, swept in.

"I dared not hope that it was you, Mr. Mayhew. With all I said to you, I maintained doubts. I—" He broke off, staring darkly at Louise.

"My daughter," Mayhew interjected by way of an introduction. He did not care for the intensity of Demming's stare.

The doctor blinked and placed a look of humor upon himself. "Of course," he said. "You have it?"

Louise reached in and removed the watch from her coat, placing it on the table. Her father had been unable to touch it, even in daylight.

Demming barely restrained himself from leaping on the watch, though from his expression he might as easily have intended to crush it as to gather it up. He seemed to forget that the dredger and his daughter still occupied the room with him; his loftier demeanor vanished, and he wrung his trembling hands and mumbled under his breath. His eyes rolled back and for a moment he struck the pose of a man lost in prayer. Mayhew noticed how dark Demming's eyelids were. Then the doctor opened the drawer of the desk and withdrew a velvet purse identical to the first one that he had given Mayhew. "You have done me an inestimable service," he said, while staring once more at Louise, this time with what might have been trepidation. "I shan't forget it." He pulled the handkerchief from his breast pocket and began rubbing at the watch case, harder than if merely polishing it.

"The watch," said Mayhew slowly, dismayed, "you sure it's the right one?" He took the purse.

"There is no doubt of that. There could be no other watch like this. And now, regrettably, I'm late for my appointments at Bethlem Hospital, so I will have to ask you to go, and take my appreciation from the money."

"Of course," Mayhew replied, goaded into recalling the class distinctions at work here. He tucked the purse away, took Louise's arm, and led her out. The liveried servant waited at the top of the stairs and showed them out onto the quiet, tree-lined sidewalk.

They walked down through the park to Birdcage Walk without a word traded between them. With Parliament in sight, Louise could no longer stand the silence. "He was a very impressive man, weren't he?" she asked.

Mayhew drew up short and turned her to him. "Don't you ever mention him again. Not to me, not to anyone. It's done, I'm paid, and I choose to forget everything, just like he wants. You do the same, girl."

"Papa—"

"No, damn you! Never!" He let go the moment she struggled, and watched her run ahead. She did not understand what he was trying to say. He lacked any real understanding of it himself. Perhaps the nightmare was still distorting his reason, and his hatred of Demming was due to the foul memory that he carried all too near the surface. He believed that, for reasons he could not explain, he had come in contact with something monstrous, something unholy, and well beyond his comprehension. The best thing he could do, he thought, was to forget it all, to bury the memory as he had buried the corpse by tossing it back into the water. This had now been done. He hastened after his daughter, to explain the way he saw things.

Returning home, he found that Louise had not gone there. She had run off to cry, he tried to assure himself. Later she would come back and he would apologize. Later. Suddenly very weary, Mayhew lay down to sleep.

When he awoke, it was past six and still Louise had not appeared. Mayhew began to worry, but anger soon tinged his concern. This was how things had gone with her before, the last time she ran away. He suspected that she might have fled back to the East End this time, too. If whoring was all she was good for, then to Hell with her; a daughter of his should be made of better stuff than that. "This time I can't forgive her," he announced to the empty room, and buried his own loneliness beneath anger. He might have made something of her, but he saw now that she would only waste his money on drink, attracting the same filth that combed the East End. He knew he had not been rough—he hadn't hit her, and he hadn't even been yelling at her, not really. He cursed her for being like her mother, cursed her mother for everything in the world that wasn't right. He dug into his pocket, felt the weight of the coins. Well, at least something was right in the world—at least he had money enough for a long time to come. A country squire, what a great man he would become. Maybe he would marry a fine woman and raise another daughter, one of distinction this time. He went and fetched the other purse, then sat down at his table and counted his way to sleep. He awoke before dawn and took a stroll, smoking a cigarette to ward off the dampness. On Webber Row he stopped into the Frog and Peach for a pint. The few patrons were all huddled in one smoky corner and whispering excitedly. Mayhew sat up on a stool and asked the man who drew his pint what was going on.

"Well, it'll be in the papers by noon, I suppose."

"What will?"

"That the Ripper's back. Killed him a woman last night in Whitechapel, just like before."

Mayhew set down his pint. "Where? Where'd it happen?"

"Castle Alley's the street as is being given. Here, where you going?"

Running at breakneck speed, past fruit vendors, fish vendors, beggars, and drunkards, Mayhew dashed headlong across London Bridge and into the East End. The visions of the day before tinged everything he saw with evil. Louise, turning from woman to carcass to bone, and in the background, Demming, always Demming. Now he forgave her, now he whined her name and begged God to forgive him for all the hateful things he had thought about her; it was really only her mother he condemned, and it always had been. Onto Whitechapel Road, shoving desperately through a line of people who waited in their own desperation outside a casual ward house to get a bed for the night. He skirted other such lines, except once to get directions to the street. The back streets were narrower, and clogged with carts, wagons, and horses. He ran past row houses, and the wide, wooden gates of pungent stable yards, then at last into the cramped corridor of Castle Alley. Wagons and carts lined one side of the road. The smell here was much worse than that by the stables. Halfway along, three policemen stood on drier stones, on small islands in the excremental sea. Mayhew grabbed onto one of them, babbling his questions between breaths. The other two pulled him off and shoved him up against a wall with a nightstick under his jaw. Mayhew began to cry. The policemen looked at one another, embarrassed to be sharing this. The one with the nightstick eased back and said, "What's the matter, then? She your strumpet?"

"Strumpet?" Mayhew rubbed at one eye.

"Yeah, you know old 'Claypipe?' "

"You was a customer, then," suggested one of the others in the hope of lightening the mood. "Must a' been a good piece to set a man weepin'."

"I—what was the name of the woman killed?"

"Alice McKenzie. She's known round here as 'Claypipe Alice.' What, did you think it was somebody you knew?"

He nodded, wiped at his face with both hands and tried to regain some equanimity. "My daughter. I heard that there'd been another murder—the Ripper."

"Oh, there's been that, right enough. His handiwork, all right. Through the throat, 'e got her, just like before. Found her between two vans, right up there." He pointed. The third policeman, silent till now, moved forward, close to Mayhew, and said, "So, you heard about a killing and you decided that it was your daughter got done. Gawd, people do go on, don't they?" He shared a laugh with the other two.

Mayhew's hand trembled and he shoved it into his pocket. He dared not tell them about Demming, about what he suspected, about his dream. They would jail him for his part in it all, he was certain. "My daughter, she lives on this street. Her name's Louise —Louise Mayhew."

He sought for their recognition and got more than he wanted. One of them became beet red and turned away as if to scrutinize the alley. The policeman who had questioned him said flatly, "Number twenty-three." He stepped back, rubbing his thumbs against his fingertips. None of them would meet his eyes now. They stepped from the walk and clomped off toward where the body had been found. Murder they could live with, but the father of a whore—the notion even that whores had families—was something they could not allow for.

Mayhew sniffled and moved quickly on to twenty-three. Not until he had his hand raised to knock, did he hesitate, turning away suddenly in indecision, pressing again to the wall. What was he going to say to her now that she was alive? His thoughts had been for a dead girl. Anything he said to her here would only shame her. If he left her alone, she might come home again; but if he left her alone . . . His wild thoughts collected like bees, and he realized for the first time what he was thinking: Demming was Jack the Ripper. How could this be coincidence—Castle Alley of all the winding corridors in the East End? Somehow, some poor bastard had discovered this—had discovered that a gold watch helped him, or made him do it, or something that Mayhew couldn't even guess at—and Demming had been unable to continue without it. That hateful watch, everything was tied to that watch; and he had retrieved it. He started back out of the grimy street, ignoring the odd glances of the police.

He wandered distractedly most of the day. Mayhew was not a man of action, nor a particularly skilled thinker. All he knew were nets and grappling hooks and the cold waters of the Thames. But he had to do something—Demming was going to kill Louise, of that much he was certain.

A drizzling rain rustled the leaves in St. James's Park and made the air smell of earth and decay. Prostitutes of a much higher class strolled by under umbrellas. One murmured to him as he passed. He kept his left arm pressed against his body to keep the item in his sleeve from slipping out. It had been a short boat hook not two days earlier; Mayhew had used a rasp file to sharpen the broken point into a needle. When a policeman appeared ahead, he ducked instinctively from sight, but in the rain Mayhew hardly looked different from anyone else in the park.

He reached Demming's street and, as he drew near the house, he saw the door open and a figure come out. The figure—a man dressed as if for a party—walked purposefully past him. Mayhew made a quick glance to determine that the man was not Demming. He glimpsed a pale, sweaty face and round, glassy eyes beneath the brim of a tall, silk hat. Demming's door thumped shut. The street was silent, no one else about.

Mayhew went up to the door and rapped the knocker. A few moments passed before the door opened a crack and one eye stared out at him. It was Demming himself. The door opened wide, and the doctor stood cavalierly before him. "Well, this is a surprise. Come to hobnob, Mr. Mayhew?"

"You're Jack the Ripper."

Demming spluttered a surprised laugh. "Am I?" He was about to go on but paused to look past Mayhew, out into the gaslit street where Mayhew could hear footsteps. "Why don't you come in and tell me about it?" Demming let him in, then led him perfunctorily up the stairs into the same office they had stood in the day before. A chair now sat before the desk, as if he had been expected. The leather was warm, and Mayhew recalled the visitor who had passed him. "Now," said Demming, "I've done a great deal of work with lunatic delusions. Why don't you tell me yours and let's see what I can do to help." He opened a box on the desk and with a steady hand took out a cigar, closing the box without offering one to

Mayhew. He leaned back against the desk, his ankles crossed. "How am I the—the infamous Ripper?"

Mayhew raised his head to meet Demming's conciliatory stare and said simply, "The watch."

For a fraction of a second, Demming faltered. If Mayhew had not been staring hard at him, he would have missed the twinge. Then Demming laughed and replied, "Mr. Mayhew, you are either drunk or mad. If the former, I advise you to go home and sleep it off; if the latter, you must accompany me to Bethlem this very evening." He moved around the desk and leaned for emphasis on the blotter, his cigar still unlit between his fingers.

Mayhew could only shake his head. He had entertained doubts till now, moments all the way here from Lambeth when he drew up short, thinking himself insane, his notions absurd at best. But he did not need to be a specialist in "lunatic delusions" to see that the doctor was lying, and prodding him to reveal what he knew in order to determine how he should be dealt with.

"You killed Alice McKenzie last night. But you were looking for Louise."

"Absurd, sir. I was at the theatre and a dinner party last night. A Gilbert and Sullivan musical. I went nowhere near your lovely daughter."

"You're lying."

"How many witnesses will be needed, Mr. Mayhew, to prove it?"

"The watch, then. Somehow the watch let you do it. When Louise wound it, I went to sleep, and you were in the dream—"

"You let her wind it?" The facade was gone: first the doctor showed fearful amazement; then his eyes narrowed with determination. He drew open a drawer and pulled out a pistol, aimed it at Mayhew, who pressed back into the creaking chair as if to escape. "You saw some things, but you haven't all the facts. Still, your zeal might be enough to set the police on me, and we can't have that, not when we're so close."

"Close to what?"

"To opening the gates, to giving me some peace. What do you do on the river, Mayhew, spend hours just sitting and thinking?" He said this with an air of humor, a hint of admiration. "I'll tell you, then—as a reward of sorts.

"I've spent much of my life studying the diseases that can afflict the mind, Mr. Mayhew, while you rowed aimlessly about the Thames. I had begun working with hypnosis to treat patients. I found in a few of them a curiously recurring set of images amidst their twisted fantasies—images of other worlds and their concomitant demons, much of which sounded like the reflections of some barbaric priest upon his drug-induced 'journeys.' Among those patients caged in Bethlem Hospital, I found one who was susceptible both to hypnosis and to this uncanny tapestry of images. I used a rather unusual watch to put him in a trance where he could describe his demons. It's Swiss, it was a . . . I once thought it was a gift. Have you ever heard the name Cagliostro? No, of course not. He was a sorcerer who followed in the footsteps of Mesmer, in Paris. The Catholics claimed all sorts of satanic things about him— even that he had feasted with the dead. The man who gave me that watch told me that it had reputedly been fashioned for Cagliostro by a corpse through the practice of necromancy, subsequently had fallen into the hands of Eliphas Levi, another infamous villain, and had passed to my acquaintance after Levi's death in '75. A *corpse*— we joked about it. Such a wild, absurd tale. And I—I wore the watch, here, in my vest. For years I wore it with not so much as a hint of its . . . God, of its power. It took a madman to do that.

"What I expected, I can hardly remember. Of course I had him stay here rather than at 'Bedlam.' Outwardly, he was passive and I felt sure he would be safe. It wasn't until the third murder that I discovered the—the connection. The watch turned up missing, you see, and while searching I found that my patient was not in his room. I did not find him that night. But early the next morning—I could not sleep—I discovered him unconscious in his bed. He had climbed in the second-floor window, which still lay open. He was wearing one of my suits, and his face, his chin and nose, had warts on it that I could not remember him having. The watch was in his—my—breast pocket. It was not ticking. I picked it up without waking him, to take it, and turned the stem just a little, casually, thoughtlessly. With a cry of absolute agony, my patient snapped bolt upright. I dropped the watch and he lay back down.

"Later that day I put him in a trance and got from him a story that I then found hard to believe. He said that the watch had spoken to him in his trance state, that it took control of him, that the fantastic demons of his dreams could not compare with the real ones inhabiting the watch. They were making him perform terrible crimes. Here it was, then: I had unleashed Jack the Ripper upon the East End. Worse, he had worn my clothes and used *my* surgical knife. I considered returning him to the hospital but I decided against this, mostly out of fear that someone else might discover what I now knew. I finally resolved to keep the watch from him while trying to cure him of his delusion. These were only East End trollops he had used in his aborted rituals—the world could do without a few of them—but I had never wanted this to happen, never. I do not know if he wrote any of the letters that the police collected.

"You will already know that I failed. He disappeared and with him went my watch. To this day I have no idea how he escaped. My suspicion is that one of my staff unknowingly wound the watch. I sought him everywhere, discreetly of course, but had no luck. Then, after the last one, the woman Mary Kelly, he returned here. I hardly recognized him. His eyes were shot with blood, and the warts had grown in clusters across his cheek. I feared that he might actually be leprous. His mind had gone, and he babbled out that he had been moments away from completing some task, from bringing the demons of his dreams into the real world, when some other spirit, as of reason, took hold of him—which I presume means that the watch had stopped. He saw what horrors he had wrought under the demons' influence and he tried to destroy the watch in Mary Kelly's hearth. It revealed the extent of its power then, and instead of being destroyed, it erupted with some terrible energy. I still believed that this was all some dark corner of his mind, with no anchor in reality. Only later did I discover that some of the things on the grate in Mary Kelly's house had actually melted, that some unaccountable force had been unleashed. At the time, as I said, I dealt only with him. He had been burned rather severely on one arm. His mind collapsed finally even as I injected him with a soporific, careful not to touch him directly. The things he said afterward made no sense whatsoever. I could no longer keep him here, and I dared never return him to 'Bedlam.'"

"You killed him."

"In point of fact he was still alive when I pushed the rented hansom off the Tower Bridge. Your river murdered him, not I."

Mayhew shook his head at this rationalization. "Then why dredge him up when he was safely put down? And that devil's own watch," he said, but the realization dawned on him even as he asked it. "You can't mean to try again?"

Demming twisted the pistol away in his sharp gesture. "I've no choice now. Those vile things of his madness have come creeping into my own dreams. Oh, faint at first, very vague; but in the past few months I haven't dared to sleep without morphine. I would never have sought you out, except that the fiends even managed to crawl through *that* barrier. God knows what they really are. The painting in the watch hardly begins to suggest . . . Mr. Mayhew, they're like worms burrowing into your brain, eating their way right through it. If you fail them, deny them, the excruciation they can induce—Cagliostro died in a madman's anguish, in prison, and I know—I know why."

After a moment, he went on more calmly. "I knew I was going insane. All they wanted—all they *demanded*—was that I retrieve the watch and continue what had begun. For any chance at peace, I hired you, I found another at Bethlem, and I set him to it just like before."

"The watch," Mayhew said, "the fella I passed coming in here—he's got it."

"You don't think *I'd* carve her up. What if she looked at me, what if the image of my face were caught in her retina for the photographers to find? Let them have some other face to identify in the dead woman's gaze."

"But why my Louise?"

"It's the damned watch, don't you see? You let her handle it, and it lives by these murders. I tried to clean all traces of her off the damned thing—you saw me do that! But the demons—their energy, their substance, must have drunk of her life in just those few moments. I'm sorry. It knows her."

"How will you kill me, Mr. Demming? That's a gun, not the Thames, you got there."

Demming looked down at his hand. "Yes," he said in sad agreement. At that moment, Mayhew flung his short spear across the desk. It smashed an inkwell on its way, throwing blackness across Demming's face, a wide gash of shadow. The point entered him below his neck and Mayhew leaped up and shoved it with all his might. Demming sprawled back, slammed into the glass cabinet of skulls, shattering it, then fell forward across the desk. Mayhew stole the gun from his twitching fingers, then made himself withdraw the boat hook from Demming. The doctor flailed briefly, then lay on his side, gasping. Underneath him, spurting blood pooled and mixed with the ink on the desk.

Mayhew did not wait to see if the doctor died. His concern was with the monster already out and prowling the night.

He ran to Pall Mall and hailed a cab, giving the driver one of his gold coins in advance for the fastest ride to Whitechapel the man could manage. The delighted driver asked no questions, and his coach skidded every turn on two wheels, plunging through the rainy night.

No one was guarding Castle Alley; the police knew well that the

Ripper did not work so regularly and never returned to the exact same location. Not before tonight.

Mayhew leapt from the coach, twisting his ankle on the ordure-slick stones. He ignored the pain and ran into the narrow street. At the other end of it, walking steadily, stiffly on, was the well-dressed man he had met outside Demming's. Mayhew slowed up, his heart and mind racing, then started ahead on the same side of the road. Twenty-three lay directly between them. He increased his pace to ensure that the Ripper did not reach it before him. With every step, he considered what to do and how to do it.

Steam rose from the sidewalk, a stench of decay. Mayhew hurriedly removed his heavy black sou'wester and balled it up around his arm. The approaching man still seemed to take no notice of him. They were close enough together now that Mayhew could see the droplets of rain on the brim of the top hat, the point of a crooked nose, the whites of shadowed eyes that continued to stare straight at number twenty-three.

The Ripper noticed him only at the last moment. Mayhew saw the face twist with hateful recognition. The Ripper's hand drew from a coat pocket a huge knife—the one that had appeared in his dream. The Ripper raised the knife and lunged at the same instant that Mayhew jumped forward and rammed his wrapped hand into the Ripper's chest. Demming's pistol made four thumping noises, quieter than if he'd knocked on a door. The Ripper stumbled back a step, staring down at himself, then up at the acrid smoke curling out from the coat. Part of his face held onto the evil scowl, but one corner of his mouth turned up as if in a grin. "Just like that," he said. He giggled, then fell over on his side. His head cracked loudly against the cobblestones and the gold watch skittered out on its length of chain, as if trying to escape into the gutter.

Mayhew looked at the body for some time before he realized that he did not see the knife. He started to bend down to search and sensed an odd coldness in his back. Reaching up, he encountered the hilt of the knife projecting acutely above his shoulder. Bracing, he pulled it free. Strange, he thought, that there was no pain. He knew he did not want to be found outside Louise's door like this; he wanted her to come home of her own volition. And she would, he pledged, she would.

The Thames was vague behind the ceaseless drizzle. Each easy pull on the oars made Mayhew grind his teeth. His shirt, under the shiny tarred coat, was soaked in blood. He had grown tired and cold, almost as cold as the burden he carried wound about in his weighted nets. He could see the dull shine of the watch where he had tied it securely to the nets. The Tower Bridge loomed out of the rain like some great, broken limb, making Mayhew think of bones rather than iron. He guessed that this was the spot more or less where he had discovered the watch. He shipped the oars and crawled back to the body. Listlessly, he took the gun, the blade, and tossed them over the side. In the coach that had carried him and his "drunken" companion to Lambeth, he had looked over at the face and wondered who the man was, what he had been. Now he no longer cared.

With the last of his energy, he grabbed onto his nets and dragged the body up over the lip of his boat and let it slide gently into the Thames. The ripples of its passing spread out across the water, disrupting all of those from the rain. Finally accepting exhaustion, Mayhew slumped back and closed his eyes, envisioning the two bodies rotting together in the coach on the bottom, the watch and the evil it contained buried in muck for all time. The tide was going out. Mayhew let it take hold of him. Slowly, he drifted beneath the jagged overhang of the bridge, cutting off the rain. He blinked the drops away like tears as the darkness crawled up him.

Afterword

From Hell Again

Okay, I'm fascinated by Jack the Ripper. I'm not alone in this. Susan Casper and Gardner Dozois, who edited the anthology *Ripper!* are also Ripperphiles. So is Harlan Ellison. So is Jack Dann, with whom I once collaborated on a comic Ripper story. When Gardner and Susan invited me to write a story for their anthology, I knew what that story would revolve around, because ever since I laid eyes upon Donald Rumbelow's incisive book it has been for me the queerest piece of the puzzle. During the final murder the Ripper committed, something was burned in a pot hanging in the hearth in that room—and it burned with such intensity that it melted the pot. No one to this day has ever figured out what would have generated that much heat, much less why the mad murderer would have bothered. It's one of those peculiar facts that sticks out, that doesn't conform to a simple explanation and never will. As for the true identity of Jack the Ripper, I think Gardner has it right when he says that if that identity were finally revealed, all who've ever speculated upon the case are going to go, "Who the hell is that?"

How Meersh the Bedeviler
Lost His Toes

YOU KNOW THIS STORY ALREADY. YOU KNOW IT
from great Bardsham's performances, which, like so many of
his skillful shadow works, portray Meersh's adventures to resound-
ing acclaim. When Bardsham controls the rods, he *is* Meersh.

There are as well the paintings collected and permanently
exhibited in Colemaigne, and from these—if you didn't know it
already—you would deduce that the events happened long ago, in
the earliest of times before all the gifts of Edgeworld suffused,
altered, reinvented every element of life in Shadowbridge. It all
took place on a span called Valdemir that has long since disappeared, collapsed into the ocean and been swallowed up, or
transformed by the Edgeworld into another place.

Meersh the Bedeviler had many adventures. Not all turn out for
the best.

*   *   *

One morning Meersh's neighbor woke him. He slept in a net
hammock that snared each of his dreams and kept him from rolling loose while embrangled in them. His dreams were as real for
him as being awake is for most of us.

The door to his house shook and rattled as if a storm had arrived
outside. Meersh sat up and glanced about.

At first he had no idea what had awakened him. He smacked his lips because he had just dreamed a great feast that he'd managed to steal from someone wealthy—a governor of Valdemir he thought it was. He could still taste the spices in the stew and the lemons in the pie. If someone hadn't pounded again on his door, he might have plunged back into the dream; dived into that vat of stew. He could do that.

Instead, he rolled out of the hammock and tiptoed to the door. There was a small window filled with multi-colored, leaded diamond panes beside it, and he sneaked a glance at his visitor.

His neighbor's name was Sun-Through-Clouds. It was she who had banged at his door. Even through the distortion in the quarrels he recognized her shape.

Sun-Through-Clouds was a beautiful woman, black-haired and golden-eyed, just as Bardsham's puppet represents. A great silver stripe ran over the top of her head and through the fall of her long hair. She'd come to Valdemir from one of the mountainous islands on the far side of the world, where trees grew as thick as sargasso and the people hacked them and roped them together into wooden lodges—at least, so she'd described to him. It was too remarkable a story to believe, but Meersh asked her to tell it to him now and again so he could sit and inhale her fragrance. He could have listened a million times if it meant he could close his eyes and breathe beside Sun-Through-Clouds. She seemed to have no idea of his devotion, which on the face of it makes her naive or else cunning. But perhaps her ignorance of Meersh's affections was due to her preoccupation with her children—two fitful demons who thwarted him every time he came near to fondling their mother.

Seeing no children but only his neighbor in all her beauty, Meersh willingly opened the door. Sun-Through-Clouds's smile drank him up. He basked in it, joyful in its radiance.

"Meersh," she said in a voice that chimed at least three perfect notes, "I'm so very glad you're home today. Have I wakened you?"

"Oh, no, sweet cousin," he said, yawning, "not at all." This in spite of his shaggy hair pushed up flat in a wedge, the result of his sleeping on it, and the fact that he was dressed only in a nightshirt which his alerted penis even now prodded toward her in its eagerness.

Sun-Through-Clouds nodded as if to say she was satisfied with his answer; in doing so she looked at the protrusion in his nightshirt, but did not react at all. "I have a difficult favor to ask," she said. "You know I would never ask anything frivolously." She met his eyes. Her eyelids fluttered like sails. Like the wings of doves.

"Anything!" he cried.

For a moment she hesitated as if weighing his devotion. "I must travel the spans for a day or more and can't take little Vek and Jurina with me. I have to travel fast, that is. And peripatetic." She was always using words like "peripatetic"—words out of some vast lexicon; especially plosives. She loved plosives. "With my wares, to make some money. And they both adore you so. And when I told them—"

"You wish for me to look after your *children?*" He was unable to disguise his consternation. It was as if she had asked him to drive hot spikes into his eyes. It was as if she desired to make candles of his fingers. It was as if she'd demanded he become a tax collector. He would have agreed to all that more readily.

"Oh, but they're *exquisite* children. Really very good. After all, they're mine. And they adore you so. Don't you, my dears?"

In unison, the two miscreants stepped out from behind their mother's ample hips. They had the same face, Sun-Through-Clouds's children: oval eyes as dark as coffee; and rings circling their eyes like some deeper pigment in their tanned skin, which had led Meersh to the suspicion that their father was a nature being, maybe a Raki. She depicted him as huge and dark and so full of malice that he'd driven her to sail across the world and take up residence here on this little circular close, where Meersh had the good fortune to dwell. Sun-Through-Clouds described her own people in something other than human terms, too; although never had the specifics of their natures been—as she might have said—pellucid. Their suggested alienness confounded Meersh: She seemed the summation of round, soft, perfect flesh. Why had someone so lucious *ever* had anything to do with such a malevolent creature as a Raki? She deserved better. She deserved Meersh.

She said, "They'll do whatever you tell them."

Meersh eyed them doubtfully.

"Won't you, my doves?" she asked them.

The children exchanged a glance and then, smiling pure innocence, nodded.

Oh, yes, thought Meersh, they'll do what I tell them.

But he had no real choice. Whatever else he was, Meersh was a creature of his appetites, and all of them were focused upon Sun-Through-Clouds. "All right, bring them in if you must—I mean, my dearest neighbor. But for *how* long are you gone?"

"Ah, possibly three days if the market is good." Sun-Through-Clouds wove baskets and chairs. She had woven the dream-catching hammock in which he slept. Her strong hands were the only rough part of her. He was certain of it.

She said, "Here," and handed him a low, ceramic jar.

"What's this?" he asked. It was covered by a paper wrapper stuck down around the mouth of the jar.

"It's their physic. Give them one good spoonful each night before they slumber. It's critical they have that much. That much and *no more*."

"Physic?" He eyed them eyeing each other. "They won't be soiling themselves, will they? Curatives always affect *me* that way— that is, I have to be very careful. That is to say . . . I must tell you, they don't look at all sickly to me."

"No, and because I give them this. Otherwise, they could never prevail in this pelagic place so unlike their natural home, so woodsy and lush."

"Lush," he repeated, with a meaning all his own.

"You mustn't forget. And feed them their one meal a day promptly then. Take good care of them, my dear, and when I get back . . ." She let the unspecified promise linger.

"One meal and a spoonful. Before they sleep," he said. "Yes," he said, "I promise." He could hardly swallow.

"You are so kind." She took a step away, but hesitated on the threshold and turned back to him. "Dearest, sweet, pliable Meersh." She leaned forward and kissed him. He hardly heard her words. He was looking down the front of her bodice and thinking of pears.

"She is gorgeous," said his penis.

"Beautiful, yes," Meersh answered vacantly.

"I think before she leaves you should have her," the penis urged.

"Have her?"

"Have her *in*. She gets thirsty like anyone. A few cups of purple wine, and who knows what might happen? What you might see, eh?"

Meersh's voice creaked with lust. Tongue-tied. He couldn't even hush his lusting member.

Sun-Through-Clouds pretended not to hear. She offered him again her promissory smile, and he hung upon it as she departed. He watched her supple silhouette shift back and forth against a view of the main avenue of Valdemir and the green distance of the sea.

When even the afterimage of her had faded from his eyes, he withdrew. The gulls on the eaves watched him charily.

He turned. The paper-covered ceramic pot was still in his hand.

The children had taken seats around his *el-quirkat* board. It sat on a low stone table, its inlaid nacreous strips gleaming. The two children were attempting to pry one of the strips out. He gasped.

"Vek," he yelled. "Jurina! Stop that, you little fiends."

How would he deal with them? He glanced around the room, at the huge pillows, the tables stacked with old chipped dishes and a cold coffee urn; at the disordered piles of antique and arcane games he collected and sometimes sold; at the burgundy tapestry curtains on brass rings fluttering lazily behind them. The scene depicted was of an excited crowd clustered upon one of the hexagonal tabulas beside a span such as Valdemir while a mountainous glowing gift from the Edgeworld was bursting into being there.

The children ran to other parts of the room. Vek picked up a pachinko machine and shook it so that the loose balls inside rolled about, mad as hornets. "What's this? What's it do?"

Alas, he couldn't say, because the knowledge of its method had never been found anywhere.

Jurina had unrolled a Hamamatsu kite, throwing up a cloud of dust. "What's this?" she cried.

Vek shoved aside an oil lamp, carelessly spilling the oil, and wrestled loose a boar's bristle dartboard. "This, what's this?" The darts stuck loosely in it fell out, clattering to the ground.

"All right!" Meersh shouted. "Enough! Put my things down. You want a game, I tell you what we'll do. We'll play a card game I know. It's called 'Lawyers' Poker.' Heard of that one? I learned it in a tavern, and it's very clever. All the cards refer to real creatures and places and concepts of day to day existence in Edgeworld. Very *funny* pictures. The original deck was found on a tabula—that's what they say. You come sit here and I'll just get them."

He set down the pot and went behind the tapestry, where his more exotic collection resided. He found the cards quickly— the last thing he wanted was to leave the two demons unattended. As he crossed the room, he said, "This game has an interesting history. The information for playing was bestowed upon a king who happened to be standing on the tabula when the original deck appeared. Oh, he wasn't a *king* at that point. The knowledge to govern accompanied this game, too. Timing is everything in life. I'm sure your mother has said." He contemplated the pot of medicine he was supposed to give them.

"What's Edgeworld, then?" asked Vek. "Where is it?"

Meersh sat cross-legged across from them. He began to shuffle the card deck as he spoke. "Well, *where* it is remains the mystery. No one sees it, you see. Its existence is hypothetical—which means—"

"It means nobody knows," Jurina interjected. "Mother uses 'hypothetical' all the time."

"Yes, she would," he muttered, "it has a *p* in it." He dealt the cards, seven to each of them. "Anyway, all the things that appear are from some other place that's nothing like our Shadowbridge. A different world."

"You're making this all up," said Vek.

Meersh glowered. "What if I am? You'll certainly never know. You don't even know how this game is played."

"You haven't told us yet."

He gave up trying to score any sort of point against the child. Either Vek was beyond insipid or else posing as a fool just to goad him. "Well, I will explain it. As we play."

The game went well for at least three minutes. He had them lay down their cards and instructed them on what they needed in order to move, what to look for when they drew from the deck, and how two players could work as a team in a four-handed match. The children questioned every detail of every rule. They teamed up against him almost immediately.

When he explained that he could block the construction of their apartment block by playing both a lawyer card and a writ card (secretly one of his favorites), they threw their hands down and pouted. "You're cheating," accused Vek.

"I'm *teaching* you, you—"

"What's a writ, then? Ha-ha, he doesn't know." Jurina joined in. They sang "ha-ha" together.

Peevishly, Meersh replied, "I'll tell you what it is. It's the past tense of 'write.' It's something that's already been writ, so it was prepared in advance, and that's how I can use it against you. There, satisfied? Look, Jurina has a Supreme Court ruling card that cancels it out. Why don't you play that and we can go on." Only grudgingly did they take up their cards again and continue.

He had to work much harder to lose than he liked.

By the end of the game they could hardly sit still. They'd lost all interest and expressed no desire to play a real hand of Lawyers' Poker—a pity, as he itched to sue them for damages. The more pressing problem was how he was going to rein them in for two days and still get any serious sleeping done.

Meersh liked to sleep more than anything else in the world, except for eating. He had a great many things to do in his sleep, projects he'd begun—like the dream-mapping of Shadowbridge. He had diagrammed the unwinding Spans, year upon year, in his sleep. The map was accessible only in his sleep. And there was that stolen feast to get back to—the wienerschnitzel wouldn't stay warm forever. He couldn't imagine so much as catnapping in the presence of the two ring-eyed demons.

Rather than let them dictate what happened next, he set the cards aside and said, "I'm feeling hungry, what say we have something to eat."

"What do you have for us?"

Meersh picked up the ceramic pot.

The children backed away as one. "Get it away," they said. "It's horrid."

"I'm required to give it to you and that's what I'll do. Let's not have any fighting."

"We're not fighting. We're running away."

"And where would you run to?"

"Back home," they said.

"Across the close? Your mother left you with me and went away."

"Back home to W——." The word splashed over him, more like a sudden chill upon the air than anything spoken. Meersh listened to his memory but the word had eluded him, eel-like. It writhed between syllables, wriggled through consonants and vowels. The very absence of its name made him set down the pot upon the table. It was nowhere on his dream map. "She's abandoning us and never coming back!" wailed Jurina. "She tricked you into taking us!"

He knew this wasn't true, despite which the words troubled him. He wanted to get on to something else.

"Look, we'll eat and you'll have your medicine afterward. I have some hard cheese—"

"You do?" they exclaimed. "We never get cheese. It's so expensive."

He thought to himself, "Never get cheese, that's ridiculous. One can hardly endure without it. It's cheese or fish or seaweed in this life." The thought made him crave some fish, but he would have had to go out for it and that was out of the question. Besides, his frying pan had cracked and he had nothing to cook in.

"Yes," he muttered slyly, "cheese first."

He brought out a wheel of bright yellow cheese and set it on the playing board. With a small knife he removed a layer of mold that coated the top of it and then cut three triangular slices, the largest for himself.

"There now," he said, handing the slices to the two of them. He set down the knife and picked up his own slice.

Meersh opened his mouth to take his first bite. The children were staring at him, empty-handed. "Where's your cheese I gave you?" he asked.

"Gone. We ate it. It was so good. Can we have some more?"

"Certainly." He set down his slice and cut two more, larger than the first but still not as big as his own. "Now, this time don't eat so fast, or you'll get sick. There's no fun in it if you don't savor the food."

They held their slices close under their noses and sniffed, nodding to one another. He watched them surreptitiously as he reached for his own slice again; but there was a moment when he had to look away, and in that moment the food he'd given them vanished.

"Oh, it's good. Give us more, *please!*" they cried. He huffed, but cut them two more slices, bigger than his. A third of the wheel was gone now, but he wanted to make sure they couldn't hide these slices. Where the cheese was going he couldn't guess.

He grabbed his own as he handed out the first one, and held it before him as he handed out the second. His eyes shifted from child to child. Jurina and her brother sniffed the cheese again, grinned to each other, then faced him, not eating.

Waiting.

Watching, he took a large bite of his slice of cheese. He chewed it, and oh it was delectable, better than he remembered. His eyes closed with pleasure. He really couldn't help himself. But when he remembered himself and opened his eyes, the children's cheese was gone, and with it went the pleasure of his own.

"More," they insisted, "give us some more."

He set down his slice. "Nope. That's all for now or there won't be any left for later, and you do want more later, don't you? I'm sure you do." They couldn't have eaten it, he thought, not that quickly. And yet . . . where else could it be?

"We want it all now!" yelled Vek.

Meersh uncrossed his legs and took hold of the pot. "Everybody wants it all now. What you're going to have now is *this*."

"It's not bedtime."

"Yes, it is."

"It isn't even dark!"

"One meal, a dose of this, and then sleep. That was my promise. Don't make me lie to your mother."

"That's not fair," they complained. However, when he pulled the paper up, they remained sitting where they were, their gazes firmly on the pot. Inside it was a thick, greenish fluid the like of which he had never seen. It had a sheen to it much like the nacreous embellishment in the *el-quirkat* table.

Meersh dipped his cheese knife into it and squinted as the gooey mass hung from the blade. There seemed to be tiny granules embedded in the stuff. It might have been made from seaweed.

He scooped it again and held it out to Jurina. Although she had protested violently before, she leaned forward and stoically closed her mouth around the blade. She drew back and the blade was clean. He repeated the procedure for Vek, who did as his sister had, smacking his lips afterward. Meersh noticed for the first time how odd his teeth were—stubby and sharp. Vek made a strange, dreamy face.

"You look more like an animal than ever," Meersh thought.

Jurina looked up at the ceiling and began to tilt, back and back and back, slowly, steadily, until her head rested on the floor. Vek placed his head on her breast, and both closed their eyes and breathed in unison. The rings around their eyes seemed lighter than before.

"It must mean they're healthier." Meersh set the pot on the table and slid over beside them. "Jurina," he said. "Vek." Neither child responded. "Well, this is perfect. I can do as I like now." He eyed the pot. He dipped his finger into it. The jelly was oily to the touch. Hesitantly he stuck his finger in his mouth. His face pinched in immediate reaction to the bitter flavor. He spat in every direction.

"Idiot," muttered his penis. It loved to make fun of him.

All he wanted in the whole world was to get rid of that taste. He jumped up and ran to his hidden cache of fermented juice, unstoppered the bottle and took a great swig. Over the bottle he paused to consider the snoozing children.

"The last thing in the world I could do after this is sleep. The flavor won't go away!" He took another long drink.

Eventually he exchanged drinking to mask the awful flavor for drinking as its own pleasure. He began to laugh: He was brilliant. He was a genius. He was soused. Eventually, in wordless bliss, he passed from consciousness.

✳   ✳   ✳

Meersh slumbered six hours. Because he was drunk, it was an aimless, directionless sleep. When he next awoke the children were still asleep. He lounged at the game table and ate his cheese, taking his time now. Then he made a search through the children's clothing, but found no trace of the cheese they'd hidden. They had to have eaten it somehow. He did find a set of bronze knucklebones on Vek that the boy must have swiped while he was picking up everything in the place. Meersh had no sympathy for them after that. He waited them out.

When they began to stir, he dipped his finger quickly into the pot and then stuck another dollop of green slime inside their mouths. They smacked their lips without ever opening their eyes and fell back to the floor.

Six hours—now he knew how long they would sleep. He really could go off and leave them without worrying. All the fermented juice was gone, and he wanted more. He prospected through heaps and layers of possessions until he found something with which he could bear to part—a collection of mahjong tiles. He set off to barter for supplies.

He was gone four hours, and returned reeling in triumph and drink. He'd traded the ivory tiles for food and juice, sampled the vintner's latest batch, and even acquired a nice new pan for cooking. He set down his goods, then stumbled about in the dark of the house until he located his lamp. After feeling his way across the house without stepping on anyone, he lit a taper out of the belly of his oven and ignited the lamp.

The children were still unconscious in a heap in the middle of the room. And Meersh thought to himself, if one dollop was good for six hours then why not another to keep them out all night? Then he could get in some really terrific sleeping. His penis, which often had a very good time in dreams, roused a little. "Why not keep them asleep till their mother gets back?" it suggested.

Meersh dipped his finger in the jar and rubbed another glob across their teeth. Jurina moaned deeply but didn't stir. Vek slept like the stone idol of an abandoned faith.

Satisfied that they were taken care of, he clambered over to his hammock again. He tugged his nightshirt to his knees, curled up in the netting and went to sleep.

The first thing he did was go back to his feast. But someone had found it by now and eaten everything. Hardly a scrap remained for him. Disappointed, he went looking for another.

He inserted himself into a world where people traveled through the air inside enormous ribbed fish, and he rode along in their midst. They held masks on sticks in front of their faces when they spoke, which made it easy for him to disguise himself among them. Their voices were all snobbily nasal. They tittered, and said such things as: "The life one leads is rarely one's real life" and "It's my opinion that madam's corset is too constricting." He suspected they were Edgeworld beings, the dreamers whose dreams, according to all the philosophers, associatively created Shadowbridge. They did have a marvelous banquet laid out, and Meersh filled himself with pickled oysters and sparkling wine whilst peering through glass portholes in the bottom of the fish. Beneath wispy clouds, bridges unwound across the globe in nautiloid spirals. For one glorious moment, as the clouds parted, he thought he saw the point of origin, the great tabula at the convergence of the lines—a place of myth that no one had ever located. He ought to have been mapping instead of stuffing his face; but he was awakened before he could start.

His house was still dark, and for a final moment he hovered airborne in the flying fish. Then someone went clomping around overhead, and he came to his senses. Someone moving across the second floor. It would be his neighbor, Sacatepequez, who woke each day just before dawn to begin pacing the floor in wait for the "dry season." There was no such season here on Valdemir and the nature of the obsessive walking suggested he'd been cursed by someone. It must have been the sound of those enormous, leaden feet that had awakened Meersh. He turned on his side to go back to sleep.

Across the room, something slapped the floor impatiently.

The children. Meersh sat up. How many hours had he been flying and feasting? He stared into the darkness but could make out nothing, not even the vaguest shape. He couldn't remember where he'd left the oil lamp; couldn't remember blowing it out. He felt around on the floor beneath the hammock for a flint and a wick.

He struck the stone until the sparks caught the waxed wick; then, as it flared, glanced across the room.

What he saw was quite impossible. Startled, he huffed and the wick blew out.

But he had seen, and an image too grotesque to be real remained with him in the sudden blackness.

Furiously he sparked the stone to light the wick. Then with one eye to the scene in the middle of the room, he located the oil lamp and touched the wick to it. Holding it aloft, he slung his legs over the side of the hammock and stood.

On the floor lay the rumpled clothing of the two children, but the children were gone. They had vanished. Poking out of the necks of their shirts were the heads of two large fish. The smaller one, in Vek's clothes, fixed its glassy eye upon him and slapped its tail weakly one final time as it died.

Meersh thought, "This must be a trick. They've put these fish here to punish me." He called out, "Jurina, Vek, this isn't funny at all!" But even as he spoke he spied the greenish jelly dripping from their inhuman, toothless mouths and he knew these were the children of Sun-Through-Clouds.

He had turned them into fish.

He sank down, stunned, staring at the pot, wondering if they'd been fish all along. But the fish had been in his dream, not outside it. Then he understood: He had tasted the awful jelly and dreamt of fish; he had overfed them the same and they had become fish. Once a day—Sun-Through-Clouds had told him to feed it to them once a day. He hadn't listened, because he wanted her and did not want her children.

What could he do now? Tell her that her children had died? He considered it seriously for at least four seconds. Then he asked himself, "What bodies can I show her?" He could say they'd been kidnapped. But she would see through it, through him. He was not a good liar. His cousins always caught him out whenever he lied, and wasn't everyone his cousin? She would know.

His best hope lay in flight. That was what the dream had augured: People in *flying* fish—yes, there could be no doubt of it.

"This is all your fault, you," he said into his nightshirt. "Wake up now, and see what you've done."

"Don't blame me," countered Penis, stirring. "However you dress it up, we were both of the same mind. If you'd listened to me in the first place, at least you could have been amply rewarded. I told you to plunge in when you had her."

"Is lust all you can think about?"

"Yes!" Penis happily replied.

"Fine, please yourself. You always do. But tell me how to get out of this."

Penis said nothing.

"Come on, what am I going to do?"

No reply ensued. Meersh set down the lamp and ran outside. The sky was just lightening, but all the houses in the close were

dark. He turned and ran down the lane, out onto the main avenue. It was nearly deserted in both directions. A few covered carts
being hauled along were all that moved. He raced to the shop of
Beedlo, the vintner. Huge, swollen bags of wine hung in the window like the carcasses of strange animals. He hammered on the
door. "Beedlo, wake up. Beedlo, help me!"

"What, are you hurt?" came the cry from the second floor.

He stepped back and stared up at a round, balding face.

"Meersh, is that you? What are you doing at this time of morning in your bedclothes? You can't have drunk up everything
already."

"No, no. It's an emergency. I've killed them! What do I do?"

"Killed whom?"

"The chil—the fish. I've got two dead fish in my house! What
do I do?"

Beedlo replied, "Why don't you fry them up? A little butter's my
favorite. And that white wine I sold you is excellent for a little
sauce."

"Fry them?"

"You've got a new pan, haven't you?"

Meersh slapped himself. "I've got a *nice* new pan, yes! Yes, that's
it. That's what I'll do. You hear that, you stupid penis? Ha!" He
bounded off Beedlo's stoop and ran straight for his lane.

"Mad as a mayfly," Beedlo muttered, and closed his shutters.

Back inside his house, Meersh took the fish out of their clothes. He
gathered up the clothing and threw it behind the tapestry. He
placed them in the new frying pan on the black stone stove and
considered them. Just two dead fish in a world of fish. That's
all they were. Well, he thought, it wasn't as if he'd wanted to kill
them.

He gutted and skinned them and tossed the heads aside where
he didn't have to look at them. Then as Beedlo had suggested, he
mixed butter and wine and began to fry the filets. The fish smelled
better even than the meal he'd consumed in his sleep. Once they
were cooking, he pulled off his nightshirt and dressed. After breakfast, he would take the remains out and throw them in the ocean.

The fish sizzled and Meersh sang a wordless song in anticipation, and between them made enough noise that he didn't hear
the knock on his door.

The room suddenly grew brighter. Meersh turned from his
cooking to see a figure silhouetted in the open doorway. There

could be no mistaking her ripe form. Sun-Through-Clouds had returned early.

"Oh, you lying children!" he cursed beneath his breath. "You evil penis!"

Aloud he exclaimed, "Why, Sun-Through-Clouds, I didn't expect you for days!"

She smiled at him—the smile that had ignited his desire on many occasions—but which faltered now as her eyes sought her children in the depths of the large room. She reached the low table and stared down at the cards and the open pot.

Meersh swallowed.

He watched in helpless horror as her hands lifted the pot. She peered into it in bewilderment, and from it to Meersh and then back again. He knew what she was seeing, what thoughts would be tearing through her brain at this very moment.

He blurted out, "I have to tell you, your children ran off. I was hoping they'd only gone somewhere to play but alas I fear now it's me—they've run away from me. I would happily help you look for them. Oh, yes, *that* stuff. You know, I tried it myself, it's not really very edible, plus I'm afraid I spilt some on the—"

Her look silenced him as severely as a muzzle. She set the pot back on the table.

He wanted desperately to turn his back on her as though he had no reason to fear her. It might have gone a long way toward reassuring her; but he couldn't. Despite her voluptuous beauty, what he saw in her eyes warned that something ghastly hid within. With one hand, a simple movement, she shoved him aside as forcefully as if she'd struck him. He skittered into a stool and tumbled headfirst into his hammock. It spun, wrapping him up like a tuna.

Sun-Through-Clouds saw the severed heads of the fish. She cried into the pan, "My children, my children!" She tried to touch the lightly browned bodies but could not. She swung about. "*You* did this. You did this to me!"

Meersh fought his way free of the hammock. The anger spreading from her heart was changing her already. She seemed to grow larger and darker, as if absorbing the light in the room. Her eyes became steel, and her body sharpened and molded into parts both flesh and metal. In places her skin parted, revealing black iron like the stove behind her. Rivets popped out along her forehead and her jaws shifted from side to side with a painful, grating squeal. Meersh knew all about shape-shifters, especially the ones who transformed in anger. They were the most dangerous.

He tumbled from the hammock and bolted out the door and down the narrow lane. He skittered into the main thoroughfare, narrowly missing a scrimshaw-hawker's cart set up at the corner. He fell on the stones, sprang up and ran. People on their knees scrubbing their stoops stared at him as he ran past. Fishmongers glanced up from where they knelt, pouring water onto the stones where they'd gutted the morning's catch. Fish blood was a libation spilt across his path—a terrible, terrible omen.

He dodged around baskets of fish, of fruit, strips of seaweed hung out to dry, a jeweler's glittering cart. To his left, the masts of fishing boats clustered motionless above the ocean. He never stopped, never slowed. Too close behind him he heard shrieks from the same people he'd passed. He didn't have to look back, nor did he wish to for fear the sight of Sun-Through-Clouds completely transformed would ground him to the spot.

If he'd had an inkling how to swim, he might have leapt the railing into the sea. He cursed himself for the life he'd wasted, rejecting knowledge and skill in pursuit of base desires of the moment. It was true, completely true, and if he could only elude this monster and relocate to some other span of the eternal bridge, why, he would definitely change his ways. Become a priest. Devote his life to charitable duties. Become the eyes for someone blind or work to feed starving children—no, no, bad idea. No children, he should *never* be allowed near children. He should go on a pilgrimage instead. *Soon.*

On his right he passed a five-story apartment building with shops on the ground floor. A turret ran up the corner. Higher towers prodded the sky above the apartments, with pennants hanging, waiting for the winds. He ran past alleys and lanes, and looked down every one for some idea of an escape. He had to get off this empty thoroughfare before she caught him.

With no more plan than that, Meersh turned down the next lane he saw, then into other, smaller offshoots—dodging blindly through a section of the span full of treacherous alleys and subversive streets. He wove in and out, hoping that such a maze might save him. Even he didn't know where he was.

He dodged around sacks of milled grain and kegs of wine waiting to be hauled in. Any other time the smells would have beguiled him.

He turned mistakenly into a stinking alley that ended in a fence. He had to throw three crates up to dive over it. His tunic caught on the rough poles and tore. He landed hard on dungy straw, amidst a flock of goats that whickered and neighed. They sprang aside, but some came back and nudged him in friendly fashion. One started to chew on his torn tunic. He shoved them all aside, waiting and listening. Hoping. Then he heard the whuffling of something rushing down the alley. Guttural, grating noises behind the fence.

A hand clutched the top of the fence. It was black and shiny, spiked at every joint and as big as his face. Smoke boiled up behind it. A colossal blackened skull with smoldering eyes peered down into the pen.

Meersh screamed. He bounded over the railing and ran on.

He ran so long that he lost all sense of what he was doing. Running became the only thing in life. He crossed the entire span that morning—four hundred *wyrths* at least—until he could see ahead the great south gatehouse of Valdemir.

The span ended in a barbican. The one tunnel going in split off into two beyond the portcullis, each with its own turnstile. A single guard regulated all traffic through the barbican, between Valdemir and the two other spans that met there. He did a comfortable business collecting bribes from those who wanted to cross for reasons they couldn't have named: Two spans ensured that he did very well indeed. He had grown lazy and corpulent from the easy pickings. His breakfast of beer and egg soup could last sometimes two hours or more. Meersh shot into the tunnel and dove over the turnstile so quickly that the guard, looking up from his bowl, glimpsed a blur that might have been a trick of light. It might have been a fluttering gull. He didn't feel like getting up for a blur.

Meersh had arbitrarily picked the right-hand tunnel. He emerged out the other side upon a span called Lukhan, where he had never been before. Lukhan was older than Valdemir and not so pleasant. Its stones were worn and uneven, the center avenue unswept and unwholesome. The tattered-awning fronted shops might have sold the secrets of dead empires. More likely they sold lies. The houses were narrow and not very high. A seedy crowd milled about, hawking and buying, cajoling and thieving. Looming above them were two great towers, linked by a narrow wall and topped with crumbling turrets. Meersh wove toward them through the crowd, putting as many people as possible between him and the gatehouse. His sorry state raised any number of scornful looks, even from those most shabbily dressed. People stepped aside to let him pass. The essence of goat manure could not have helped.

Almost beneath the towers, he entered a smaller, tighter throng that seemed as ragged as he was. A few men in tidy, black uniforms hemmed them together. He slipped deep among them to hide himself. The beggarly throng moved slowly but steadily away from the barbican and toward the twin towers, for which he gave thanks.

A moment later his pursuer emerged.

The iron monster had reverted. She'd become her own beautiful self again. Crouching low, Meersh was well hidden among the beggars, and they behind the looser crowd. Yet Sun-Through-Clouds stared straight at him across the plaza. To his amazement she smiled. Her smile flew to him and whispered in his ear, "A poor fate you've picked, dear Meersh. I won't set foot in there to retrieve you. My punishment would have been quicker than death in Lukhan." Her fingers pressed and moved as if snapping a wishbone. She turned on her heel and walked back into the tunnel.

Meersh cheered. He had won. Sun-Through-Clouds was giving up. Now he could slip away, start over somewhere else where she would never find him. He straightened, straightened his ripped tunic, pushed his mane of hair into some kind of order, and tried to depart from the shuffling throng.

A large hand fell upon his shoulder.

"Where you think you're going, louse?" asked a voice as large as the hand.

"Hey? I, ahm, forgot something, cousin," he said.

The hand spun him around. "I'll bet you forgot to bathe." The hand belonged to one of the uniformed men. He'd closed in from the side. His sleeves sported lightning bolt patches. "And what an appalling pong. Taken a goat lover, have you?"

"No, I forgot something important."

"Didn't we all? Else we'd be off somewhere with the living. Maybe on that span over there, heh?" He pointed to the bridge span Meersh had not chosen. Brightly festooned with banners and flags and pastel spires, it receded sharply into the mists, much more inviting than the dark towers looming overhead. The hand on his shoulder turned him again.

In front of him lay a black hole cut in the wall between the towers. As he looked on, the beggar at the head of the line stepped into and was swallowed by the blackness.

"No," Meersh protested fearfully. "I *am* living. I mean, I should be somewhere else than this, cousin."

"Sure you should." The hand slid from his shoulder to the back of his neck, where it clamped tightly. "If you want to be excused, *cousin*, at least come up with something original." The guard hauled him around the others ahead of him. "Special acknowledgment, louse, of your special stink. You move to the head of the line. Bye now." He propelled him into the blackness.

Meersh dropped like an anchor, straight to the center of the world.

*   *   *

At this point in his performances, Bardsham blows out the lantern behind his screen and all is dark. The audience shifts edgily, wondering if a tale can end at such an unsatisfying juncture: They know Meersh gets into trouble in every story, but they expect some resolution—a satisfying conclusion. Bardsham is a master at sensing their collective mood.

At the very moment when they would begin to leave, a dull red light comes up behind the screen—the lantern now enclosed in red glass—and the audience settles back.

Meersh's figure comes into focus against the screen, but it's a pthisic shadow now, wasted as if by disease. The leather of this puppet's torso has been hammered so thin that the light passing through it reveals the thicker shadow of his skeleton. Years have passed in no time at all. Press-ganged into the mines of Lukhan, he has outlived those who fell in with him and others thrown in later, mainly because he willingly ate anything—absolutely anything in order to survive. Propped up around the edges of the screen are the corpses of unfortunate pickers.

The mines of Lukhan were as ancient as the world. Indeed, much silver and marble had been recovered from them, some at one level and some at another. Levels were used up and then sealed off to allow a new crop of metal and marble to grow.

Over centuries, the mineshafts sank ever deeper until finally, inadvertently, they broke through into the Land of the Dead: A wall collapsed.

For the abject miners, life was already death, but the collapse brought the dead directly to them. On the other side of the large hole, the dead drifted in to watch the miners work themselves into the afterlife. The manner of dying seemed to fascinate them.

The dead were most peculiar. Their features often were flat, as if lightly drawn upon a smooth face. They were adorned as in life: Clothing shifted form with memory, as spirits reminisced. Except as memory, time did not exist in the Land of the Dead. The future would never arrive. For the ghosts, as for the miners, time ended with the present.

The Land of the Dead appeared to be a vast grotto receding into infinity. Figures wandered aimlessly throughout, dressed in costumes of ancient times, of other spans and stranger places. In the opening to the grotto, Meersh beheld strange finery every day: linen robes and striped headdresses beside smudges that looked like tail coats and ruffles, bustiers and hoop-skirted ball gowns, liripipes and lithams. They might have included spirits from the Edgeworld. He couldn't say.

An aura surrounded each of them — a sphere of influence that gained dimension the closer one came. From a distance it was a bright mist, but closer it took on detail, becoming a mutable view hovering about the spirit.

One ghost that drifted past the opening had no hands but strange boxes on the ends of its arms with glowing centers that projected bluish, moving images and music and voices as if each contained a tiny world of its own. A jungle aura hung around it.

The Land of the Dead as he knew of it was surrounded by molten rivers and guarded by monstrous creatures. Yet nothing seemed to separate the dead from the miners. Nothing except fear, and that derived mostly from stories about hapless fools who'd attempted to escape through the opening.

"What happened to them?" Meersh had asked his rheumy-eyed neighbor, a miner who died two weeks later at his side.

"Become ghosts themselves, the instant they crossed over and stepped on that misty, green floor. Like that." He snapped his dark fingers. "Ate 'em right up."

Looking upon the suffering, slope-backed filthy workers around him, Meersh had replied, "That might not be so terrible." Nevertheless, he thought no more about sneaking into the grotto of dead souls — until the day the shades came looking for *him*.

The pickers — those who tore the silver from the open seams — worked constantly throughout the day with only one resting period, when the food was brought around and they sat and ate, hardly speaking to one another, barely looking at each other. Speaking would have taken too much energy.

Meersh sat against a rock and wiped his grimy fingers across the tin pan on which he'd been fed. He licked the grease from them and leaned back to enjoy a minute's peace. As he did, he spied two figures hovering at the edge of the fissure, watching him.

They were small, their faces oddly pointed, their eyes at the side instead of straight ahead. They looked a little bit like fish. He hadn't eaten fish in a very long time, and his stomach growled with longing. Their clothing looked vaguely familiar. And the blurry aura hanging between them—didn't it remind him of the interior of his house? His house. The recollection stirred memories a thousand years old.

Yes, of course they looked like fish.

He glanced around to be sure none of the guards was about, then crawled near the collapsed cave wall. "Vek!" he whispered. One of the two fish-spirits floated nearer.

"You know us?" asked a voice so icy that his head froze hearing it. But, like the clothing, it was familiar to him.

"Yes, cousin, I know you."

"We know you, too," accused Jurina. "You're the god of sleep who put us here." She asked, "When is our mother coming to get us? We don't like it here."

"Wake us up! Take us home, please."

"It's not so easily done. As you see." And he dragged his leg up to let them behold the shackles on his raw and festering ankles.

"We want our mother!" They began keening like the lost souls they were.

"Hush," Meersh hissed. If they kept on wailing, he would be in plenty of trouble; the guards would take away his meal and work him 'til he dropped. He glanced around at the other weary pickers, most of whom sagged over their tin plates, too exhausted to take interest. Almost dead themselves.

A plan took shape in his mind—an escape, at least a possible one. "Children," he said, "go back into your world there and find me one of my former cousins from this mine. Quickly now if you want to get out."

"Why? There are plenty of them behind you," complained Jurina. Vek had already turned and moved off as fast as spirits could do.

"Yes," he told her patiently, "but look at them. They have no thought any longer of escape—not dead, but hardly alive. They're ruins."

"Why?"

"Civilization used them up."

She stared at him silently—at least he thought she was staring. It was hard to know for sure with her goggle eyes.

Vek came back shortly, towing another spirit behind him. Unlike the children this one was accompanied by a wide, crisp aura in which Meersh recognized an avenue of Shadowbridge. "Then it's you," said the spirit.

"And who would you be that you know me?"

"You know perfectly well, trickster."

Meersh recognized the voice of Rheumy Eye, the miner who'd died beside him, but the epithet troubled him. He remarked, "Your condition looks much improved."

"I'm dead, you bastard. How much improved is that?"

"You tell me. But first tell me what happens if I step across into your grotto. The truth now."

"Thinking to leave the mining profession? Escape your condign punishment?"

"I did you no harm in life. Why gibe me? Tell me is the story true."

"I see into you. They're too young to have the skill, but I know your lazy soul. You *will* nothing. You create good things and evil things all across the world, but you perceive none for what it is. You know no morality, and kindness comes only when you want something. Like now."

Meersh hung his head. He didn't have to try very hard to look despondent. "Have pity. Isn't this punishment enough?"

"Pah."

"Show me so that I can escape this dreaded place that killed you. So that I may take these poor little fish—er, children—back to their mother, who even now grieves at their untimely loss." He worked up tears, and slapped both hands to his face, shaking as if he wept. He peered at the shade between his fingers.

"What's the good of that? They're dead, same as me," argued the ghost. "Same as you soon enough."

"I can save them if we hurry," he blubbered. "They're barely anchored. We can bring them back, you and me. Just *tell* me."

Rheumy Eye's aura now projected images of the mine itself. Meersh knew his resistance was breaking down. "Won't do you any good anyway. The story you have was put about to keep pickers from shambling off through the hole. If someone was to slip in here, they wouldn't know which way to go. Be lost forever, which ain't long, considering. Death does come for you. But slow and steady. Comes crawlin' up you from the ground, till your whole body is pale as the moon and cold as night, and you lose yourself in what you knew. So it's no lie, what the guards say. Just not so quick."

"But *you* know how to navigate it."

The ghost bobbed agitatedly. "What if I do? I can't leave. *I'm* not lightly dead. I'm *very* dead."

"But you can show me—show them—the way out so that I can rescue them. Don't you see?"

"Like I said—if you was to save these two, it'd be an accident of saving yourself, else there's more to it than you're telling."

He had to laugh at the reversal of things: The ghost could see right through him. He dropped his pretense of misery. "Happenstance, so be it," he said, "let accidents occur and fortuity reign. Who cares for my motives? Let them be *saved*. You alone can do that."

In the tunnel far behind him he heard the snap of a whip. The return of the guards. The daily meal was at an end. A hundred men groaned as they found a little more strength and got up on their swollen feet. Meersh hurried to collect small scrapings and nuggets of silver he'd concealed nearby while he dug. Over time he'd acquired enough silver to fill his pockets until his hips bulged on each side.

"You've been planning."

"Escape was inevitable—just a question of how and when. Let's go."

Rheumy Eye shook his pale head at fathomless self-interest, then leaned down and wrapped an ethereal hand around the shackles. The iron froze, becoming instantly frangible. Meersh pulled his ankles apart and the chain snapped. The leg irons split. Quickly, he bounded into the grotto beside the ghost. The bottoms of his feet burned as if seared. "Yiiiee! Hurry now." He reached for the children's hands but then stopped himself, recalling what had happened to the leg iron. "You stay close to me—not too close, Jurina—and I'll take you to your mother."

They trekked across the Land of the Dead. Meersh yipped and hopped as coldness like frostbite wormed through his feet. "Gods, this is excruciating," he hissed.

"It's your greed. All that silver weighs you down, you mire in death the faster. If I were you, I'd get rid of it."

Meersh shook his head defiantly, but soon the pain attacked his ankles. He thought, "I can do without some of it," and he reached into his pockets and sprinkled a few of the nuggets around him, where they dissolved instantly, leaving only icy puddles to mark where the ground had resorbed them. He was dismayed by the dissolution—leaving silver behind was one thing, eliminating it another. But like a balloon that's cast off ballast, he rose above the chill of death. His ankles felt all right again. Death stayed confined in the bottoms of his feet.

Deeper into the grotto, they encountered clusters of ghosts surrounded by small villages of their own dreaming. The proximity to other eidolons with shared memories redoubled the power of their projections. Their collective aura extended well beyond them, forming a landscape that might have been real. He walked through a farrago of places as alien to him as the realm of death itself was: a place where the houses stood on legs, shifting from side to side, and could run away from floods; another where people in close-fitting silver and gold costumes strolled arm in arm as if in a processional along a broad avenue overarched by impossible trees. A world underwater: Sunlight rippled eel-like across everything and the phantoms floated above the floor, swimming through the air. There were hundreds of such scenes; thousands more he might have beheld if he'd elected to remain.

Death soon imbrued his legs again. He groaned as it climbed his calves. He could no longer feel his feet.

"Throw away that silver," his penis begged. "Do you want to lose me, too? If it gets any higher, you'll be sorry!"

Peevishly then, he flung away more of the silver. In his anger he threw a large lump at a nearby group of ghosts. It struck one of them on the back, and the whole group turned as one. Their vague features darkened. Their heads followed him. He crept closer to his guide for protection.

"Really asking for it, ain't you?" said Rheumy Eye.

"It's because of this damned place that I have to give up my hard-earned riches. I have a perfect right to be upset."

The ghost made a grunt of dismissal and continued on. Beneath his temper, Meersh noted that his feet were still blue and his ankles still burned with cold. He pondered the dead man whom he'd struck. That fact was, the lump had *hit* him. It hadn't dissolved.

Meersh withdrew more of the silver from his pockets and said, "Vek, Jurina, you carry these for me, will you? It won't harm you as it does me."

The fish-children accepted the riches; he was careful not to let them touch him. Vek commented sharply, "Now maybe you won't slow us up so much."

"I? I've all but led this flight. Remember who arranged this for you."

The boy made no reply.

They came upon another cluster of ghosts, whose ambit was a desert land filled with towering temples and statuary. Some such spirits had passed them previously, dressed in the same linen skirts and headdresses and necklaces of lapis lazuli. In this group, how-ever, Meersh spotted two—a bearded man and a woman—seated on cushioned chairs in front of a board game that he had never seen before. He could not help but intrude. The ghosts took on def-inition. Both the man and woman had dark makeup circling their eyes. The woman wore a gold band around her head, and her breasts were exposed. He barely noticed the inclination of his penis at the sight of her. He was staring at the board. It had three rows of ten squares each. Four of the squares had markings on them. The playing pieces were black and white carved figures of mythological creatures. He watched the woman take four thin dice and throw them. The dice were curved along one side and flat along the other. The curved side was black, the flat side white. The woman moved one of the white pieces forward.

"What is it called, this game?" he inquired of her.

She looked up at him as if she hadn't noticed him before. "*Senet*," she replied. It was a game he had never heard of.

Behind him Jurina asked sharply, "What are you doing? We're carrying your silver; you should be going faster!"

Rheumy Eye replied, "He gives into his urges wherever he goes. His appetite for games is stronger almost than his instinct for sur-vival. He gives you his silver to stay alive, then dallies here to watch stones pushed along a board." He came up beside him. "You want this for yourself, pawky?"

"It's exquisite."

"Take it, they won't miss it."

Meersh stared incredulously at the miner's ghost.

"Don't trust me? Think I might treat you the way you do every-one else?" The ghost laughed. He stepped in and whisked away the board. He handed it to Meersh. There was a drawer in one side of it for storing the pieces for safekeeping, but the pieces had disap-peared. When Meersh glanced back at the couple, the board and pieces lay on the table in front of them as before. Rheumy Eye chortled at his confusion. "Time," he said. "It's no river here."

Meersh's feet were burning again because of the weight of the board. He handed over the last parings of silver to the children.

"Not much farther," promised the ghost.

The burning cold did not abate, but Meersh would not part with his board. Pretty soon one of his toes fell off. He yelped and picked it up. It was frozen solid. He put it in the drawer of the game board. Before long he lost another.

They headed for a heap of loose rock leading to a cavern wall.

"That's your way," their guide said. The last of Meersh's toes came off. He put it with the others in the tiny drawer; now with every step he stumbled off-balance.

Rheumy Eye drew up. "I'm too much dead to go further than this. The climb is yours to make, all the way to that tiny dot of light up there. You do good in taking these children with you, even if it's that box full of your toes that moves you to it. Your reward suits you." He left them.

Meersh quickly climbed off the floor of the grotto and up the rock face. The children kept with him but not through any effort on his part. If he'd still had his toes on his feet, he might have climbed fast enough to leave them behind.

The circle of light grew brighter as it grew larger. It played across them in their ascent. The shades of the children brushed up against him. He cried out in fear at their touch, but nothing happened to him. Steadily, they took on form and definition. They were no longer fish, but were becoming something else animal-like. As they tired of the climb, they grabbed onto his legs and hung from his pockets. To brush them off, he would have had to let go of the rock face or the game, and he would do neither. He dragged them along as fast as he could go.

At the top Meersh poked his head out into the light. He found himself overlooking the whole of a span. A gull squatted beside him, watching him incuriously. "Hello, cousin," he said to it. The gull disdainfully ignored him and walked away. He pulled himself halfway out of the hole, enough so that he could fold himself over the lip of it and free his hands. He set down the *senet* board and took hold of each child, one at a time, and drew them out over his head. They were wholly transformed. They had round, furry faces, and black rings encircled their eyes, though that might have been soot. When they looked at him, they showed their tiny, sharp teeth. At least, he thought, they weren't fish anymore. He climbed out after them and snatched up his game board before anything happened to it.

He stood on a ridge of clay pantiles along the peak of a house. He was battered and torn and covered with greasy chimney soot. A great vista surrounded him: the vast ocean; the great broad span with its single main avenue off which capillary lanes twisted every which way; the high, cupola-topped towers where the wealthy and the governors dwelled, many of whom had paid handsomely for his games and his knowledge. A thousand rooftops distant stood the weathered twin towers of Lukhan like two smudges impressed upon the clouds; and, directly below, a small circle of houses like petals on a sunflower. "This seems awfully familiar," he remarked.

Vek looked up, disgusted. "We're on top of your house," he said. "How do we get down?"

"Call for help I suppose." He was dismayed by their location. But, sure enough, what they had emerged from was his chimney. He peered into it, at the edges of blackened bricks dwindling to darkness.

The children cried for help, which brought some of Meersh's neighbors with a ladder; it also caught the attention of people on the main avenue, who gathered close to the railing and pointed and watched as the three of them clambered to the edge. Word of them spread like disease.

The children refused to be quit of him then. He pleaded to his neighbors, "Cousins, please, someone take them over to their mother, she only lives across the way. Isn't she home? Well, let them *wait* for her, then." His rescuers plainly felt they'd done enough in helping him climb down two stories. "You'd have been able to shimmy down the drain if you took care of yourself," one of them told him. "You're starving to death, Meersh." And, "What's happened to your feet, then?"

With the greatest reluctance, he took the children inside. He inspected the interior. The pot of green jelly was gone. There were no fillets in his frying pan, no fish heads beside the stove. He hazarded a look behind the tapestry where he'd stuffed the children's clothing, and the clothes were gone, too. These miracles left him addled.

There came a loud knock on his door. Thinking it was one of the neighbors, he flung it back to find Sun-Through-Clouds standing there. Her look changed from fury to joy as she spied the animal-children behind him. The thunderhead vanished; the sun broke upon him. "Oh, my darlings!" she cried and swept in while he leaped as far from her as he could. But he couldn't balance without his toes and fell into the hammock she'd woven for him.

Sun-Through-Clouds dropped to her knees and hugged her children to her. She kissed their faces, inhaled them, her babies, her Raki babies. They whispered excitedly to her, words on top of each other, the way children do.

She looked over her shoulder at Meersh with large and liquid eyes. He untangled himself from the hammock, clutched the game board tightly to his chest, and took a step toward the door.

Sun-Through-Clouds rose and barred his way. "And you!" she

cried. "You are my *hero*. You penetrated the realm of death to bring them back to me, just like in great stories. How I misjudged you, my dear." Her arms circled him and her mouth sought his. He remained rigid with terror. She pressed herself tightly to him. His penis had nothing to say about her now. It had retreated as far as it could. Had it been able, it would have detached, slid surreptitiously down his leg and scooted under the nearest heap of games.

Her nails raked his back. Didn't she notice the soot and grease, how awful he smelled?

"I swear to reward you with every pecant pleasure you desire, my dearest, dearest Meersh," she whispered in his ear. Her thighs wrapped around his leg. Her teeth pinched his earlobe. All he heard was the whuffling, creaking breath of the monster that had pursued him across the whole of Valdemir.

She pushed him back with one hand. The other caught the drawstring of his trousers. He fell again into her net.

His penis screamed, and he fainted dead away.

* * *

The articulated puppet lies swinging in the hammock. The other figures—the beautiful woman and the transformed children—silently withdraw. Then he rises from the hammock to take his bows. There's always plentiful applause and cries of "Pe-*nis*, Pe-*nis!*" more often than not, until it, too, appears, rising from his torso. Both sexes, all creatures, cheer him. They know he speaks the truth about the caprices of life.

The lamp goes out on the shadow-puppet screen.

Bardsham emerges to more applause. His assistants hang back behind him.

When the theater empties, they jump to action. One takes down the curtains and collapses the framework. One replaces all the puppets in neat piles in their cases, ready for the next performance. There will always be a next performance somewhere. And there will always be another story of Meersh. Meersh did many things, awake and asleep, in the earliest times on Shadowbridge. He did everything. His escapades are cautionary.

Bardsham will leave them to dismantling. If they're performing in a hall, he goes to the tavern; if they're in a tavern he goes to the bar. If he's lucky, someone will show her interest. If she lingers before him, he'll smile and do his best to enchant her. Though he tells many tales, it's Meersh who's won him fame. Meersh she'll ask about. He's not a handsome man, Bardsham, and it's a rough life, traveling the spans. Closed up playing in a space not much larger than two kegs, he probably stinks as bad as Meersh did climbing out the chimney. By the time she finally accompanies him, he's often five parts drunk as well. But in his room, there's the magic of love and laughter. He'll strike up a conversation with his own penis to entertain her, and it will answer always in the affirmative. Always "Yes!" it wants her. "Yes!" it loves her. "Yes!" it adores her. Yes, it is no different for him.

Meersh the Bedeviler speaks the truth. Here and there and halfway round the world. Truth is usually good for a night.

Afterword

Meersh the Bedeviler

I've been working for a few years now on a project entitled "Shadowbridge." The world of Shadowbridge is a place where mythologies, legends, and fables of every sort find purchase, but in a somewhat altered form. Meersh, who began life as a shadow puppet, is a variation on Coyote the trickster, who invariably responds to his basest desires and generally is punished (if not killed) for his misbehavior. I decided to write a shorter work from this world at the urging of Michael Swanwick, and so I owe him a debt of thanks for this, because I probably wouldn't have given Meersh his own tale otherwise. I'm sure he'll have many more adventures and behave just as irresponsibly in each of them as he does here. I am tempted to take a poll and find out just how many babysitters and former babysitters at one time or another wanted to cook their charges.

Afterword:
The Damned Human Race

I WRITE THIS IN THE WEEK FOLLOWING THE 2004 U.S. presidential election, won, after a campaign of lies and character assassination, where citizens were not allowed to attend his campaign events unless they signed a loyalty oath, by George W. Bush, arguably the worst chief executive to sit in the Oval Office in a century.

What does this have to do with the stories of Gregory Frost? More than you might imagine. But first, in the interests of full disclosure, let me reveal my acquaintance with the accused.

I first met Greg Frost in 1982, when I moved to Raleigh from Kansas City. I came here to begin my career as a teacher at North Carolina State University. Greg was working in the university bookstore. Knowing no one in the science fiction world in North Carolina, I looked up Greg and some others in the SFWA directory and threw a party. We quickly developed a friendship that has lasted more than twenty years now. Over that time we have shared manuscripts, aspirations, joys and sorrows, worked our way through the permutations of our families, written one story together, watched the men in our mirrors go from late youth to middle age, eaten a few meals together, and drunk more than a few bottles of wine.

What can I tell you about him? Gregory Frost is a master of the anecdote, and a superior teller of jokes. He can do dozens of voices and accents—you have not lived until you have heard him recite "The Love Song of J. Alfred Prufrock" in the voice of Elmer Fudd. He has played small roles in several awful movies. He has read a much broader range of literature, from all nations and at all levels, high and low, than I have. He has the largest music collection of anyone I know. He is a font of historical and other arcana. He's a pretty good cook. He is one of my dearest friends.

And, to bring us back to my opening paragraph, Frost is also a keen observer of the American scene, a man of passion and humane commitment, evident, in a dozen ways, in the stories in this book. Frost's fiction is charged by an awareness of the idiocies, cruelty, prejudice, and ignorance of what Mark Twain called "the damned human race." I sometimes think that his sensitivity to these sad realities gives him physical pain, and if I were allowed no more than one word to describe the large body of Frost's fiction, the word would be "angry."

Stories like "The Madonna of the Maquiladora" are powered by rage at the injustices we visit upon each other, or that are visited upon us by God (if She exists). Frost identifies villains in high (and low) places. He excoriates organized religion. He reveals to us "The secret inner life of the masses," and what we see there is seldom pretty.

Yet what I like about Frost's stories is the bruised heart they reveal beneath the rage. Anger can fuel art, but anger alone will not make good art. What captures me is how these stories tread the edge of a decent and humane despair: despair at the way we destroy ourselves, at the yawning gap between what we might be and what we all too often become, at the ways we might reach out to one another, and at our common failure to do so. Frost tells certain hard truths about America. I see him falling in a line of story-tellers from the American gothics Poe, Hawthorne, and Melville, through Twain in his supernatural mode (see "The Mysterious Stranger") to oddball writers like Nathanael West (1903–1940), the author of that quote above about "the secret inner life of the masses."

Back in graduate school I wrote a paper about West in which I invented a category for his writing: "American Social Surrealism." I haven't thought about that for thirty years now, but rereading Greg's stories in preparation for this afterword, it comes to me that he is West's legitimate heir. Unlike the social realists who domi-nated American fiction of the 1930s (think John Steinbeck) West wrote odd novels about a suicidal advice columnist, about a man who takes a tour of the inside of a giant wooden horse, about hangers on in an apocalyptic Hollywood, and about a Horatio Algerish young man who might have made it big if he hadn't lost his eye, his teeth, his scalp and eventually his life in the pursuit of the American dream. West could be cruel to his characters and always twisted the bounds of realism in doing so. He was comic but dark dark dark.

Frost's "Touring Jesusworld" occurs, metaphorically, just down the street from the movie studios of West's *The Day of the Locust*. The photographer of Frost's "The Madonna of the Maquiladora" works in the same newsroom as West's *Miss Lonelyhearts*. Lemuel Pitkin in West's *A Cool Million* drops body parts in his road to success as readily as Frost's family members waste away in "Collecting Dust." Both of these writers are cool observers of the American scene, horrified by its callousness, who turn to fantasy to depict a reality that cannot be caught in social realism. "Collecting Dust" opens a window on the bleeding heart of America, yet at the same time Frost is wielding a scalpel on this typically dysfunctional middle American family, he sympathizes with the human beings caught up in it, who do not even understand how they are being destroyed.

"The Bus" is a simple fable of winners and losers in America, direct as an arrow, funny and sad and ultimately horrifying. The engine that powers the bus we're riding on is fueled by the bodies of the people we discard. Those of us enjoying the amenities up front don't spend much time thinking about the costs others must pay. We try hard to ignore the fact that we are likely to end up paying that cost ourselves, that there but for the grace of God (and a few breaks, and a few more years on the calendar) go you and I.

Before this all gets too grim, however, let me say that if you allowed me a second word to describe Frost's work, that word would be "funny." Sometimes Frost's humor can be very dark indeed, as in "The Girlfriends of Dorian Gray," but in another mood Greg can deliver "The Road to Recovery," a farce that no one else could write, the best Road movie never made. Or combine vicious satire with a Warner Brothers cartoon of the racist South, as in "Attack of the Jazz Giants." Or give us the wry sadness of "A Day in the Life of Justin Argento Morrell," which evokes sympathy for its tormented space farers at the same time it mocks the standard tropes of Star Trek interstellar sf.

Finally, a third word I might use for Frost's stories would be "crafty"—even "beautiful." Let me commend to you the quieter side of Frost. You will not find a better example of the unforced use of the second person narrative than "The Madonna of the Maquiladora." You'll not read a more heartfelt story of love and loss.

It's a pleasure to have these stories in once place at last, and to hope that perhaps the appearance of this collection will reveal to readers how much has been going on so quietly in Gregory Frost's work, and how coherent and telling and emotionally moving a vision of humanity it presents.

John Kessel
Raleigh, NC
November 2004

Two thousand copies of this book have been printed by the Maple-Vail Book Manufacturing Group, Binghamton, NY, for Golden Gryphon Press, Urbana, IL. The typeset is Electra with Antique Olive display, printed on 55# Sebago. Typesetting by The Composing Room, Inc., Kimberly, WI.